Homecoming for the Chocolate Girls

Birmingham Rose
Birmingham Friends
Birmingham Blitz
Orphan of Angel Street
Poppy Day
The Narrowboat Girl
Chocolate Girls
Water Gypsies
Miss Purdy's Class
Family of Women
Where Earth Meets Sky
The Bells of Bournville Green
A Hopscotch Summer
Soldier Girl
All the Days of Our Lives
My Daughter, My Mother
The Women of Lilac Street
Meet Me Under the Clock
War Babies
Now the War is Over
The Doorstep Child
Sisters of Gold
The Silversmith's Daughter
Mother and Child
Girls in Tin Hats
Black Country Orphan
Secrets of the Chocolate Girls
Wartime for the Chocolate Girls

ANNIE MURRAY

Homecoming for the Chocolate Girls

MACMILLAN

First published 2024 by Macmillan
an imprint of Pan Macmillan
The Smithson, 6 Briset Street, London EC1M 5NR
EU representative: Macmillan Publishers Ireland Ltd, 1st Floor,
The Liffey Trust Centre, 117–126 Sheriff Street Upper,
Dublin 1, D01 YC43
Associated companies throughout the world
www.panmacmillan.com

ISBN 978-1-0350-1993-9

1 3 5 7 9 8 6 4 2

A CIP catalogue record for this book is available from the British Library.

Typeset in Stempel Garamond by Jouve (UK), Milton Keynes
Printed and bound by CPI Group (UK) Ltd, Croydon, CR0 4YY

Visit **www.panmacmillan.com** to read more about all our books
and to buy them. You will also find features, author interviews and
news of any author events, and you can sign up for e-newsletters
so that you're always first to hear about our new releases.

I

1946–7

One

December 1946

Joy crept along the hall towards the kitchen and slipped quickly inside, pulling the door shut behind her. The room was full of the noise of children and of her elder sister Sheila's bad temper, as well as the fug from a pan of boiling potatoes.

'For heaven's sake, Patty, stop that banging!' Sheila erupted, swinging round with a rolling pin in her hand. 'Take that off her, Elaine, before I go mad.'

Joy's little girl, Patty, twenty-two months old, was safely strapped into the high-chair. Her brown frizz of hair stuck out endearingly round her head, and she was banging a spoon on the tray as if attempting to raise the dead.

Sheila's two children – Elaine, six, and Robbie, five – were on the floor, squabbling over who could play with the tin teapot.

Sheila had never been one to hide her moods. Now, with her sandy-brown hair scraped back each side into kirby grips, and wearing her old slippers, once pink but now almost grey, and an apron tied tightly over her frock, she looked the picture of martyrdom.

At least your husband is alive and well, Joy thought, at the sight of her sister's glowering. What the hell have you got to moan about? Whereas her poor husband, Alan, was in the front room, poleaxed by a day's work and looking

3

like a death's-head. And how he looked was only the start of the problem. She had to do everything she could to keep the racket and the unpredictable movements of the children away from him.

Sheila clamped her hands on her hips.

'It's bad enough that we all have to be caged up in here and not be able to . . .' She stopped, waving a hand towards the back room, where Alan was. 'So where're the greens you bought this morning? I need to put them on.'

Joy's mind went instantly blank. Greens?

That morning she had taken Patty, wrapped in a blanket in her pushchair, up to the shops in Cotteridge in the freezing wind. 'It'd be nice if the weather would at least make its flaming mind up,' she muttered, leaning on the pushchair against the raw force of the gale. A few days ago it had been as mild as anything.

Thinking back now, she could remember having the ration books and buying butter, cheese and a couple of tins. She had gone on to buy a loaf of bread and potatoes. She definitely remembered those. And a swede. Her mind pulsed with panic. She couldn't remember anything after the potatoes. Had she bought greens?

She was so tired. And she felt so tense all the time – it was as if her mind was shattered into little pieces.

The actual bombing might have stopped long ago, but Joy still felt as if bombs were going off around her all the time – or were about to. She had become vague and forgetful. She may have been the younger sister, the pretty, dark-haired one whose brown eyes and feet could both dance beautifully, but these days she felt like an old woman – the faded, forgetful one of the two of them.

'Well, I'm sure . . .' she began, not sure at all.

'Yes, but where did you *put* them? Elaine, no, leave that, you'll cut yourself . . . Yes I know you want to help, but

4

not with the knives . . . I can't cook them if I don't know where they *are*, can I?'

Elaine's face began to crumple.

'No, don't cry. Just don't.' Sheila was getting near explosion point. 'You forgot them, didn't you?'

'I . . . Sorry, Sheila, I think I might have.'

Her apology was drowned out by a blood-chilling yowl from elsewhere in the house.

'Oh God, not again!' Sheila looked wildly round the kitchen. 'Where's Robbie? You stay there, Elaine.'

Joy felt the horrible, familiar clutch of dread in her belly. She and Sheila dashed into the front room, to find Robbie howling in terror. Sheila fell on her knees next to her distraught little boy, pulling him close and defensively shutting the rest of them out.

'Al?' Joy moved forward cautiously.

Alan, her once lively, brown-haired and blue-eyed best pal – her husband now for nearly six months – looked like a shrunken old man. He was doubled over in the chair with his face in his hands, which were resting on his painfully bony thighs. Joy could see, without touching him, that his whole body was shaking.

'Al. I'm coming to sit by you, OK? And I'm going to touch you. It's all right. Don't worry.'

Slowly she knelt on the floor at his side, only daring after a few moments to lay her hand, very gently, on his back. He was trembling so much she could almost hear his bones rattling. He should never have gone back to work, she thought. Not yet. It was too soon.

The Cadbury works had kept open returning servicemen's jobs for them. As employers, they had been good to Alan. He had gone back to the box-making department. If he felt bad, he could go for a lie-down in the sickbay. And they were even giving him sunray treatment. He, among a group of other men, would sit down, bare to the waist and wearing special goggles, under a sunray lamp. The firm did everything it could think of to help.

But these remedies could not heal Alan's shattered mind. It was too soon for him to be working, but he had insisted that he wanted to go back to the job he had done for years. He was desperate for things to return to the normal he remembered. And most days, despite the look of him, he did actually manage to work.

'Alan? Can you sit up?'

Joy had almost forgotten about Sheila until she heard her sister say, from the doorway, with a sob, 'I can't live like this. I just can't.' Sheila went out abruptly, with a howling Robbie clinging to her. Joy gave all her attention to Alan.

He sat up gradually. And Joy was shocked when she saw his face. There was a sallow yellowness to it that had not been there when he left this morning, and the shaking was not simply upset, as she had thought. Her young husband, twenty-five years old – only a few months older than she was – already looked twice that age since he had come back from being held in a Japanese prison camp in the Far East. On top of that, he now looked really sick.

'I never meant to hurt him,' he said through chattering teeth. 'Only I was asleep and he – there was a bang . . .'

Robbie and the others had been warned time and again not to creep up on Alan or make loud noises around him. But it was a hard thing for a little one to remember and Robbie had evidently slipped out of the kitchen to come and find one of his toys in the front room.

'I'm sorry.' Alan sounded close to tears. 'I never meant to frighten the kid.'

'Shh, I know,' Joy soothed him.

Often she felt she had two children instead of one.

Except that Patty, though sometimes waking at night, did not make the other demands on her that Alan did.

'Robbie just made you jump, I expect. You look really poorly, love. Could it be malaria again?'

Alan nodded, shaking convulsively. 'Think it must be.'

Joy got wearily to her feet, praying that Patty would be all right in the kitchen for now. She could hear the spoon banging again.

'Come on, Al – let's get you up to bed.'

Joy and Alan were sharing what had been the bedroom of Joy's and Sheila's parents – Ann and Len Gilby – before the two of them finally admitted that they needed to separate and be with the people they truly loved. All of this would have been completely unthinkable before the war. But now, well, how things had changed, and their family was no exception.

Having settled Alan in the bed, Joy fished out the cold rubber hot-water bottle from under the covers.

'I'll go and do you a hottie – be as quick as I can,' she promised, as he shuddered in the bed.

She found Patty in the steam-filled kitchen, still in her high-chair, with Elaine standing in front of her. On her food tray were two clothes pegs and a muddy carrot. Patty's face was smeared with mud, but she was happy enough. Where the hell was Sheila? She must have taken Robbie upstairs to mollycoddle him, Joy thought crossly. She rushed to move the stew off the gas and put the kettle on it instead.

'Good girl, Elaine – thank you.' Joy kissed the top of her niece's head. 'You're a good little helper.'

'I'm keeping her busy,' Elaine said seriously. She seemed a rather old child for her six years these days. 'Where's Mom gone? She went outside.'

7

'Outside?' Joy was saying when the front door opened.

'Sheila?' The voice of Kenneth, Joy's brother-in-law, came from the hall.

'Daddy!' Elaine charged out to greet him. Now that her father was home for good, after his war in the RAF Air-Sea Rescue, Elaine was glued to his side whenever he was available.

Joy followed, watching with a tense smile as her tall brother-in-law – fair, blue-eyed and now broader, some-how bigger all over than when he had left to go into the Air Force – scooped his little girl up into his arms. Elaine was very like Kenneth and it was always sweet to see them together.

'All right, kid? Where's your mother?'

'We're not sure,' Joy said. 'There was a bit of upset.' She rolled her eyes towards upstairs. 'Alan's gone down with malaria again.'

Kenneth's eyes clouded and he nodded. 'Right. Down you go, Lainy. Good girl. I'll go up and see him, shall I?'

'Hang on, let me fill this hottie to take up.' Joy dashed into the kitchen, then stuck her head out again to say, 'Sheila won't have gone far, I'm sure.'

Two

Sheila clutched Robbie so tightly to her that he squeaked in protest.

'Sorry, lovey,' she panted, hurrying along Beaumont Road in the cold, smoky darkness. 'We're just going to pop in and see Nanna.'

Len's parents, Margaret and Cyril Gilby's house, was further along Beaumont Road from where they lived in Bournville, a few miles south of the middle of Birmingham.

Sheila rapped so hard on their door that she skinned her knuckles and instantly regretted it. No good taking out all her frustration on her grandparents – certainly none of this was their fault.

'Who is it?' It was her grandmother's voice. With a pang, Sheila heard the quaver in it. Nanna Margaret and Grandpa Cyril, both seventy-eight, were ageing fast these days. They had weathered a good many things without it seeming to make any difference to how they looked. But towards the end of the war they had suddenly become bent and fragile and, when it was all over, they had aged further, suddenly and rapidly, as if they had been holding everything off until peace was declared and they could relax into old age.

'It's only me,' Sheila called out, thinking, with the self-righteousness she was rather prone to, no wonder they had aged, with all the hoo-ha this family had put them through.

Margaret's strong-boned face, which Sheila's own strongly resembled, appeared in the gloom of the doorway.

'I thought it must be one of those blokes selling things.'

Every so often lately men were turning up and knocking at doors along the street, toting suitcases full of nylons and silky-smooth underwear. Given the shortages these days, even worse than those during the war, these items seemed nothing short of miraculous, but it did feel funny buying undies off some strange bloke on the doorstep.

Margaret stepped back to let Sheila in. Cyril was by the gas fire in the back room. Sheila put Robbie down, the boy blinking in the sudden light.

'All right, Grandad?'

'All right, Sheila? Hello, Robbie lad.' Cyril put his paper down, peering up at them and adding cautiously, at the sight of Sheila's face, 'Social visit, is it?'

'I'm going to go mad – I can't stand any more.' She burst into tears.

'Here, lad.' Cyril, instantly relegating this situation to 'women's business', got creakily to his feet and held out a hand to Robbie. 'I'll take him and show him my special box.' He had a little wooden case full of interesting bits and pieces: a magnifying glass, a big shiny beetle in an old Fisherman's Friends tin, a paper knife with a carved handle. 'You talk to your grandmother.'

Sheila saw her grandmother's face take on a less-than-grateful expression for being left with this. Margaret sank into a chair, then arranged the bobbly green wool of her skirt over her knees. She drew the edges of her cardi around her, as if preparing for the worst.

'Sit down, Sheila. What's the trouble?'

As if she didn't know, Sheila thought. 'I can't go on – not in that house, with *him*.' The words rushed out. 'If Kenneth hadn't been demobbed as well, I'd take the kids and go and stay with Audrey again. But I can't just go off and leave him, and I don't want to. Why *should* I!'

Sheila had spent months during the war as an evacuee,

with Elaine as a baby, living in a Berkshire village with a woman called Audrey Vellacott. Audrey, now a widow, had become a friend and they knew each other's children well. She was always pleased to see Sheila.

But Sheila had not spent the war aching to have Kenneth back home, only to go and leave him again. Even if sometimes it felt as if he had not come back – not completely. Not as he had been before.

'I know Alan can't help it. At least . . .' She bit back the words, *though sometimes I wonder*. 'But the way he is, with Joy tiptoeing around him all the time. He's so unpredictable! Robbie went into the front room and must have made him jump, I suppose. Alan screamed as if someone had dropped boiling water all over him. Frightened poor Robbie to death. The kids can hardly breathe in that house and it's not fair on anyone.'

'He's been through a lot, Sheila. You only have to look at him.'

'But it's not as if we even know what really happened – with the Japanese and all that. Alan won't say a word. And Joy's not much better; she can't hold a thought in her head. I send her out to do the shopping and she comes home without half of it, so I have to go again or do without. I'm a nervous wreck. I know we're on the housing list with the council, but it's all taking so long.'

Nanna Margaret was staring back at her and Sheila could see that the look was not wholly sympathetic.

'We don't know the half of it, Sheila.'

'I know, but . . .'

'If Alan doesn't want to talk about it, who can blame him?'

'Sometimes I think he just needs to pull himself together, like the rest of us,' Sheila burst out.

She had never voiced this before, but she was becoming

more and more resentful of everyone tiptoeing around Joy and Alan. She had a husband who had returned from the war as well, and no one took any notice of him! Kenneth had come home and got on with things, without all this fuss.

How they had all longed for the end of the war, and now none of it was turning out anything like she had hoped or expected. Kenneth was not the same, either. She felt like a sulky little girl.

'You saw the state of Alan when he first came home,' Margaret said. 'I think you need to try and be a bit more understanding, Sheila. Even from the little we know about those camps, you wouldn't have wished it on your worst enemy. That's not what Kenneth's war was like, and you know it.'

'I know. I do.' Sheila wiped her eyes. 'I just . . . I thought when the war was over, things would be – better. I'm sorry, Nanna.'

'It's not like you to be so . . . well, like that.'

There was a silence.

'You'll get a house sooner or later, and then you can all get on with your lives. You'll simply have to be patient. It was much the same after the last one.'

'Huh, yes – "homes fit for heroes"! Don't make me laugh.' Sheila twisted her wedding ring round her finger, keeping her eyes down. 'I know things are difficult for Joy, with all that to cope with, and Patty not being Alan's child on top of everything else. It would be better for them to be on their own, without us all round them. I was thinking . . . I could help you and Grandpa – Kenneth and I both could. Maybe for a while, couldn't we all move in with you?'

In the silence that followed, Sheila dared to look up. Her grandmother, instead of glaring at her as she might have expected, was looking away from her, towards the curtain-shrouded window. She seemed to be considering.

Sheila's own annoyance melted at the sight of the softening skin of her grandmother's face, the little puckers of wrinkles on each side of her mouth. Her hair was now entirely white, still thick, pinned up as usual in a loose bun. Time takes its toll slowly, Sheila thought. A tiny bit, day by day, until suddenly we all notice a change. And Nanna looked so tired. Already she felt guilty for asking, but she wasn't going to take it back. They had to get out of that house.

Her grandmother's attention snapped back to her. 'Your grandfather and I have talked about it,' she said. 'He's worried about that lad – the state of him. And Joy. And the rest of you, of course,' she added quickly.

'I know it's a lot to ask,' Sheila said. 'And I never would, if things weren't so difficult. But if we kept to the attic, the way we do in—'

She had been about to say 'Mom and Dad's house', but of course it wasn't any more. No 'Mom and Dad' as one unit any more. A pang went through her. All that had happened still seemed like a bad dream they were all going to wake up from.

'In the other house,' she finished. Her mother, Ann, was for the time being staying in Southampton with Tom Somers, the man she had first met during the Great War, and whom she loved. And Len, Sheila's father, had moved into the house owned by his fiancée, Jeanette, not far away in Maryvale Road. Neither couple was married yet because they were waiting for divorce papers, but with the pressure on housing as bad as it was, there was nowhere else for them to go. The whole situation was very embarrassing. It had set some of the neighbours' tongues wagging and made Sheila burn with shame.

Margaret got to her feet, as if she had suddenly decided. 'I can't say yes without asking your grandad.'

'It's a lot with the kids, I know. But with Christmas coming, I can help with everything – do the shopping and . . .' Sheila trailed off.

'Well,' Nanna Margaret said, unable to disguise the weariness in her voice, 'I suppose they'll help keep us young.'

Sheila looked into her grandmother's eyes, her own face crumpling again. 'I wish Mom was here.'

Three

'Thank you again, Doctor. I'm ever so grateful.'

Joy went to close the door behind Dr Saloman, a thin, stooped man in his sixties, with the wispy remains of grey hair and a soft German accent, whom she had come to love out of sheer gratitude for his kindness. Dr Saloman had fled Germany for England with his wife and two children in the early 1930s and was much loved in the area. There was great upset among his patients when Dr Saloman and his family were interned on the Isle of Man in 1940 and he was only released later in the war. Everyone who knew him recognized a transparently good man.

He had been to the house many times now to see Alan. 'Any time, my dear,' he had said to her when they first called him out. That time Alan was writhing on the bed with his latest attack of dysentery.

On his way out, downstairs in the hall, Dr Saloman had gently touched Joy's elbow. 'Might we speak for a moment?'

They went into the front room. Joy was so relieved to have someone talking to her properly about Alan that she was in tears before Dr Saloman had even begun.

'I know, my dear, it is very hard. And you will have to be brave – as I can see you are being. Your husband has been through ordeals that none of us can ever fully know or understand.'

Joy's eyes welled with more tears. The first weeks of her marriage had been so full of bewilderment and fear of what would happen next, with this stranger of a man she had married. Although she was beginning to get used to certain things, it had only got slightly better.

'Sit down, my dear.'

Dr Saloman sat down opposite her. She liked the way he wasn't afraid to say things and was straightforward. He didn't brush it off saying, 'Oh, I expect he'll be right as rain soon' as most people did, because they had no idea.

'It is not going to be easy, Mrs Bishop. Your husband has a number of physical conditions that will probably stay with him for the rest of his life. With luck, some of these will lessen over time, as he grows stronger and his body can resist.' He looked into her distraught face. 'It is possible to recover – at least partially – from some of these problems. However . . .'

Joy wiped her face, drinking in his every word.

'As you have no doubt realized, a large part of your husband's affliction is as much in his mind as in his body.' Dr Saloman hesitated. 'His actions, perhaps lashing out or behaving unpredictably, are not fully under his control. They are reactions that have been caused by the harm he has suffered. They are not directed at you – not in reality, though I am sure at times it feels as if they are.'

Joy looked down into her lap. Why did it feel so shameful talking about this? Alan could be sweet and tenderly loving towards her, and he was often full of apology after one of his outbursts. At other times he was like someone she did not know at all: angry, violent, terrifying, seemingly locked into some nightmare in his head that she could not understand. If only she could find the key to making him better.

'He will probably not want to talk about any of it,' Dr Saloman continued gently. Joy looked up at him again. 'It might be better not to ask questions. If he is ready to

16

talk, he will probably let you know. And if he ever does, it might not be for a very long time. I'm sorry, my dear – as I say, I know it is all very difficult.'

Joy nodded. She felt bad enough about all this. But there was the other thing that she really could not bring herself to talk to Dr Saloman about. Thin and weak as he appeared, Alan craved sexual relations, almost endlessly. At least twice a day was not unusual. He seemed primed for it virtually all the time. He was never rough or forceful; he was sweet and said loving things. But it felt too much. It felt driven and strange, as if it was not about her or about love, but as if Alan was fixed on something quite separate from her, which he had to prove. And she was exhausted. But none of this could she force through her lips, even to Dr Saloman.

Cheeks aflame as certain memories came into her mind, she only just managed to meet the doctor's pale, kindly eyes.

'You will have to be patient – and not take it personally, that would be my advice.' Dr Saloman got to his feet. 'And they advised you never to give him rice to eat?'

Joy stood up as well, bewildered. They? Who were they? No one had told her anything.

'No. I mean, we don't really eat rice. Only rice pudding.'

'Even that – don't give it to him. These men were fed almost nothing but rice by the Japanese. They can react very strongly to the sight of it.'

'Oh,' Joy said. 'All right. Thanks. And, Doctor, thank you for talking to me.'

As he went to the door, he patted her shoulder. 'It is nothing. Give it time, my dear, for him to heal, at least as much as he can.'

Now, seeing Dr Saloman out of the house again, she thought, He has no idea how much help he is. This time

Alan had malaria and it was a question of giving doses of something called chloroquine. ('I thought they were supposed to drink tonic water?' Kenneth had said. Which, Joy thought, annoyed, showed how much he knew.) Thank God for dear Dr Saloman.

While Alan was ill upstairs, Joy always left a light burning in the bedroom once darkness had fallen, and made sure Alan knew that she was coming in. She even knocked on her own bedroom door to warn him. No sudden movements or surprises – she had learned the hard way. Any shock, however innocent it seemed to anyone else, could reduce her husband to a shrieking, trembling mess. Sometimes he would hit out at her. It would take each of them time to recover.

Tonight he was shaking with fever. Once she was in the room and undressed, Joy said, 'Alan? I'm going to get into bed now.'

He turned, his face slick with sweat. 'OK.'

Despite the illness, he seemed calm and she got under the covers. He was ill, so surely he would leave her alone tonight? Usually, as soon as she got into bed, he was up against her, his bony body pressed against her, aroused and ready to make love almost instantly. Often it did not feel like love.

'Here, let me help warm you up.'

'You gonna set fire to the bed then?' he managed to joke between chattering teeth.

'Maybe not quite.' She smiled down at him. Even though he was sick, this was a good moment. There *were* good moments, she reminded herself. Of course there were. Alan could still be sweet and funny. It was just that the rest was so bewildering, so heartbreaking, that sometimes she felt she did not have a husband – an equal – but rather a burden to carry. She felt a hundred years old. 'Can I turn the light off?'

'Yes.'

She clicked off the light and snuggled up close. The fever was shaking his body, but he seemed clear in his mind. And was not trying to push into her. It was calm, nice. This was a good moment. She should ask him now – about work.

Alan and Kenneth had both gone back to their jobs, Alan at Cadbury's and Kenneth at the cycle factory where he worked in Greet. Kenneth had enjoyed going back and seeing the lads who had returned and those he knew. But after the initial settling-in period, he found his work life incredibly frustrating. He had had a bigger life in the Air Force, in Air-Sea Rescue, and had travelled to Italy, flown over the Mediterranean. He was bored and straining at the bit for something bigger. Alan, on the other hand, seemed quite content to do something familiar and the same, day in, day out.

'Al, d'you think you did go back to work too soon? You're ill so often.'

A faint sound came from him and Joy realized, to her surprise, that it was a kind of chuckle.

'I've had to work when I was worse than this,' he said, through chattering teeth. 'They'd never let you go off sick unless you were at death's door.'

The temptation rose once again to say, *Tell me about it* . . . But as soon as she ever asked, Alan would clam up again. And did she want to know, really and truly?

'They're good to me at work – when I'm not well.' There was a pause as he shook again convulsively. 'It's all right being back. Earning a wage. Better than just sitting at home.'

'OK,' she said doubtfully. 'As long as you think so.'

He pulled her closer. 'Joy?'

'Yeah?' He sounded sleepy.

'Sorry. I don't feel up to . . . you know. Tonight.'

'That's all right,' she said, in absolute relief.

Alan turned on his side and was soon breathing heavily and regularly. Joy wished she could fall asleep as easily as he could.

Many nights she had lain awake once Alan slept, often after his frantic love-making, staring up into the dark.

Alan had spent his first few weeks, after release from hospital, at his family's house in Ladywood. It had been awful. Ivy Bishop, Alan's mother, and his sister Irene had looked after him, trying as best they could to cope in the cramped little terraced house. None of it would have been so bad if it had not been for Alan's father. Arthur Bishop was a dishonest, manipulative man who had been in and out of prison and had already reduced Ivy to a nervous wreck.

As for having a son coming home in that state, Arthur Bishop had no patience or sympathy with it, and not the least idea of what was going on. His way was to try and bully his son back to health – taunting him one minute for being weak, and trying to force him the next. Ivy and Irene had spent all those weeks fending Arthur off.

'We can't go on like this,' Irene told Joy when she visited, as she did as often as she could manage. 'The old man got hold of Alan yesterday and yanked him to his feet as if he could just . . . I thought he was going to hit him.'

She shook her head, losing words in her upset and fury. Irene was a strong, energetic young woman – or had been – but there were so many things in her life to grind her down.

'The only thing we can do is get married,' Joy said. 'Then he can come and live with us.'

Alan had been just about well enough for them to marry in July and they moved into the family's old home in Beaumont Road with Sheila and Kenneth, while Ann, their mother, was, for the moment, living with Tom Somers in Southampton, waiting to be able to marry and become Mrs Somers.

Joy, Sheila and Martin, their younger brother, had seen their parents, Ann and Len Gilby, trying to do the right thing and hold their family together for years. Now, despite all their efforts, they had finally admitted that they needed to call their marriage a day. While they waited to be properly divorced, Ann was with her beloved Tom in the house he had inherited from his father; meanwhile Len, their father, was with Jeanette, a friend of the family who, like Len, worked at Cadbury's.

Joy was glad for her mother – mostly. Mom kept saying she would not be down in Southampton for ever; they were making arrangements to sell the house. But Joy missed her mother terribly, especially now.

She had written a quick note to her before coming to bed, trying to make the best of things and sound as cheerful as possible. But now, lying in bed, she found herself composing the letter she had really wanted to write: '*Oh, Mom – things are so hard, I don't know if I can stand it. Alan is so poorly and difficult at times and everyone's tiptoeing around us in the house. It's not nice for Sheila and the kids. But I can't really do anything about it. And the other thing is, he won't leave me alone . . .*' No, she could not write that to Mom. What in the world was she thinking?

They were not taking precautions. Alan wouldn't hear of wearing one of those rubber things. So far there was no sign of her getting pregnant, and Joy wondered if that lay at the root of a lot of this. Was Alan worried that all he had suffered in the prison camp had left him infertile?

'*I'm worried about Patty too as she gets older,*' her fantasy letter went on. '*She needs a father, and Alan takes no notice of her at all – he's far too wrapped up in his own problems. I love him, I do . . .*'

Even in her head, she hesitated now. Would she ever say *any* of this to her mother?

'*Sometimes I wonder if I've made the biggest mistake of my life not going to America with Hank, when I had the chance. At least Patty would be with her real father, and Hank was healthy and, well . . . I feel so terrible saying this. I didn't want to go over there and leave you all, but what sort of marriage am I going to have now? Alan's changed so much and it feels as if he's a huge weight on me – as if I am the one doing all the giving all the time.*'

Tears started to roll down into her hair.

'*I feel so bad for Alan – for whatever these men suffered. But sometimes I feel as if I've let myself in for a prison sentence there's never going to be an end to. Oh, I'm so terrible to feel like this. I feel so guilty. I love him, I do . . .*'

She turned, pressing her face against Alan's shuddering back, and he stirred and muttered. Poor Al. Poor, poor Al.

Of course she would not write any of this to her mother. She would carry on writing nice letters, not ones full of these awful, dark night-thoughts. Something more cheerful.

But please, please, Mom, she begged, there in the darkness, *I do wish you'd come home soon.*

Four

Ann Gilby surfaced from sleep, reaching out to rest her palm on Tom's back, lean and warm beside her. For a moment she listened to his steady breathing. It was the greatest comfort she could imagine. The only light in the room was the faint outline at the edges of the heavy crimson curtains, pulled across the window of the spare room of Tom's parents' house in Southampton. Tom's house now, since his father died. And now, for the last few months, the house the two of them shared.

Here, for this blissful time, even with all the tasks Tom needed to get done, they had been luxuriously free to get to know each other in a day-to-day way that had never been possible in all the thirty years since they first met. There was time to make love, to lie in each other's arms for hours at a time, if they so wished. Simply to be Ann and Tom. *Ann and Tom* – she often said these words to herself, in wonder. At first they sounded so strange, those names together. One day soon, she thought, when we can get married, someone will address our first envelope to us as Mr and Mrs Somers.

Sleepily she let her mind run on its usual course. A kind of radar, she thought sometimes, circling around her family. Where is everyone? Are they all right?

Sheila and Joy were in the house in Beaumont Road. A churning anxiety began within her. Things were hard, she knew. Alan – the poor lad, the state of him when he came home. He had gained some weight, it was true, and had managed to stagger through the wedding. But anyone could see he was a wreck, and poor Joy was having to brave it out.

During the last years of the war Joy had heard nothing from Alan, who she had known at Cadbury's for years, who had been her pal, her shiningly brilliant dance partner and then her fiancé. The Japanese officers in his camp had not permitted letters – or at least if anyone found the wherewithal to write one in the first place, they had cruelly never been sent.

Joy had slowly given up hope. Alan must surely be dead. Finally, when Hank Eklund, a big, handsome, doting lad (Ann had always thought of him as being like a large dog) from Philadelphia had asked her to marry him, Joy had agreed to, when they got the chance. Not only that, but she had borne his child, little Patty – and they had been all set to cross the Atlantic to a new life in America, when news came that Alan was alive. He was back in England and in hospital.

Leaving the camp where all the GI brides – and fiancées like Joy – were being processed to leave, Joy came home with Patty and joined her fate and her future to Alan. Sick, traumatized Alan. Even though she had been overjoyed and relieved that Joy and Patty would be staying close by, Ann worried constantly about her younger daughter.

Ann knew Sheila was struggling as well – but, she had to admit, Sheila was reverting rather to the heavy-weather person she had been before the war. What did Sheila really have to worry about now? She and hundreds of other couples in Birmingham did not have a house of their own, but she was better off than most. The girl needed to be patient, although, being down here away from it all, Ann never knew if she was hearing the full story anyway. Were they keeping their struggles from her so that she didn't know the half of it?

She saved her thoughts about Martin for last. Age order, of course – he was the youngest. But she knew, as her hand caressed Tom's back, that there had always been a special poignancy in her love for Martin. A passion and a guilt – because he was Tom's son and not Len's, the girls' father.

Where was Martin this morning, her lad? Her Bevin Boy, sent to mine coal by the government. He was still down that pit, living in a hostel in a Nottinghamshire mining village. It had felt as if his name had been picked out of a hat; it made so little sense, when he thought he was going into the RAF.

Ann had been worried to death about Martin, though she tried not to show it. He was a slender, clever boy, good at passing exams. How on earth was he going to manage in a coal mine? To her surprise, once the shock was over, he had seemed content to set off for training and give it a go. And he had never once complained about it. He told funny stories, of course, and it all sounded very tough. But he coped with it all amazingly well. Of course he was very pally with that Jack Thorne lad, who had been with him since the beginning.

The few times Martin had come home to visit, he was almost like another person. For a start, he was huge, his shoulders looking twice as broad as they had before. His whole body had expanded, iron-hard with muscle. Her boy and Tom's was suddenly a big, brawny man, not a boy any more. He was handsome, and confident in himself. And yet she felt he was fast slipping away from her and she was losing him.

And since she had been with Tom in Southampton, Martin had not once come to visit, to try and get to know his father, even though she had written and asked him to come several times.

She inched closer to Tom now. The air felt cold outside

the bed and she brought her face up close to his warm back. Once Martin was released from his government duties – when the Bevin Boys could get away – then surely he would have to come home. And then he and Tom could really start getting to know each other . . .

This thought cheered her and she smiled as she slipped back into sleep again.

'Ann? Tea for you.'

Ann surfaced from sleep to find Tom placing a mug of tea on the table on her side of the bed. She heard the faint click of the mug, then he leaned down and kissed her on the temple. Ann rolled over, opening her eyes, and smiled up at him.

'You're a wonder.'

And he was a wonder, managing to do so many things with only one arm, carrying the mugs up carefully, handles clenched in one hand. A tray was much trickier.

'My pleasure. It's lovely to see you sleep.'

'Even though you have woken me up,' she teased, sitting up and taking the mug. 'Ooh, just what I need.'

Tom climbed into bed and they snuggled close, drinking tea in companionable silence. Every morning felt like a miracle to Ann, waking here with Tom. Her Tom.

'Seems so strange, doesn't it,' she mused, sipping her tea. 'That we've known each other for thirty years this year. And I feel I know you so well – when we've hardly even seen each other.'

'D'you think it's a record?' he said. 'Waiting thirty years to get married?'

'Well, we're still not that. We're living in sin.'

'Ah,' Tom said, grimacing at her. 'Sin. Yes.'

'Not for much longer, I hope.'

It felt very uncomfortable, and not how she had ever

26

expected things to go in her life. All that really mattered now was to be with Tom. And she wore a wedding ring to fend off gossip. But of course people talked. They could be very nasty. It would be so much better once they were legally divorced and free to get married. And until then she thought it might be better to keep well out of the way down in Southampton and not bring embarrassment on the rest of the family.

Ann thought back, uncomfortably, to the office of the solicitor that she and Len had visited to request a divorce. The sombre, lean-faced official had looked like an undertaker. When each of them confessed that they had committed adultery and had a child by another person, Ann thought the man was going to swallow his fountain pen. Outside, Len had seemed shell-shocked at first.

'God,' he said, looking pale and shaken, 'that was horrible.'

'What a pair we are,' Ann said, as the knots in her stomach gradually loosened, on getting out of there. *Divorce.* The very word so terrible and shameful.

They had looked at each other and managed, after a moment, to laugh.

'Stick around, though, won't you?' Len said.

Ann's face sobered. They would miss each other in some ways, she knew.

'I'll be back,' she said. 'Anyway, Jeanette's one of my best pals.'

'If this is what sin feels like . . .' Tom's voice brought her back to the present. She could hear the smile in his voice without looking at him. Cuddling closer, she marvelled once again that they could be together now, like this: sitting in bed drinking tea, warm and loving. Able to be a couple, ordinary and happy.

Tom, with his missing left eye and left arm (he had been

left-handed), the price he paid for his survival at Gallipoli. Tom, older, his hair thinner and wearing specs now. But Tom – still the man she had fallen in love with in 1916 at Fircroft in Selly Oak, one of the houses the Cadbury family had given over as a convalescent home for the duration of the war. She had never known him any other way than with the injuries he had sustained, and had always loved him just as he was.

'Oh, I forgot – there's post.' He fished an envelope out of his dressing-gown pocket. 'Sorry, it's a bit crumpled.'

Ann looked at the handwriting. 'Joy.' With her heart beating a little faster, she tore the envelope open.

Before she had even read it, she felt the guilt rise in her again. Here she was in Southampton, in the huge house that had been owned by Tom's family and was now left to him. Unlike much of the ravaged city, and the dock area in particular, it had survived the bombing. It was far too big for the two of them. Tom and his sisters had grown up there, but lately, before Tom's father died, it had been only the two men rattling around there together. And then Tom had been left alone.

And here she was, living what felt to her like an endless honeymoon with Tom, when Joy and Sheila were going through who knew what?

She read hungrily – and nervously – through the letter.

'Everything OK?' Tom asked.

'What d'you reckon?' Sounding troubled, she handed the brief letter over, watched him read:

Dear Mom,

Just a few lines, now I've got Patty to sleep. She's full of beans and Elaine's very good with her. Alan's in bed as well, as he's gone down with malaria again. He had to come home from work early. Dr Saloman came and gave

28

him his medicine. He said sometimes people get over
malaria in the end, but not always.

Sheila is talking about her and Kenneth and the kids
moving in with Nanna and Grandpa. First I heard of it
was this evening, and she says they'll be going tomorrow.
I am not sure about this – it seems too much for them to
me: Nanna and Grandpa, I mean. If only S and K could
get a council house.

Otherwise we are all going along – not much news.
Have you heard from Martin? We haven't heard a word
from him here.

Hope to see you soon. Regards to Tom, and bye for
now.

Love from Joy

Tom read, then folded the scant letter and handed it
back to her.

'Reading between the lines, I'd say . . .' But Ann was
already in tears. 'Oh, love.' Tom leaned round, pulling her
close with his good arm. She sobbed into his chest.

'I'm sorry,' she said, once she could speak. She pulled
back and sat up. 'It's not that I don't want to be here with
you. I *do*. It's been just the happiest time. It's heaven.
But . . .'

'Your children need you. The girls anyway.' He stroked
the top of her head.

'I don't like being so far away when they've got so
many problems facing them – and there're the grandchildren as well.'

'Ann, we can go back to Birmingham whenever you
like. I never, ever want to be the one who separates you
from your family – you know that. And there's nothing for
me down here now. The business is almost wound up, so
one way or another, I'm going to have to look for work.'

29

Ann could hear the doubt in his voice even as he said it. Since his disabling war injuries Tom had been forced to give up his beloved career as a marine engineer. Instead he had been managing his father's chandlery business.

'Love,' Ann leaned round and took his hand, 'work is something we don't really need to worry about. You'll find a job – of course you will. And for the time being, I'm perfectly happy to go back to Cadbury's. There'll be plenty to do there.'

Tom looked doubtfully at her. 'I don't want you having to work, Ann.'

'I don't mind.' She smiled, realizing that she missed the works and all the chit-chat on the line. 'Actually, I like it. It's company, being with the other girls. So let's not worry, eh?'

'Well, if that's what you want. At first anyway. I don't want people saying I'm a kept man. But of course we must go. My home is where you are, my love.'

'Oh, Tom, you are so kind.' She flung her arms around him. 'And I do want to go back – as soon as we can. Could we get there by Christmas? I know it's not long, but we can put this house up for sale. And . . .' Her thoughts from earlier that morning came back to her. 'I hope soon you'll be able to see something of Martin as well. I'm sure he'll be back, when he can.'

'Yes.' Tom stroked her back. 'I know. Give him time, my love.'

Five

Martin threw himself onto the hostel bed, its springs screeching as he did so. The hut slept twelve of them, with six black iron bedsteads along each wall.

He lay with the letter pressed against his chest, all churned up inside from reading it. Eyes closed, he tuned into the thrumming physical exhaustion of his body, which came over him after every shift down the pit. His every muscle was clamouring for rest. And yet it was a good feeling. As if he was really living in his body, working it. Being a man – strong and in command of himself.

He drew in a deep breath, laced with the smells of smoke and men's sweat and damp socks that pervaded the room. And coal dust – always that; so familiar now that it seemed to coat the inside of his nostrils and every other surface, so that he no longer noticed it. In any case, his mind was on other things.

Home. Mom. The letter was asking – not begging, but asking mildly, in Mom's careful and unselfish way – that he come and visit. A short visit, at least? She knew Southampton was a long way, but they'd happily pay his fare if that was the problem.

They: Mom and Tom, this man whose presence in his life hung over him, heavy and full of dread. Why was that? Martin did not understand himself. But Tom, his actual blood father, was someone he would always rather avoid thinking about. Even though – as the pounding of his heart and his racing blood told him – somewhere deep within him, it mattered. And he could not avoid it for ever.

'Mart?' Jack's voice sounded along the space between the beds.

There was a stove in the middle to stave off the worst of the cold, its chimney poking out through the roof. All right in October, just about, but when real winter set in again . . .

'Um?'

Martin opened his eyes and Jack was standing over him, imposing as ever, tall, lanky, with a dark lick of hair falling over his eyes. Handsome. So handsome. For the umpteenth time, Martin felt his innards somersault at the sight of Jack Thorne. Jack – confident, clever, happy with himself. Very different from how Martin felt inside.

'You coming? I thought we were going to the pub?'

'Yeah. Course.' Martin made himself sit up, belly muscles jerking.

'What's up?' Jack pointed at the letter, pulling the corners of his mouth down. 'Mama again?'

Martin lowered his feet to the floor, nodding. Jack's mocking tone grated on him, but this was the tension he lived with: Jack versus home.

'She's only asking when I can get over to see them.'

Jack stopped joking then. He could be sensitive in reality. And he was the only person on earth in whom Martin had confided about his father. Or fathers, rather. In the early days of intimacy with Jack, Martin had felt stripped naked as a babe – physically and mentally. He told him everything, and he believed that Jack had done the same. It was the miracle of his life so far, that this man could feel something for him. That they were lovers, best friends, no matter what the world might say if it knew. Except that it was absolutely vital it did not.

'You're going to have to go sometime, aren't you?'

'I suppose so.' Martin leaned on his aching thighs, gloom-struck. 'They're just not like your family.'

'Well, no – hardly.'

'But they're all right,' Martin said, defensive again as he saw his mother's loving face in his mind's eye. 'I mean, Mom is. She just worries.'

'A mother's job,' Jack said. He reached out a hand. 'Come on – a pint or two'll cheer you up, old thing.' He fumbled in the inner pocket of his jacket and brought out a tight roll of paper. 'Thought I might get the odd sketch done.'

Martin got creakily to his feet and their eyes met. For the moment there was no one else in the hut, even though outside they could hear the voices of other Bevin lads approaching. They leaned in, snatched a kiss on the lips, then drew back, making scared faces.

'Naughty,' Jack said, with a grin. And Martin instantly felt better.

They settled in one of Eastwood's street-corner pubs, warm and fuggy, with a beer-laced male intimacy. It was Jack's turn, and he brought watery pints to the table, the two of them squeezed into a corner by a tiny round and very stained table.

Jack fished for his charcoal – what else could you draw miners with? – and his untidy roll of scraps. Despite paper being in such short supply, he always seemed to have some: sent from home, he said, as there was always loads of it stashed away there. Jack's mother, Charlotte, had a hoard of paper, going way back.

Keeping the small sheet of paper, only about six inches by six, flat to the table, Jack would sketch while casually looking around, fixed on one person who, because he could chatter away at the same time, would never realize a portrait of him was being created. They never found out if anyone would mind, because so far no one had noticed.

'Ah, marvellous . . .' Jack fixed on his subject, an elderly, knobbly-faced miner across the pub, sitting back in his cap, a pint raised to his lips. And off he went. He was a good artist, very good. Martin was amazed by the skill with which he could create a whole impression of a person with only a few sketched lines.

'One day, when I have a house of my own, I'm going to put your pictures all over the walls,' Martin told him.

Jack glanced up at him, the charcoal still moving across the paper. He smiled. 'You're sweet,' he said.

Jack Thorne came from London. His mother Charlotte was an artist and his father, Dr Henry Thorne, taught history at one of the London universities. By the sound of it, they were what people called 'bohemian'.

Martin did not feel inferior to Jack. Not mentally. Jack was exciting, artistic, free in himself, but Martin knew that he himself was clever. It was just a different sort of clever – and Jack's family sounded quite different from what he was used to.

Jack described his people as artistic, living very much in their heads while keeping a chaotic household in a big Hampstead house in North London. His mother's oil paints and canvases, two hairy dogs, stray guests, hangers-on arriving at odd hours, as well as Jack and his two sisters, had all been chivvied into some sort of functioning order by a long-suffering housekeeper called Madge – 'a treasure', Jack's mother called her. That was before the war. But Madge, still only in her late thirties, had departed for the ATS.

It all sounded rather odd to Martin. But refreshing.

34

And vague as they apparently were on the domestic front, Jack's mother and father were married and seemed to show every sign of wanting to remain so. And what was more, they did not seem at all troubled by Jack being just . . . Jack. This was breathtakingly astonishing to Martin.

'But do they really *know*?'

He kept asking Jack this, because he could not believe anyone could be accepting of something that everyone considered so utterly terrible and shameful – not to mention illegal.

'They do,' Jack said, after considering for a moment. This first conversation was when the two of them had still been in lodgings with Nancy, whose husband was away – she thought in North Africa and, later, Italy.

Martin and Jack had shared a room barely big enough for a put-you-up that had a habit of collapsing into itself in the middle of the night, plus one hard, narrow bed. The two of them often both ended up squeezed into that. They could not have moved the beds together, even if they had been the same height or safe to sleep in. That would have been a bridge too far for Nancy, who spent a lot of her time flirting with them – Jack especially. Even though she must have been thirty, Nancy seemed to have no idea they were not interested in her, and never would be.

That first time the two of them lay on the hard little bed in each other's arms, everything about life felt like a miracle to Martin. This frankness. The way he could be truthful about himself for the first time ever, because this amazing and handsome man liked him and saw something in him. Loved him. Wanted him. Their gazing at each other, with Jack's blue-grey eyes holding fast to his, had said more than they ever could with words.

'But do they *really* know?' Martin insisted.

There was a silence, Jack stroking his arm for a moment.

'When I was fifteen there was a girl at home – one of Mother's art students. At the school, I mean. She was for-ever round, wouldn't leave me alone. It was pesky, I can tell you. Rosamond, she was called. All long, wavy hair and brooding eyes, very Pre-Raphaelite.' Jack laughed. 'I had to get rid of her somehow, so I told her fibs about this girlfriend I had – I called her Sarah. I've no idea if she really believed me, but she stopped hanging about. And Mother said afterwards, "Poor old Rosamond. She really couldn't see that you'd never go out with her, could she?" And she gave me this look . . .' Jack paused for a second. 'And then she said, "I think your friend Sarah is going to be rather useful, don't you?"'

Martin had lifted himself up on his elbow, suddenly hearing an edge of tears in Jack's voice. He stroked Jack's cheek, full of tenderness.

'That's so . . . good. Astonishing.'

'Yes.' Jack recovered himself. 'My mother's a brick like that. Of course there are a lot of queer chaps around, if you're an artist. But I suppose she could see – had done for a while. We never said any more; never have. They sort of let me get on with it.'

Martin lay down again, full of wonder. He could not imagine ever saying to his mother, or to his 'father' – 'Len', as he now called him in his mind (his 'actual' father, Tom, did not yet count, because why should he care what he thought?) – 'Well, the thing is, I'm not ever going to get married or have the sort of life you think I should, because I'm—'

No. There was no word he could use. No way he could bring this out into the open. Not like that.

Jack was putting the finishing touches to his sketch. All around them in the pub was the loud blare of male conversation and bursts of laughter. Someone was playing a mouth organ.

'D'you think they will nationalize the mines?' Jack asked, smudging the charcoal into shadow. He was good at doing two or three things at once.

'Probably,' Martin said. 'It's going that way, isn't it?'

'No one seems all that interested.' Jack looked round.

'They will be, if it improves pay,' Martin said.

He could understand it, even after their short time of working in the mines. They were not colliers. Only the older and more experienced men actually dug at the coal face, not the Bevin Boys.

They had started their working life in the freezing cold of pit bottom, waiting for the empty coal tubs to descend for filling. Now they had been moved to the junctions of different roadways within the mine, dealing with the lines of tubs that moved coal along the shafts – unhitching and redirecting them. It was hard and heavy work, but at least there was enough height to stand; and the junctions were airier, unlike some of the narrow passages, where you had to stoop or even get on your hands and knees. Here you could breathe better.

What a life it was, down there: dark, tough, too hot or too cold, relentless and cut off from any other existence. Even when the war had still been raging, a lot of the miners scarcely seemed to know or care how it was progressing. Many simply wanted to lift their hours of freedom above ground, by betting on horseraces and sweepstakes or going to the pictures. Martin had started to feel rather the same. The outside world and all its turmoil were far, far away, and in the hours of freedom from that dark underground world you wanted to let up and enjoy yourself.

Jack was saying something else to him, but Martin,

sipping his pint, found that his mind was wandering elsewhere. *Mom*. Should he – could he – go and see them?

How was he ever going to cope with this father who
had arrived out of the blue? And were they ever going to
cope with him, as he really was: the Martin Gilby that he
himself knew he was supposed to be?

Six

'What is it – what's the matter?'

Joy could hear the panic in her own voice as she rushed into the front room holding Patty, who was still gulping and hiccoughing after knocking her head against the kitchen table. She found Alan sitting bent over, hands over his face, weeping and rocking.

Last night he had writhed violently in bed, screaming in utter terror. She had had to put the light on to chase away whatever horrors were haunting his mind, to hold and soothe him. She was already exhausted and wrung out. But now it was as if those same horrors had followed him into his waking hours.

'Oh, Al love – what's wrong?'

No one else was in the house, so she could not hand Patty over to anyone. For a moment Joy felt she was going to explode. Her panic increased when she realized that her feelings were not only ones of sympathy for him. She was sorry and sympathetic, of course she was. She was overflowing with sorrow for her poor, poor Al – so broken and suffering so much – for all that they had done to him. Even now the very sight of his terribly thin body gave her a jolt. But right at this moment she felt desperate, as if this was the last straw.

Oh, what is it now? she thought. Can't you be strong and be the one helping me for once? Is it always going to be like this?

Forcing back her own tears, furious with herself for

such selfish feelings, she went over to Alan, putting Patty down cautiously on the floor.

'It's all right, sweetheart.' She stroked Patty's leg. 'Daddy's just feeling a bit sad.'

Patty stared open-mouthed, silenced by the sight of a man sobbing. Although Alan could be very odd and contrary in the daytime, he was not usually in a state like this.

Joy knelt down and carefully took him in her arms, keeping her voice low and calm.

'I'm sorry,' he spluttered. He was so broken, so defenceless, like an old man and a little child all at once. It wrung Joy's heart. 'It's all because of me . . .'

Immediately she realized what was wrong. Sheila and Kenneth had moved out the day before, taking Elaine and Robbie to Nanna and Grandad's house because, as Sheila had said a number of times, she could not stand any more.

It had not been very nice, how it all happened. Joy was still stinging from the words she had exchanged with her elder sister.

Sheila had turned on her, two nights ago when they were upstairs. They had had an angry conversation, trying not to let any of the others hear, though the sound of Kenneth in the attic playing 'Santa Lucia', one of the records he had brought home from Italy, on his gramophone helped to drown them out.

'I just can't stand any more,' Sheila hissed at Joy, her face hard and tense. 'I know Alan can't help it, but it feels as if we're all in prison – we can't move a muscle in this house without some sort of upset. And he's scaring the children.'

Joy, already at screaming pitch herself, wanted to shriek at her, *Oh well, poor old you – you're all right, you don't have to deal with any of it, do you? You and your perfect little family!*

But shrieking was the last thing that would help. And Joy could see that these words she wanted to hurl back at Sheila, to hurt her, were not even true. Things weren't easy between Sheila and Kenneth, however much they tried to hide it. Kenneth had changed as well. He seemed in his own world a lot of the time, and there was all this music. He played the records endlessly. He might as well still be in Italy, she thought sometimes.

All the same, she was brimful of rage that Sheila could simply go – could walk away with her healthy husband – when she could not.

'I hope you know what you're doing to Nanna and Grandad,' Joy retorted. 'You're being selfish: they're too old for all this.'

But she said it quietly. She felt suddenly limp, as if all her energy had left her.

Sheila looked away and Joy could see that what she said had hit home. A moment later Sheila was in tears.

'I don't know what else to do. It's Kenneth, he . . .' She stopped herself, as if she had said too much. Wiping her eyes, she looked back at Joy. 'I'm sorry, Sis. I just . . .' She trailed off, shaking her head.

'Me too,' Joy said, her voice flat. Because she *was* sorry. But what could she do – about this. About anything?

They did not say any more about it. Sheila carried on packing up their clothes, and Elaine and Robbie's toys and Kenneth's gramophone, and off they went, along the road to Margaret and Cyril's house.

'Al?' He was calming as Joy knelt, holding, rocking him. 'Look, it's no one's fault. It's just there aren't enough houses. That's all.'

She felt him nod, against her chest.

'Yeah.' He surfaced, looked up at her. 'But I feel so useless. A waste of everyone's time. The Japanese should've done for me, like they did for—' He stopped, his face haunted.

'For?'

There was someone he had mentioned, a friend called Joe. Whatever had happened to Joe seemed to be unspeakable.

'There were so many – died,' he managed to say. 'So many lads.' His eyes filled. 'I keep seeing . . .' But again he could not bring the words out. Whatever images haunted his mind, it was as if they had to be swallowed down, for fear of bringing them to life again. 'Why am I one of the ones still here? Me? What's the point of me?'

He gave a despairing shrug, his watery eyes boring into hers, as if willing Joy to give him an answer that would lay this agony to rest.

'I don't know, Al,' she said carefully, trying not to feel hurt. Wasn't she supposed to be part of the point: the girl he had longed to come home to? 'All I know is, I'm glad you are. All that time, I was afraid – I thought . . . But you came back to me. My love, you're my love.'

They were both weeping now, their arms around each other.

As she held Alan's bony frame, the tears coursing down her cheeks, Joy thought, This is another day, that's all. Today is all I can think about. All I have to do is keep going for today.

'Things'll get better,' she murmured to him, praying inside that she was right. 'They will – you'll see.'

A week later, Mom and 'Mr Tom', as Joy had come to think of him, arrived and moved back into the house.

Mom had sent a note saying they were planning to come back immediately. Joy was so relieved.

'Mom – oh, Mom!' She flung her arms emotionally round Ann as she came through the door that afternoon. And almost did the same to Tom, though she held back, feeling suddenly shy. She liked what she knew of Tom Somers. And while she was of course still loyal to her own father, Tom seemed a nice man and was good for her mother.

'Hello, Joy,' Tom Somers said, as they all stood in the front room. She liked his voice. It was smooth and kindly. 'I feel as if I know you already – your mother has talked so much about you all . . .' He trailed off. Adding 'for the last thirty years' would not have been tactful, even though she could guess that was what he had been about to say.

And in some ways she felt the same. Not that Ann had talked about Tom. But that one letter she had found in Mom's drawer while she was in hospital, after being caught up a bomb blast during her WVS days – that letter from Tom had been so full of gentleness and love.

She was shocked, all the same. She had vaguely known Tom Somers had injuries; after all, Mom had met him when she was helping to nurse him, and they all knew what some of the injuries from the Great War had been like. But as she watched Tom and Alan shaking hands, she had to get over her shock: the eye-patch behind his spectacles, the left sleeve of his coat hanging limp. This was a man who had been through a lot, she saw, in a way that she had never realized before.

Alan shook Tom's hand and was looking at him with a mixture of curiosity and, Joy could see, a kind of hunger. Was it the sight of another man in the house who was a casualty of war – unlike Kenneth, who seemed to have come through almost unscathed?

43

'All right?' Alan said. And they talked about surface things, like the journey and how it was good that they had come back to Birmingham. But Joy could see the need in Alan's eyes.

'I'll put the kettle on,' she said, going to the kitchen.

'Oh,' Ann was peeling her coat off, 'I've brought our tea ration – and a few other bits and pieces. Here, I'll come and give you a hand. Where's little 'un – asleep?'

'Yes, she's been down a while. I expect she'll last another half an hour,' Joy said as she and her mother escaped to the kitchen, with Ann pausing only to hang her coat on the newel post at the bottom of the stairs, as she had always done when she was in a hurry. This house had been her home for years – and now she was back.

In the kitchen, Joy could feel Mom examining her closely.

'You're looking very thin, love. I'd say Alan looks a bit better, if anything – it's you I'm worried about.'

Joy's throat ached as she made a huge effort to hold back her tears.

'I'm all right.' She kept her back to her mother as she lit the gas and fussed with the kettle. 'Alan's getting over malaria.'

'I thought he looked a bit green round the gills.'

'Well, yellow maybe.' Joy turned round and forced a smile.

Ann was not taken in. She looked really concerned. 'How are things, love?'

Joy leaned against the stove, looking away towards the window, battling hard not to spill out all her anguish.

'Not now, Mom, all right?' But she could not hold back her tears and her voice broke. 'I'm so glad you've come home.'

*

44

Carrying the tray of tea into the front room, they found Tom and Alan sitting facing each other, leaning forward to talk. Tom's face was very grave; Alan's looked hungry, desperate. But the two women coming in was like a switch being turned. Both men stopped talking and sat back, trying to put on social faces.

'Ah,' Tom said, as Ann put the tray down, 'I could do with that.' He turned to Joy. 'Now, where's that little girl of yours?'

'She's napping,' Joy replied, pouring the tea. 'I don't know how long she'll last.'

She handed Tom a cup, having the strangest feeling as she did so. He knows everything about me, she thought. Well, not everything; but he knows my mother and who my father is, and that Dad's going to marry Jeanette. And I suppose he knows all about Hank and my nearly going to America, and about Patty. And about Alan. There was something restful about not having to explain everything. And something about him: a strange rightness about him, as if she had known Tom already for a long time. And now that she had actually met him, she felt comfortable with him.

But as she sat down with her cup of tea and Tom was asking Alan about the garden, and then Mom touched Tom's hand when she wanted to ask him something, she thought, That's what it is. It's him – with Mom. Her mother looked different; even her face had changed. She looked complete somehow, and more relaxed than Joy had seen her in a very long time. Happy – that's what it was.

Joy sat back in her chair. I'm glad for her, she thought. I can see Mom's in the right place. And please God, let them coming back help make things better for Al and me as well.

Seven

'For Pete's sake, can't you stop that child making that flaming noise?' Kenneth snapped.

Sheila scooped Robbie up from the floor of Margaret and Cyril's back room. It was bedtime and the little boy was overtired and howling. He writhed in her arms.

'No-o-o! Don't wanna go to bed!'

Sheila felt as if her head was going to explode. Robbie's shrieks grated on her nerves and now Kenneth, who had not had to deal with any of this all day, had marched in and come out with that.

'Robbie, stop it,' she snapped, which only made him bawl all the more.

'Here, let me take him,' Margaret tried to intervene. 'He just needs to calm down . . .'

'No,' Sheila said, fighting to stop Robbie wriggling from her arms. 'His father can take him – here.'

She went to thrust him at Kenneth, but Robbie screamed in real alarm.

'No! Not Daddy! Don't like Daddy.' He clung to her like a monkey and suddenly she felt like crying herself, in utter despair.

'It's all right, babby. Elaine, I'll come back down for you, love.'

Elaine nodded, without looking up from where she was playing with her doll by the fire. She looked subdued and miserable.

'Sheila?' Kenneth stepped forward, trying to touch her shoulder. 'Look, sorry. It's just, that racket . . .'

Sheila swerved furiously out of his reach and carried Robbie out of the room. A bit late to be sorry, she thought, as she stomped up the stairs.

Up in the dark of the attic, she rocked her tired little boy, whose grating cry soon ran down like a clockwork toy into muffled sobs, before he dozed off in her arms. Sheila sat, tears running down her cheeks. She felt so unhappy, but did not feel she could show anyone else.

She laid Robbie at his end of the little mattress that he shared with Elaine and sat on her own bed, her chest heaving. Was this how she had dreamt things would be, once the war ended? All those years of yearning for Kenneth to come home, for them to be together as a family – and now look at them. Nowhere of their own to live; more shortages than ever, so that getting a meal together every day was a major challenge; and this man she loved was not quite the Kenneth she remembered from before the war.

The old Kenneth had been a blond and handsome (he was still those) but steady and biddable man. He hadn't wanted anything except to marry her, do his job in Greet living near both their families, and play the occasional bit of football or a darts game at the pub.

But now he was always going on about new things – Italy, and those flaming records that he played, over and over again! The first thing he did when he got home was buy a second-hand record player. He had carried the records home with him, heavy 78s weighing down his pack, and had played them incessantly ever since. 'Santa Lucia', 'Funiculi, Funicula', 'Torna a Surriento' . . . And he kept saying he'd like them to go and see an opera. What on earth was all that about? And where the hell did he

47

think they were going to do that? It made her feel shut out, ignorant. And he seemed so unsettled, as if none of them were good enough for him.

But all these things seemed small compared to what Alan had apparently gone through, so Sheila never felt she could complain. Wasn't this what a lot of wives were finding? People did keep talking about having to 'readjust'.

Pull yourself together, she muttered to herself, wiping her eyes. She was about to go down and wash her face when she heard Kenneth coming up the attic stairs.

'Why is it a wooden hill?' she heard Elaine saying.

'Well, I s'pose because the stairs are made of wood and they're like a hill.'

'No, they're not.'

'You have to go up them – like you go up a hill?'

'Oh,' Elaine said, doubtfully.

They paused outside the door.

'D'you think Robbie's asleep?' Sheila heard Kenneth say softly. Her feelings of desperation lessened. Kenneth and Elaine got on well most of the time.

'Yes,' Elaine hissed, 'If he was awake, we'd hear him blarting.'

The door opened, letting in a faint wedge of light.

'Mommy?' Elaine was trying to make her out in the dark.

'It's all right,' Sheila whispered. 'He's asleep. Have you done a wee-wee?'

'*Course* I have,' Elaine said, so imperiously that Sheila could not help smiling.

'Come on then – hop into bed.'

After they had both kissed Elaine goodnight, Sheila felt Kenneth reach for her hand and squeeze it. It was an apology, a promise. Because they both knew there was nowhere they could talk for now – not with Elaine's ears flapping in their bedroom.

'Here.' Margaret put Kenneth's tea down in front of him. The rest of them had eaten earlier with the children. 'They're a bit tough, I'm afraid.'

Pigs' hearts. Sheila made a face at him. They didn't even try and make the kids eat this sort of thing – she had bulked out an egg for them, frying it, poured over potato slices and a bit of carrot.

'Thanks.' Kenneth smiled at Margaret, whose eyes met Sheila's for a moment.

Sheila dragged a smile onto her face. 'It's all right, Nanna.'

'Busy day, lad?' Cyril asked, from the armchair. He was all chirpy, back from singing with the choir of retired Cadbury workers that he went to every week. It did him good.

Kenneth pedalled across to Greet each day to the James Cycle Co., to the frame-building shop where he had been before the war. He spent each day building motorcycle frames or the chassis for sidecars.

'Much as ever,' Kenneth said indistinctly, trying to get through a mouthful of the rubbery meat.

Cyril looked up from his paper and gave Kenneth a wry glance. 'Like summat from Dunlop, those hearts, aren't they?'

'I did my best,' Margaret said, rolling her eyes. She sank into her chair, pulling one of her crocheted blankets over her knees.

'It's all right, love – no one could have done better,' Cyril said quickly.

Sheila swelled with affection for both of them. Joy was right – it was an awful lot to ask two people in their late seventies to have their whole family move in. And Cyril and Kenneth did their best to have man-to-man conversations about work and football. But Cyril, like Sheila's father Len, had worked in the chocolate-making department at Cadbury's – 'up the wet end', as they called it, where there was liquid chocolate. That was very different from making bikes.

'The nights are drawing in all right now,' Margaret said, to no one in particular.

'I'm sorry, Sheila.' Kenneth reached for her in the darkness once they had gone to bed.

Hearing the genuine apology in his voice, Sheila found herself in tears again. She turned to cuddle up to him. 'It's not fair, shouting at them like that when you've been out all day,' she said into his chest. 'It's not fair on me, either.'

'I know. It just . . . when the lad makes that noise, it goes right through me – winds me up something rotten.'

Sheila pushed herself up into a sitting position. The kids were both fast asleep, so there was not much danger of waking them, if they kept their voices down.

'You aren't like you were – before. You're . . . I don't know. You've changed.'

There was a silence before Kenneth said, 'So've you, you know?'

'Have I?' She thought for a second. 'Yes, I s'pose I must have done.'

'You're more—' Kenneth stopped, obviously trying to put this tactfully. 'You've got more fight in you. You answer back more.'

'You mean I'm not such a good wife?' She said it teasingly, but there was an edge to her voice.

'No, I just mean . . .'

'And you seem fed up all the time. With me – with all of us.' Her emotion rose again. At last she was beginning to say what she needed to say. 'As if you don't really want

50

to be here, and you want to go back there.' Into another silence she voiced her worst suspicion. 'There wasn't – isn't – someone else, is there? In Italy?'

'What? No!' Kenneth shot upright beside her, putting his arm round her. 'Course not! God, Sheila, how can you even think that? It's not that at all.'

'Well, what is it? Just me, the kids?' She spoke with dread. The way she had been feeling this week, and the fact that she had missed her monthly twice – there were not going to be only two children . . . She was going to have to find the right moment to tell Kenneth, but this did not seem to be it.

'No. It's . . .' He withdrew his arm and seemed to be thinking. In a low, serious voice, he said, 'I s'pose, when you're away a long time, you forget what home's really like. All we could think of was getting back: home, family and that. And then when you get here . . . It's not you, although the kids – I mean, I love them, course I do, but it all takes a bit of getting used to, when you haven't . . . And living here. No place of our own. But it's work as well.'

His thoughts came tumbling out now.

'I've spent these war years doing something different. Seeing and learning new things. It was exciting, in its way, although it was dangerous. We were outside a lot, and at sea. And then Italy . . . Oh, I'd love to take you there, Sheila.'

He reached for her hand and squeezed it.

'It's poor all right – really bad in some parts. But it's so beautiful. And the weather's lovely and warm. The trees smell beautiful. And they drink wine: real rough stuff, you know, but even that's not bad. And now I'm back on the factory floor, same thing day after day. This small life. I never saw it that way before, but now I can see years of it stretching ahead, with nothing much new happening. And the food's terrible – we were better fed in the forces, I can tell you, and we had fags, unlike here. And England's so bloody cold and dark and miserable.'

He almost sounded close to tears himself. Sheila listened, full of a mixture of sadness and indignation. She had had to be here through all this cold and rationing and misery that he was moaning about – all of them had. Kenneth was home and he was going to have to get used to it! But sadness filled her, because he had changed – he had changed a lot and so had she, and there was no going back.

'I see,' she said woefully. 'Well, I'm sorry you feel like that, but I don't think there's much we can do about it.'

'Well, there is one thing.' She heard the change in his voice beside her, a rising excitement. 'I didn't dare mention it before, because I didn't think you'd like it. But you have changed – my missus.' He hugged her close and Sheila had a sense of being sweetened up for something.

'What?' she said in a dull voice.

'These passages they're offering: ten quid to start a new life in the sun. We could go. It's the ideal time, while the kids are small. They could grow up as little Ozzies.'

'You mean, Australia?' Her voice rose so high for a second that she actually put her own hand over her mouth. Having to whisper, she could barely contain her outrage. 'What – go and live over there, miles away from everyone? Have you gone completely mad?'

Eight

'I see you worked on fillings. Oh, nursing at Fircroft . . . munitions. You seem to have done it all.'

The woman in the office in the Lodge at the Cadbury works looked up and smiled at Ann over her spectacles. She was a softly-spoken older woman, who Ann vaguely remembered seemed to have been here for ever.

This was reassuring, though Ann's hands were clammy with nerves. She was almost a divorced woman, and was already living with the man who was to be her husband. Not that she was going to volunteer this information. She'd never lie, but at the moment she was legally Mrs Gilby and still married to Len, wasn't she? That was all they needed to know. But it was a long time since her family had fitted in with the strict brand of morality espoused by the Quaker Cadbury family. It seemed a bit late to worry now, as she had worked here for so long. But worry she did, and she didn't like the thought that she might be deceiving anyone.

But there were not many questions.

'We are glad of recruits – the war workers who were brought in have mostly gone home, and of course not all the men who were here before . . .' The woman trailed off, without going into that. 'A lot more women like yourself are coming back to work part-time. We're glad to have you. If you did want full-time work you could go back on fillings – or there are vacancies on the line in the Roses department?'

Ann hesitated. She had said to Tom that as he had yet

to get a job, she would go back to work first – Cadbury's was very good about taking back its former staff. For the moment they needed the money. And Tom could then take his time finding employment that his injuries would enable him to do.

'Yes, full-time,' she agreed. 'I'll go on Roses.' Why not? Roses chocolates were a nice brand and it was something new, so it would be a change. No good thinking things were ever going to be as they were before, with her old pals. She hardly saw any of them these days.

'Right.' The woman flicked through her cards. 'You know the routine. I'll send you your letter to sign. It'll be with you this week. Best now if you start after Christmas?' She smiled. 'You'll miss Pudding Week, I'm afraid.'

In the week leading up to both Christmas and Easter a lot of Cadbury workers put in as many extra hours as they could, to earn extra money for the season.

'Oh, well – can't be helped,' Ann said. She had a job, that was the main thing. 'Thanks very much.'

As she stepped out into the biting air, the 'bull' – the factory siren – rang out to announce the dinner break. She smiled to herself at the sound. The sky was blustery with clouds, with a watery beam of sun managing to penetrate for a few seconds. She walked round and looked out over the men's grounds, at the playing fields and along the elegant brick face of the Cadbury works, where she had spent so many years of her life; where she had met Len, had laughed and chatted with her friends – Hilda especially, and then Jeanette, in the girls' grounds on the other side of the road. It was all so familiar, and now that the camouflage was no longer draped over the buildings, everything seemed to be returning to a normal they recognized.

Feeling contented, she walked out to Bournville Lane. She was home again and it felt nice. Maybe now her lovely

Tom might be able to find a home here. But her smile faded and her pulse speeded up as she thought about what she needed to do next. It was not all going to be easy or comfortable, settling back into her own neighbourhood.

'Oh, Ann. You'd best come in.'

Margaret's face had turned solemn when she opened the door and saw who was on the step.

Ann felt shocked at the sight of Margaret. Even in these few months she had been away, her mother-in-law – for Margaret was still that, as things stood – had aged noticeably. She had lost weight, making her face appear longer and the skin on it hung more loosely.

As Ann stepped inside, Margaret closed the door on the grey heaviness of the day, saying, 'Joy did say you'd be back. You haven't brought him with you then?'

'Well, no,' Ann said. *I must go and see them first*, she had told Tom. He was nervous about meeting Ann's in-laws, Len's parents. But meet them he would have to, as they were all going to be living in the same street.

The last time Tom had seen Margaret was when he visited Ann in the hospital ward where she was recovering from being caught up in a bomb blast. Margaret, who until then had known nothing of Tom's existence, walked in and saw the two of them together – loving, close – before they caught sight of her. It must have been obvious what they were to each other, and it had been a terrible shock for Margaret.

'Hello, bab, fancy seeing you!'

Cyril got out of his chair. He was so obviously pleased to see her that it warmed Ann's heart. She had always loved Margaret and Cyril and had been closer to them than she had ever been to her own family. It had felt terrible to cause them such sadness and distress by all that had happened.

'Sit down. I'll brew up,' Cyril said. 'Sheila's not here at the moment – she's taken the kiddies up to the Green, to the shops.'

Ann sat. The familiarity of the room, which never seemed to change – the table by the wall, the armchairs, with Sinbad, the black-and-white cat, curled up in one, plus Margaret's colourful crocheted blankets, the picture over the fireplace, the mantel clock – filled her with an almost painful sense of comfort.

'He'd like to meet you,' she said cautiously as Margaret shifted Sinbad, who moved grudgingly and settled back straight away on her lap as she sat down. 'Properly, I mean,' Ann added.

There was a silence. The clock ticked. Margaret said, 'Have you seen Len?'

'No, not yet.'

Poor Margaret. Over the past years, all her previous ideas about how things should be – the ordained order of things – had been challenged and turned on its head again and again by those closest to her.

First of all there was Ida, her elder sister, who had disappeared from Margaret's life when she was a small girl. She came across Ida again – now calling herself Lizzie – in a church in Balsall Heath, where Margaret had volunteered in 1940 to help people who had been bombed out. She learned from Ida, who was now strange and childlike, that she had been 'put away' after having a baby, aged seventeen. Margaret had had no idea, and this completely rocked her view of her mother and father. How could they have been so cruel?

And then Ann and Len, married for well over twenty years, were both, it appeared, involved with other people. By the time Margaret found out about all this – and that the father of her beloved grandson Martin, Ann's youngest, was not in fact her own son Len, but Tom Somers – Martin had been fifteen years old.

And Len had had a child, little George who was six now, with a woman called Marianne. But Marianne was not to be relied upon and had left Len, who, feeling hurt and betrayed by both women, had then fallen in love with Jeanette, Ann's pal who worked at Cadbury's. Len and Jeanette, like Ann and Tom, were now waiting to be able to get married.

This merry-go-round of carry-on had, in Margaret's and Cyril's eyes, been a complete disgrace. All of it. Margaret had not held back from telling them how disgusted she was with them. But what could she do? Lose her only other remaining son? Her eldest son, Ron, had died on the Somme. And lose Ann, the daughter-in-law she had loved as her own all these years – and her grandson Martin, clever lad that he was?

'How long will it take. This . . . *divorce*?' Margaret could hardly bring herself to say the word, so that it came out sounding like a curse or a dirty word.

'A few months. It shouldn't be too much longer.'

There was a pause. Margaret picked something off her cardigan.

'You'll see Jeanette, I suppose?'

Ann's friendship with her had been the reason Jeanette had visited Ann and Len's house so often during the war. She would come round for Sunday lunch, bringing her rations, and they had all enjoyed having her there. And then, gradually, Jeanette and Len . . .

'Yes. Course. I'm going back to Cadbury's, for a bit anyway, until Tom gets set up with something. He's over there now, seeing what they can give him.'

'Oh, Jeanette's not there now,' Margaret said.

'Isn't she?'

'She says she's had enough of work, after all these years. You can hardly blame her. At least she'll have time to look after Len properly.'

Ann was still stinging from the barbed nature of this comment when Cyril came in, carrying a tray of tinkling teacups.

'Here you go.' He poured and handed Ann one and smiled with genuine warmth. 'It's nice to see you, bab.'

Ann returned the smile, feeling emotional. Cyril, though bewildered by events, had always been kind and loving to her. He kept out of any emotional hoo-ha – he liked a quiet life.

'It's good to be back. But . . .' She took a sip of tea. 'I'm sorry. About Sheila, putting you in this position.'

'Oh, don't you worry about it.' Cyril eased himself into his chair, holding his cup and saucer. 'Needs must.'

Margaret shot him a look as if to say, *It's all right for you.*

'They need you, your girls,' Margaret said. 'Even Kenneth seems . . . what would you say, love?' She looked at Cyril.

'Like a cat on a hot tin roof?'

'And Alan, well, the poor lad's in a bad way. It's not easy, for either of them.'

'No.' Ann sighed. 'I don't suppose it is.' She looked out of the window, distracted by unusual movement out there. 'Oh, look, it's snowing!'

A few moments later they heard sounds at the front.

'That'll be Sheila,' Cyril said, getting up. 'I think I'll just . . .' He left his half-drunk tea and slinked off to go upstairs.

Margaret gave Ann a comical look, out of habit, before remembering that she was with her disgraceful daughter-in-law and looking away again.

Ann got up and hurried into the hall as Sheila came in. Through the open doorway she could see the swirl of snowflakes.

'Nanna, it's snowing!' Elaine cried, seemingly forgetting that she had not seen Ann for weeks.

'Elaine, you've got wet shoes,' Sheila scolded.

'Hello, darling – hello, Robbie!' Ann kissed them both and they ran into the back room calling, 'Hello, Nanna' as if she had never been absent for a day. She heard them chattering to Margaret.

'Hello, Sheila.' Ann held her arms out to her daughter in her snow-wet coat, but Sheila had her arms full of shopping.

'Oh, Mom!' Sheila's face crumpled and she burst into tears.

'Oh dear,' Ann said, putting her arms round her daughter anyway. This was more like the old Sheila before the war, for whom everything was a heavy-weather crisis. Things must be bad, if she was carrying on like this again.

Sheila promised she would come round later for a proper chat. When Ann left the house it was still not midday, and she decided to get all the visits over in one morning. Tom was out, trying his luck at the works, and she still had time before dinner.

Snow was still drifting down in big, fat flakes and the sight of it lifted her. It was settling just enough to lay a light frosting on everything and turn Linden Road and the Cadbury grounds into a picture postcard. Ann crossed the road, feeling the tickle of the flakes against her cheeks, loving the sight of it. She had treasured her time alone with Tom in Southampton, but this was where she really belonged – here, in Bournville, with her family. She was smiling again as she made her way to Maryvale Road.

Nine

Ann knew that Len would be at work now, so she could pop in and see Jeanette on her own.

She and Jeanette had started work at Cadbury's when they were fourteen, as had Ann's other old friend, Hilda. Though she had seen less of Hilda over the years, Ann and Jeanette had worked together in the waterside munitions huts at Cadbury's during the war and had spent a lot of time together.

Jeanette used to come round regularly – Sunday lunch, cups of tea – and share everything with herself and Len, with Sheila when she was there, and with Joy and Martin.

Ann had taken a long time to realize that Len and Jeanette had become more to each other than friends. It was a huge, stunning shock at first. But as things stood, she never felt in a position to judge anyone – not with her own love for Tom, which was seemingly unstoppable, always humming in the background to her everyday life. She did not bear any ill-will towards Jeanette and was looking forward to seeing her and chatting with an old friend.

She knocked on Jeanette's door – Jeanette and Len's door, she corrected herself. Originally the house had been Jeanette's mother's, and Jeanette had continued living there after her mother died. It was a modest-sized terraced house, very calm and neat inside.

Jeanette soon appeared. She was a gentle-looking woman, her fair, shoulder-length, wavy hair pinned back and wearing a neat tan-coloured skirt with a cream blouse and a dark-green cardigan over it. Ann knew there was more to Jeanette than her mild appearance gave away – she could be very sharp and shrewd. Even so, she was not expecting what happened next. Ann beamed at her. 'Hello, stranger.'

Her smile was not answered, at least not straight away. For a second she saw something in Jeanette's eyes, a glint of something she could not interpret, before her old friend's face lifted into a more welcoming expression.

'Ann, I didn't know you were here.' Jeanette seemed put out or something. Maybe just surprised, Ann told herself. After all, Jeanette probably thought she was still in Southampton and was startled to see her.

'Well, I am. We've come to live back in the house – with Joy and Alan. Sheila's moved in with Len's mom and dad.'

'Oh.' Jeanette definitely sounded put out, but she recovered enough to say, 'You'd better come in.'

Jeanette stood back and ushered Ann into the front room, which was plainly furnished with pale-brown furniture and a neat tiled fireplace, the fire laid but not lit.

Jeanette sat down and gestured for Ann to do the same. The room was really chilly, but she made no move either to light the fire or to offer Ann a cup of tea. She sat forward on the chair, rather primly, her knees clamped together.

'So, how are you both?' Ann asked, trying to inject some warmth into the situation.

'Yes, we're very well,' Jeanette said. Her cool manner seemed to thaw a little for a moment. 'Yes, thanks. Getting along very well.' She looked down at her hands for a moment.

Ann studied her. She had always liked Jeanette, but suddenly she seemed a complete mystery. She was so pale, so cool. She found herself imagining Jeanette's long, slender legs, her white thighs; Jeanette and Len lying together, naked . . . She forced her thoughts to behave themselves. This was all going to be more difficult than she had imagined. And as if her mind was making mischief of its own, she found herself saying, 'So, how are things with *her* – and George?'

Afterwards she realized this had been an attempt to make herself and Jeanette allies. But if that was what it was, it certainly didn't work.

She – Marianne – was the woman Len had met at the Cadbury's grounds at Rowheath and had had an affair with, which led to the birth of little George in 1940. Because of George, Marianne was someone that neither she nor Jeanette was ever going to escape completely.

The mention of Marianne and George seemed to freeze Jeanette even further.

'They're all right,' she said. 'She's still in Nottingham. At Boots. Doing quite well for herself, I believe.'

'Well, that's good,' Ann offered.

'George comes to stay – now and then.'

'He gets on all right with Elaine, if you ever need company for him,' Ann said.

Jeanette looked at her, very directly suddenly. 'We manage very well, thank you. Without—' She stopped.

Without any more of your family butting in, Ann thought. That was what she meant.

'Well, I'm glad it's going all right,' she said, trying to be helpful. 'He's not a difficult child, from what I remember.'

There was another silence before Jeanette said, 'So are you . . . staying then?'

'I think so.' Ann suddenly doubted herself. Jeanette sounded so hostile. But why should she not stay? This was her home, after all.

Jeanette did not ask after anyone else, and Ann did not know what else to say. She was getting very cold sitting there, even though she was the one who still had her coat on. It was not only the temperature in the room that was freezing her out. So she got up.

'Well, I'd best be off. Maybe I didn't catch you at the best time, Jeanette.' She could hear a sharpness in her own voice, even though she had not intended to let Jeanette know she felt hurt and offended by this chilly reception.

In the hall, Jeanette said, 'Ann . . .'

Ann, who had been heading for the front door, turned. Jeanette's face was solemn, cold.

'Things can't just go back to how they were before. As soon as Len and I can marry . . .' She looked away for a second. 'We think we might move on – somewhere.'

'Oh,' Ann replied. This pained her far more than she would have expected. 'Where?'

'I don't know,' Jeanette said.

'Well,' she said, trying to sound cheerful. 'It shouldn't be too long now. Good to see you, Jeanette.'

And she was outside in the cold again, feeling unexpectedly tearful. Because it had felt even colder inside that house.

Walking slowly towards Beaumont Road she thought, Jeanette has always had a hard side to her. It had surprised her before, when she saw it. A sharp, hard realism, and she had certainly seen it today.

Then she gave herself a ticking off. What on earth did she expect? Jeanette had finally found someone she loved, but she had to put up with the fact that her relationship with Len had all these other people hanging off it. There was Ann herself, soon to be Len's ex-wife, plus all their children and grandchildren. And on top of that, Marianne and George, Len's young son. That was a lot to take on. Even so, Ann felt hurt and annoyed.

'Just because you don't feel you've got the right to

judge anyone,' she muttered to herself, 'doesn't mean she's not going to.'

All the sins she had heaped on her plate, because of Tom, had meant she was careful not to blame other people. Even if Jeanette did manage to run off with my husband, she thought, righteous anger surging through her for a moment. Even then, she had not judged – or tried hard not to.

But that was what most people did, didn't they? she thought bitterly. Judged other people, even when they hardly knew the first thing about them. She felt cold and sad, her tears near the surface – even if this was what she might have expected.

And then, coming along the street in the opposite direction, she saw a familiar figure, the sight of whom made her spirits soar again.

'Tom!' she waved, saw him wave back and they hurried towards each other.

'Are you all right?' He looked closely at her face.

'Yes, course I am.' She tried to banish her bitter feelings and took his arm. 'Where have you been then?' she said, adding cheerfully, 'Oh, by the way, I have a job.'

Tom smiled at her. 'So have I.'

'What – where?'

'Well, Cadbury's has found a place for me. In engineering supplies. It's what I've been doing, more or less, in Dad's business. It'll suit me down to the ground.'

Ann looked anxiously at him. 'Will it? I know really you're an engineer – and you can't . . . I feel badly about it.'

'It's not your fault I had my arm blown off, is it?' He looked teasingly at her. 'Anyway, it's a long time ago, and a one-armed engineer is not a lot of good. I'm pleased – they were very nice. They even seemed glad to have me, which was gratifying. They said they employ quite a few people

64

with injuries and handicaps. I'm to go in before Christmas in fact, to get the lie of the land.'

'Oh, I'm so glad!' Ann threw her arms around him, feeling so happy for him and relieved to be with someone who was warm and loving to her, after the freezing shower of Jeanette.

'And you?'

'Full-time on the Roses line – but I'll see how long I last full-time.' She took Tom's arm again. 'Still, we could do with the money, and being out of the house might not be a bad thing either, the way things are.'

Tom released his arm and put it round her shoulders, pulling her close.

'It'll all work out,' he said in his calm way, which always made her believe him. 'You'll see.'

Ten

Christmas Day 1946

Joy surfaced in the dark of early morning, immediately becoming aware of Alan's hands moving over her body. He worked his way in under her nightdress and up to her breasts and was reaching round between her legs . . .

She almost groaned out loud. Not again! Whatever was the time? It felt like the middle of the night. Alan's insistence on such frequent sexual relations had seemed a tender, sweet thing at first. He was hungry for her, had so much time to make up and he was proving himself as a man.

But now, after a few months of it, she was not sure it felt like love. Sometimes it was more of a frenzied habit, like someone who drank too much. And it was yet another thing she had to do to look after him, to make sure everything was all right. Because without his dose of intercourse – that was what it seemed like – Alan might be grim and sulky for the rest of the day.

And still she wasn't pregnant. She did not especially want to be and was certainly not craving it, because it would have felt like another thing that she had to contend with. It was just something she took for granted would happen, and she thought it might calm Alan down. But so far – nothing. It made her feel she had failed.

He was thrusting now, against her back.

'What time is it?' she managed to say.

'I don't know. Let me, Joy – come on . . .'

He was tugging at her nightdress. Resigned, Joy pulled it up and arranged herself so he could enter her. It did not take long. He writhed, groaned with the effort of it and was soon finished. She pulled the Winceyette cotton down again. Their love-making did not really touch her own feelings or excite her in any way. She really was not in the mood.

'Thanks,' Alan murmured as they both sank back towards sleep, his arm lying heavily over her. 'You're the best, Joy. I love you . . .'

'I wanted it to snow!' Elaine announced as the other household from Beaumont Road rolled in before dinner time: Sheila and Kenneth and the children, and Margaret and Cyril.

'Never mind,' Ann said, kissing her. 'I expect there'll be a bit more snow before the winter's over.'

Joy watched as Nanna Margaret stiffly accepted Ann's welcoming kiss and 'Merry Christmas'. Ann didn't add 'Mom', as she once would have done. It was bad enough that Margaret was having to come here, to a house where her own son no longer lived, but instead a strange man did. But she wanted to have Christmas dinner with her grandchildren – not just with Len and Jeanette on their own.

Margaret and Tom had been introduced, and Margaret was polite and as pleasant to him as she was able. Now she gave him a nod.

Joy, with an excited Patty in her arms, joined in the general greetings.

'Merry Christmas, Sis,' Kenneth kissed her cheek and Patty's. 'Something smells very nice. Is that beef cooking?'

'Yes, it's been in the oven for hours,' Joy said, smiling,

seeing that her brother-in-law was making an effort. She and Sheila exchanged Christmas kisses as well.

The children were in the front room, jumping about, peering at the presents under the little tree that Ann had bought. It was squeezed right into a corner now, as they had laid tables in the front room for everyone to eat on and there wasn't much space left.

'Careful, you two,' Ann called to Elaine and Robbie.

'Come on – out of there,' Sheila said. 'You'll upset Granny Ann's table.'

'Where's Alan?' Margaret asked, looking round.

'Oh, he just popped out for a wander round,' Joy said.

In fact she had been relieved when he said he was going out. He was stronger now, physically, and liked to take himself off for walks. But he had been quite a long time, she realized. She felt the beginning of a pulse of anxiety. Surely he'd be back any minute? He must have gone out at eleven, and he knew it was Christmas dinner, though she wondered, with a sinking feeling, whether Christmas might be a stumbling block for him. The more time she spent with her husband, the deeper she realized his problems were. There were the physical scars, the recurring illness – but the worst of it was on the inside.

'Come on, everyone, it's all ready,' Ann said. 'My spuds'll be black, else!'

They were all squeezed in around the tables, with Kenneth doing the honours, carving.

'Not something I can tackle, I'm afraid,' Tom joked with him.

Joy saw her mother and grandmother watching the two men. Ann's eyes were full of affection, pride. She looked happy – there was no getting away from it. Nanna Margaret was still trying to get the measure of Tom. But the

68

thing was, there was nothing about him not to like. He was a nice man. He was polite, kindly, funny at times, and did not push himself on anyone. And his injuries from the first war were something people felt respect for, no matter what else they thought.

Everyone had pooled their rations and saved up the very best they could for Christmas. They served up crispy potatoes, carrots and sprouts. There were cheap crackers to pull – Joy laughed, watching Grandad Cyril and Robbie tugging one between them, with Cyril pretending to be too weak to pull properly and Robbie giggling. But all the while, the chair between herself and Tom, where Alan should have been, remained empty.

They had all been trying not to notice or say anything, but eventually Ann leaned round from the other side of Tom.

'Where d'you think he's gone, love?' she asked quietly.

'I've no idea.' Joy was getting angry. Alan had suffered terrible things, it was obvious, though he was so tight-lipped about it all that she still had little idea exactly what had gone on. But everyone was dancing around after him, day after day – could he not at least have thought about everyone else today?

'I expect he'll turn up in a minute,' Tom said quietly. He seemed to have some understanding of Alan, even though he admitted that Alan had said very little to him, either. But from his own experience of war and its horror, he had more chance of guessing how Alan might feel. He gave her a smile. 'Don't fret, Joy.'

She smiled back, fighting tears.

'Right, let's have a toast!' Cyril said. Grandad couldn't bear any moods or emotion – he always tried to jolly everyone along.

They were all raising glasses of beer, cider (Tom's

favourite) or cordial for the children, when Joy heard the front door open. Her heart started thudding like a drum. She was pushing her chair back, for some reason full of dread, when Alan appeared in the doorway in his damp coat.

'I'm ever so sorry,' he said, looking at Ann. 'I went for a walk and went too far – it's taken me an age to get back. I'd have got a bus, only there aren't any.'

Joy felt her panic and rage subside. It was a genuine mistake, something anyone could have done.

'Never mind, love,' Ann said. 'Come and sit down – we've only just started.'

A moment later, after shedding his coat, Alan was beside Joy, with a plate of food, smiling at her.

'Sorry,' he said quietly. 'Been away too long – I'd lost my sense of direction.'

Relief surged through her. This was more like the old Alan, his blue eyes looking into hers.

'Don't worry,' she whispered.

'Right,' Cyril persisted. 'Now we're all here, let's toast. A happy Christmas – and let's hope things settle down in the New Year, eh?'

'And to absent friends,' Ann added. 'Martin, for a start.'

'Such a shame he can't be here,' Cyril said.

'He's coming soon,' Ann replied. Joy could hear a forced cheer in her voice. Martin had been away for such a long time. 'There's only so many of them can leave at Christmas – he'll come in a couple of weeks, he said.'

'And to Len,' Margaret added pointedly. She and Cyril would be going round to see their son later.

Joy looked round at Tom, uncomfortable at the way Nanna was forcing this on them all. But he sat there quietly.

'To Len,' they toasted obediently. Joy and Sheila both said 'Dad'.

'And to peace from now on,' Nanna Margaret added pointedly. 'At home and abroad.'

It was a happy day, on the face of it, but Joy still found it a terrible strain. Now that Alan was stronger physically, she was beginning to realize how little interest he ever took in Patty. He was not her real father, of course. Patty's blood father was Hank, the American GI that Joy had almost gone to join in the USA. Alan had been very forgiving when he first knew about Patty. Children, life – let's have it, all of it!

But in reality he did not know Patty, or try to get to know her. He only truly had energy for himself, for trying to deal with his own recovery and the haunting memories he carried with him. For all the times they had made love since he came home, so far there was no sign of a child of his own appearing. Joy was relieved, in a way. But was this a further toll that the camps had taken on him, robbing him of another part of his manhood? Nowadays it was something never far from her thoughts.

After Christmas dinner they cleared the tables out of the way. The children sat on the floor with their new presents, with Sheila watching, feeling queasy as she often did, on and off during her pregnancies, as Kenneth played with them. Especially with Robbie's little train set.

'Two kids together,' she remarked to Joy.

Looking at Sheila's pale face, Joy thought, She looks as if she's expecting again. But Sheila had not said anything yet, and Joy knew better than to ask.

A pang of sad envy went through her. The thought of having another child was so exhausting – but it would bring her and Alan closer, wouldn't it? Make him feel stronger as a man?

Joy helped her mother bring in cups of tea, and they

all ate the mince pies Nanna had made. Alan and Tom sat together in one corner, talking quietly. Joy went over with a cup of tea for each.

As she approached, she heard Tom ask something that ended in 'Chindits?' And Alan answering, 'January forty-four – that's when we went into Burma. And then, well, a few of us ran into a group of them in March: an ambush sort of thing. And that was that . . .' He looked up and took his tea. 'Thanks, love,' though Joy did not feel that he really saw her. He was too intent on what he was saying to Tom.

She carried on serving tea and looking over to see that Patty was happy with Nanna Margaret, building towers with little wooden blocks. She took no notice then of what Alan had said. It was only much later that what she had just heard him say forced its way to the surface in her mind, slicing her open like a knife.

Later, when nearly everyone was in the front room, Joy noticed that both Sheila and Kenneth had disappeared. No one was in the kitchen and Sheila would not have gone out, so Joy went upstairs. She found Sheila in Martin's old room with the little lamp on, lying on her side on the bed, staring across the room.

'Sheila?' Joy went in and perched on the edge of the bed. 'Where's Kenneth gone?'

Sheila shrugged. She and Kenneth had had words earlier. Elaine and Robbie had got a bit over-excited and he had lost his temper and stormed out of the room.

'Probably gone out for a smoke,' she said. 'As usual.'

Joy looked cautiously at her. She could not remember Kenneth smoking before the war, but now he – like so many people – hardly ever stopped. Mom, who did not smoke, had never liked cigarettes in the house, and so anyone wanting a smoke went out the back.

Joy could see that her sister was upset, but there was so much that neither of them ever confessed about their husbands that she didn't know where or even whether to begin.

Sometimes she ached to pour out all her troubled feelings about Alan to someone – almost anyone. Even with Dr Saloman there were things she would never say. She and Sheila had hardly ever been close, exactly. And it felt so disloyal to discuss Alan. Joy kept soldiering on, trying to be the perfect wife to this injured hero. But she could see there were things Sheila was keeping to herself as well.

'Sis?' She spoke very gently. 'You can tell me to mind my own business . . . Are you expecting again?'

Sheila nodded without raising her head. Her face crumpled then, and she buried it in the eiderdown and started sobbing.

'Oh, Sheila.' Joy shifted closer and stroked the side of her sister's heaving body.

After a moment, Sheila heaved herself up and turned to sit on the side of the bed next to Joy, who waited until she was able to speak.

'I feel terrible,' she sobbed. 'I mean I don't feel well, either, but what I mean is . . . I don't want another baby – not now. Not with Kenneth the way he is.'

Joy was not sure what Sheila meant. Even having lived with the two of them until quite recently, all she had noticed was that Kenneth smoked a lot and seemed to have a short fuse and a craze for Italian songs. But she hadn't known there was anything really wrong. Compared to Alan, Kenneth seemed pretty normal.

'You mean . . .' she tried, feeling out of her depth.

'He's not like he was before,' Sheila said. 'He used to be – I don't know.' She shrugged despairingly. 'Easier. Happy, just to go to work and be with me and . . . I don't

73

know. He seems angry all the time and now . . .' Her voice broke again. 'He says he wants us to go and live in Australia!'

'Oh my word,' Joy said, genuinely shocked. She had had to face the thought of emigrating to the USA when she was going to marry Hank. And it had been terribly hard. She really could not imagine Sheila adapting to something like that.

'And yesterday he said that if I didn't want to go and bring the children, he'd go anyway – by himself!'

Eleven

January 1947

Ann and Tom were in the kitchen having breakfast, the windows steamed up and the room full of the smells of porridge and warm milk. The remains of Patty's porridge were congealing in her little bowl on the side.

Alan had gone to work, and Joy was upstairs getting Patty dressed. Now and then Joy's voice or Patty's gurgle of laughter drifted down to them.

'Happy little soul, isn't she?' Tom said. He had taken rather a shine to Patty. And she was a jolly child. But Ann wondered if Tom also saw Patty as another outsider, like himself, and if it drew him to her.

'She is, despite it all,' Ann said, getting up. 'Toast?'

'If we can spare it.'

Ann laughed, pushing the slices of the so-called National Loaf under the grill.

'Course we can. We eat more bread than before it was rationed.'

'Yes, the ration's pretty generous. Good for us too, they say – even if rather heavy-going.'

Ann turned and they looked at each other for a moment, exchanging a smile, as they sometimes did, tinged with disbelief. *We're here. We're really here together.*

It had been strange at first, Ann had to admit, living back in this house, which she had shared with Len and the family for so many years. It had felt wrong. Ghosts wandered the landing and slipped in and out through the door of the bedroom that Ann had shared with Len throughout their marriage. She had not been able to face it: that room, where she had hidden Tom's letters all those years. Where she had lived with (and loved, it was true, as she had loved Len in a way) her husband, while yearning for Tom.

When Sheila and Kenneth moved out, they had switched the house around so that Ann and Tom shared the room in the attic. Joy and Alan were now sharing the old bedroom. Now and again Ann and Tom were woken by Alan crying out in the night on the floor below, tormented by hauntings of his own.

And there were other ghosts: the children when they were small. When they, the Gilbys, were a family unbroken by unfaithfulness. But now everything was different, had to be different, and Ann found that she and the house began to change together.

She was here now, with Tom. Sometimes her own contentment pricked her with guilt. Her daughters were going through such difficulties. But at least, she told herself, her own happiness meant that she had energy to spare for them.

'Here you go.' She handed Tom the plate, toast and margarine. He picked up the jar of Marmite. Ann reached over and unscrewed the top for him. 'Come on, let me spread it.'

'Thanks. You know,' Tom said, nodding towards the window, 'I keep looking at that garden.' Since Len moved out, almost nothing had been done to it. 'It's a bit of a waste. It needs all the dead stuff taking out and a good dig over. I can't dig – not without a hell of a struggle. But maybe Alan and I could tackle it between us? Do him good?'

'That might be nice – if he's up to it,' Ann said uncertainly.

With Alan, you never knew how things were going to go. He might love it or storm off at the very suggestion. With a pang, she had one of her moments of wondering whether Joy might have been better off going to America with Hank. But then they would have lost her – and Joy loved Alan, had devoted herself to him.

'Yes. Poor lad's not in a good way,' Tom said. He looked troubled, as if unsure whether to speak.

'What?' Ann could see it in his face.

'It's just, what he said the other night. He was a Chindit – one of Orde Wingate's lot. I'd never realized that. And what he said – something about it didn't add up.'

'How d'you mean?' But Ann was distracted by the sound of the letter box clattering. She went to the hall and rushed back excitedly, tearing open an envelope. 'It's from Martin.' Her eyes scanned the letter feverishly, her heart racing. 'He's coming home – this weekend.' She looked across at Tom, suddenly stricken with fright. 'Oh God, I hope it's going to be all right.'

Tom got up, his own face shimmering with emotion. He reached for her and pulled her close.

'We'll do our very best to make it all right.'

Even the sight of the front door made Martin curl up inside. The door he had known all his life. He had been home very few times since his Bevin days began. Yet every line of the door – the spotted marks of the paint, the chipped lower left-hand corner, the lock with one screw slightly proud, often catching tiny fragments of wool from their garments as they went inside – was almost as familiar as his own body.

Home. You were supposed to long for home. Yet all he wanted was to turn and run.

'Let's get it over with,' he muttered.

His mother answered, so fast it was as if she had sprinted to the door.

'Martin, at last!' She pulled him in and into her arms. 'My boy, you're finally home!'

He writhed inside. The sight of her was a shock. She looked older, and much, much happier – radiant, you could even say – which made him both glad and furious.

'Not for good,' he said, pulling away.

'No, I know, but it can't be long now.' She gazed at him. Adoringly. She was wearing a shade of plum-red lipstick that he had never seen before, and he wondered if she wore it all the time now, when she never used to.

And someone was coming out of the kitchen. *Him.* Tom Somers. Also older and somehow milder-looking than Martin had expected. And despite the eye-patch and glasses, even he could see that he himself did look like Tom. The way his hair fell, with a cowlick on the left side that always wanted to stick up, the colour of it, his skin.

'Martin,' Tom said quietly. 'I'm so glad to meet you.'

He put his hand out. Martin found himself thinking, It was lucky he lost his left arm, or shaking hands would be very awkward. Which was ridiculous, because Mom had told him Tom was left-handed, so losing his left arm had made life especially difficult for him. Martin shook the hand and nodded, awkward, angry. Not wanting to give.

'I went to see Dad – first. And Jeanette.' He spoke while looking at Ann, saw her eyes flicker with pain. How ungracious, how deliberately unkind he was being. But he could not seem to help it. As he had grown older, he found he had less and less in common with Len, who was not even his father. But still.

'How are they?' Ann said carefully, shepherding him into the front room.

'All right.'

Martin sat down. They sat down. God, this was awful. Excruciatingly, horribly awkward. What now: were they supposed to sit and make conversation as if they were in a railway-station waiting room? In that situation Martin would, in any case, have got a book out, to avoid being chatted to by strangers. Which was not something he could resort to now.

'Fancy a cuppa?' Ann got up.

'I'll do it, if you . . .' Tom began.

'No.' Martin saw his mother put a hand on Tom's shoulder and she left the room.

Oh, hell. Now they would have to talk. Martin had no real idea what he felt about Tom, the man from whom he had obviously got his looks – even he could see that – and supposedly his brains as well. It was something he had pushed far from his mind all the time he had been away. After all, what with Jack, he had had other things going on. He had tried not to think about home, and suddenly here he was and he was not prepared.

Tom sat calmly, looking at him. Martin couldn't help admiring the man's quiet sense of himself. Some men would have been babbling at him, trying to get him on side, to suck up to him.

'So,' Martin said sarcastically, 'I suppose you're going to ask if I had a good journey?'

'No.' Tom looked mildly surprised. 'I assume it was reasonably good or you wouldn't be here, would you?'

Martin was taken aback. He almost laughed.

'No – I suppose,' he admitted, feeling silly. He wasn't sure what to say.

It had been just as bad with Len. He didn't mind Jeanette, as she was a nice woman and he found her easy enough. Len had asked if he had a good journey.

'It must be hard to know where to begin,' Tom said.

'Twenty years of your life and suddenly you're confronted with a man who says he's your father.'

Martin felt the most terrible swell of something inside him. As if his veins were about to burst and he could hardly breathe. *Stop!* he wanted to shout. *Stop talking!*

Everything about the house felt too small, as if he could not move his limbs. All his old selves were here, like a stack of Russian dolls. But he was expanded now, in mind and body. He was dense with muscle, from the mining life. His mind had travelled into areas that none of them could ever guess – his body as well, though he was certainly not telling them that. But now it felt as if someone was trying to press him into a trunk and slam the lid shut.

It was not as if he was close to his father. Not his father; Len, the man who had brought him up. As he grew older, Martin had found less and less to say to him.

In fact, he had a father by blood who had also had a wider life, more education – or at least more in the way of skills. A nice man, whom he longed to hate. But found he couldn't. And he didn't want to have to deal with this, wanted to get up and walk out . . .

'I have the advantage over you,' Tom was saying. 'Your mother told me about you so long ago. Well, not at first actually. I didn't know straight away that you were my son. I had no idea – not for years.' He sounded awkward now. Embarrassed or sorry. Or something. 'But once I did . . . She told me, kept me in touch.'

Martin gave a harsh laugh. Tom was so direct. He felt like crying suddenly, which was horrific.

'Well, lucky you,' he managed.

Tom did not say more. Didn't force anything. And again Martin felt a grudging admiration for this.

'How did you lose your arm?' he asked. Because

somehow, whatever else he felt, you had to respect someone who had come through the Great War.

'Shell – coast of Turkey,' Tom said. 'And this.' He pointed at his eye. 'I was lucky.' He didn't sound as if he wanted to talk about it any more.

'One of our lads lost a leg a few months back,' Martin found himself saying. 'He was hit by a line of tubs deep in the mine – it went over his shin.'

Tom winced. 'Yes, you don't have to go to Gallipoli for that.' He looked directly at Martin. 'How've you found it?'

'OK.' He knew this, but still found himself surprised by what was coming out of his mouth. 'It's all right actually.'

Ann came in then with teacups on a tray, an anxious look in her eyes, which seemed to relax slightly when she found them talking quietly.

'Joy and Alan have taken Patty out for a while – and Sheila and the others are coming up for a bit of dinner. Everyone's dying to see you. And tonight . . .'

'Oh,' Martin said quickly, 'I've got to go back late this afternoon. I'm on shift tomorrow.'

It wasn't true, it was his escape hatch. Something they could not argue with. He glanced away from the wounded look in his mother's eyes.

Twelve

Once the others came over, it all became much easier and Martin was able to relax. He stopped being so aware of Tom Somers. And he gave up wondering whether his mother found him different. Could she spot it: that he was Jack's, that everything had changed, and not only the size of his muscles?

But Joy and Sheila hugged him, Alan and Kenneth gave him manly pats on the back, and he now felt like one of them: a grown man.

'All right, Mart – good to see you,' Alan said. His face creased into a smile and Martin could see the bones moving under his skin. The state of Alan, even now, came as a shock. Even though he looked better than he had at his wedding to Joy, he still looked like an old man to Martin.

'Good to see you, Alan.' He had not known Alan well before the war, but he had always liked him – he seemed like a good bloke. But Martin found himself speaking a bit too enthusiastically. It sounded false and he was furious with himself.

Sheila looked fed up, Martin thought. But maybe that was just Sheila, and he hardly had time to notice because Elaine launched herself ecstatically at her long-lost Uncle Martin. He was able to romp about with Elaine and Robbie and Patty, and then Ann brought the dinner in – a shepherd's pie with the mince bulked up with vegetables and somehow, with everyone there, it was all right.

'Does it feel strange to be home?' Joy asked.

She had come as another shock: his pretty older sister. God, he thought, when he first saw her, she looks nearly as bad as Alan does! She was so thin and hollow-eyed. But she laughed and joked with him as ever. It felt really nice.

'He has been back, once in a blue moon,' Sheila pointed out, spooning peas onto the children's plates. 'Yes, Robbie, you do have to eat something green.'

'The strangest thing is having all these pesky women around,' Martin joked.

It was the first thing that came into his head – but it was true. His had been a man's world, these last two years. A world that suited him. Not that he didn't like his sisters or women in general, it was just that . . .

'Ah,' Joy said. 'Poor old Mart. What – none at all?' She winked at him. 'No one special?'

'Well, there was Nancy,' he said.

'Naughty Nancy?' Joy grinned at him.

'She was our landlady,' he found himself explaining to Tom, then realized that he probably already knew. He found himself wanting to seem nice, despite everything. And he realized, with a pang of shame, he wanted to sound . . . normal. A normal red-blooded lad, chasing girls, as they all expected.

Tom smiled. He was still calm, seemingly unbothered that Martin had totally ignored him since the rest of the family arrived, up until now.

'Her husband came back and we moved into the hostel – so there are women in the canteen . . .'

'So,' Joy insisted. 'You didn't answer my question.'

'Older than Mom, though,' Martin said, returning the grin.

'Oh, leave him alone,' Sheila nudged Joy. 'Nosey.'

Mom was smiling at him, seeming pleased at the sight of him here, finally. And again Martin was pierced with guilt at the way he was running away sooner than he really needed to. He was owed some days off – he could easily have stayed.

He managed to smile back, to salve his conscience, while the well of his feelings overflowed both with love and with a spiky, angry discomfort. *You lied to me. Betrayer, unfaithful woman – how dare you be so obviously happy now? With a man who seems* nice?

Unreasonable. Unkind. But it was how he felt.

Everyone had eaten up their portion of shepherd's pie except Elaine, who was fiddling about with the remains of hers on her plate.

'Eat up, pet,' Sheila said quietly, nudging her.

'There's a tiny bit more, believe it or not,' Mom said, standing up, and Martin was looking at her hopefully – he was forever starving hungry – and of course she immediately beckoned him to hand over his plate, beaming at him, when Martin felt a jerk of the table and Alan leaping to his feet.

'For God's sake, eat it!' he shrieked at Elaine, seemingly beside himself, the veins standing out on his neck. 'Stop messing about and eat it, you silly girl!'

Elaine jumped in shock and her face crumpled.

Joy leapt up too. 'Al . . . Don't.'

'For goodness' sake.' Sheila leaned round, pulling a sobbing Elaine from her seat and onto her lap. 'Don't take any notice, Lainy – you know what he's like.'

Alan was trembling. He was in some strange state, distant from the rest of them, seeing things none of them could see. Martin felt his belly clench. Alan looked like a madman or some kind of feral animal. It was horrible to see.

'It's all right, Alan,' Mom was saying calmly. Martin realized they were used to this, had seen it all before. 'It's all right, Elaine – you know Uncle Alan's not well . . .'

And Joy had her arm round him and was leading him from the room.

Mom sat down, leaning forward, and said in a low voice, 'That's partly why Margaret and Cyril didn't want to come over – they find it all a bit difficult.'

'Bloke's been through it, whatever it was, in those camps,' Kenneth observed. He looked different now as well, Martin thought, with appreciation. Blond, blue-eyed and now strong and fit – ready for anything.

'Well, there's no need to shout at a child like that, whatever he's been through,' Sheila said crossly. 'It's horrible. He needs to start getting over it.'

Kenneth looked at Tom. 'You must've seen plenty of it – in the last lot.'

Tom nodded, his face serious. 'It'll take time. He may never really . . .' He stopped, realizing this was not what anyone wanted to hear.

Moments later Joy and Alan came back in.

'Sorry.' Alan lifted his head a moment to look round the table. 'Sorry, Elaine. I shouldn't have shouted at you.'

'Don't worry, Alan,' Mom said.

And they all carried on as if nothing had happened.

Later, Martin called in to visit Nanna Margaret and Grandad Cyril. That was the easy bit, apart from seeing that they were growing old, because they had always been there and he wanted them to be there for ever, the same, always in the same place in their house along the road, even if he was hardly here himself.

'Look at you, lad!' Cyril said proudly.

'Feel his muscles!' Nanna squeezed his arm.

And they sat and asked him about the mine and day-to-day things, and nothing that gave him any difficulty.

Then he was back home for a quick cup of tea, saying

goodbye – hugs for his sisters, nods to all the men, including Tom, just like the rest. He appreciated Tom not trying to lay any special claim on him. And Mom.

She came outside, hugged him in the street. He knew she was sad. Was she disappointed, wanting a big, loving father–son scene where everything was rounded off and happy?

No can do, he thought bitterly. The bloke's all right, but what's he got to do with me?

'Come again, won't you?' she said and he could hear the tears behind her words.

'I'll try,' he said.

'If you wanted to bring anyone . . .'

'Yeah,' he said. Then, 'No. Don't think so.'

I'm not who you think, he thought. I'm a queer. Tell that to Tom Somers. Your queer son, who lies with a man – exactly like you lie with him. He felt a delight in how harsh and crude his thoughts were. He could never, ever have thought like this before. Before Jack. Back then (despite Ian, his school friend, and all he had felt), Martin could not have admitted the words, even to himself. *Homosexual. Queer.*

'See you then.' He pecked her on the cheek and shrugged his coat closer around him.

'Here,' she handed him a little package of chocolates. 'These are for you. Roses: that's the line I'm working on. They're nice. We have little ration tokens for the shop now – different colours, depending on what they've got going. There's not a lot, so you take them.'

'Thanks, Mom.' He pushed the chocolates into his pocket, feeling like a child again. 'That's nice.'

They'd all grown up on stuff from the seconds shop, using the Chocolate Card that entitled workers to go in for a share. And it tasted just as nice, whatever odd shape it was. He felt bad. Things were difficult – for all of them, he could see. But in any case, he told himself, there was nothing he could do. If he came home to live here, he'd be another person taking up space.

He could almost feel his mother's eyes drilling into his back as he walked away, exactly like when she sometimes used to stand and watch him when he was younger, when he was going somewhere a bit out of the ordinary, like the Cadbury's young people's camp.

It wasn't because she was worried, he thought, with a stab of guilty pain, but because she loved the sight of him, her boy. And did she love me all the more because I was *his*? All Martin's thoughts were so tender and angry at the same time that he wanted to banish them from his mind.

When he'd gone some way along the street, he forced himself to turn and wave at her, saw her raise her arm, then put her fingertips to her lips and blow him a kiss. And he waved quickly, then turned back and walked away even faster.

Ann stood in the street's winter dusk, watching as her boy strode away into the thicker gloom. Such a big, solid man now. She had to stop herself running after him.

All she could feel was a piercing sense of sadness and disappointment. She had not expected him to be instantly close to Tom – it wasn't that. It was just that she had thought he was coming for the weekend, that they could all have a cosy evening together, with Martin sleeping back in his old bedroom, breakfast together, maybe a little walk. It would have felt nice and right, having them all under the same roof, even for one night. You had to treasure these brief moments when you could. But no. It wasn't to be.

She had shown him his bedroom, how it was exactly the same. A strange expression came over Martin's face as he wandered into the room, almost as if he had never seen it before. He picked up the little painted figures that Cadbury's had given away with cocoa when he was small – the Cococub club animals.

'For heaven's sake, why've you still got these?' He sounded almost angry.

'Well, it's not my room,' she said, sounding hurt. 'They're your things. I didn't feel I could get rid of them.'

He put them down, looking round at the desk where he had worked for so many exams, the chair, the bed with the pale-blue candlewick bedspread.

'I thought you'd like me to keep it the same.'

He had been so stiff with her. He forced a smile. 'No need,' he said finally. 'Just do what you like with it. It's not as if I live here any more.'

It was cold outside and Ann pulled herself together and went inside. As she went into the living room she could see Tom searching her face. He sensed her upset, she knew. She put on a bright smile, trying to cover the tears that wanted to fall.

'It's bound to happen – two years away and he's in a tough environment,' Tom comforted her as they lay together in the attic bed that night. 'He's had to grow up fast.'

'I know.' She felt sadder than she could say, though she did not want to cry. 'It's all happened so suddenly. If he'd been here, I'd have seen Martin grow up gradually.'

'Not if he went away to university, like he said he was going to.'

She hadn't thought of that. 'Does he still want to? Did he say?'

'Not to me. I didn't ask. We don't know when he'll be released from the mine – it's turning into their National Service, isn't it?'

'Yes,' she said crossly. 'And you'd have thought they'd given enough by now.'

Her anger spread – with everyone, herself, Tom, Martin, life in general. Then it went out, like a match blown out. None of this was anyone's fault.

'Just the damn war, breaking up people's lives,' she murmured. 'He was always such a sweet lad. Sweetest of the three of them, really.'

'He's alive – that's the main thing.'

'Yes,' she sighed. 'I know. You're right.' Only it was so hard to let go of him, her lad who had gone away as a boy and now seemed like a stranger. After a moment she said, 'Don't you feel sad? Don't you want him to like you? Actually I thought he did seem to like you – I mean, more than like?'

'Ann,' Tom pulled her closer and she could feel the warmth of his breath on her neck. 'I have no right to expect anything from him. He's a lovely lad. I know he's my son – by blood. But what's blood, if you've never spent any time together? I'm not sure how much that means.'

Ann stirred, turning onto her back. 'But I hardly spent any of the last thirty years with you – and I knew I loved you.'

'And I loved you too. It was just . . . well, one of those mysteries. But it's different. Martin was a child; and children need people there, day in, day out, steady like the furniture. I didn't give him that. If one day we can be some sort of friends, well, I'd be very happy. But we'll have to wait and see, Ann, there's no hurrying it.'

She snuggled up closer to Tom. She knew he was the wise one, but her heart was still aching.

Thirteen

The 'bull' sounded across the works for the dinner break and Ann straightened up, flexing her back. Time to go home. It was late January and her third week back at work.

'Regretting it, are you?' Molly, one of the other married women, asked as they went to take off their overalls. Molly, like Ann, was in her early fifties with three grown-up children, though she looked so young that Ann sometimes found this hard to believe. She had more than a few grey strands in her own hair, whereas Molly's – without any assistance from a bottle, it seemed – was dark chestnut, very curly, and she had big teeth, which made her look cheerful, whether she was or not. Though mostly she was.

'To tell you the truth, I'm glad to be out of the house for a bit.' Ann rolled her eyes. 'And it's nice to be back. When I walked into the Crush Hall the first day, it felt as if I'd never been away.'

The Crush Hall was where they assembled before going off to their departments. Back in the old days, George Cadbury had prayed with the staff before work, but they no longer did that. The war had changed a great many things.

She and Molly were working in the Roses chocolates department. The chocolates had been introduced as a new brand the year before war broke out and were proving very popular.

The fillings were done in another department and arrived with each filling already sitting on the bottom part of its own chocolate shell. Row after row of them, all the different flavours, were carried by conveyor belt through the chocolate enrobing machine, which laid a blanket of liquid chocolate over the top.

Ann and Molly sat in a line of women marking the tops – in Ann's case, strawberry – with a tool that made the little raised pattern across the top. Molly was on limes.

After that, the chocolates were cooled and fed through the wrapping machines, before being sorted into brass cups, which rattled loudly along their conveyor to the boxes, ready to be filled at the far end. Ann was glad she was not working at that end, because some people said the constant clatter of the cups could make you feel a bit sick.

Now in their coats, the two of them left U-block and headed outside.

'Oh!' Ann exclaimed, feeling the tickle of snow against her cheeks. Big flakes were drifting down again in an unhurried way. 'Well, the kids'll be pleased anyway!'

'I hope it lets up soon,' Molly said. 'It's all right for a day or two, but it gets to be a right pest when you're slipping about all over the place.'

They walked along Birdcage Walk, between the factory and the green expanse of the men's playing fields. Once on Bournville Lane, they parted with a wave. Molly turned the opposite way, towards Stirchley. 'See you tomorrow!'

Ann watched her as she went off in her belted black coat. Molly was good company, but with a feeling of actual pain inside her, she missed her old friends.

She did see Hilda, whom she had known years, from the time when they started as green fourteen-year-olds at Cadbury's. Now and again anyway. And Joy and Hilda's daughter, Norma, had been lifelong friends. The only trouble was that Hilda was helping look after Lizzie and

Gary, Norma's kids, and Joy had her hands quite full enough with Patty – and Alan. It was easy to drift apart.

But her biggest stab of pain came from thinking about Jeanette. As she walked towards home, with the girls' grounds on her left, where they had all spent so many happy breaks during the war, for a moment she felt close to tears. Maybe she had been naive in thinking that she and Jeanette could stay friends, once Jeanette was with Len.

After all, Ann found herself thinking bitter thoughts again, she was the one who ran off with my husband. Why is she giving me the cold shoulder all of a sudden?

But she knew it was more complicated than that. She had hurt Len terribly by loving Tom all these years. By being unable to help it. By having Martin. Of course Jeanette thought badly of her. And Jeanette was offering Len a new start. She didn't need his ex-wife – or soon-to-be ex – and family hanging round her neck for evermore.

But still, Jeanette's coldness when she had gone to see her still stung. Ann had tried to be fair on everyone, when it all blew up and Jeanette and Len admitted they were in love. Tried to talk about things. Be a friend. It didn't seem as if Jeanette was going to offer her the same in return, and she couldn't help feeling hurt – and lonely. Instead, she had lost a friend.

She had nearly reached the main road when she realized someone was hurrying to catch up with her.

'Ann?'

Len. She still hadn't seen him, since coming back from Southampton. She had thought to go round, be friendly, but that visit to Jeanette had been so off-putting that she had decided to keep out of their way.

She found her heart thumping uncomfortably hard, as if she was being accosted by a stranger. Len was so familiar, and yet now suddenly they were awkward with one another, like two people who barely knew each other. Snow trickled down in the air between them and the pavement was filmed with white, patterned with the shoeprints of workers heading home.

'You're back then?'

'Jeanette must have told you I came round?' The kids had been to see them of course, at Christmas, with Margaret and Cyril – but not Ann.

'No.' Len looked genuinely confused. 'When?'

'Ages ago. Before Christmas. But she was . . .' Ann stopped. She didn't want to stir up trouble. 'Probably best if I don't call, though.'

Len looked uncomfortable. 'Yes, well. Nice to see Martin, though? Seems to be all right?'

'Yes, I think so.'

They walked slowly, and a silence grew that she wanted to break.

'I suppose our papers will be through soon?'

'Yeah. I s'pose.' Len sounded almost shifty. There may have been more people requesting divorces these days, certainly since the war, but it still felt a very shameful business.

'And you and Jeanette will get married?'

Len nodded, but didn't ask about Ann and Tom, and she felt annoyed.

'Thing is, when I marry again I'll have to change my name.'

'Oh,' he said. 'Yes. I s'pose so.'

It felt like dragging words out of him. How did I live with this man all those years? she found herself wondering. These days she was used to Tom, who was so quick and always had something to say.

'I don't know how it'll go down at work.'

She could see that Len did not know what to say. Being

93

a man, it was not an issue for him. Len Gilby he was, and Len Gilby he would remain.

'It'll probably be all right,' he said eventually.

They exchanged a few more comments about the children. There seemed absolutely nothing else they could say, and soon Len turned down Maryvale Road.

'See you around,' they both said, like acquaintances who had met only a few times.

Ann was still recovering from this as she turned onto Beaumont Road. One of the houses still had a string of bunting sagging across the front window, all grey now, with little icicles hanging from it. It gave her a pang of sadness. The end of the war, the bonfires and dancing happiness of those days seemed so far away now. And everyday life was back with a vengeance, all around, having to be dealt with.

She was glad Len lived close by, so that the children could all see him and things would be as normal as possible. In most respects, she did not regret her marriage to Len for all those years. And yet . . . Even if the past had been all right – good even, a lot of the time – somehow she didn't want it to keep turning up, to bump into it in the street and have to look it in the face. Suddenly she had a bit more of an inkling of how Jeanette must be feeling.

'I made some soup,' Joy greeted her, doling it into a bowl. 'Here you go. Leek-and-potato.'

'Nice,' Ann said carefully. And it was. Tasty, with thin curls of leek.

Patty was excited about the snow. She kept kicking her plump legs, staring at the window as Joy tried to feed her.

'Oi, you,' Joy ticked her off, fondly. 'I'll take you out to see it a bit later, but you need to sit still.'

Ann watched her daughter. Her thin arms, bony face. Her natural rosy prettiness had shrunk back and she looked so strained. But she didn't seem to want anyone to ask. Thank goodness for that nice Dr Saloman, Ann thought. He was so kind, and she realized Joy could probably talk more to him about Alan than to anyone else. It wasn't as if Alan could hide much anyway, Ann thought. Or so she imagined then.

Ann and Joy shared out the housework between them, and the two of them muddled along quite well. Now Tom had a job, they were not desperate for Ann's wages, but she was happy to be working at Cadbury's – to get out and give Joy some time with no one else about. Even when Alan was at work as well, somehow there was a feeling of tension, which Joy herself could never seem to shake off.

By the time Tom and Alan came back from Cadbury's that evening, the snow had been falling again for a couple of hours.

'I hope it's not going to last,' Ann said as she and Tom got ready for bed. The wireless had said there were terrible storms down south.

'Oh, I don't s'pose it will. At least we've nearly finished the digging.'

As he had suggested, Tom had got Alan to help, and between the two of them they had started to get to grips with the garden. Ann had watched now and then through the window, wondering at the strangeness of men. Alan was doing the digging and Tom was clearing out weeds and brambles.

If that was two women, she thought, they'd be nattering away. As it was, the two of them worked in complete silence, unless some instruction or question was needed. She couldn't fathom it – she only hoped it was doing both of them good. They seemed to enjoy it anyway.

'The last bit can wait.' Tom pulled his pyjama top on

awkwardly, swinging round so that the jacket covered the rough scars of his left shoulder. His arm had not been amputated; it was blown off. Ann had never known Tom without this wound, but every time she saw it, she would feel a pang of dread. How easily he might have died. But he was here. Blessedly here.

'This is my favourite time of day,' she said, getting in under the covers. Downstairs there was no privacy.

'Mine too.' Tom peered out of the window. 'It's still going strong out there.' He closed the curtain and got into bed with her. She lay on the left side of the bed and he could lie on his side and wrap his right arm around her.

'Is work all right?' she asked anxiously. Even though Tom kept assuring her that he was quite happy in his job at Cadbury's, she still worried. He had come here for her – she didn't want him to be unhappy.

'It's fine,' he said. 'Everyone's been very kind. They're good people. I ran into a fellow today, face a terrible mess . . .'

'Oh, I've seen him around,' Ann said. 'It's awful – he's all scars. But I'm sure he can work all right.'

'He's German, you know?'

'*Is* he?' Her head shot up. 'How strange.'

'Yes. Does a good job, though, I gather. How's life in the Roses department?'

'Oh, it's fine.' She laughed. 'I mean, they're not quite what they were – powdered milk and all that. They just can't get the fresh milk, and haven't for years.'

'Getting parts is the devil as well.'

'Did you know, they're named after Miss Dorothy Cadbury's favourite flower? The Roses, I mean?'

Tom laughed. 'No. But that's nice. I saw her today – I think so anyway. Cycling along the Lane, on her bike with an umbrella up.'

'Oh, that'll be her,' Ann laughed. 'Bit of a character. I always used to be a little scared of her, but she's quite nice really.' She turned to him. 'Tom, is it really all right?'

'Ann, it's more than all right.' Tom kissed her. 'Where else would I be but here? And they've given me a chance. It's wonderful.'

'OK.' She turned the light off. 'I love you – so much.'

Tom pulled her close. 'My darling.'

Ann settled down, but her mind was racing. Thank heaven for Tom, always so grateful for each day as it came. She didn't need to worry about him, which was a blessing, because she had quite enough on her mind with her children.

Fourteen

'Where's Alan?' Tom asked, bringing in the last of a pile of firewood that had been stored inside the old air-raid shelter at the bottom of the garden.

'Gone to see his mother and Irene,' Joy said. She was sitting with Patty, both of them wrapped in a blanket, reading her a story.

'What, in this?' Tom was dusted with fast-melting snow. He knelt to deposit by the hearth the firewood he had been able to gather in one arm. 'I'll bring in what more I can. It'll have to dry out a bit.'

'Why don't you leave it for Alan to do?' Ann said, coming in.

'I can manage,' Tom replied. Joy heard, *Don't treat me as if I'm incapable*, and saw her mother button her lip.

'It never seems to stop.' Ann looked out, watching Tom make his way through the inches of snow already in the garden. 'There's hardly any coal to be had. We should've got that wood out of there ages ago – I s'pose your father put it there.'

'I hope Al's going to be able to get back all right,' Joy said. 'Are the trams still running in this?'

She felt all the time now that she never knew what Alan was going to do next. He would disappear for hours at a time, when he was not at work, and all the while he was gone she was filled with unease. She didn't really know why – he always came back. He was just so strange sometimes, and she could not work out what was going on in his head.

'He'll be all right, don't fret, Joy.' Ann came and sat on the other side of Patty and caressed the little girl's hair out of her eyes. 'D'you want to come and help Nanna in the kitchen, sweetheart?'

Patty nodded, solemn. She liked 'helping' – playing with a bowl of water or a few pegs and other things from the kitchen.

'Thanks, Mom.' Joy sat back and looked out at the whirling snow and darkening afternoon. 'It's not got above zero for days.'

Alan did come back, reporting that the trams and buses were still running, but that soon they would be having to dig them out if it didn't stop snowing.

But it did not stop. The weather went on and on, snow and blizzards in the countryside, high winds building huge drifts and blocking roads.

Every morning Ann, Tom and Alan set off for the Cadbury works and managed to stagger back again after their shift. There was more than a foot of snow in the garden. Everyone in the street tried to sweep or shovel their bit of pavement to keep it clear. To Joy's surprise, Alan got up every morning and shovelled the snow outside their house and cleared the front path and steps.

'Well, Tom can't do it, can he?' he said. She realized he had gained a deep respect for Tom, and it made her even more grateful to her stepfather.

The bad weather went on and on, with forecasts only promising more of the same. Coal was rationed and sometimes there was none to be delivered. They only ever heated the front room, and going to bed was misery. Joy would get Patty ready in front of the fire, put a hot-water bottle in her cot to warm it and then hurry upstairs to wrap her up warmly.

Their own bedrooms were icy cold, the windows white with ice on the insides when they woke in the morning. Icicles hung from the gutters, the air was bitingly cold, and every morning they went staggering along, trying not to slip and fall after each night's freeze. Pipes froze, even birds froze. There were pictures in the paper of just the roofs of buses showing in deep snowdrifts out on country roads. And the days turned into weeks.

Joy hated being cold and couldn't see the point of winter at the best of times. But now with the sheer misery of frozen feet, being stuck inside all the time – and often she didn't feel that much warmer in than out – and rationing, and nothing much to look forward to, she felt really low.

But what surprised her was Alan.

'The sheets are like ice,' she moaned one night, shivering as if she had a fever as she hurried to get into bed.

'Come on, I'm warming it for you.' Alan pulled the cover back. 'Jump in.'

She hurried up close to him, so tense with shivering that it took her ages to get warm enough to relax her muscles.

'I can't stand it,' she said, her teeth chattering. 'Aren't *you* cold?'

'Yeah,' he said, 'Course.'

He was very thin. She had already bought him some long-johns, knowing that winter was going to be hard for him. And yet he was making less fuss than her. And Alan was up, shovelling snow in the freezing dawn, and as these weeks of appalling, extreme weather passed he seemed almost cheerful.

*

The snow went on and on into February. One morning she woke to find him already up and gone. Patty was awake, so Joy got out of bed and carried her downstairs.

'You'll have to learn to walk down by yourself soon, little pickle,' she said fondly. Patty had just turned two.

In the kitchen she found a big pan piled with snow on the lit stove and Alan halfway through the door with another bucketful.

'What on earth?' she said. 'Oh, don't say . . .'

'Yep. Pipes are frozen. I was going to make you a cuppa, but no dice.' He turned the tap to demonstrate. Not even a drip came out. Joy groaned.

'That's all we need.' A thought struck her. 'What about the lavs?'

Alan shrugged. 'Buckets of snow water, I suppose.'

She stared gloomily at the melting snow. 'I hope it's not going to poison us.'

'Oh, I don't suppose so,' he said. 'I've drunk worse, believe me.'

'Yes – well, that's why you've got dysentery,' she retorted.

He turned. 'C'mere.'

She still had Patty in her arms. They huddled together in a hug.

'You're very cheerful,' she said.

'Yeah.' Alan sounded puzzled himself.

His strangely buoyant mood continued. Joy was glad of it – he was so cheerful suddenly – but something about it did make her feel uneasy. He went striding off to work, shovelled snow, boiled up meltwater in pans on the stove. He and Tom even went off round the parks, trying to find wood to boost their meagre supply of coal. They came home with a few wet bits of branch and twigs, which had to dry out for ages before they would burn.

'You want to tell that lad of yours in the mines to get digging,' Alan joked with Tom over tea one night.

Tom smiled. 'Martin's not a collier – they're the ones who actually dig it out. But yes.'

'I keep thinking about him,' Ann said. Joy could see she was worried. 'What must it be like over there?'

'Good job it's hard work,' Tom said. 'Help keep them warm.'

Ann looked reproachfully at him. She was the one doing all the worrying. It was as if all these men actually *liked* things to be difficult.

'He'll be all right,' Alan said. 'Strong lad, he is.'

Joy watched Alan, eating fast as he always did, almost like a dog, as if he was afraid someone else might steal his dinner from under his nose. It was disturbing and she looked away.

He's enjoying this, Joy thought. Maybe 'enjoying' was not the word – but something. Almost as if he needed things to be hard and horrible, and living in some kind of crisis made him feel more at ease with things.

'You know, you two,' Mom's voice cut into her thoughts, as she looked back and forth between Joy and Alan, 'you haven't been out and had fun for ages. I know you've got Patty, but when this lot's cleared away' – she nodded towards the window – 'why don't you go to some dances? You used to love it, both of you. And Tom and I'll be here. We're not going anywhere, are we, love?'

'Not as I know of.' Tom smiled.

Joy felt her spirits lift for a moment. Until now it had never felt as if Alan was well enough to think of doing anything like that. But dancing was what had brought the two of them together. Alan had been a wonderful dancer and, for her, dance was the breath of life. It was an age since she had been able to dance – to go out and have a good time – and she could feel herself getting excited at the thought.

'Oh yes!' she said. 'That would be . . . Oh, Al – let's!'

But Alan's face had turned wooden, stiff, as if he was shrivelling in on himself.

'Nah,' he said. 'Don't think so.' He had already finished eating, before everyone else, and put his knife and fork down and got up. 'Not any more.'

And he left the room.

It happened that night. Joy was still angry with Alan for the way he rejected even the idea of doing something she might enjoy. Afterwards she wondered if that had been the reason it occurred – as if things had been stirred up in her mind.

She was lying in bed, trying to drift into sleep. The room was so cold that when the light was on, they had been able to see their breath. She could feel the chill pressing on her face and ears and she shrank right under the covers, trying to warm herself with her own breath. It was hard to fall asleep completely, and her thoughts swam in and out . . .

It was not a dream, exactly. Words began repeating in her head, insistent and clear. It was as if they had been waiting, lurking there deep in the folds of her mind. Something she did not, could not, understand – like something pressed down underwater, which had suddenly rushed to the surface . . . Weeks ago she had heard Alan say these words, but only now did they seem to ring out and she began to take in the meaning of them.

Tom and Alan had been sitting there, heads close together, talking. Tom had asked something that ended in 'Chindits?' And now Alan's reply came echoing after it along the tunnel of time: 'January forty-four – that's when we went into Burma. And then, well, a few of us ran into

103

a group of them, in March: an ambush sort of thing.' That was when he had been captured by the Japanese. *Forty-four . . . Forty-four . . .*

Sleep snatched itself back, like someone twitching away the covers. Joy was wide awake, her heart pounding. She grabbed Alan and shook him hard, for once not caring whether she scared the living daylights out of him, because *by God* he had some questions to answer. Alan let out an anguished shriek as he jerked upright.

'Just shut up, it's me,' she hissed furiously.

'For God's sake, Joy.' She could hear him panting. 'What the hell's going on?'

'You tell me? Right – listen. You said, to Tom, that you went into Burma in January forty-four?'

'Yeah?' He sounded completely bewildered, and resentful.

'And you were captured in March? Nineteen forty-four.' She already felt as if her head was going to explode. She could hardly breathe. '*March nineteen forty-four.*'

There was a long pause. She realized the penny had dropped. He knew what she was about to say. She felt him shrink from her physically in the bed.

'The last letter I had from you was in March *nineteen forty-three.*' The silence expanded beside her. She could only just hear his breathing. 'So for a whole year, when you couldn't be bothered to write and tell me you were still alive, *what the hell were you doing?*'

Fifteen

It took Alan time to splutter into speech.

'I was . . . We were . . . training.'

Joy was holding onto herself very tightly. She had actually wrapped her arms round herself, to keep warm, but also to hold herself in. She was glad she could not see Alan. She kept quiet; she was not going to help him, not after all this.

'We were in Ceylon first – then they moved us to India.'

He seemed to have been everywhere. Unlike Kenneth, who had stayed in Italy once he was abroad.

'A bunch of us went to Bengal; it was all different, see, the way we were organized then. We ended up with that nutter Orde Wingate.'

Joy knew who he meant. Orde Wingate, the famous Major General – hero or crazy man, it seemed, depending on your point of view – had created the forces known as the Chindits and led them into Japanese-held territory in Burma.

'And?' Impatience flared in her. Alan was saying things step-by-step, as if taking care not to say anything that would drop him in it. She could tell he was evading the real meaning of her question, and she could not make sense of any of it. 'Did he forbid letter-writing or something?'

Another silence. Why wasn't Alan answering? Yes or no to that? What the hell was going on?

'So what were you doing. Before that? Did you meet someone else or what?' As soon as she said it, she thought,

What other reason could there be for what felt to her like his cruel silence?

And now another silence, which went on, gave him away.

'What – was that it? You met some woman?'

Alan lowered his head.

'And you just . . .' She could not get the words out. 'Threw me away? Left me here thinking you were wounded or dead? Out of my mind with worry? Was that it?'

Did she want to know any more? She did. She could not stop now.

'Who was she?' Again, a silence. Joy elbowed him, with force. 'Alan, answer me!'

'She worked for the Red Cross. In Calcutta. A sort of secretary, I think.'

'Oh, you think? And did she have a name?'

'Joy,' he protested. 'You went with someone else. You had a baby . . .'

'Because I thought you were dead!' She was screaming now, hysterical, out of control. Yelling at the top of her voice. 'I waited for every post, every day, for months and months. But nothing. You couldn't lift a finger to write me one measly letter! And I trusted you; I believed you'd write if you were OK, not leave me thinking . . . How *could* you? You bastard, how could you do that to me: just not bother, let me think you were dead?'

She was shrieking, sobbing and then Patty woke up, howling at being startled out of sleep. Joy was climbing out of bed to reach her when she heard feet running up the stairs and a knock on the door.

'Joy?' Her mother's voice in the dark. 'What on earth's going on? Is it Patty?'

'It's all right,' Alan tried to say.

'No, it's not all right!' Joy was still yelling, hysterical

now. She could not control it; it all poured out of her. Patty, in her arms, was beside herself.

Her mother, wearing only her pale-pink nightdress, clicked the light on and held her arms out. Patty almost fell into them to get away from the terrifying banshee her mother had turned into.

'Ask him.' Joy pointed, with a hoarse shriek. 'Ask him what he was doing for a *whole year* while he let me think he was dead. Or had left me . . . because he had!' She knew she was not making much sense. Her mother stood, eyes wide with shock, jiggling Patty and murmuring to her, 'It's all right, pet. Don't you fret' and kissing her. She was barefoot and starting to shiver herself.

'Joy, it's one o'clock in the morning.'

'I don't care what sodding time it is,' she ranted, turning on Alan. '*You* tell her, you bastard. Why should I have to flaming well tell her the truth?'

Alan sat in bed, hollow-eyed, looking terrible – but not completely sorry.

'There was a war on,' he said stubbornly. 'We went for a dance, a drink now and then.' He looked up at Joy. 'Didn't you ever dance with anyone else?'

For a second Lawrence Dayton flashed into her mind, the lively, brilliant dancer she had become close to during the war. That brilliant dancer who also turned out to be married. She hesitated, before the reality came back and smacked her in the face. Alan was not getting away with that!

'That's not the point.' She was almost raving. 'Yes, I danced with someone else. A friend – just a friend. But I *wrote* to you, waited for you, all that time, worried to death until it had been so long that . . . What else was I supposed to think?' She was really working herself up again. 'I thought that if you were OK, you would let me know; that you'd bother. I trusted you. And you just cut me off – threw me away like a bit of rubbish. I only met Hank after I thought you were never coming back and that you must be dead.'

Ann, seeing how serious things were, sank down on the bed, a snivelling Patty in her lap, and pulled the eiderdown around them both.

'Tell her the truth, Alan,' she said. And Joy could hear that her mother was too tired to sugar-coat anything. 'Everyone's sorry for all you've been through. But you owe this to Joy. She was worried to death about you for months on end. Come on – out with it.'

Alan was looking resentful now. Trapped. But orders from his mother-in-law were rare, and he could see that he had to face it.

'She was a secretary . . .'

'Name?' Joy barked. At this moment she did not feel like crying. She was too full of rage. And there was something strange and energetic about the anger that filled her. As if she felt more alive than she had in months.

'Noreen. Smithson.'

'I bet you've got a picture, somewhere.' Joy was relentless.

'No.' Then, 'Yes,' he admitted.

'Get it.'

'Joy, is there any point in—' Ann tried to say.

'Yes, there is! If he wants me to run round and look after him for the rest of our lives, then I want the truth. That's all. Did you decide she wouldn't make a good nursemaid in the long run then?'

'No, it wasn't like that.' Alan had got out of bed. He opened his bottom drawer, where he kept a box of his army bits and pieces, then stood up slowly. He handed Joy a photograph, about three inches by two.

Looking back at her was a dark-eyed, very pretty young woman with full lips and beautiful, thick long hair. Joy's head shot up.

'She's Indian?'

'Her mother was.'

She stared long at the photograph. The girl was so lovely-looking. It was like being punched. Without thinking, she handed it to her mother.

'You were in love with her.' Her voice was low now, as if the wind had been knocked out of her. 'How could you not be in love with her?'

'I just . . .' He was speaking honestly now and sounded wretched. 'I mean, I suppose I was. It was an odd sort of time, treading water before they sent us north for jungle training. And when we managed to get into town I s'pose I went a bit crazy. It was an . . . a what-d'you-call-it?'

'Infatuation?' Ann said.

'So you went crazy for this woman – and I didn't exist any more? On the other side of the world?'

He looked up at her. 'It did feel a bit like that. Another world.'

'And you had done away with me.'

That was how it had been, she could see. In Alan's mind, he had left her behind. It was a horrible clear, hard moment.

Alan had got back into bed and spoke, looking down at the rumpled blankets and eiderdown.

'After they captured us, of course I had plenty of time to think about all of it. About you. But they wouldn't let us send out letters.' His face creased, Joy wasn't sure whether with loathing or sorrow. 'So I couldn't . . .'

Abruptly, from anger and bolshie self-pity, he was crying.

'I swear to God, Joy – all that time, it was you I was thinking about. Dreaming about.'

'Well, that was bloody nice of you, after not bothering yourself with me for a whole year,' she spat back at him.

'Home,' he choked out. 'You. And home – you *were* home, for me.'

There was a silence. Almost silence. Patty, still awake, cradled against Ann, watched tear-stained, but no longer crying. Alan wept quietly. Joy was dry-eyed now. She thought about Lawrence, and what she had felt. About Hank, whom she had tried to love, to persuade herself that she loved (because that was the truth, deep down) and could make a life with in a far-away country. Had to, once she had borne his child.

She felt weary to her bones. What could be done now, about any of it? But that was still not enough. It wasn't Alan falling for someone else. That was not the worst thing.

'Are you even sorry?' Her voice was quieter now and sad. 'I could forgive what you did – but not for not writing when you were alive. Just letting me think . . . That was so cruel.'

'I'm sorry, Joy. I really am. I wasn't thinking. Not properly. It didn't feel like real life out there. We'd been in so many places. Home felt so far away, like another life. I didn't know if I'd ever see it again – or you.'

Joy sank down onto the bed now, next to her mother.

'Come here, darlin'.' She took Patty, who was growing sleepy again now, and cuddled her, rocking her.

'Let's get some sleep,' her mother said, getting up stiffly. Joy noticed that she did not add, as she had often done when they were children, 'It'll all look different in the morning. Shall I put her down?' She looked at Patty.

'It's OK – I'll do it. Come on, pickle.'

Her mother left the room wearily, without saying any more. Joy laid Patty in her cot and she did not protest.

'It's all right, little one,' she murmured. 'You go to sleep now.'

She switched the light off again and climbed into bed next to Alan. After a moment he reached out and stroked the contours of her body as she lay turned away from him. She flinched, trying to move out of his reach.

'I'm sorry,' he said. 'I am.'

Neither of them said anything else.

Joy lay curled up tight, such a long way from being able to sleep. An image of the future unfolded before her, stretching ahead like in a show at the pictures: a country road, long and endless, with farms and barns and cottages, telegraph poles flashing past each side. Their future. It felt endless and inevitable.

She would have to forgive him, she knew that. Try to forget, somehow. The rage and hurt she felt cut so deep. It was not so much the girl, Alan needing some love and comfort in a far-away place. It was that he had not given her even a thought, or how she would feel. It was enormous. Monstrous. That was the truth of it.

But now here they were and what could she do? Somehow they had to go on.

Sixteen

It was tea time and Sheila felt as if her nerves were all standing on end. In fact these days she felt like that most of the time.

'Don't like it,' Robbie said in a tiny voice. They were all struggling through a watery stew Sheila had made. Even she had to admit the mutton scrag-end was hard-going, and Robbie looked ready to burst into tears at the very sight of it.

Kenneth gave him a look, but didn't say anything. Sheila tensed up even more.

'Eat up,' Nanna Margaret wheedled kindly, seeing Kenneth's face. 'It's nourishing. It'll make you a big strong boy.'

Robbie gave her a look of extreme doubt and slid a tiny morsel into his mouth.

'That's it, kid,' Grandad Cyril said, raising his glass of water. 'Bottoms up to you!'

Robbie grinned suddenly. 'Bottoms up!'

Sheila tried to force a smile to her face. That was what Nanna and Grandad had been doing for weeks now – trying to jolly everyone along.

She felt very grateful. And guilty. And angry with Kenneth that he kept letting her grandparents see their problems. He had flared up and lost his temper quite a few times. Sometimes she wondered what had happened to the easy-going, steady man she had married. But it was partly just the way things were, she could acknowledge that. He had changed – but she was not the easiest-tempered person these days. She felt queasy, what with the coming baby. And trapped.

'I don't like snow,' Elaine grumbled. It was late February; the snow had lain for nearly a month and the novelty had long worn off. So far in 1947 there had been nothing but bad weather. A few days of snowmen and snowball fights and sliding about on a tin tray had been fun at first. But now they were all sick of it. The cold pressed down on them, made everything a miserable struggle – getting up, going to bed, stepping outside the house.

'We've all had enough of it,' she said.

'When's it going to stop?' Elaine held her hands out with the melodrama of a seven-year-old.

'We don't know. Eat your tea,' Kenneth said.

Elaine scowled at him. Sheila found herself praying inwardly, *Please don't say, 'I don't like you, Daddy.'*

Day after day, the snow kept coming. There were blizzards, and pictures in the paper showed astonishing, house-high drifts in some country places. But it was bad enough here. Getting anywhere was an ordeal. They didn't have the right shoes. Sheila and other mothers tied newspaper round their kids' legs to try and keep them warm on the way to school. Coal was in extremely short supply – both for industry and at home. They all ended up huddling in one room until they could face going up to bed.

The pavements were like an ice rink after the dark, frozen nights. The wireless gave reports of trains and buses unable to reach towns and villages. And everyone was either struggling to work to be cold there or was trapped, chilled inside their houses. Imprisoned by the weather.

And all Mom could say was, *Poor Martin – whatever must it be like for the miners?* At least that was all she said, until Joy and Alan's row erupted; according to her, in the middle of the night. Mom had come round, very upset, and poured it all out to Margaret and Sheila: what Alan had done, what he had not done. How hurt and angry Joy was.

'Doesn't Joy mind you telling us?' Sheila asked. She was not so keen on airing her problems, and Kenneth's, all round the family.

Mom shrugged. The three women sat huddled close to the feeble fire. Mom still had her coat on.

'She said you might as well know. You'll find out sooner or later. She can hardly even look at him.'

'Fancy,' Margaret said. 'I mean Joy's not been snowy-white – but Alan keeping her hanging on like that all that time – I can hardly believe it.'

'Sounds as if he left her,' Sheila said. 'Sort of. Forgot her. And then changed his mind when it suited him. That's terrible.'

They all agreed it *was* terrible.

'But we're all living under the same roof,' Mom said. 'So one way or another they're going to have to sort themselves out.'

And, Sheila thought afterwards, of all people, Mom would know about having to make the best of things.

It was so cold that she and Kenneth had to cuddle up together for warmth, even if they were in a bad mood with each other. It helped make things better. Made them make love sometimes, even when they had been fighting, because lying close like that, one thing led to another.

Tea time had not been easy, or getting the kids to bed. They filled hot-water bottles and slid them into their beds. At least their pipes weren't frozen, like they were in Mom's house.

'I don't want to get undressed,' Elaine had protested, earlier on at bedtime, sitting as close as she could to the fire.

'Oh, just get on with it,' Kenneth ordered.

Elaine started crying.

'Leave it,' Sheila snapped at him. 'You're only making things worse. Go somewhere else 'til I get them down.'

'What's that supposed to mean? Where am I s'posed to go?' Kenneth said, leaning close to the wireless to try and tune in. A scrambled mix of foreign words poured out. He found some music and sat crouched, listening. Cyril, who was in his chair, kept out of it.

Sheila and Margaret exchanged *oh dear, someone's in a bad mood* looks.

'Come on, Elaine.' Sheila drew on every reserve of patience she could find, even though she felt ready to explode. 'Soon as you've got changed we'll run upstairs – and I've done you a nice hottie.'

And now, lying together with the children breathing steadily across the room, things felt better. There was a warmth between herself and Kenneth as they spooned together, despite the room being like an ice-box. Sheila pulled the sheet up as high as she could. Every morning there was ice inside the windows – beautiful, it was true, but she had never known it this cold. Kenneth kissed the back of her neck.

'Always waiting for something, aren't we?' she said. 'The end of the war. The end of the snow. The end of rationing. A house . . .' She turned over and snuggled close again. 'Things will get better, won't they? Tell me they will!'

'Yeah. Flaming hope so, anyway. I'm sorry, Sheila. It's not that I'm not grateful to your nan and grandad. But we're all so cooped up. At work as well – that's how it feels. Sometimes I can hardly stand it.'

'Waiting again.'

'Yeah.' She heard his voice gain energy, and a curl of

dread started in her belly. 'But what're we waiting for? In the long run? If we ever get a house – I mean, I'll still be stuck in the same job and—'

'You could get a different job?'

'Yeah, I s'pose. It's just . . . there's so much more to life. Going to work, the factory, coming home. We could see the world: get out there. When the kids are older we could take them to Italy. It's beautiful. I mean, it's poor, but it's different.'

'Yes. That would be nice,' she said politely, not really having any idea or believing it would happen. 'Look, maybe I could take them down to Audrey's – give you a bit of a break?'

'You can't go down in this.'

'No, when the weather picks up.'

'Yeah, if you want.' But that was not what he was interested in. 'Sheila. About Australia. I meant it.'

The dread unfurled like a fern and spread. She was a wife; you were supposed to follow your husband wherever he went. She couldn't speak and the silence got longer.

'You know,' Kenneth said eventually. He sounded shy suddenly. Awkward. And she felt closer to him again. 'About Joy. And Alan. I never did that. Got involved with anyone else. I never would've.'

Sheila was moved. She could hear how difficult it was for him to talk about things.

'I know,' she said. Even though she had wondered, a little. Everyone must wonder, she thought.

'I'd never have done what he did. The way he didn't let her know. It's . . . well, it's shocking. But somehow, after what he's supposed to have gone through, not that we really know anything . . . it makes it hard to say anything against him really, doesn't it?'

'It's between them,' Sheila said.

'Yeah. But I just want you to know, that's all. I'd never . . .'

She hugged him. Thank God he'd got off the subject of Australia.

'Thanks,' she said. 'I know. I believe you.'

'Will you think about it?' he said. 'Us going over there – Australia?'

She so badly did not want to. Everything in her rebelled against the idea. But he was being so loving and she could hear the longing in his voice.

'Can we think about it after the baby's born?' she asked. 'Please? I don't think I can cope with it when I'm like this. It's only a few months. Another September baby.'

'All right, yeah.' He kissed her again, sounding pleased. 'That's all right. But promise me you won't just say no – we'll find out more. Think about it properly. A new start: an adventure.'

Against everything she was feeling, she said, 'Yes. All right. But, Kenneth? This baby, it should be our last, don't you think? Three's enough. Specially if you want to go abroad.'

'Yeah. All right.' He was drawing even closer to her now, happy, ready to make love. She kissed him back, feeling closer than they had been in a while.

Oh well, she thought, as their kissing became more passionate, I'm already expecting anyway. At least that was one thing she didn't have to worry about.

Seventeen

'When will this ever end?' Ann groaned. 'It's colder now, if anything. My feet have been like blocks of ice all day.'

It was March and the weather was still terrible. Ann and Molly were creeping along in front of the works in a bitter wind and between piles of snow, trying not to fall over. Day after day Ann stood on the Roses line, working away marking the chocolates, with the sweet smell of them all around her, stamping her feet to try and thaw them out. Thank heavens there were the others to have a moan and a laugh with! The freezing weather had gone on and on, getting suddenly even colder again over the last couple of days.

The sky was leaden and looked as if more snow was about to fall. Everywhere, as far as they could see, was muffled white.

'I've got chilblains on both feet,' Molly complained. 'They're murder – and I've got rehearsals tonight. I bet my flaming feet'll be itching all through it!'

Molly, who had a lovely singing voice, was part of Bournville's Musical Theatre Company and always seemed to be practising for something or other. The society was almost completely made up of Cadbury workers, although a few others were allowed in, if necessary.

'Sounds nice,' Ann said vaguely, her mind wandering to what was waiting for her at home: the atmosphere between Joy and Alan was still very strained. It had made her even more thankful to be able to come out to work, despite the struggle to get here. And what were they going to have for tea?

'At least we don't have to rehearse in the air-raid shelter any more,' Molly said, laughing. 'Oh yes, it keeps me going, singing does. It's marvellous. We have a lot of fun. D'you know, before the war they even hired a donkey once and brought it on the stage.'

Ann forced a laugh, which stopped abruptly as her foot skidded and she nearly fell over. Her body felt jolted all over and for a second she felt like bursting into tears.

'Careful!' Molly grabbed her sleeve. 'Got you. Are you all right, Annie?'

Ann's eyes filled, despite herself. 'Yes, I am really. Just a bit of bother at home. I'm sure it'll blow over.'

'Look, why don't you come to the show next week? You and your husband? I can get you tickets. We're doing *The Geisha* and I'm singing in a group with some other girls – one of the songs is called "The Amorous Goldfish".' There in the street she started singing a song that was so absurd, and she was so funny singing it, that Ann burst out laughing.

'See?' Molly grinned. 'It'll cheer you up. The concert hall will be freezing, I expect, so bring blankets. But it'll take your mind off things.'

'All right,' Ann laughed. 'I'll think about it – I'll see if Tom wants to come.' She still felt a little thrill when she said his name like that. *Ann and Tom.* Soon, eventually, he would be her husband – not that she went round mentioning to anyone, not even to Molly, that he wasn't already. Despite everything else, this warmed her inside.

'I'll get you two tickets,' Molly said, turning off along Bournville Lane. 'No arguments!'

*

Ann reached home at dinner time, frozen to the marrow. She stamped the mucky snow off her feet on the mat. Even though the house was cold, it still felt warmer than outside. She slipped off her wet shoes and pulled on her slippers, hearing little noises from Patty in the front room.

Putting her head round the door, she found Joy and Patty by the electric fire they had resorted to buying. It felt as if you couldn't win – you could burn coal in the house, or the power stations could use it to generate electricity for your fire, but either way there was still never enough to go around.

The whole situation was a mess, with everyone complaining about Manny Shinwell, the Energy Minister, though Ann couldn't help feeling that it was hardly his fault that most of the coal was frozen solid. All of them wondered how Martin was, but he hardly ever let them know.

Patty was playing with a doll that Elaine had given her – 'I'm too old for that now I'm at school' – and Joy was trying her best to join in, except that Ann could see she was miles away.

'Cuppa?'

Joy jumped. 'Oh, I didn't hear you come in.'

'There's a drop of soup – come and have it.'

The three of them sat around the kitchen table. Life was easier when the men were out. They both got on with what had to be done. But it was now a week since Joy had confronted Alan and the atmosphere was horrible whenever Alan was in the house. He and Joy had locked themselves into a silence – guilty and resentful on his part; enraged, bitter and jealous on hers. And Ann and Tom had to live with it.

The two of them found themselves discussing it every day.

'That was grim, what he did,' Tom had said last night. 'Terrible. And rotten for Joy. When you're at war, it can feel as if your real life doesn't . . . No, not that it doesn't exist,' he corrected himself. 'But that it's stopped for the moment and everything you do in between, before you get home and your real life starts again, doesn't really count. D'you see what I mean? That's how some blokes I was with behaved, anyway.'

'But it does count – for her,' Ann said.

'Yes.' Tom was silent for a moment. 'But they're here now, aren't they? That's the reality. They're either going to have to get over it or . . .' It was hard to finish that sentence.

Now, looking across the table at Joy slowly sipping her lentil soup, Ann thought, How thin she is, and she looks so unhappy. It brought tears to Ann's eyes. Joy had once been so blooming and pretty, with her lovely clothes and dancing feet. It wrung her heart to see her like this.

'You can't go on like this, love,' she said gently. She glanced at Patty. The little girl was too young to understand this conversation, or so Ann hoped.

'Eat your toast, pet.' Joy zoomed a piece of toast towards Patty's lips like an aeroplane. 'Before it flies away!'

Patty chewed obediently.

'I know.' Joy's eyes filled. 'It's not the affair – that's not the main thing.' She shook her head, tears welling up.

'It's the not writing to you?'

'He went on as if I didn't exist!' The bottled-up words came pouring out. 'He didn't give a thought to how things were for me: all the worry, waiting every day and praying for a letter. I know what men are like – with women, I mean. But it's Alan treating me as if I didn't matter any more, didn't even exist.'

She wiped her face and looked across at Ann, her big

brown eyes still swimming with tears. 'I don't know if I'll ever get over that. When I think . . .'

She paused to cut Patty another finger of toast and held it up to her, bravely trying to smile. Ann waited.

'When I was at Tidworth in the army camp, waiting to go to America and marry Hank, and Irene came and told me, I'd have done anything for Al. Anything. When I saw him in the hospital, the state he was in, and he clung to me as if I was the most important thing in the world . . .'

She laid her hand on her heart.

'He was so broken up. And he needed me so much. I felt as if my heart was melting for him. Nothing would have made me go to America after that. But now,' her voice was hard and angry as she finished, 'I feel as if he tricked me. Not tricked – not on purpose, but . . . I should have gone and married Hank. Al hadn't really loved me and thought about me, the way he made out he had.'

She broke down then and cried, broken-heartedly, with her hands over her face.

'Mom?' Patty gazed, full of dismay. 'Mommy?'

Ann got up quickly, walked round the table and put her arms around Joy.

'It's all right, darling.' She drew Patty into the hug as well. 'Your mom's just feeling a bit sad.'

She held Joy as her grief and anger stormed through her.

'I don't know if I can ever forgive him,' she sobbed. 'I don't know how to get past it. Alan says he's sorry, but it doesn't seem to mean anything – not after all that. It's just a word, isn't it, easy to say?'

'Speak to him, will you?' Ann said to Tom later. 'We can't go on like this. If I try and say anything I'll lose my temper. I know Alan's been through a lot, but still – I can't bear to see Joy like this.'

'I need a word, Alan,' Tom said that evening. He led Alan into the front room while Ann and Joy stayed in the kitchen. If the weather had been different he would have taken him out into the garden, spoken while they were busy with something perhaps. But yet more snow had fallen during the day and the house felt muffled and wrapped in silence, as if they were separate from all the world outside. There was no going anywhere.

Tom and Alan sat on each side of the hearth. Alan was shivering, huddled up as close to the fire as could get. He was so thin that he found it difficult ever to feel properly warm.

The lad's in a state still, there's no doubt, Tom thought, looking at him. And he knows something's coming.

'Look,' he said, 'none of us know what went on in those camps.'

'No, and no one wants to, do they?' Alan erupted. It was the first sign of energy he had shown all week. He had seemed locked inside himself. 'No one wants to hear a thing about it!'

'I know.' And Tom did. The light, polite way that people would say you were free to put it all behind you now. People who had no idea. 'They don't,' he agreed. 'I know. I used to feel angry about it. People talking about all sorts of nonsense, yet never asking about those things that were . . . Well, you couldn't imagine them unless you were there. Things you . . . As if it was some dirty secret that we can't —'

He had to stop, his throat tightening. He was startled at his own words, and at the old emotions suddenly surging through him. Alan's head jerked up, and Tom could tell that the thickened sound of his own voice had betrayed what was happening to him. There was a link between them. An understanding.

'I've had longer to think about it,' Tom went on, when he could speak again. Even so, he felt suddenly as frail as a twig – a feeling he had not had for some years now. It was going back over it, that was the trouble. He tried to pull himself together. 'They can't imagine it, that's the thing. But over the years I've started to think, Wouldn't it be worse if they could? If what happens in war was normal, so that anyone could easily imagine it? If that ever happens, we're all done for, I'd say.'

Alan stared at him, sunken eyes huge in his gaunt, haunted face.

'It's lonely,' he whispered. 'Knowing. The worst. The most . . . Animal – no, worse than animal. Evil.' He cringed, as if some memory was assaulting him. 'I don't want to know. I want it to be taken away.'

'And compared with that, your little . . . fling with a woman,' Tom could not keep the bitter criticism out of his voice, 'you not telling Joy anything, not writing ever, to let her know how you were – that seems nothing, in comparison?'

Alan's face darkened. 'She just needs to get over it.'

Tom stared at him, trying to control his fury. Feelings surged from what had undoubtedly been the worst time of his life. He had met Ann, the beautiful nurse he had fallen deeply in love with in 1916, while he was a patient at Fircroft, the convalescent hospital in Birmingham, only to find she was engaged to another man. He had had to go back home to Southampton, his missing eye and arm meaning he could not do the work he loved – with no hope of Ann. That time back at home had been hell. Worse than the war. He was lonely and felt he had no future. But he had tried so hard not to take it out on his father and sisters. To behave as they needed him to. Because this was life, wasn't it – normal, safe, often monotonous life – not the hell he had come back from? No one needed to know about hell unless they had to go there.

'How can she get over it, Alan?' Tom found himself having to hold on to his temper. 'For Joy, it was a torment. Just because you have been through the worst doesn't mean no one else has been through anything. You caused her terrible suffering.' He swallowed. 'Can you remember what the King said, when the war ended? That we should try not to do anything unworthy of those who died for us?'

He saw a kind of writhing in Alan's face for a second. A memory. He knew what he said had hit home.

'You need to apologize.'

'But I *have*,' Alan snapped, getting to his feet in a rush. 'And I don't need you to—' He bit back whatever he was going to say. 'I keep flaming telling Joy I'm sorry, and she won't take any notice. What more does she want?'

Tom sat back, keeping his gaze firmly fixed on Alan.

'She needs you to mean it.'

Eighteen

'Oh, Joy, I'd forgotten – Molly gave me these.'

Joy took the two tickets her mother was holding out without much enthusiasm. She knew Tom had had words with Alan the night before, but still he was as cold and sulky as he had been before – it didn't seem to have changed anything. What the hell did he have to sulk about? she thought.

'You and Alan have them,' Mom was saying, lighting the gas under a pan of snow-water. 'Do you good to go out. Molly said to take warm clothes to the concert hall – a blanket even – although I think it's warming up a bit. I don't think I'm imagining it. Heavens, I hope so anyway. If the song Molly showed me was anything to go by, the show will be fun.'

Alan came in then, on his way out to the back garden for a smoke.

Joy held the tickets out. 'Mom said we could go and see this, if you like.'

She knew her own voice sounded dull, as if she already knew he wouldn't go. So far Alan had refused point-blank to go out dancing, which was the thing that had really bound the two of them together as youngsters, before the war. Joy thought he was embarrassed by the way he looked – as scrawny as a skeleton. But she knew it was more than that. He had changed so much. Before the war there was a flame of pleasure and lightness in Alan that had made him light-footed and skilled and fun. That had been

126

extinguished. She wondered if it could ever be lit again. But she knew she had to keep trying.

He looked at the tickets quite amiably and her heart lifted. But a second later, '*The Geisha?*' he burst out. He was almost frothing with rage, his face red and contorted. 'That's *Japanese*! You want me to go and watch *them* – those fucking . . . torturing bastards!' His eyes burned into hers. He was shaking.

'Oh,' Joy cried, horrified. She felt terrible. She hadn't even realized.

'Heavens, I'm ever so sorry, Alan. I didn't think,' Mom was saying wretchedly.

Of course there were no real Japanese people involved – it was Mom's friend Molly and other people from the works. It was all meant as a light-hearted bit of fun. But between them, she and Mom had made a terrible mistake.

'You've no idea, have you – you *stupid bitches*.' He hurled the tickets to the floor and slammed out into the dark garden.

'Oh God.' Joy put her hands over her face and sank into a chair. It was as if they had both been assaulted: by Alan's rage, his filthy language.

'I'm sorry.' Mom was patting her shoulder, sounding miserable. 'Oh, good Lord, I'm so terribly sorry.' She made as if to open the back door.

'Leave him,' Joy snapped. 'It won't do any good.'

'*We* might as well go then,' Ann said to Tom the next evening. 'It'd be a waste not to.'

Tom was quite happy to go to the musical with her, but what previously had felt like a bit of fun was tainted now by Alan's response. It was understandable, Tom had said. And Ann had apologized for her thoughtlessness, and Alan for his outburst, when he eventually came inside from smoking in the garden. And both of them meant it.

'All the same, I'm glad to get out for a bit,' Ann said as she and Tom set off arm-in-arm along the road in the twilight. 'All this walking on eggshells is exhausting.'

When Joy was about to take Patty upstairs to bed, Alan was outside smoking yet another cigarette. With Patty in her arms, Joy opened the back door.

'Say goodnight to Daddy,' she instructed Patty mechanically.

To her surprise, Alan ground the stub of his cigarette under his foot, came up close and kissed Patty's cheek.

'Night, little 'un.'

'Nigh-nigh.' Patty waved her hand at him.

Joy's heart lifted again in surprise. She did not expect anything from Alan when it came to Patty, but it was so nice to see him respond to her so warmly.

'Won't be long,' she said.

After she had settled Patty she came down, put the kettle on and looked into the front room.

'Want a cuppa?'

'Yeah, please.' Alan smiled at her.

This was encouraging as well. Maybe last night's outburst had cleared the air, made him think about things a bit. She made tea, then listened at the foot of the stairs to make sure Patty wasn't stirring. But as she was carrying the tea to the front room, all the lights went off.

'Oh, not again!' she said, groping her way along. 'Here, help me put the tea down.'

'Never mind.' Alan was on his knees by the fire. Joy was always struck by the way he seemed better in adversity, when there was any kind of struggle. As if it was more comfortable, everyday life he couldn't stand. 'There's a few bits of kindling and coal.'

Now that they had the electric fire, they weren't using the fireplace as much, so they had saved some fuel. And at the weekend, Alan and Tom had finally resorted to chopping up a mouldy old table that had stood outside at the back. Len had used it for potting in the garden, and it was well past anything else. At least it offered something else to burn on the fire.

And Alan's offering to make a fire felt romantic – a peace offering.

He got a little fire burning, Joy lit a candle and stuck it on a saucer in the hearth and they sat on the hearth rug, cuddled up together under a blanket to drink their tea. It felt friendly. There was something about sitting on the floor that made it feel almost like a game: children pretending to go camping.

'Nice to have the house to ourselves for once,' she said, trying hard to make the evening pleasant. 'I s'pose we'll get our own place eventually.'

Alan nodded. He leaned forward to put his cup down and took hers as well.

'Look,' he said, sitting back. For once his eyes met hers directly. Even in the flickering light she could feel the strength of his gaze. 'I want to say sorry, properly.'

Joy tensed. This was such tender ground. She felt so hurt and was nursing a deep wound inside her. She didn't want to fight, but she was afraid that whatever he said would not be enough. That it might make her feel worse.

'Don't,' she said, fighting tears, 'unless you really mean it.'

'I do.' His eyes bored into hers. She realized then how long it was since he had really looked at her. 'I s'pose I didn't realize what it was like for you.'

'You didn't think.' She wasn't going to let him get away with it. All at once she was furious again. 'You didn't *realize*? You only had to imagine just for a moment how it would be, what I would think, if you suddenly stopped writing. And don't tell me you were in the camp then, having horrible things happen to you. No, that didn't start 'til 1944. You were in India, having an affair with that girl – and not giving me one thought. You were a selfish' – she groped for a word she never normally used – 'bastard!'

Alan looked away. She thought he might fight back, argue. She didn't care now if he did.

'You were carrying on with someone else without a care in the world. *And . . .*' She got up, suddenly not wanting to sit next to him, making out that everything was all right and they were close. 'You didn't care about me. That's the truth of it.'

She paced the floor behind him.

'And now,' she was starting to lose control, all the hurt and frustration of the last few months erupting in her, 'I'm expected to look after you and care for you for ever and ever. Even when you scream at my child and expect every-one else to tiptoe around you all the time, as if you're some sort of flaming hero and no one else's feelings matter. All you wanted me for was as a nursemaid, when you found yourself back here and there was no one else!'

She sat down on the sofa suddenly, as if all the energy had gone from her legs.

'That's not true.' Alan turned and crawled over to sit by her feet. He did actually sound upset. 'When I was in the camp, I only thought about you. It's the truth, I swear. Noreen was just . . . I suppose I got carried away. It was . . . India's so . . . Anyway, once I was away from her, it was a bit like a bubble had burst. It wasn't real. She was Indian – half anyway.'

'And pretty.'

'Yes, but we had nothing in common. And then I was back to my real life. And you. And home. And you *were* home, all that time. I swear to you, Joy.'

He sounded genuine now. Broken and upset.

'I know I'm too wrapped up in myself. There were things there, in the camp. Blokes who . . .' He shook his head in distress. 'I don't want to talk about it. I *won't*. I won't bring it back – I don't want it here, outside me. I've got to keep it inside or it'll just—'

Alan looked up at her. She could not see his face at all in the shadows, but his voice was full of fear.

'I want to be home. To be me again. But I can't seem to find myself.'

He was being truthful now. About all of it. But she could not give in and comfort him, not yet. She had been pushed too far down, was too hurt and angry. She sat stiffly, her arms tightly folded.

'I'm sorry,' Alan said at last. 'For not writing. It was a terrible thing to do.'

'You had left me, that year – before you were captured,' she said, hard and relentless. 'Hadn't you?'

He hesitated. 'I suppose.'

'And then you changed your mind.'

For a moment Lawrence Dayton came into her mind. His dark, lively eyes. Their nights of dancing, that final kiss before he left. Lawrence, whom she had loved but held back from. She wanted to ask, 'Did you sleep with her?' She had not given herself to Lawrence. He had a wife, a child. Of course Alan had slept with this half-Indian beauty, with her long black hair, hadn't he? Or perhaps Noreen was a careful girl, unprepared to risk any sort of disgrace? Either way, this was more than she wanted to be told.

'I suppose,' Alan admitted, 'in a way. But I wasn't thinking straight. It was the other side of the world. And it was then, when everyone was . . .' He moved closer, laid his hands in her lap. 'I am sorry, Joy. I am so, so sorry for being such a selfish idiot. I don't know what else I can say.'

And he did mean it, she could hear that.

'And thank you. For waiting for me. For not going to America. I don't know what I would do without you – I honestly don't.'

He knelt up and slowly, grudgingly at first, she allowed herself to be pulled into his arms. He wrapped them round her tightly and hugged her to his chest, cradling and rocking her until she started to relax.

'I suppose we're all we've got now,' she said, her voice muffled against his jersey. 'You've got me and I've got you.'

Instead of answering, Alan released her and got up. He moved the half-burnt candle up to the mantel and clicked the wireless on. He twiddled the knob until some slow dance music came from it. Even broadcasting was limited by the power shortage, but they seemed to be laying on a stream of music. A waltz, she thought, already measuring the rhythm in her head. He stood in front of her and held out his arms.

'It's been a long time,' he said. 'But I think I can remember.'

They began very gently and slowly, getting the feel of each other again in the limited span of the room, waltzing tiny steps in a tight ring between the sofa and fireplace. The music changed and although it would have been good for the cha-cha-cha, there really wasn't the space. Instead they held each other, rocking from foot to foot.

It felt so familiar, a link to their young past. A time when things had felt so much more straightforward.

'We had some fun, didn't we?' she said, looking up at him.

Alan smiled. 'Maybe we'll have some more. We should go out – like your Mom said.'

'What, dancing?'

'Yeah.' He seemed light-hearted, and Joy's spirits soared. 'Why not?'

When Mom and Tom came back later, Alan and Joy were still dancing to the wireless, gently stepping round and round the room, finding each other again. And when they walked in finding the two of them, Joy saw her mother's face light up in a smile.

Nineteen

'It's raining again,' Margaret called from the front door. 'Cats and dogs.'

'Well, that makes a change,' Sheila said, bundling Robbie into his coat. 'It's melting fast now.'

The thaw began in the middle of March and from then on, it rained and rained. Rivers were bursting their banks, already defeated by gallons of meltwater, and now the rain poured down on top. A pipe had burst in the other house and water dripped through the ceiling. The plumber who finally came to fix it said he had never been so busy. At last, though, Ann's household had running water again instead of the chore of heating snow, which put the gas bill up, and all that running about with buckets.

The snow had shrunk to a few mucky clumps of ice and the world had gone back to its usual green and grey of winter, with bulbs starting to peep timidly through the ground.

'I've got all the ration books in my bag,' Margaret said. 'You nearly ready? There'll be nothing left, else.'

'Coming.' Sheila was gathering up her bag and umbrella when she heard Margaret say, 'Morning' and then, 'Oh, thank you.' She came back along the hall tearing open a letter, a frown on her face, which deepened from puzzlement to concern as she read.

'It's from the Home,' she said. 'They say she's gone downhill and won't last . . .'

Sheila looked bewildered.

'Ida. My sister.' Even the mention of her brought shame to Margaret's voice. 'They call her Lizzie.' Again she stared, baffled, at the letter. 'This is from Rednal – they must have moved her.'

Margaret stood, dithering. She looks old, Sheila thought. Her grandmother suddenly seemed frail, even though she was a well-built woman. Dithering was not what she usually did. Grandad was out. Now it was safe to walk the pavements again, he had gone to meet a couple of his old pals in the upstairs bar at the works, so there was no turning to him for his thoughts.

'Never mind the shopping,' Sheila said. 'You must go and see her.'

'I suppose,' Margaret said. She looked as if she needed to sit down, but she leaned against the wall. 'Though I don't know what good it'll do.'

'Come on, Nanna.' Sheila took charge, thanking heaven she wasn't feeling quite so queasy with the baby any more. 'Joy'll look after Robbie for a bit. I'm coming with you.'

They took the tram down the Bristol Road. Everything and everyone smelled of damp. Even though it was a sad occasion, Sheila enjoyed sitting next to her grandmother as the blurry images of the city beyond the steamed-up windows became gradually greener and more spacious.

It was an unexpected break from the kids and she felt like a little girl going on an outing to the Lickeys – the hills directly south of the city, where so many people went to have a day out in the countryside. An outing with her grandmother.

'You all right, Nan?' she asked. Margaret was staring ahead of her, her face sad. She tried to rally herself.

'It's silly of me, I know. But there hasn't been a day

since I came across her, in that church, when I haven't thought about her, about how her life must have been.'

The two sisters, Ida a decade older, had met again after more than sixty years, when Margaret was volunteering at a church looking after people who had been bombed out.

Margaret stared down at her lap, seeming washed in shame and sorrow. Sheila touched her arm. It was clear what a burden this was to her grandmother, even though she was only seven when Ida was put away in a home by their parents.

'There was a time when I might even have thought it was' – she was whispering now and Sheila leaned closer – 'if not the *right* thing exactly, just the only thing you could do. A girl having a baby out of wedlock.' She shook her head. 'So terribly shameful. They were such straitlaced times.'

She drifted for a moment, turned to look out of the window, but there was nothing to see through the grime and condensation.

'It was cruel, really. Everyone always blamed the girl, as if the man had nothing to do with it. Rules are rules and all that – no one thought any differently. Of course I never had a daughter, but when I look at you and Joy, see you grow up and imagine, *What if anything like that happened to either of you?*' Her eyes filled. 'Would we have done what my mother and father did to Ida?'

'Mom wouldn't,' Sheila said immediately.

'No,' Margaret agreed. 'Ann would have brought up the baby and supported you, whatever other people said. She's staunch like that.'

'But I suppose plenty of people still disown their daughters.'

'Yes, I suppose.' Margaret gave her a sad, guarded look. 'Where's the love there?'

Sheila had struggled hugely with her mother's own secrets – with finding out about Tom, with discovering that Martin was only their half-brother. It seemed appalling and wasn't something she exactly wanted to broadcast. But now she had Elaine: supposing, when she was older . . . ? No, her mom would never have thrown them out like some people, leaving them alone to fare for themselves – and she wouldn't do that, either.

She laid her hand on her grandmother's.

'None of this was your fault, Nanna.'

Margaret's eyes filled and she patted Sheila's hand. 'I know, bab. It's nice of you to say. But it's terrible – all of it.'

Sheila was filled with dread as they approached the Home, not knowing what to expect. As they went in, a couple of women who must have been Agatha Stacey Home inmates watched them in fascination and giggled together. They were plump, looked middle-aged, but it would have been very hard to guess how old they were.

When Margaret told the matron why she was there, they were taken straight upstairs. Sheila took Margaret's arm as she climbed, her stiff hip making the ascent slow.

'I'm afraid Lizzie is no longer conscious,' the matron told them.

Sheila looked at her grandmother to see how she would react to this, but she did not show any change in emotion.

'Her name was Ida, you know,' she pointed out. 'Not Lizzie.'

'I'm sorry,' the woman said stiffly. 'We've only ever known her as Lizzie. She's our oldest inmate – she's lived a good long life.'

Has she? Sheila wondered. Long, certainly, that was

true. She realized, with a shock, that her grandmother's sister must be coming up to eighty-nine years of age.

The next jolt was going into the room – a little infirmary at the side of the building – and seeing Ida. Sheila saw the shock on Margaret's face too. In the bed was a tiny, wrinkled old lady. The room smelled strongly of disinfectant, along with a whiff of urine. Ida was clean and looked comfortable, but so shrunken and defenceless against the white sheets.

As Margaret went forward to sit on the chair by her bed, Sheila searched the old lady's face for any resemblance to her grandmother, or to anyone. But she could not see any. Ida's mouth was sunken in – if she had false teeth, she did not have them in her mouth. Her hair was wispy, almost white with remaining streaks of grey, her features smaller, altogether different from Margaret's. You would never have known they were sisters.

'Ida?' Margaret took her bony hand between both of hers. 'Can you hear me, love?'

Sheila stood awkwardly at the foot of the bed. The whole place made her feel heartbroken and uncomfortable and she couldn't wait to get out.

'You're her sister?' the matron said. 'She always spoke about you so proudly.'

Margaret ignored her. Sheila knew this had been one of the things Margaret found the hardest – how pleased and proud Ida had been, if she came to visit.

'This home is quite new,' the woman informed Sheila. 'We've not been open long.'

'Oh,' Sheila said, 'I see.' She wished the woman would go away.

'I'll sit with her for a few minutes, if you don't mind,' Margaret said pointedly. And at last the woman took herself off, with a promise to show them out afterwards.

Sheila sat down on the bottom of the bed. Ida did not stir.

'Well,' Margaret said as they waited at the tram stop afterwards, huddled under an umbrella. 'I've said my goodbyes, for what it's worth.'

'Oh, Nanna.' Sheila put her arm round Margaret's shoulders for a moment. The day was heavy and grey, with water everywhere. It all felt so bleak and sad.

The tram appeared in the distance, trundling along, and they got on.

'Now,' Margaret said, briskly, 'enough of all this. Tell me about you. What's going on with you and Kenneth?'

There did not seem much more to say about Ida. It had not felt as if she knew Margaret was there. On the way out, Margaret had said, 'Let's hope she just slips away now.' So Sheila felt that she could start telling Margaret about things, and her grandmother seemed astonished when it all came pouring out.

'Australia? What does he want to go there for?'

'I don't know,' Sheila sighed. 'Well no, I do: wide open spaces, sunshine, oranges on the trees, he says. And jobs – there're supposed to be all sorts of opportunities. A bigger life, Kenneth says. He's been keeping on about it even more because of the weather, and us all being cooped up. He's fed up with the job, says England is so small and narrow-minded, wants to get out and see more of the world . . . He was never like this before the war. Has Grandad ever wanted to up-sticks and go somewhere else?'

'No. Not as far as I remember. Birmingham's home – always has been.'

'I made Kenneth promise we wouldn't say any more about it until after the baby's born.' Sheila gave a brave smile. 'So I can have a bit of peace for a few months at least.'

Twenty

'Oh no, I thought I could smell that!' Joy came into the kitchen carrying Patty. 'Snow-ek? Snoyk? I thought we'd seen the last of that – it smells as bad as it tastes.'

She stood with Patty on her hip, looking over Ann's shoulder as she stirred the grey, oily snoek fish into a sauce. A pan of mashed potato and swede stood alongside to go on top.

'I found it at the back of the cupboard,' Ann said. 'Waste not, want not . . .' She made a wry face. 'I think Martin might have hidden it.'

They laughed.

'He really hates it, doesn't he? Oh, Mom, by the way, have you got any elastic left?' She made a comical face. 'My knickers are falling down.'

'No such luck – and you can't get it for love or money. Not coupons, either.' She laughed. 'It's safety pins or nothing, love. I can find you a couple of them.' She turned from the stove and looked over at her daughter, carefully.

'I'm glad you and Alan seem to have turned a bit of a corner.'

Since that night when Mom and Tom had come home to find her and Alan dancing, things had been a lot better.

'I hope so.' Joy sat down at the table and put a wriggling Patty down on the floor. 'I don't know if I forgive him yet.' Her face clouded. 'I still can't believe he just didn't think about how I might be feeling. Doesn't that seem . . .' She shrugged, running out of words.

She saw Ann hesitate. She knew Mom must think it had been thoughtless and horribly selfish of Alan. All those years, Joy thought, she and Tom never forgot one another. But Mom was careful with what she said.

'Well.' Joy could see her resisting the temptation to say, 'You've made your bed and now you'll have to lie on it.' It was an expression Mom especially disliked. But that was what she meant. 'This is where we are now, I suppose. You've both got to find a way of getting over it.'

'Yes.' Joy smiled. Alan had been especially tender with her in bed last night. Not only demanding, but really loving, as if they were drawing close again. She had lain and sobbed next to him afterwards and he had held her, kept saying he was sorry. Her eyes filled for a moment at the thought, but she rubbed the tears away and smiled. 'Step by step. Hope so.'

'I wouldn't be so sure,' Tom said that night when he and Ann were alone in the attic. Tom was already in bed and had picked up a book about boat-building to read, but had not opened it. Ann climbed in with him.

'What d'you mean?'

'Just . . .' He leaned to put the book on the bedside table. 'It's not likely to be a straight road, that's all. Thinking of lads I knew, from the last lot.'

Ann jumped onto her knees and started tickling him, poking him in the ribs.

'Aargh! Stop it!'

'You can be a right gloomy so-and-so,' she laughed, tickling him even more.

Tom was squirming and laughing. He grabbed at her hands with his one arm. 'Will you stop it, woman – this is not a fair fight for a one-armed bandit like me!'

She gave in and cuddled up next to him.

'I hope the very best for them,' Tom said. 'All I'm saying is that there will probably be a lot more ups and downs yet.'

'Well, all right,' Ann conceded, yawning. 'But at least things are looking up. Alan's even said he'll go out dancing. They always loved dancing.'

Tom leaned over to switch off the light. 'Well, that's good,' he said carefully, kissing her. 'One day at a time.'

Now the thaw had come, the news was all about floods. Low-lying land near rivers was swamped with meltwater and the endlessly falling rain. The sky was like a grey, heavy lid, and it was so wet that whereas previously the freezing cold and ice had trapped everyone in their houses, now they were all stuck in because of the pouring rain.

Joy saw Alan off to work that morning, huddled up in a big raincoat and cap. As soon as the front door opened there came a sound of sheeting rain.

'You'll be soaked,' Joy said, kissing him goodbye. This was new – the closeness that meant she stood at the door with Patty on one hip, seeing him off. Often beforehand he had slid out to work, only calling goodbye as he shut the door, if at all.

'I'll be all right, don't fuss.' But he smiled, put one hand on her shoulder and kissed her and stroked Patty's face, before pecking her cheek as well.

'Ta-ta!' Patty waved.

'Don't be late,' she joked. 'We have a date tonight!'

Alan gave a grin and put one thumb up to her. Then he hunched his shoulders and set off into the deluge.

Joy watched him. 'Bye-bye, Daddy,' she said softly to Patty. 'That's your daddy.'

Her mother and Tom set out for the works soon afterwards, arm-in-arm under an umbrella. Joy closed the door behind them. Tom seemed happy enough with his new work, even though Mom said he would still have been an engineer, and far more hands-on, had he not lost one arm. Joy wondered if Tom was happy. He really did seem content; he was never one to complain about anything.

'Right,' she said to Patty. 'Well, we're not going out in that – we'll see if the rain ever clears up. You come upstairs with me and help me choose a dance dress.'

It wasn't as if there was much choice, she smiled to herself. If she'd known they were going out, she might have tried to make up something new or altered one of her old dresses. She still had two – and one of them she had had since before the war. But when she opened the wardrobe, Patty looked as excited as if they were opening a treasure box.

'This is my oldest dress,' she said, showing her daughter the silver-grey one, the skirt as light and diaphanous as dragonfly wings. 'And this is my other one . . .' Also a filmy silver, with a plum-coloured underskirt. 'That was the one I wore to get married to Daddy – do you remember?'

Patty looked blankly at her.

'No, you were very little,' Joy laughed. She felt younger suddenly. A little more like her old self.

She laid the two dresses on the bed.

'Daddy and I are going out dancing – tonight. At a dance hall in town. It'll be lovely, because your daddy is very, very good at dancing and . . .' She sat on the bed and grinned at Patty. 'You don't know this, but Mummy is too. So which dress shall I wear? Either one is going to hang on me,' she murmured to herself. The strain of the past months had sucked the flesh from her bones.

'That,' Patty pressed her little hand on the plum skirt, as Joy guessed she would. Patty loved colours.

'Yes, I think you're right,' Joy said. She got up and held the dress against her, looking in the mirror. A variety of memories assailed her: her wedding day, the emaciated, strained-looking man she had married. And before – dancing with Lawrence Dayton . . . That seemed like a fairy-tale time now. Locked in a safe place, even at the time, because each of them knew they could not have each other, not in the long run.

'And how should I wear my hair?'

She put the dress down and caught her hair up, twisting it into a rough knot on her head. It felt so strange doing this – it was so long since she had dressed up to go any-where. It was like a forgotten life.

'Like this? Does Mummy look nice?'

Patty, who did not have the words for any kind of hairdo, smiled and nodded.

Joy looked in the mirror and felt excitement tingle through her. A dab of make-up and her hair up, and she would look almost young again. She *was* young, she reminded herself. Nearly twenty-five, that was all. Except most of the time she felt about a hundred years old.

Now, though, she and Alan were going to reawaken their youth. She couldn't wait to see him smarten up to go out. She was so thrilled that he had agreed to go dancing, finally.

'You don't look that thin any more,' she had told him. This wasn't quite true and he had been terribly self-conscious about how he looked before. The sick, skeletal man he had been. But no one was carrying much weight these days – there wasn't enough food to get fat on – and now he did not look all that much thinner than a lot of other skinny men.

'It'll be all right,' he said. 'My suit's baggy on me, but it'll do.'

Joy could see he was trying very hard – to do it for her. They both knew they needed this, a chance to rekindle things for the future.

'Now,' she hung the dresses up again, 'later on we're going to pop round and see Norma and you can play with Gary.' The two children were close in age and got along – mostly. 'You'll be staying in with Nanna tonight, and Daddy and I are going out on a glamorous date!'

She laughed as she helped Patty climb back downstairs. Her heart felt lighter than it had in a very long time.

Twenty-One

'We'll have tea a bit early,' Ann said. 'Tom won't mind, and then you and Alan can get your glad-rags on.'

'Thanks, Mom,' Joy said, putting some squares of bread and butter thinly smeared with golden syrup in front of Patty. She beamed, excited. 'I can't wait.'

Her mother smiled at her. 'You look radiant already. It'll do you both good.'

Joy gave Patty a bath, sitting her in the little galvanized baby bath inside the big bath, and sat down on the floor, watching her daughter splash and play. She sang songs to her, enjoying being with her little one, and through it all feeling the hum of excitement and anticipation. She and Al were going out dancing!

'Come on, miss – that's enough.' She lifted a squeaking Patty out of the water and wrapped her in a towel. 'No, you can't stay in there. The water's getting cold.'

As she was crossing the landing she heard Tom come in and Mom's voice, 'So where've you been today?' He often had to travel around, speaking to different firms they were ordering supply parts from, for Cadbury's. He seemed to like being out and about. But his reply was muffled as he walked into the kitchen.

Joy settled Patty in her cot, reading her a story. She and Alan would have to get changed to go out quietly, but once Patty was off, she slept like a log and it took a lot to wake her. Joy sat by her cot, singing more nursery rhymes and lullabies until the little girl's eyelids were heavy. Then she crawled over to the door and crept out of the room.

'Al?' She put her head into the kitchen.

'Not yet,' Mom said. She looked at the clock they kept on the windowsill and frowned. 'He's late, isn't he? You seen him, love?' she asked Tom.

'No. But I came from the station tonight, so I probably wouldn't have done.'

Joy felt a bit deflated. She wanted Alan to be as excited as she was about the dance. The West End Ballroom – what a long time it was since she had been there! She wanted to spend time with him beforehand, enjoy getting ready and looking forward to setting off, not have to do it all in a big rush, as if he wasn't really bothered about going anyway.

'Never mind,' she said, trying to stay in a good mood. 'We need to let Patty settle before we can change. And we'll have tea first.'

She sat and chatted with Tom, but most of her mind was listening out for the front door opening and Alan coming home. Inside, she was getting more and more tense – angry, in fact. He could have made an effort, just this once, she thought.

Mom kept glancing at her, and Joy knew her face must be giving away some of what she was thinking. She was starting to feel like a little girl who has been promised a treat and then had someone snatch it away.

'He'll be in any minute, love,' Ann said kindly.

But as the minutes passed, they all started to quieten and listen out, wondering.

'It's not like him to be this late,' Ann said, her eye on the clock again. 'He won't have forgotten you're supposed to be going out, surely?'

They all knew there was no good reason for Alan to be kept late at Cadbury's. It never happened. The shift ended and he came home. He was never late – not like this. He wasn't the sort to wander off to the pub with some pals; he never did that, either. Alcohol no longer agreed with him, and Alan found it hard to cope with being sociable.

'The tea's ready,' Ann said uncertainly. 'What shall we do, go ahead or wait?'

They all looked at each other. Joy glanced at their faces and in that moment her anger started to fade and be replaced by a turning worm of real worry inside her. 'We'd better wait a few more minutes,' she said.

After another hour, by which time they had given up and eaten their tea – not that Joy could get much down her – no one was pretending they were not worried. There was no reason for Alan to be at work, though Tom even offered to walk up to the works and check if he had been kept back in the packing department for some reason.

'He won't have been, will he?' Joy said. She was trying not to cry, the huge disappointment she felt mixed now with worry that was growing more pressing with every moment. 'And he won't be hanging about out there, will he? It's horrible.' She nodded towards the window, through which there was nothing to be seen but darkness and the spatter of rain on the outside of the panes.

'There's probably a good reason,' Tom said, trying to sound reassuring.

Joy was grateful to him. But as they all sat together in the kitchen, unable to move away and get on with anything else, they all knew there wasn't any reason – not that any of them could think of.

'Right,' Tom said, when the time had crawled to nine o'clock, 'I'm going to go and telephone the police.'

'I don't think . . .' Ann said. Joy watched her mother struggle to find the best way of saying this. 'I mean, from the police's point of view, it's not long. The pubs aren't even shut.'

'Alan won't be at the pub,' Joy said. She had been crying, unable to help it. It was awful, sitting there and not being able to do anything.

'Yes, we know that,' her mother said uncertainly, as if she wasn't sure she did. 'But that's what they'll think.'

So they waited. And waited.

Tom did go out to the phone box at half-past ten, when Alan still had not come home. Ann thrust an umbrella into his hands. He came back in and shook his head.

'You were right – the police weren't keen to take it seriously, not yet. They said someone's not usually considered missing unless they've been gone for at least twenty-four hours.'

They all looked at each other.

'Shouldn't we go out and search for him?' Joy said. But she knew they were not going to. It was pitch-dark and pouring with rain – and where would they even start?

Her mother shook her head. 'Look, I think the only thing we can do now is go to bed.' She came over and wrapped her arms round Joy, who could feel how upset she was. 'I'm so sorry, love. I just think we are going to have to wait until the morning. Alan does wander off sometimes, doesn't he? He might be back by then.'

Joy knew she was right. She went up to the bedroom, feeling utterly drained, but full of a horrible tense energy. She knew she would not sleep.

Switching on the little side-light by the bed, she was about to climb in, when she noticed that the bottom drawer of the chest of drawers was open a crack. This was not especially unusual, but it was the drawer Alan used for his things, and for want of anywhere else to look she squatted down to open it. Might there be a clue: all his clothes suddenly missing, perhaps?

Nothing looked different. An old, slightly moth-eaten green jersey that he was fond of. A couple of folded shirts. To the left, the old shoe-box that he kept his bits and pieces in – souvenirs from the war. She never looked in there. Ever. Because she was afraid of what she might find. Things to do with *her*: the girl, the photograph. What Joy really wanted was to take the box out and burn it.

The lid of the box, she realized, was not set tightly on the bottom, as if it had been hurriedly shoved back on. With dread, but unable to stop herself, she drew back the lid. Sure enough, there was a little bundle of papers, typed ones, from what she could see.

She reached for the top one: Alan's demob papers from the RAF – the letters of thanks. And sure enough, underneath, the little black-and-white photograph of the girl, Noreen. Joy picked it up and stared at the sweet, mischievous face in the picture, thinking that had she not wished to slap her hard, she might have got on rather well with the cheeky-looking Noreen. Was that where Alan had gone? she thought, her mind rushing round insanely for answers. Was he on his way back to India – to find Noreen?

She put the little picture back. If that was the case . . . Despair washed through her. It would be far too late for her to do anything about it.

Next to the papers there was nothing. The end third of the box was empty. It looked odd, as if something had been there that had been taken out, leaving a gap. She closed the box and the drawer, feeling helpless.

As she lay down to try and sleep, she felt as if Alan – the man she had known for so many years of her life, the man she was married to – was someone she did not know at all.

*

Tom set off for work the next morning, promising to get word to them immediately if he heard anything.

'I don't think I can stand staying in,' Joy said to Ann. 'It's not actually raining. I'm going to take Patty out for a walk.'

She stormed along the road with Patty in the push-chair, down to the boating lake in Valley Park, where they watched the geese and ducks gliding on the dark water. She came back via Bournville Green, to fetch a few groceries.

When she got near the house, Joy found herself break-ing into a run. He'd have come back by now surely, while she was out. Alan would have come in, explained to Mom where he had been and why . . .

But her mind snagged on this. What possible explan-ation could there be? And when she got home, Mom shook her head before she had even opened her mouth. No, of course he was not back.

Sheila came round, and Nanna and Grandad, and they all sat around and did their best to entertain Patty, but every so often someone would say, 'There must be some explanation' or 'Wherever can he have gone?' And they would all sit quietly for a while, pulled back into the worry, and the bewildering reality that Alan had vanished, it seemed, into thin air.

Twenty-Two

Three agonizing days passed.

The police started to take the situation seriously. Ann and Tom went to the packing department at Cadbury's to see if anyone could tell them anything. Alan had been into work the day he disappeared, one of the men told them. At least until the middle of the afternoon. It seemed he had walked out of the works without even clocking out, at around three o'clock. No one had noticed anything in particular, and no one had seen him since.

'How did he seem?' Ann asked. 'He wasn't unwell, going to the medical room?' They knew that Alan was sometimes unable to work for a whole day and had to go and lie down for a time. The factory allowed for that.

'No, not so's you'd notice.' The man shrugged. 'So far as you can tell with him. He seemed all right, to be honest – much as ever.'

'So,' Joy said, when Ann told her, sitting in the front room with Patty. Even to her, her voice sounded lifeless. She felt numb and absolutely exhausted. 'He left work because he wanted to. And he went – somewhere. He hasn't told any of us where he was going, or anyone . . .' Her tone cranked up several gears abruptly, until she was shrieking. 'And he hasn't let us know where he is, *again*.'

She broke into distraught sobs, unable to help herself, even though Patty was there.

'He's just a selfish—' She thumped her hands down on the sofa with a strangled cry of rage and frustration. 'He never thinks about anyone but himself!' She tried to pull back from sounding so self-centred. 'I suppose he can't help it, after everything, but . . .' She was overtaken by emotion.

Her mother was on her knees beside her immediately.

'Oh love, love.' She held her, rocked her. But, Joy noticed, she did not say anything to contradict her. What were any of them supposed to make of all this?

The days of pouring rain that followed trapped them all inside, making the world beyond feel alien and unreachable and only adding to the sense of catastrophe.

On the Friday afternoon Joy was upstairs putting Patty down for a nap. She didn't even hear the knock at the door, but suddenly Mom was in the room with her. Her face was stony-solemn and she beckoned Joy out to the landing.

'You have a little nap, sweetie,' Joy said to Patty, her voice trembling. She closed the door quietly behind her and faced her mother.

'The police are here.' Mom spoke in a very low voice. 'They've . . . They think they've found him.'

As Joy went down the stairs, even the odd cotton-wool feeling in her legs did not seem real. In the front room were two policemen in rain-shiny uniforms, holding their hats in their laps. As soon as she walked into the room, they stood up, one tall, young, ginger-haired and looking terrified, the other shorter, older and stocky, with a round face and thinning brown hair. He had a calmer air of experience and did the talking.

'Mrs Bishop?'

Joy nodded, hearing her mother come into the room behind her.

'Married to a Mr Alan Bishop?'

'Yes,' she said faintly. She could see, from their faces,

that they were about to say something terrible. It was just a matter of waiting for a few seconds to pass.

'We have bad news, I'm afraid.'

'Do sit down,' Mom said quietly.

The policemen resumed their seats, and Joy found herself ushered to a chair and discovered that she was sitting in it.

'I gather Mr Bishop was reported missing on the night of the twenty-fifth?'

'Yes,' Joy agreed. 'Tuesday.'

The policeman nodded. 'A . . . person has been found answering his description. In the countryside to the south of the city.'

'Person?' Joy stared at him.

The man looked down for a second, then up again. 'Body, I'm afraid.' He shook his head.

Joy looked at her mother. As their eyes met, Ann also shook her head slightly. Joy felt she had already heard this, that she already knew that there was no doubt. They meant dead. The 'person' was dead.

'How do you know it's Alan?' she managed to ask.

The policeman looked at his young colleague, who fished in his pocket and brought something out from it; an odd, twisted brown thing. He gave it to his superior, who handed it to Joy.

'He had this on him. We have been able to dry it out a bit.'

Joy's eyes met his as she took it from him.

'Most of the fields out there are flooded. Someone saw him in the water.' He cleared his throat. 'There was a bus ticket as well, but I'm afraid it disintegrated. Midland Red.'

'Bus ticket?' Joy echoed. For a second she felt like laughing. Why were they being so apologetic about a Midland Red bus ticket? She held the brown twisted thing in one hand. It felt like a scrap of shammy leather. Her mind was trying to piece all this together.

'So, he went on a bus. And then he must have . . . I mean he does go off sometimes. He must have decided to go for a walk or something. And you mean – he fell and drowned?'

There was a long moment of ominous silence.

'I'm afraid it's not quite that.' The older policeman brought out each word as if it pained him. 'There's something else.'

'Well, what?' Joy's voice was high, wild-sounding. She wanted to tear the meaning of all this from their throats. She could feel her mother, to her left, leaning in and sensed that whatever they were about to say, she did not know what it was, either.

'He didn't exactly drown – not initially anyway,' he went on. 'There was a wound. Gunshot.' As if this would clarify everything, he added, 'We have the weapon back at the station.'

'Weapon?'

'Revolver. Enfield, army-issue,' the policeman said in a mechanical voice. Seeing that Joy was about to ask where he could have got such a thing, he added, 'Far too many of them about among the populace, I'm afraid. Not difficult to get a hold of.'

An image flashed into her mind of the box upstairs, that empty space at one side, as if something had recently been removed from it . . .

Before she could say anything else, both men stood up.

'We'll leave you to take all this in, Mrs Bishop.'

As soon as he said these words, Joy thought of the other Mrs Bishop – Alan's mom. And Irene, his sister. She was going to have to tell them.

'We shall be in touch – about identifying the body, in

due course. But we don't believe anyone else was involved, in case you're wondering. Perhaps, once we've gone, if you undo that, in private.' He pointed tactfully to the twist of brown leather. Gesturing with his helmet in one hand, he said, 'May I offer my sincere condolences.'

The young ginger-haired constable nodded hard as well, not knowing what to say. Joy saw his Adam's apple move as he swallowed. Poor things, she thought, having to do this.

'Thank you,' she managed to whisper, before her mother showed the two men out. She sat, numbly holding the odd, ragged thing, until she realized her mother was back in the room with her. 'Shall I open it?' She found she was afraid, although the thing was such a pathetic scrap, it couldn't be anything much.

It had been twisted round and round, the ends folded in to make an effective little watertight pouch. Now that the leather was dry, it had gone crisp. Joy realized the police had already opened it, knew what was inside and had looked after it for her, by drying it out and twisting it closed for her again. For some reason she felt touched by this.

Inside was a sheet of lined paper torn from a notebook and it had obviously suffered damp. The writing on it was barely recognizable as Alan's. It was big and scrawled, as if he had done it on his knee – maybe even on the moving bus.

'*My wife*,' it said at the top. And their address: *Beaumont Road, Bournville.*

> *I love you, Joy*
> *but I'm sorry*
> *I can't.*
> *Alan*

Ann came over as she sat, staring at the note. Joy handed it to her, watched her face as she read, solemn, then tenderly anguished.

'Oh,' she said. She handed it back and knelt beside her. 'The poor boy. I'm so, so sorry, my love.'

Twenty-Three

Martin was glad of the walk home along Linden Road once he had got off the tram. He wanted time to prepare himself, ease himself back into his home city before having to step into the house and face them all – not to mention facing this terrible thing that had happened.

It was raining, again. The wet seeped down the back of his neck and into his old shoes. He smiled, thinking how indignant he would once have been at feeling wet and a bit chilly. It wasn't even cold now, not compared with the winter they had all come through. Now this felt like nothing. He wore a cap, something Jack had taken to doing and he did the same, whenever they were out and about in Nottinghamshire mining country. It made it easier to blend in, even though he had not been a wearer of caps before and Jack certainly hadn't, he was sure.

His long, powerful strides – how his body had changed and developed in these four years! – along the sedate Bournville Street took him to Beaumont Road. The long curve of the terrace opened out in front of him as he turned the corner. It was undoubtedly rundown after the long years of war and neglect, paint chipped, windows cracked and even a few boarded over, potholes along the road, rags of decayed bunting here and there, yet still it felt solid, respectable and safe. Full of memories: fond ones of his childhood, his grandparents. And yet, at this moment, somehow enraging, suffocating, making him want to turn and run.

You're here for Joy, he reminded himself. Stop thinking about yourself all the time.

'I must go to the funeral,' he'd said to Jack. 'Joy's the person I'm closest to in my family.'

Or was once, he thought, apart from Mom. He didn't say that. Not to Jack. It sounded sissy. And he didn't feel it was true any more. Mom – someone he had thought was so reliable, unchanging and true – now felt alien, a betrayer. Not who he had once thought she was.

'Martin.'

Ann opening the door like that jarred his thoughts. But in a way it was a relief. So many times when he had come home he felt Mom had been waiting, all excited to see him. Wanting to spend every moment with him, and sad and disappointed – even though she tried to hide it – when he had to leave. This time she had other things on her mind. This day was not about him. It was about poor Joy and Alan, and he could merge into it all, stay around the edges, which suited him perfectly well.

'Mom.' He stepped in and kissed her, though the rain gave him an excuse to keep his distance. 'I'm wet, I'm afraid.'

Normally she would have kept on about why he never had the sense to carry an umbrella. Today she barely seemed to hear. Her face was pale and tight.

'You'd better hang it up – but we're going soon . . . Joy will be down in a minute.'

Nanna and Grandpa were in the front with Sheila, Kenneth and their kids. Sheila was having another one, he saw at a glance. She seemed old to him. A matron, these days. All that – family, children – seemed so far away from him.

'Come and sit here, bab,' Nanna Margaret said, after everyone had hugged him, looked at him with their sad

159

eyes and said he felt damp, he must come and sit by the fire. 'I want to look at you.'

'Got some muscles on you, lad!' Grandad said, as he always did whenever Martin arrived home.

He perched on the edge of a chair, leaning towards the electric fire, legs spread wide, feeling manly and too big for the room.

'Your fellas aren't digging fast enough,' Grandad joked, nodding towards the cold hearth. 'You want to get your finger out.' Then remembered why they were all there and that this was not the moment for jollity. His face turned solemn again.

There was a silence.

'Poor Joy,' Nanna said, after a moment. She sighed. They all sighed. Then they heard feet on the stairs.

They all came in at once: Mom and *him*, as Martin thought of Tom, and Joy carrying Patty. The first thing he saw was how thin and pale Joy was, but she looked pleased to see him.

'Mart.' She came over, and the two of them and Patty all hugged. 'I'm glad you came.'

'Sorry, Sis,' was all he could think of to say. 'It's rotten for you.'

'Yeah.' She nodded and looked down. She seemed stunned and blank as if, for the moment, she had gone beyond emotion.

He shook Tom's hand stiffly. Behave, he told himself inwardly. Today is for Joy.

'We'd better walk over now,' Mom said. Quietly to Martin, she added, 'Len's meeting us there.' Not 'your father', but 'Len'.

Bournville, Martin found himself thinking again, as he took his place in a pew. His childhood home seemed so unchanged. Quiet, green, moderate. No extravagant housing. Nothing out of place. Nice little shops on the Green. It was pleasant. Everything measured and right. Stifling. Martin felt he couldn't stand it.

Stop thinking about yourself, he ranted inwardly as they sat in the parish church, St Francis, right up close to the Cadbury works. He was moved to see Dr Saloman come in and sit in a pew on the other side of the aisle. How kind of him to come; he had always been kind to Joy. For a moment the sight of the stooped, grey-haired man did lift Martin out of his own obsessions. He was being ridiculous. Not everything here was bad, he knew that perfectly well really. People were kind and nice.

Even so, while the prayers were read and he heard muffled weeping around him, Martin mostly kept his head down, feeling as if he was going to explode.

He had still not met Jack's family. But Jack had painted to him a London upbringing full of colour and freedom: a house full of interesting and eccentric visitors, his mother too preoccupied by art to be much of a housewife, but somehow they all got fed – even extravagantly. A goose! Pâté and feather-light wafers of toast! Trifles laced with sherry (which was not how trifles tasted, in his experience; more of a jelly and custard, with a few tinned pears and a glacé cherry or two, sort of experience).

And London: art and museums and plays and – for some reason, this felt very thrilling – the Underground trains whisking everyone through the intestines of the city.

Martin felt excited, and very nervous, about meeting the Thorne family. (Or rather, Jack's father was Dr Henry Thorne. His mother had done something utterly unthinkable and kept her own name: Charlotte Gordon. For her art, Jack said, but this seemed somehow terrifying. And it led to thoughts about his own mother, who would be changing her own name again soon, wouldn't she? His mother and he would not have the same name . . .)

But what he was more nervous, and definitely not excited about, was the thought of Jack meeting his family here in Bournville.

Soon they would be released from the pit. Their term must be almost up. And then what the hell was he going to do? For the last four years – miraculously – he had been able to find himself, be himself . . .

Even in the worst cold of the winter, everything had felt like an adventure. At times no trains could get out of sidings to deliver coal, even had they been able to dig it. Everything was frozen, with drifts deep as houses across the countryside and up to the pithead. On days when they had been able to work, the pit bottom had been cold beyond belief. And when they were having to melt the winding gear with braziers at the pithead, the meltwater rained down on them. Once, as Jack was working, a massive icicle crashed down beside him, frightening him to death. It was so close that it could easily have done a lot worse than frighten him.

'That would've killed you,' one of his working companions remarked, matter-of-factly.

Martin was proud of himself for having survived such masculine hardships.

There had been the beauty of some of it, too. Their lamps shining on the snow in the darkness. Hoar frost in the trees. Early mornings of undisturbed snow, when the black of the winding gear stood stark against it.

Jack had done beautiful charcoal drawings, a few sketched lines across a white page capturing the scene perfectly. He was good at what he did, there was no denying. Martin carried one of these sketches of Jack's with him all the time. Sitting in the church, he reached inside his coat and felt the reassuring crackle of paper in his breast pocket. It helped to make him feel as if Jack, and all he had become by being with him, was here, safe together with him.

On the first day of this year they had all gathered at the pithead. There had been a band and a huge banner was unfurled: 'This colliery is now managed by the National Coal Board on behalf of the people.'

'We're the bosses now,' some of the lads joked. 'Does that mean we wear a bowler hat down the pit?'

As he had stood in the cold, greeting the events of this momentous day of nationalization, with Jack beside him, Martin felt powerfully that he was part of a family of sweat and effort and triumph. Everything else – his own blood family especially – felt a very long way away.

And here he was now, sitting in the heart of that family, behind the man who was supposedly his father. His blood. He found himself studying the back of Tom's slender neck and was filled with revulsion and shame. He knew, without ever having seen it properly, that his own neck looked very much the same. Slender, the hair lying in the same way. That hair seemed to stand up on the back of his neck at the thought of who else might be noticing this. Mom's friend Hilda and her daughter Norma, Joy's friend, were behind them and they *knew*, which somehow felt even worse.

Len, the man who brought him up, was at the front on the other side of the aisle, with that woman, Jeanette.

Here they all were. The mess that was his family. Bitterness rose in him until he wanted to explode. A family of cheats and liars. Especially Mom. And *him*. If it hadn't been for them, maybe Dad – Len, he corrected himself – would not have felt forced to behave the way he did. All those lies over all those years.

What was worse, and what made him feel as if his skin

was too tight for his body, was that he was forced to lie too. How could he possibly tell any of them who he was? *I love men. Not women. That's who I am, I'm afraid, so you'll all have to get used to it.*

Here, in this green, respectable suburb of Bournville, nothing ever seemed to be rocked by anything. If there was anything untoward, it would have to be kept firmly behind closed doors.

Imagine Mom's face as he came out with the truth. *Your father will be so disappointed . . .* Which father? It didn't really matter – both, he was sure.

No, he could never be himself here. He could not be here.

Martin clenched his hands tightly together between his knees as he leaned forward, head down during the final prayers. They stood to sing 'Abide with Me'.

Everyone was in tears. The hymn was almost impossible to sing without weeping. By the end of the first verse, '*When other helpers fail and comforts flee, Help of the helpless, O abide with me . . .*', Martin was already choked. How Alan must have felt, in the end, to do such a thing to himself. How broken and trapped and helpless.

And he himself, that was exactly how he felt – helpless.

Tom tried to get him alone to speak to him, when they were back at the house, but Martin wasn't having any of it.

Mom, Nanna and all of them had scraped together their rations for a few sandwiches and a cake. Fish paste, madeira cake with a few scattered currants, a jelly – all very plain.

Len and Jeanette came back to the house as well. Martin found it awkward beyond endurance and avoided all the 'parents' for as long as he could. He chatted to his grandparents and Sheila, keeping things light. Then he followed

Joy to the kitchen, where she had gone to fetch something for Patty. He hugged her again. Joy raised her head to look at him properly now.

'You're such a big man, little brother. I can't get over it.'

He was touched, and enjoyed her hugging him. 'It's men's work all right,' he said. 'I've learned a lot.'

She was looking right into his eyes. So pretty, he thought. Those dark-brown eyes and the slight wave of her hair. Joy had always been lovely and even now, when she was haggard and full of grief, she was beautiful.

'I suppose we've all learned a lot,' she said. He knew how sad she was, but she managed to say it with a humorous twist, as if to say, *God help us – what kids we were before.*

For a moment he wanted to pour out everything to her. To be able to say, to at least one person in his family: *This is who I am. Look at me. Accept me.* But of course even if he did ever decide to tell Joy, this was definitely not the moment.

'I hope one day . . .' he began hesitantly, hardly knowing how to finish the sentence.

'Oh!' She drew back with a surge of bitterness, assuming what he was going to say. 'Don't you start! Don't you think I've had enough of men? No.' She kissed her daughter's soft head. 'It's just going to be me and her from now on. I want a bit of peace.'

Martin smiled, unsure what to say. 'Well, you deserve it,' he managed. Which felt feeble.

Joy seemed about to say something else, when Martin realized they were not alone. Tom had come in. He stood humbly, waiting for them to notice that he was there.

'I wondered if I could have a word with you, Martin?' he said.

Martin suddenly found that Joy had melted away and he

was standing, alone, with his father. He shrank inwardly, wanting to run away. Instead he raised his head and stared insolently into Tom's eyes. The bloke was so annoying. So calm. Comfortable with himself. He wanted to make Tom lose control – to rouse him into a temper.

'Yes?' he said rudely.

'Martin . . .' But Tom seemed to lose courage and this was annoyingly disarming. It took him a second to look back at him again. 'I thought I knew what I wanted to say, but I don't.'

There was a split second of opportunity, Martin realized afterwards. He could have waited, been kind, done a hundred things differently. Instead he felt all his angry defences rise up in a moment. *You don't want to know me. Don't even try – you won't like what I am!*

'Well,' he said acidly, stepping round Tom to leave the room. 'Probably best not to bother then.'

It was really only on the crowded train going back towards Nottingham the next day that something came home to Martin. He learned it in that moment, if he was truly honest.

His mother's double life during his upbringing was a problem to him. It made her seem mysterious in a nasty way. Deceitful and cunning. Things he would never, ever have said she was before.

Tom coming into his family – they weren't even married yet, for heaven's sake, and were openly living in sin; Tom trying to own him, as if he had some rights as a father – these were the things Martin told himself were the problem. Even though his better, kinder self knew, and in some ways understood, what had happened.

He knew that each of them, in their own way, had struggled for years to do what they felt to be the right thing. He knew they were good people and that even good people, at times, get themselves into terrible messes.

But in that moment he learned what the problem was. It was him: he himself. *You will never accept me, so I can never tell you who I am. I can never be here – not any more.*

That's what he told himself. Because a little while after he had walked away abruptly from Tom's attempt to talk, Mom had taken his hand and all but dragged him back into the kitchen, so the two of them could be alone.

'Look, Martin.' Not 'love', he noticed, not the way she would have before. 'I understand you find it difficult to see Tom here. To accept what's happened – how things are. And I'm sorry, I really am.'

She didn't sound sorry, he thought defiantly. She seemed exhausted and cross.

'But I'm afraid this is how it is. You may not like it, but you're just going to have to get used to it. Bearing in mind that you have hardly set foot in the house since you were eighteen, and you scarcely ever bother to write a letter home, d'you expect me to arrange my whole life for your convenience, the very few times you do deign to turn up?'

She couldn't keep up the anger then. She burst into tears. 'Oh, I didn't want to say that. But honestly, you're going to have to get used to things – like them or not.'

This time she didn't hug him or try to baby him with comfort. She walked out of the kitchen, wiping her eyes.

Now alone, and already travelling away from them all again, Martin sank deeper into the corner of the chilly railway carriage and pulled up the collar of his big coat. If he had been alone, he would have wept. As it was, he swallowed hard on the aching lump that had come up in his throat and stared out at the sodden landscape speeding past the window.

Twenty-Four

Joy was sitting at the kitchen table and at first Ann could not tell whether she was laughing or crying. She had her face in her hands and her shoulders were shaking. She was feeling very raw. Alan's funeral had been only two weeks ago and she was on a constant see-saw of emotions.

'Love?' Ann said cautiously, at that moment spotting an envelope torn open, the sheet of paper between Joy's elbows.

Joy sat back, lowered her hands – her face was wet with tears, but her laughter was bordering on hysterical. She pushed the letter across the table to Ann, who stared at it. Pale blue. Airmail.

'Hank?'

'Of all the moments to decide to write! I've written – I sent him pictures of Patty. Nothing. Not for two years. And now . . .'

Hank's letter included a photograph of himself, his arm round a small, dark-haired woman with a pleasant face, holding in her arms a baby of two or three months. The short letter said that he and Dorothy were getting along very well, that they now had little Hank Junior and were living in Philly, and that he hoped she was well and happy.

'He doesn't ask about Patty – not once!' Joy said, her eyes welling up.

'I think . . . it's well intended,' Ann said carefully. 'He wants to let you know that he's got a new life and he's not bearing any grudges, doesn't he? So far as he was

168

concerned, you had promised to marry him and go and join him over there and you dropped him for someone else.'

'Someone else who came before him.'

'Even so.'

Joy sighed and folded up the letter.

'I suppose so. But it would have been nice if he'd shown one tiny bit of interest in Patty.'

'He's married someone else. Just let him go, love.'

Joy hesitated. She took the letter and photo out again and looked at them for a moment. Then tore them up. 'Yes. You're right.' She dropped the pieces in the waste-bucket. 'No good dwelling on any of that.'

'And, Joy,' Ann stopped her as she was about to leave the room, 'we'd better talk properly soon – about what exactly you're going to do.'

Along the street, another very different letter had arrived. A brown envelope, which Sheila sat staring at, neatly placed on the kitchen table, the top carefully torn open. The queasiness she always felt in the first months of preg-nancy had worn off and now she felt as if her innards were doing a different sort of dance of their own. Turning somersaults almost.

She could hear her grandparents moving around upstairs, their footsteps and the creaking of the house. Robbie was up there with them. It would soon be time to take him out to the little playgroup they went to.

It was she who had heard the post arrive. The enve-lope addressed to Mr and Mrs K. Carson. Should she have waited until Kenneth got home? She felt suddenly guilty. But it was addressed to her as well. Didn't she have a right to open it?

'Please,' she found herself praying out loud, 'let this

make all the difference. We'll get our own place, we'll find Kenneth another job – please don't make me have to go to Australia. I can't stand the thought.'

There were feet on the stairs, Nanna saying, 'Come on, Robbie, no messing about. Your mother's waiting to go out.' And Robbie making silly noises and jumping down each step with both feet, then stamping along the hall until they were in the kitchen.

'I'd best get up to the village,' Nanna went on, reaching up for the ration books. She only ever shopped in Bournville. Years of habit. Nicer shops than Cotteridge and anyway they knew her. She glanced round at Sheila. 'What's up with you?'

'Nanna – look.' She tugged the letter out of the envelope and passed it over, her heart thudding. Her grandmother read it, took a moment for the penny to drop, then looked up at her.

'A *prefab*?'

Sheila nodded, her excitement overspilling now. 'It's going to be ready very soon. We can move in – into our own place. And you can get shot of us!'

There was no denying the relief that passed across Margaret's face at this. It was a lot, two people in their late seventies having a young family move in with them. She put the council's letter back in the envelope.

'Well, all I can say is I hope you don't freeze to death.' Then she smiled. 'I'm pleased for you, love.'

II

1950

Twenty-Five

Summer 1950

'Here comes your mummy,' Ann said, hearing the front door open.

'Hello-o – I'm home!'

Joy peeped round the door of the kitchen, her face lit up and cheerful. Her dark hair was still drawn back and fastened low in her neck after wearing the Cadbury cap all day, and her skin had a glow to it.

She looks lovely, Ann thought, smiling at her. She's coming back to us. At long last they were starting to see the pretty, vivacious Joy who had seemed to get lost during the long years of the war and all the sorrow and tragedy that followed it. A flame of happiness had been reignited in her. What a long road it had been, with so much sadness. But Joy was young and was naturally a buoyant person. She was recovering.

Patty, now five, was at the kitchen table. While Ann got the tea ready, she was bent over a colouring book, trying desperately hard, in her careful way, to colour inside the lines of a big teddy bear with a straw hat on.

'Hey, missy, I'm home.' Joy made a mock pout.

'Hello, Mom.'

Patty glanced up at her mother, as if Joy was a piece of furniture – perhaps a hat stand that had wandered in – then went back to her colouring.

Ann shrugged, and she and Joy made a face at each other.

'At least I know she's perfectly all right with you!' Joy joked. 'I can tell you've missed me, muffin.' She kissed the back of Patty's neck until she squirmed. 'How was school?'

'All right.'

'Her class teacher said her reading's coming on no end,' Ann said. 'Tea's nearly ready – d'you want a cuppa?'

'Please. If there's one on the go.' Joy sank down at the table and her face lit up even more. 'I didn't get to tell you last night . . .' She had got in late the night before, then left for work in a rush that morning while Ann was seeing to Patty, so there had been no time to talk. 'They've asked me to be a demonstrator!'

'What, at the Western?'

'Yes. I think it's after I won that ballroom cup – they said they've had their eye on me. And if I do all my exams, then I can be a proper dance teacher.'

This had been Joy's ambition since she was a little girl and had first started learning ballet. And from then on she had learned tap and ballroom, and every other kind of dance she could. But of course until recently this had been buried beneath all her other worries and responsibilities.

'Oh, that's marvellous,' Ann said, putting two cups of tea on the table. 'I'm so pleased for you.'

'And we've got the tea dance this weekend,' Joy went on, full of enthusiasm. 'I know it means you having Patty again . . .'

'At Rowheath? I could bring her along for a while. Let her see her mother strutting her stuff.'

Joy laughed. 'That'd be lovely – and Kay'll help look after her. Maybe you and Tom could come and have a dance? Now that you know he actually can.'

Some months ago, before she really got going on her dancing again, Joy had switched on the wireless in the front room. There was dance music on, and she said to Tom, 'Come on, you can help me get back into practice.'

Ann, who was sitting with them, watched in amazement as Tom managed, with only one arm, to keep a grip on Joy with his right arm and cha-cha-cha and waltz across the living room and out into the hall, with quite a bit of flair.

'You can dance!' Ann cried in amazement.

'I don't know what you're sounding so flaming surprised about,' Tom replied indignantly. 'Most people can manage a few numbers, if they put their mind to it.'

'Well.' Ann clamped her lips shut. She had been about to say, 'Well, Len can't – he's got two left feet.' Instead she said, 'You just never told me, that's all.'

'Ah,' Joy said. 'So you two can go out dancing as well now!'

After Alan's death, Ann had agreed that she would give up work for the time being and look after Patty. Joy had no husband to support her now and she needed to earn – as well as get her teeth into something.

'We don't need the money half as much as she does,' Tom had said. 'We do all right on my wages. I know you like doing a bit at Cadbury's, but maybe you can put your feet up now, at least for a bit.'

'Put my feet up? Ha-jolly-ha,' Ann said. 'Here speaks a man who has never looked after a five-year-old.'

She had Patty for the rest of the day, once she had taken her to school and collected her again. Joy often had to be out in the evenings. And now and again, when she was tired, Ann found herself thinking, Oh, this again – having brought up three of her own already, and having had Sheila at home with her two for a long time as well, she seemed to be forever looking after children.

But mostly she relished it. Patty was a sweet little thing, who seemed secure in herself, despite what had happened. She had not had a lot of fathering from Alan, but she had her two 'grandads', Tom and Len, and her great-grandad Cyril, as well as Ann and Joy. She was a happy soul.

And it made Ann feel useful. Bringing up kids became a habit, she realized. And even if it was tiring and aggravating at times, there were not many jobs that felt more worthwhile.

'She'll be all grown-up in no time,' she said to Tom. 'I might as well make the most of it.'

She soon got into a routine. There was school and then, in holiday times, she would take Patty to the shops, and one morning a week to a group of mothers and children who met in each other's homes. She was by far the oldest, but it was still good to be there. She enjoyed chatting with the young mothers. And after dinner back at home, she and Patty would sit with the wireless on for *Listen with Mother*. It was lovely snuggling up with the little girl. Sometimes Patty felt asleep on her lap, soft and warm as a bun, and Ann would have a doze as well.

It made up for things, just a little. Stroking Patty's soft hair, feeling her slender little limbs, inevitably reminded her of her own children when they were small – but of course now they were having to deal with all the difficulties of being grown-up. Sheila, she knew, was having a tense time with Kenneth. Then there was poor Joy and all she had gone through. Ann realized she was destined to worry about her girls. It seemed to be her mother's role. But they were here, close by, for her to keep an eye on, and she got on well enough with each of them, despite everything.

Then there was Martin. Since he had come home for

176

Alan's funeral, he had not been back. Not once, in three years. He wrote very occasionally. She and Tom had so wanted to go to his graduation – at the Albert Hall, of all places! – and be able to stand proud, parents together, and see him collect his degree. But Martin had written and said he was not even going to the ceremony himself. He and Jack were going abroad: Spain, he thought. And that was that. He was gone, her boy. A rift had opened, for which she blamed herself fairly and squarely. Every time she thought of him, it was with an actual physical pain inside her. Tom's boy. Her boy. No longer.

She would cuddle Patty and think, At least I have her – and Sheila's three as well. Martin's a man: he has to go his own way. But it only partly made up for the pain that crouched inside her, waiting to jump out whenever she let her thoughts go in that direction.

At first, Joy had been like a little waif, so thin and pale and sad.

'I keep thinking, If only I had asked him more – got him to get it out of his system, instead of bottling it all up, maybe he wouldn't have . . .' Her eyes would fill every time she spoke about poor Alan.

She talked to both Ann and Tom about it together. Ann was happy that she trusted Tom and liked him enough to be so open with him. And they both knew that Tom and Alan had had a special bond – men who had seen things, been through terrible experiences that the rest of them could not understand.

'Alan said a few things: about Denis, his friend who died. Like once, he said Denis came out from . . . somewhere; it was something "they" – that's what he called the Japanese – had been doing to punish Denis. And when Alan saw him, he didn't recognize him, as if he was a completely different person. He wouldn't say any more. It felt as if anything he said was like . . . what's the word? When there's a lot worse that he won't say?'

'Tip of the iceberg?' Tom suggested.

Joy nodded, solemnly.

'Yes,' Tom said, quietly. 'I expect there was a lot more.'

'Did he say much to you about how it was?' Joy's big eyes pleaded for something.

'Not much,' Tom said. 'I think,' he hesitated, choosing his words carefully, 'from what I gather – not just from Alan – that what went on in those camps, the men's camps especially, was some of the worst of the war. Almost beyond belief. I think they're afraid people wouldn't believe them. And they're ashamed.'

'Ashamed?' Joy frowned.

'Of having been captured. Of being . . . ill-treated. Having things done to them. It's hard to explain, but it makes men feel deeply humiliated. Being completely in someone else's power, I suppose. As well as all the illnesses and so on, being starved and weak, and vulnerable like that.'

'That day when I got to the hospital in London and saw Alan.' Joy spoke, staring ahead of her. 'We got there, Irene and I. And when I saw him, he looked like . . . he was all yellow. And I couldn't tell it was him, not at first. He was like someone else. It must have been like when he saw Denis.'

She sat for a moment, then nodded slowly, with sad recognition.

'I suppose that was it, really. He was someone else. I married someone else, not Alan, the Alan I knew. But I knew I had to . . .'

Ann and Tom sat and listened, very still. It was Joy who looked ashamed now.

'I owed it to him, even though he'd . . .' A bitter expression passed over her face for a second and then she looked resigned. 'He did try. I know he did. But whatever they had done to him, he had changed into someone else. I s'pose I thought one day he might change back into the Alan I used to know.'

They all sat silently. Joy turned and smiled at them, though her eyes were full of sadness.

'I'll never know now.'

Twenty-Six

When Joy had received her employment letter from Cadbury's, it felt strange – almost like going back to school, only better. She had been employed at the works from the age of fourteen and had done weekly classes in the Day Continuation College, as all the school leavers did to enable them to develop their education while working. It felt so familiar and – just what she needed at the time – comforting.

The last time she had worked there was during the war when she, like Ann, had been one of the employees transferred to work for Bournville Utilities, doing subcontracted munitions work for the duration of the war. Parts of the factory had gone over to making aircraft gun magazines for the Austin works. Others worked for Lucas's, making Sten-gun magazines and rotating gun turrets. Ann had spent part of the time filling anti-aircraft rockets; and Joy, before she gave up work, expecting Patty, had been covering petrol tanks with rubber from Fort Dunlop.

She looked fondly at the letter stating her terms of employment – timekeeping, very strict! The hour in the factory was divided into ten six-minute parts, with all production carefully calculated. It outlined details of her Women's Pension Fund and the availability of dental treatment and the sports facilities.

It all felt very strange, as if two severed parts of her life were, at least partly, being reconnected. And it felt good.

The factory itself seemed more or less back to how it

had been before the war. A few ragged posters remained about the place, admonishing everyone about waste and careless talk. But the work went on: the lines and lines of chocolate, the enrobing and wrapping machines, the bars of Ration Chocolate, the selection boxes, the Easter eggs . . .

All the shortages of milk and the difficulties in obtaining cocoa, plus the fact that rationing had not yet ended, meant the company still had to offer fewer lines. There had been a quick flurry of excitement last year when sweets came off the ration – only for this to be reversed a few weeks later. In the factory the struggle to access ingredients was something they were aware of; it came echoing down from higher management but, on a day-to-day basis, they could not do anything about it.

Joy's job this time was on wrappings, on a new line called Milk Fudge – a fudge finger, in a half-circle shape, with a red wrapper. It was very nice, she concluded, when she first tried it. But her favourite was still a Flake.

She liked being back among the other girls, new people she had never met before who did not know anything about her.

'Oi, come on, black eyes – stop slacking!' Jill, her neighbour on the line, called out to her.

'I've got things on my mind, that's all.'

'Oooh – what things would those be? You got a bloke?'

The others laughed and ooohed.

Joy replied firmly, 'No!'

'Well, why the hell not, with looks like yours? You want to get out there, girl.'

Being at work helped her. The repetitive tasks, the chats with other girls on the line, the jokes and teasing and singing all distracted her and helped her gradually climb out of her sorrow. Now and again she ran into Len, her father, who still worked 'up the wet end' in the chocolate-mixing department. Here, at work, they sometimes found time for a little chat.

And it was at Cadbury's that she met Kay.

Kay Tarrant worked on the new Milk Tray Bar, which had come in the year before the Fudge, in 1947. So they did not meet on the line. They got to know each other at one of the tea dances in the Rowheath Ballroom.

Amid the steam from the tea urn and the smell of powdered-egg sandwiches and cake, the low murmur of chat under the music and the shuffling feet of couples stepping round the long room, Joy spotted Kay's lithe figure, topped by fashionably cut, shiny bronze-coloured hair.

Kay was about as tall as the man she was dancing with. Her wiry hair was cut shorter than Joy was wearing hers, tucked round her head in a neat style and curled at the ends. It looked lovely. She looked lovely altogether – fresh and lively and fun. Joy immediately decided she wanted to cut her hair. The man Kay was dancing with looked a good deal older than she was, and his dancing was not bad. But it was Kay who stood out: laughing, vivacious and just good at dancing. Joy went up to her afterwards, as everyone was helping themselves to tea and cakes.

'Hello,' she said as Kay turned, holding her plate with a couple of neat little sandwiches on it. 'I wanted to say you're a very good dancer.'

'Me?' Kay laughed. She had a very infectious laugh, and her freckles made her look jolly too. 'Well, that's nice – especially coming from you. You're Joy, aren't you? Gilby?' Joy decided to let that go for the moment, even though her surname was Bishop. 'You're one of the best dancers around, so I've heard.'

'Have you?' Joy was genuinely astonished. It felt so

long since she had done much dancing. 'I'm out of practice now, though.'

'Well, I tell you what,' Kay said, as Joy picked up a cup of tea and a scone. 'Shoot me down if you don't fancy it, but how d'you fancy going out one night? Up the Western or the Tower, or somewhere? I've got no one to go with, and I feel a bit of a chump turning up on my own.'

'I'd love to!' Joy said, a surge of excitement going through her. 'I haven't got a partner, either. My husband . . .' It was too late as she said it, realizing the impact it would have. 'He was a good dancer, very good. But he – died. Recently.'

'Oh.' Kay's face fell. She looked terribly shocked. 'For heaven's sake. How awful. Was he . . . ill?'

'Yes.' Joy said. That seemed to sum things up. 'Yes, he was.'

'Well, you definitely must need cheering up then,' Kay said. She was never downcast for long. 'How about Saturday?'

The two of them both worked full-time and they often met up at dinner time in the girls' dining room. The more Joy got to know Kay, the more she liked her.

She still saw her old friend Norma at times, but Norma had three kids now and had not been back to work at the factory. Norma was all about children and home – which was lovely for her, Joy knew, but somehow these days they had less in common.

Their mothers had once been very good friends, but the friendship had been blown apart in the end by Ann and Len splitting up. Hilda and Roy and Ann and Len had been friends as couples for years – since they were young. Now things just could not be the same. Hilda found all the changes unpleasant and hard to cope with. And Ann 'living in sin' with Tom, on top of waiting to be divorced, was too much for Hilda, even though part of the problem was that there were so few places available to live that it made it hard to do anything else. But inevitably spiteful tongues would wag whenever anyone stepped out of line. And the end of it was that Ann and Hilda didn't see each other these days.

Finding Kay, who was not only a keen dancer, but someone who was turning out to be a really good friend as well, had been a wonderful thing. Kay was easy to talk to and a genuine listener – and she was fun.

They started going out to dances regularly across Birmingham. Anything from the big ballrooms to dances in church halls. Joy loved dancing any time and anywhere; she always had.

Kay was never short of a partner. She was so lively and good-looking and friendly, and her family were happy and close. She lived with her mother and father and had two older married brothers. Kay was the baby, much adored by everyone.

'You must come and meet my mom and dad,' Kay said, soon after they met.

The family lived in Dawlish Road in Selly Oak, and Joy found herself welcomed by Mrs Tarrant – 'call me May, for heaven's sake' – who was also a lovely-looking woman, an older version of Kay, and her father, Bob. He worked at the Battery Works by the canal, which produced brass and copper tubes. He was a cuddly character with tar-black hair, jolly in a sidelong sort of way, who liked imparting information: 'The Gibbins family, who set up the firm, they gave the library to Selly Oak, and the park. Did you know that? It's not all just the Cadburys, you know.' This, over tea, in their snug back kitchen, the first time Joy visited.

Joy laughed and said, no, she hadn't known that.

'I s'pose you'd be more interested in frocks and such,' Bob Tarrant said lugubriously, his nose disappearing into his teacup. 'You girls.'

'Ignore him, Joy,' Kay said. 'He's a terrible tease.'

'I suppose I am,' Joy grinned. 'But I have got a tiny bit of space in my head for other things.'

'Ah,' Bob said, reaching out a sizeable hairy hand for a slice of bread. 'Well, you're better provided with cranial space than my daughter then. Did you know—'

'Dad, stop it!' Kay said, exasperated. 'Joy doesn't need you drowning her in information all the time!'

Bob Tarrant crumpled into silence.

'So, what about your family, Joy?' May asked.

Oh God, Joy thought. Where do I start?

'Well, nearly everyone's worked at Cadbury's,' she said, trying to keep things on safe territory.

'Oh, I was a chocolate girl, before I was married,' May said. 'I liked working there. I was in the offices. I suppose now the children are older . . .'

'You could help earn a crust, instead of leaving it to your poor, harassed old husband,' Bob said.

May whacked him round the ear, gently, with the tea cosy.

'And I suppose you're going to cook and clean, and all the rest?' she demanded.

Bob subsided again with an exhalation, as if someone had stuck a pin in him.

Joy laughed. It was fun being with the Tarrants. It all seemed simple and calm – and at least she had managed to get them off the subject of her own family. There was a can of worms that she could live without having to explain. Certainly for the time being anyway.

*

The more she and Kay went out dancing, the more Joy felt as if she was getting back on form in every way. The steps to all the dances she had known were rusty at first, but soon came back to her. And she was keen to add new ones – the Lindy Hop and jitterbug, dances imported from the USA, and calypso dancing, which had come with people who had arrived to work from the Caribbean. Any dance that came along, Joy was keen to learn it.

'You're so quick,' Kay said to her one evening. 'You learn ever so fast. You could be teaching dancing for a living.'

Joy knew she could dance well, but this was the first time she had ever dared, in reality, to think anything like that, thanks to Kay. Teaching dancing as a way of earning money, how wonderful that would be!

'So are you,' she said. In fairness, Kay was a wonderful dancer too. 'Maybe we should go into business?'

They both laughed at the idea – then, anyway.

But it encouraged Joy to make a decision. This is what I'm going to do, she decided. Get better and better at dancing and bring up Patty, and that's that. That's all I need – not men and marriage. Though it was not always so easy to persuade some of the men she danced with of that.

Twenty-Seven

'Sheila? SHEI-LA-A-A!'

Sheila stopped sweeping and rushed, still holding the broom, to look out of the front door.

It was a lovely June day. Jonny, the baby, now approaching three, was in the garden playing in his little car. A row of bronze wallflowers and marigolds was blooming in the bed along the back fence, and they had planted lavender and bush roses along the front of the house. The air smelt of cut grass, and all the gardens of the neighbouring prefabs looked neat and well tended.

The only thing that did not look quite so shipshape was Sheila's neighbour, Beryl Phillips, who was standing in her garden next door, right up by the fence. Her black hair was a bird's nest, there were milk stains on her blouse and in each arm she clasped a grizzling baby. She also, unmistakeably, had a black eye.

'Take them off me, will you, Sheila – just for a few minutes? Or I swear to God, I'm going to throw them both out of the window.'

There seemed to be some bawling going on in the house as well. Sheila stood the broom against the inside wall and suppressed a sigh.

'Come on then – just for a bit. I've only just got in with Jonny.'

She had been up to the welfare clinic in Selly Oak for his orange juice and rosehip syrup – all things that the new National Health Service had decided were good for

nourishing the next generation of children. Of which –
at the rate Beryl and Sid Phillips next door were going,
with four kids under five already – there were going to
be a good many. And the strain on them appeared in the
bruises Beryl wore on her body. Sheila was already struggling to keep her trap shut when she was anywhere near
Sid Phillips.

'Sally, Maryann – stay where you are!' Beryl yelled into
her own prefab, before kneeing open the gate and arriving
with the squalling pair.

'Just take them.' She thrust the little boys, Charlie and
Richard, at Sheila, who found herself weighed down by an
indignant infant in each arm as Beryl strode away again.
'I'll be back . . .'

It was not the moment to ask what had happened or if
Beryl was all right because she wasn't, that was clear. Or
to ask whether *he* couldn't look after them for a bit. *He*
being old man Phillips, Beryl's father-in-law – 'the grumpy
old sod', as she referred to him. Alf Phillips lived in a back
house on a yard near Gooch Street, but most days he rode
out on the tram to inflict his presence on Beryl. He had
given up work at sixty-two because of his lungs and sat all
day: inside if it was raining, outside if not, smoking like
a stack. He would finally wend his way home via a pub
or two, only to come back the next morning like a bad
smell – literally. The kids all stank of smoke, mixed with
the smell of the chip pan.

'Have you fed them?' Sheila called after her.

'Course I have – what d'you take me for? Only I don't
know what they flaming well want now, and Maryann's
hurt her finger and I haven't got enough hands . . . Back
in a tick.' And off she went.

Sheila tutted. 'Jonny, come in here, will you?'

She wanted to be able to keep an eye on him – not that

Jonny would run off, as he was a placid little lad – but she also needed his help in entertaining the babies. He came hurrying over in his too-big shorts, his blond hair gleaming in the sunshine.

'They blarting again?'

Sheila smiled. He was so solemn, like someone confronting a serious repetitive problem, like, is the water pouring through the roof again?

'They are,' she said. 'Come and play with them, eh?'

Inside, she lay both boys on the sofa.

'Now,' Jonny said to Richard, who was flat on his back, face screwed up ready to roar again, 'you need to stop that.'

Sheila burst out laughing. Jonny was always coming out with quaint little phrases. He spent his life trying to keep up with Elaine, who was ten and Robbie, eight, and he seemed old for his age.

He was a sweet lad – had been a real joy ever since he was born, Jonny had. Crossing the room, Sheila looked at the photo they had on the little mantel of Jonny's christening. She was standing outside St Francis's in her hat and coat, holding Jonny wrapped in a fine white blanket that Nanna Margaret had crocheted for him. Kenneth was smiling down at him on one side of her, and Joy on the other, both lit up. It was a lovely picture of a happy day.

She had had a good birth with Jonny – in hospital this time – and it felt as if his arrival had marked the beginning of a more settled, happy time.

'Let's sing them a song, shall we?'

Sheila sat on the sofa, leaning over the babies, and Jonny stood nearby. They sang 'Baa Baa Black Sheep' and 'Mary Had a Little Lamb' while Sheila tried not to think about the fresh bruise on Beryl's face; and until the twins, overcome by the novelty of the situation, stopped bawling and stared in surprise.

'There,' Sheila said. 'You little monkeys, giving your Mom the run-around.'

'Are they naughty?' Jonny asked.

'No, they're just babies,' Sheila said.

At that moment Beryl was back. 'Knock knock!' at the front door. A moment later she came in with Sally, three, and Maryann, two, tear-stained and with a plaster on her finger. 'They've stopped! Oh, thank God for that. Thanks, Sheila. I thought I was going mad.'

'I'll get the kettle on,' Sheila said. Obviously she wasn't going to get much more done this morning.

Sheila gave Jonny, Sally and Maryann each a biscuit and they went out to play in the garden. She and Beryl settled, each with a cup of tea and a baby on their lap.

'What happened?' Sheila asked. It wasn't as if you could hide a black eye. And Beryl was not one to pretend she had walked into a cupboard door.

'Oh, the usual,' she said wearily, looking down at Richard in her lap. 'Yes, you're quiet now, aren't you? The kids were playing up and I got between him and Maryann.'

Sheila watched her. She was appalled by Sid Phillips. And by the way Beryl was so matter-of-fact about Sid using her as a punchbag whenever he found life frustrating. He seemed to have it in for little Maryann, and had hit the child hard, more than a few times. Maryann was a cowed, angry little girl.

'You can't go on like this,' Sheila said. 'Four's enough – 'specially that close.'

'Try telling Sid that,' Beryl said, rolling her eyes. 'Making babies is about the only thing he's any good at.' She seemed to wither then, and looked at Sheila, ashamed. 'Thing is, I'm so . . . We just seem to make a lot of babies, the two of us. And he can't cope.'

Sheila bit back the obvious response to this. After all, she and Kenneth were determined that three was enough for them – they planned to keep it that way. But this all seemed a bit too personal to go into, even with Beryl.

Sheila and Beryl and their families had moved into the new prefabs in The Grove within days of each other.

That winter, when they arrived, the place had been so new and raw. The prefabs had been built quickly to ease some of the pressure on the city's housing. Although Sheila took to the compact little house straight away, the gardens had been bare then, muddy rectangles, and they and their neighbours had all worked really hard to get proper gardens going for the children to play in. There were also allotments to each side of the prefab site, and playing fields at the back, so although they were in Selly Oak, it had felt almost like moving to the country.

Beryl only had Sally then and things had been a lot easier. She and Sid were delighted to move out from her mother's cramped little house in town. Beryl had not been able to get over having her own bathroom, with running water and a lavatory inside – 'no more running down the yard!' – as well as a proper kitchen and a neat, tiled fireplace. She adored her house.

Everyone had set to and turned their prefab into the little palace they felt it to be. They were new and clean and cosy. Sheila stitched curtains – pink-and-white candy stripe for the bedroom and a soft green for the living room. She collected knick-knacks for the mantelpiece, wooden candlesticks and some china geese: a mother and two goslings. And she bought two nice little rugs off the market to have on each side of the bed.

Of course the walls were not very thick. Silverfish bred in the bathroom and there was ice inside the windows in winter (those things were true of most houses anyway) and it was a long walk back and forth to the shops. But it was a new start, with neat gardens to tend and grow your own vegetables, and they all took pride in them.

Sheila loved it there; everyone was friendly. It wasn't too far from the family in Bournville. They often came to visit – even Margaret and Cyril occasionally, both curious about these new houses. Now that Mom had given up work and was looking after Patty, she often popped up to see Sheila, who would also go down to Beaumont Road to let the cousins play together.

And she and Beryl had hit it off straight away. Beryl was always chaotic and seemed to tumble from one crisis to another, but she was kind and cheerful and good company.

Sheila had not been too sure of Sid from the beginning. Even though Kenneth and Sid had both been in Italy during the war, Sid still did not seem to have a word to say about it – or about much else, either.

'Have you got anything out of him?' Sheila asked Kenneth when they had all been there a few weeks. 'He hardly seems to say a word.'

'Not a lot.' Kenneth grinned. 'He asked me if I'd got a spare fag. That's about it.'

'Just like his old man,' Sheila said.

'Well, she does all the talking for both of them.'

'Now, now,' Sheila said.

She kept off the subject of Sid with Beryl at first, as she was not sure what to say. But Beryl was an open book.

'I met Sid at the Austin,' she said, soon after they had started getting to know each other. 'I was working in the canteen. We only went out three times and then he was called up. In 1941. I waited for him – all through the war.' She took a thoughtful swig of tea before adding, 'Dunno why I bothered really.'

Sheila was startled, then laughed. She liked Beryl. It reminded her of chats she had had with Audrey Vellacott, the woman she had stayed with when she and Elaine were evacuated from Birmingham during the war. A frankness had grown between them, so that they could say almost anything to each other. She missed Audrey, she realized. They had talked more than she and Kenneth ever did. Although they exchanged letters now and again, the months slipped into years and they had not seen each other. She dragged her attention back to Beryl.

'Oh dear, like that, is it?' she said carefully.

'He's all right, most of the time,' Beryl conceded. 'Only I could live without that grumpy old sod of a dad of his turning up all the time. He all but lives with us – and I can't always get him to smoke outside. Place stinks like an ashtray. His only saving grace is he doesn't eat much.'

Beryl's and Sid's children had arrived in short order: Sally, Maryann, then the twins. And things went downhill between them. Sheila often found herself being a listening ear. She also found herself having to button it around Sid, who, she finally concluded, was a bully and an idiot, for all he had a winning smile.

Gradually, as they got to know each other, Sheila had opened up about Kenneth. He had kept his promise about not mentioning moving to another country or anything drastic while she was expecting Jonny. And then they got the prefab, which felt like a fresh start. Kenneth said he was bored with his job and it was a good way, heading over to the cycle firm in Greet. Sheila had suggested Cadbury's, but he said cycles and transport were more up his street and he managed to get taken on at the Austin, making cars instead.

The new place and new job seemed to settle him for a bit. The Austin faced shortages, like every other firm in the years after the war, and there were strikes over piecework rates. But business was booming, the factory was modernizing, and Kenneth, working in the press shop, was kept very busy. Which was exactly what Sheila wanted him to be. Anything to keep his mind off leaving the country.

She suggested that they get an allotment and they shared one with another bloke, so Kenneth got cracking on that as well. He was still keen on his Italian records and kept talking about going back to Italy one day. But for a couple of years things had settled. But then he started to get restless again. He wanted to be off, here there and everywhere, and was talking about getting a car.

'I s'pose the novelty's worn off now,' Sheila complained, rolling her eyes at Beryl. 'He's got ants in his pants again.'

Kenneth wanted to take off nearly every weekend. Doing the garden wasn't enough. They went out to Bridgnorth and Stratford and Lichfield – all just to wander around, Sheila thought. It was a big effort for her, packing up picnics, getting all the kids onto buses and trains, then bringing them home after a day when they were tired, sometimes cold and often bored.

Lichfield had been their last day out, a couple of weeks back. Lichfield Cathedral did not hold much charm for little ones, even though it was beautiful. Amazingly so, Sheila had thought. She would have enjoyed it, had she not had two fed-up little boys to try and keep happy. Elaine said she liked it. But it was all about what Kenneth wanted. She had to work hard to get him to go into a park where the kids could have a swing or a slide.

'I just need to get out of here,' he would say. He seemed about to burst with frustration. As if Birmingham was a tight jumper that he had got his head stuck in.

The visit to Lichfield had been so fraught that by the

194

time they got home, with everyone tired out and scratchy, Sheila was at screaming pitch.

'Look, if you want to go places at weekends, go and do it,' she snapped at Kenneth. 'I've had enough. It's too much for the kids.'

'Oh, come on, Sheila,' he said. He had a way, these days, of making her feel like a boring stick-in-the-mud with no interests. He was a man who had seen the world, after all. 'Don't you want to get out? Do things as a family.'

'Yes – to do *family* things,' Sheila said, getting heated. 'That the kids like as well. Not dragging them round a whole lot of things you've suddenly decided you should see. You just do whatever you like, and I have to try and keep them occupied. I've had enough. From now on, you go where you want and I'll take them over to see Mom or one of my friends who've got other kids. Then everyone'll be happy.'

Kenneth shrugged. 'I thought you had more sense of adventure,' he said, turning away sulkily.

Sheila stared at his back, anger swelling within her. She managed not to snap back at him. He never used to be like this, she thought. Another thing the flaming war had done. They had hardly ever quarrelled back then.

And she . . . Sheila thought back. In all honesty, she knew she had been a mouse in those days – a worrier, scared of all sorts of things. She had changed too. She wasn't prepared to put up with as much, and would answer back.

And now this morning, sitting with Beryl, there seemed no more that she could say to her about Sid. It was their business, she told herself. Nothing she could do. So they sat chatting about everyday things, while Beryl fed first one baby and then the other – 'They're drinking me dry, these two' – and it was Beryl who brought up the subject.

'Kenneth still going on about Australia?'

Sheila felt a stab of dread at the mention of the word. She wiped away a spot of milk from Richard's cheek.

'Um. Now and then.'

'You can't go. Leave all of us. You don't want to go, do you?'

Sheila looked up at her then. 'I feel as if I'm holding him back. As if we all are. He used to be happy with anything – before the war.'

'Ah well, before the war,' Beryl said. Her face creased a moment and Sheila thought she was going to cry. It was unusual, Beryl showing emotion like that. Usually she soldiered on, making light of everything. No choice.

They were quiet for a moment. A seagull shrieked above them, its feet clattering on the roof.

'I just feel I ought to go. I'm his wife, aren't I? I'm supposed to go where he goes. Where the work is.'

'There's plenty of work in Birmingham,' Beryl said. She eased Charlie off her breast. 'That's enough, my lad.' She settled him on her arm and looked across at Sheila. 'That's not an excuse he can use for dragging you all off to the other side of the world.'

A few days later, Sheila waited with the children at Selly Oak station. She had written to Audrey, asking her to visit, and Audrey seemed to have leapt at the chance. It was still the summer holidays and she had two lads to keep occupied.

'I'm afraid I've nowhere for you to stay,' Sheila wrote. 'I wish I had.'

Audrey wrote by return of post, saying they would come up early, for the day.

When she got down from the train with two boys – Edward, who was seventeen, now taller than Audrey; and Charlie, fifteen, about the same height – Elaine, who was ten, stared fearfully at them. She was the only one who might remember the Vellacott boys at all. Sheila laughed at the look on her face.

'Did you think they'd still be little boys, Lainy?' she teased.

There were hugs and greetings. Edward and Charlie were shy, but nice lads, Sheila thought, remembering the tense, angry boys she had first met when she moved to live with Audrey and her husband.

'You do look well, Sheila,' Audrey said as they exchanged kisses.

'So do you!' Sheila said. Audrey looked every bit the country gentlewoman, in her hat and twinset. Sheila felt suddenly shy again – of seeing her, of showing Audrey her own place. It was the first time they had ever met any-where except on Audrey's ground.

'Oh, Lainy, look at you!' Audrey exclaimed, cuddling her. 'And Robbie! And this must be little Jonny. Oh, you've a lovely family,' she said as they started walking. 'And I can't wait to see this little house of yours.'

They went home and spent time chatting, catching up. Audrey looked round the prefab, saying nice things, but Sheila knew how small and basic a place it was, compared with Audrey's own sprawling, rose-covered country house. Beryl came in to say hello – and the two were polite, tongue-tied in fact, and had nothing to say to each other.

'Goodness,' Audrey said afterwards. 'She's had her children terribly close together.' There was a faint tone of disapproval in her voice, which Sheila noticed.

'Well,' she said, 'she's got that sort of husband.'

But she could see that Audrey was like a fish out of water here in Birmingham, however hard she was working to be polite.

Things were easier in the afternoon, because Sheila had organized for them to go on a tour of the Cadbury works. They all looked fascinated as they were guided round the different departments, seeing the endless flow of bars of Cadbury's Dairy Milk – 'CDM!' Sheila said, laughing – as they poured along the belt. They walked the grounds, with Sheila showing them the girls' grounds opposite, then going through the tunnel under the road to reach the beautiful green space.

'It's not what I thought a factory would be like,' Charlie said.

'It's not what most factories are like,' Sheila said. 'You feel lucky if you get to work here.'

It was a lovely day and they sat outside and ate chocolate and chatted. The little ones ran about and looked into the pond. Edward and Charlie got up and had a wander round as well.

'You all right, Audrey?' Sheila asked, feeling suddenly shy. Now that they shared no day-to-day tasks, it was hard to find common ground and there was a distance between them that felt sad, when they had once been so close. Audrey seemed more closed than she remembered, stiffer somehow.

'Me? Oh yes,' she said breezily. 'No more chaps, if that's what you're asking.'

Sheila laughed, then realized that might have been tactless. 'Oh,' she said. 'Sorry.'

'Not while the boys are still at home,' Audrey said. 'When I got them back, I decided I'd put any other sort of life for myself on hold. After all, I don't seem to have much luck in that department, do I?'

Sheila realized there was a bitterness to her that had not been there before.

'They're lovely lads,' Sheila said. 'A credit to you.'

Audrey smiled briefly. 'Yes.' The smile faded. 'But they'll soon be gone. Then I'll be left with flower shows and cleaning the church.'

Sheila was not sure what to say. It was so easy, in Birmingham, to say, 'Get a job' – if you wanted one. But in a small country village, things were very different.

'I expect something will turn up,' she said, feeling silly as she said it.

Audrey looked across the girls' grounds, towards the trees, stirring in the breeze. To Sheila's surprise, she said, 'Perhaps you're right. You're lucky, though, Sheila, d'you know that?'

Later, when she saw Audrey and the boys off again, 'Do come and stay?' Audrey said. They had been down once, after the war.

'That'd be lovely,' Sheila said, but in her heart she knew it would not happen. Too much time had passed. 'You look after yourself.'

As they left the station and walked towards home along the Bristol Road, she was sad to realize that what she felt was relief that Audrey had gone. The visit had felt strained. It was a sad thing, but she had to recognize that their friendship was a thing of the past, pressed on them by the war, and good while it lasted. But it was not going to survive – not as anything more than the occasional letter or Christmas card.

'Come on,' she said to the children. 'Let's go home and see Beryl, shall we? And you can play with Sally and Maryann.'

Twenty-Eight

'Tom?'

It was a bright Saturday morning, still early. Ann and Tom were having breakfast, the smell of toast drifting through the house. Even Patty was still not awake, having been up in the small hours, and Joy was sleeping in from her busy night of dance, after coming in not long before the milk.

They had heard the sound of the letterbox clicking and the slap of something falling on the mat.

'I'll go.' Tom got up and went to the hall. He didn't come back. Ann waited, puzzled. She thought she heard him go into the front room. She finished her mouthful of toast, took a sip of tea and got up. She pushed the door of the front room open.

'Love?'

Tom was sitting on the edge of the sofa, bent over, poring over something. There were letters beside him on the seat, brown envelopes – nothing exciting. But he was staring at a card.

Ann went and sat beside him, worried by the way he was looking. Had something terrible happened?

Without looking round at her – which was very odd – Tom handed her the postcard. Immediately Ann recognized Martin's writing and her heart started to thump even harder.

It was addressed to Mr and Mrs Somers, which seemed encouraging. Martin had at last addressed it to both of them. She flipped the card over and saw a picture of a church. On the back it said, *Santiago de Compostela.*

> *Hello – we are exploring the north of Spain. It's very wild and interesting. Have reached Santiago, the old pilgrim city, and this is the cathedral. It's an amazing country. Terribly poor, but beautiful. We are travelling a mixture of buses and thumbing lifts and my Spanish is coming on. Just to let you know we are OK. Hope all's well with you – Martin*

Ann stared at this impersonal and not especially affectionate message. 'Well, at least we know he's alive and well,' she said, trying to sound cheery.

It was only then that she realized what a state Tom was in. He was still sitting hunched forward, and she could see he was fighting back tears. Seeing that was like a stab in her heart. She had not seen Tom weep, ever, since he was in hospital in those very early days when she had first met him. He had been struggling to come to terms with the loss of an arm and an eye – not to mention his future livelihood as an engineer.

'What is it?' she asked gently, stroking his back. Though in a way she already understood. Her wretchedness over Martin was something she tried to keep hidden, but she knew Tom must be aware of it. And he felt terrible about it.

She and Tom had married in the late summer of 1947. Martin had not come to the wedding, saying there was some appointment he had to go to at the university.

Ann had chosen to believe him – there was something urgent that he really could not get out of – and not to let it cloud what had otherwise been a beautiful day. But underneath what both Sheila and Joy put themselves out to make a day of real celebration, there was a deep pang of sadness. Her children were like the three legs of a stool and, with one missing, nothing felt completely right.

It was a very small, simple wedding. Ann and Tom sealed their vows at the Registry Office in town: it did not feel right to make too much fuss. It highlighted the friends who had been lost – Hilda especially. So it was only close family, those who showed them love and support. Just Sheila and Kenneth with Elaine and Robbie, and Joy with Patty. Tom was not close enough to his sisters – who were also busy with families – to ask them to travel up.

As Ann and Tom waited to say their vows, holding hands, Tom had looked down at her, his face full of tender emotion. He did not need to say anything. At last after all this time, all these years of loving her, they could be fully and legally together. She squeezed his hand. *Thank you, my dear love . . .*

Their made their vows and exchanged a loving kiss. Elaine started clapping and the others, unsure at first, joined in. Ann, with tears in her eyes, hugged every member of their tiny gathering.

'Thank you, loves,' she said. 'Thank you all so much.'

'Now,' Kenneth joked, 'back to the pub!'

'You'll be lucky, in Bournville!' Sheila said. 'Come on – we're going home. Nanna and Grandpa said they'd pop in.'

And all afternoon they had eaten and drunk the humble wedding feast they had scraped together. Margaret and Cyril had said they did not want to come to the wedding; that would have felt wrong. But they came in for a drink and to wish Ann and Tom well.

Ann looked round at her family, and for a moment her heart ached. *Oh, Martin, Martin . . .* She longed for him to be here. Margaret, who was sitting next to her, leaned close, seeming to read her mind.

'He'll come round, bab. Give him time.'

Ann looked at her, welling up. 'I hope so. And, Mom, thanks for being here. It means the world.'

Margaret gave a stiff little nod and looked at Tom. 'He's a good man. I can see that.'

'And Len is too,' Ann said quickly.

'I know.' Margaret nodded sadly. 'But this is how it is. So it's no good keeping on.'

Ann met Tom's eyes across the room as he saw her talking to her former mother-in-law. He smiled. *I love you.*

Ann smiled back. *And I love you, my dearest.*

They had not seen Martin since the day he stormed out after Alan's funeral, more than three years ago. All they ever heard from him was the occasional card, like this one today from Spain. It was a constant source of grief to Ann. None of it was Tom's fault, but she knew he blamed a lot on himself.

'If we'd . . .' He had difficulty speaking. 'Left things as they were. Let him carry on thinking Len was his father. Just let it be, like that. He wouldn't be like this now, would he? You'd have your son – your lovely boy.' Tom knew how much Ann adored Martin. He turned to her and she could see all the pain this was giving him. 'I've driven a wedge between you and him. It's all wrong.'

'Oh, love . . .' Ann put her arms round him tightly for a moment and kissed him, tearful herself. 'You're so kind and good to me.' She sat back and looked at him. 'Whatever's happened, I wouldn't have wanted to be without you for a day longer than I had to. I love you so much – you know that. It does hurt, the way Martin's carrying on.'

She sat back on the sofa, tugging at Tom's arm until he sat back with her. They held hands.

'And I'm not sure it's true – things wouldn't have been easy, whatever we did. Martin wasn't getting on well with Len before, either. He's at that age . . .'

She knew she was trying to convince herself as well. She was terribly hurt by Martin's behaviour and sometimes felt very angry with him. He was grown-up now and surely he could come to terms with things and behave better? But she still wanted to make excuses for him.

'He's been very busy, doing his degree, living in London . . .'

'This Jack bloke – they've been pals for a long time.' Tom said. 'I wonder whether it's him as well, whether he's a bad influence.'

Ann sighed. 'I don't know.' And I don't know *him*, she wanted to add, not any more. He left here as my sweet lad, barely eighteen, when he was called to go down the mines. And I've barely seen him since. Day after day she thought about it, turned things over in her mind. It hurt so much. But she did not want to lay her sorrow on Tom.

'I don't know what goes on in his head. I just think he needs to come to terms with things, and one day he'll come back.'

Tom stared ahead of him sadly. 'I feel I've made a complete mess – of all of it.'

'No, you haven't.' Ann stroked his thigh, feeling really upset. Tom had never said anything about what he hoped for, or expected, from them telling Martin he was his natural father. But it was Tom's one chance – his only child in the world. And usually Tom was the one who could step aside, try to help her see things in a more hopeful way. But today he looked devastated and so sad.

'It'll be all right, in the long run,' she said.

Deep down, she did hope this. That Margaret had been right. Martin had been such a loving son. Even though sometimes it felt as if they had lost him for ever, she felt she knew her boy, every inch of him, inside and out. And that he loved her. 'He needs to grow up a bit.'

'I hope you're right, Annie.' Tom gave a sigh from the depths of himself and she saw a nerve twitch at the side of his mouth. 'I don't want to feel I've ruined everything.'

'Why d'you keep blaming yourself?' she asked. 'It took two of us – every time. When I went to that hotel with you . . .' She paused. 'God, that was nearly twenty-five years ago! It seems like another life, doesn't it? But all I could think of was you. I wanted you, so don't keep on as if you forced me to do what we did. It was . . .' She blushed, embarrassed, as she never normally talked like this. 'Beautiful. It was. That's how I'll always remember it. And Martin came out of it and he was beautiful too – I always had a piece of you.'

Suddenly Ann was crying, at the clash of the memory of that time of her loving little boy, with this young man who seemed unable to bear being anywhere near her – or either of them.

Tom put his arm round her and pulled her close while she had a little cry. He kissed her forehead, then gently wiped her cheeks.

'My dear, dear love,' he said. 'I'm so sorry.' And she knew he was not apologizing this time, just sympathizing.

They heard feet on the stairs then, and a moment later Joy came in, with Patty clasped to her hip. Joy wore a pink dressing gown and looked tousled, pink-cheeked from sleep and very pretty – as did her little girl.

'Gamma!' Patty said, bouncing on Joy's hip. Ann could not help smiling.

'I woke up smelling the toast. Oh dear.' Joy grimaced,

but there was a twinkle in her eye. 'What's up with you two?'

Ann handed her Martin's card from Spain. Joy read it, still holding Patty, her dark eyebrows knitting together as she got to the end. She turned it over, glanced at the picture, then handed it back.

'If I could get hold of him, he'd get a piece of my mind, I can tell you,' she said briskly. 'Going off in a sulk like that.'

'It's rather a long sulk,' Tom said gloomily.

Joy was the one of Ann's children with whom Martin had by far the closest and frankest relationship. She visited Len, her own father, of course, although these days she tried to see him on his own. She had got on well with Jeanette before, but these days, as a stepmother, she found her sharp and unwelcoming. However, she had a good relationship with Tom.

'I can see you're both happy,' she had said to Ann. 'Tom's a lovely man and you're much happier than before – so that must be a good thing.' And Tom was very fond of Joy. He knew he had been lucky with her.

She smiled at Tom now. 'Silly little sod needs to get himself here for a visit and stop messing about.' She went to the door. 'Is there any bread left? I danced non-stop last night and I'm starving.'

Off she went and they heard her rattling about in the kitchen. Ann and Tom exchanged looks. Joy's attitude to her brother had cheered both of them. They smiled at each other. What could be done, except wait for Martin to come round in his own time?

Twenty-Nine

Martin lay in the dark barn on the pile of musty straw. The woman had hastily scattered it for them to sleep on. But he couldn't sleep for scratching, his legs and body hot with bites. Fleas! Everywhere you went in Spain there seemed to be fleas. And heat pressing down like a flatiron.

But the toughness of everything else was much like being in the mines, and he and Jack had soon got used to roughing it again. The stomach problems were another thing, though. Finding water that was drinkable and didn't send your guts into alarming contortions was a daily challenge. They ended up building fires out in the open and boiling up cans of water, just to try and stay in reasonable health.

That night, for once, they had eaten well. They had set off walking south from Santiago de Compostela – 'You really have to *walk* in and out of Santiago, surely?' Jack had joked. Even though they were not really any kind of pilgrims on a *camino* route, it felt wrong to travel any other way. Then they had hitched a lift, squeezed together into the cab of a clattering truck, whose engine had sounded as if it was about to go up in smoke at any moment.

The driver, a middle-aged man with a drooping moustache, had eyed up the two of them in a feverish way while they tried to talk in rough Spanish. Martin and Jack exchanged looks, as the man's right thigh pressed closer and closer to Martin's – he was squeezed between the driver and Jack on the hard bench seat.

'OK! *Vale!*' they said, somewhere in deep countryside north of Ourense, pressing a few pesetas onto him. '*Bueno. Aquí!*'

The driver looked even more mournful – in fact deeply disappointed – as he rammed down the shrieking brake pedal and let them out. As he drove away, Martin and Jack looked at each other and started laughing hysterically.

'Poor bloke,' Jack spluttered. 'He's probably got a wife and thirteen children.'

Martin laughed at the awkwardness of the situation, but he also felt uneasy at the way Jack talked about the poor man. What was he supposed to do in this old-fashioned country run by Catholics and fascists? It was one of those moments that had begun to happen more and more often, when Jack mocked people. Martin used to find it funny. Now it made him uncomfortable. It's all right for you, he found himself thinking.

They had walked into this dusty village at dusk. The woman who had taken them in seemed to be in charge of a smallholding. There was no sign of any man around. This country – like so many countries since the war – was full of struggling women. The Civil War had already taken many of their men, as well as the ones who had joined various armies during the Second World War, such as the Blue Division fighting for Germany against Russia; and the exiled Republicans fighting against the Nazis in France.

'Why would you want to go to a fascist country like Spain?' Charlotte, Jack's mother, had asked them before they set out. 'We've just fought a war to get rid of all that.'

'Because it's fascinating,' Jack said. 'The art – and everything.'

'Maybe we can learn how to avoid it,' Martin added. 'Fascism, I mean.'

Spain was huge, isolated and mysterious. They wanted

to see the old Spain and what had been done to it: the Spain of Franco.

And they found fear and sorrow, and many widows and single women. The mother and daughter here, seemingly alone, were both dressed in dusty black and looked sad and as thin as broom handles. But they lit up with smiles and almost leapt on these two young men who needed food and shelter.

They had hens and whipped up omelettes, a giant mis-shapen tomato sliced on a plate and iron-crusted bread. They scattered straw on top of even older straw in the barn. And Jack and Martin smiled and thanked them and paid as much as they could manage, feeling for the women. They seemed to enjoy their company as well.

Martin lay, eyes open in the total darkness. There was a dusty smell of ancient straw and grain. Creatures rustled about. There must be rats and mice, he knew, but it was far from the first time he had slept in places like this and no harm had come to them.

He thought about Jack, who had fallen asleep almost instantly, and he could hear his steady breathing, strong and regular like the healthy animal he was. What adventures they had had together all these years. And yet . . .

The name of the young woman here was Paula. They never discovered the mother's name; she was just the *señora*. Paula's age was hard to guess – perhaps in her early twenties like them, but she seemed both older and younger. And Jack had flirted with her. It had made Martin uncomfortable, enraged even.

Paula, thin, haunted, with huge soulful eyes, had sat with them as they wolfed down the food. Jack had prob-ably made her day – year even. Perhaps he had made her feel livelier, attractive, young again. It didn't mean anything; they would be gone the next morning. Jack did not want her; it was not in his nature.

But Martin had felt a petulant, childish part of him wanting to yell at Jack, 'How dare you flirt? With a woman? With anyone? You're with me!'

He knew really – had learned by now – that Jack loved attention from anyone. He needed people to love him. In the mine he had got recognition by sheer hard work, which was always respected.

Martin watched him reeling Paula in, this strong, handsome-looking man, tall compared to the men she would be used to. A little overwhelming. And Martin wanted to shout at him, *Stop showing off. Stop making such a spectacle of yourself!*

It took him a long time to calm down and speak. He knew he would not say anything to Jack. Jack would laugh. *What's the harm? We're never going to see her again and she knows that.*

But it was one of the cracks in their relationship that, after all this time, seemed to be growing wider.

Martin had started his degree in chemistry at King's College, London, in the autumn of 1947. He was uncomfortably aware that the reason he had been able to work himself into this privileged position was because of the money Tom Somers had been putting aside for him – generous amounts – ever since he discovered that Martin was his son. It was something he mostly chose not to dwell on. When he did, it was with a mixture of defiance – well, he owes me, doesn't he? owes all of us – and plain gratitude that this man had enabled him to follow his ambitions. And this gratitude was not easy to deal with.

Jack, meanwhile, had gone to Chelsea College of Art. They had tried to find rooms to rent in Lambeth and other districts south of the river, but there was such a shortage of housing and, as Charlotte said, 'You shouldn't be taking a place off a family who might need it, when we've got room here.'

So they paid a minimal rent of half a crown a week to live in the attic in the Thornes' huge, rambling house. Charlotte organized the means for them to be as independent as possible. She was not keen to play mother and cook for them. Both of them could get a canteen meal during the day. They had a little plug-in stove and heated up food out of tins in the evenings, only joining Jack's parents for meals at weekends.

They were busy years – and in the main, happy. Martin's course was demanding: 'Oh, not in the labs all evening *again*?' Jack would complain. 'You need to lighten up a bit.'

It's all right for you, Martin thought, for not the first or last time. Jack's course seemed very free and easy in comparison; or maybe it was Jack's attitude to it – among all the arty types, who of course socialized together in the evenings, which was something Martin mostly missed out on.

Chemistry was much more exacting; they were all heading out to industry and needed to be prepared to take on serious, responsible jobs. As he occasionally pointed out to Jack, who would tell Martin not to get heavy.

'I see your family's factory background is coming out,' Jack would tease. 'You can go back and work at the jolly old chocolate factory again, after all this – they always need chemists, I suppose.'

The last time Jack said something like that, Martin felt a cold bolt of rage go through him. More and more since they left the mine – where they had clung together, Bevin Boys in the same boat – it was coming home to Martin

that their backgrounds and expectations were very different. That Jack, for all his talk of socialism, looked down
on him. And, Martin felt, he wasn't having that. He really
wasn't.

Now and again he fought back with Jack. 'At least,
where I come from, people do something useful.' Then he
would feel a bit petty afterwards. Or with Jack's family
at Sunday dinner he would make sure he threw in some
piece of information like, 'Ah yes, the Crystal Palace. Of
course all the panes of glass for that were made by Chance
Brothers in Smethwick.'

And Jack might roll his eyes in a comical way. But his
mother and father were genuinely interested, because they
were the sort of people who took an interest in everything,
and that rather took the wind out of Martin's sails.

He liked Jack's family. They were educated, cultured
in a way that his own was not. At times he felt ignorant and as if he did not quite know how to behave. But
he learned a lot from them – about art, and history. Dr
Thorne was a gentle teacher, good at explaining things in
a clear, simple way. They were relaxed, confident people
and they were good to him, never seemed to look down
on him. But they were certainly different.

The more Martin stayed in the Thornes' house, the
more he was drawn into their orbit. Going back to Birmingham and his family was already difficult. He could
not work out what he felt about anyone: his mother, his
'father' apparently – Tom Somers, Len and Jeanette. He
wasn't sure Len was all that happy with Jeanette, either.

And the thought of taking Jack back there and introduc-
ing him, 'This is Jack, my . . .' what? Friend? Boyfriend?
His family were not Jack's – who either accepted or chose
to ignore their son's preferences, he was never quite sure
which. Martin felt accepted, so although nothing was ever

mentioned, it seemed Jack's parents were quite at ease with it. But his own family: all in all, it was easier to stay away. So months and years passed, and he avoided it. Avoided what he felt about it.

And they had had a lot of fun. London, like everywhere, was struggling to emerge from the rubble and recover from the war. Despite everything – housing shortages, the endless rationing and the lack of money – everyone wanted a good time.

He and Jack did all the free things they could find: museums and art galleries. He learned a lot from Jack, who was not arrogant when talking about art – just enthusiastic. They went to the occasional show, made friends, and a few of the chemists and art students got on surprisingly well.

It was a good time, those three years. And when they emerged at the end, the thought of more freedom, of not being hemmed in by the walls of regular work that would go on and on for the next however many decades, of taking to the road, was irresistible. And, Martin realized, by going away he could avoid his graduation – having to deal with his mother and *him* coming along, all so proud. The thought made him curl up inside.

But travelling did not mean that they left themselves behind. In fact, some things about their individual personalities became starkly clearer now the daily routines were stripped away. Jack's cheerful, confident way in the world, which Martin had loved, had a side to it that Martin had already begun to see, but had tried to ignore. An arrogance that overrode other people – including him.

Thirty

'Now, girls – first position, second position . . . No, Susie, feet apart. That's right – on we go, Mrs Parsons . . .' Joy turned and smiled at the comfortable middle-aged lady who played the piano for her classes. 'Third, fourth, fifth. Yes – well done, children.'

She gave the little group of girls, all between the ages of five and nine, a broad smile. They beamed back at her. The girls loved her, she knew, and she had a good relationship with them.

'Now, show me your points . . .'

She pointed her own right foot in her pink ballet shoe and all the little girls, in a line, followed suit.

'No need to bend your knees quite that much, Shirley – yes, that's better. Right, we'll dance alternating points. Here we go.'

Right point, left point . . . The girls jumped up and down on the wooden hall floor, copying Joy as Mrs Parsons tinkled away in the background.

'Very good!' Joy told them at the end of the class. 'What lovely ballerinas, like little swans. And next week we're going to learn to do something called a *plié*. See you then, girls. Thank you, Mrs Parsons?'

'Thank you Mrs Parsons!' they chorused, before they scattered, giggling, as their mothers came in to fetch them.

Mrs Parsons wore a tweed skirt and pale-green blouse and arranged her grey hair in a stylish bun. She had told Joy she used to dance as a young girl, but her knees had let her down. She liked to be part of dance lessons, even if she couldn't do it herself any more.

'They're coming on, aren't they?' she said, gathering up her music. 'Even if Shirley has got two left feet!'

Once everyone had gone, Joy sank down onto a chair and took out her cheese-and-onion sandwich. She was in a church hall in Northfield, one of two halls she hired out each week for two lessons a week. The other was in Stirchley, and she had two children's and two adult classes. The number of students was growing, but it was summer and she hoped the autumn would bring even more people in.

She had an hour off before teaching the ballroom-dance class for adults and it was nice to have a sit-down in peace in the musty-smelling hall. Mom had handed her a flask of tea as she ran out, and she poured the dark brew into the cup and pushed her nose into the sugary steam.

'Ooh,' she murmured, 'I could do with this.'

She had been on the Milk Fudge line at Cadbury's all day, as she was every weekday. On top of that, she was now running four different dance classes as well as acting as a dance demonstrator at the West End Ballroom. She was also working her way through her dance teaching exams, and life was exhausting – but it was also exactly how she needed it to be.

'If we go on like this, we'll soon be able to set up our own little school,' Kay kept saying.

Kay, also still working full-time at Cadbury's, was running a few dance classes as well and the two of them had dreams of starting their own business. But they knew this was a little way down the line yet.

The only drawback was that Joy did not see enough of Patty. Sometimes she had started to feel that her little girl was closer to her mother and Nanna Margaret than to her. She had started bringing Patty to the dance class in

Stirchley, which was lovely. The only thing was that, both days when she taught, she had to stay on and teach adults afterwards, so Mom had to traipse all the way to Stirchley to pick up Patty and walk back with her. It was tiring for both of them, but Patty said she liked it.

'It's all right,' Ann said. 'While the weather's OK anyway. Come the winter, we might have to rethink.'

Mom had been so good, doing everything she could to support her, but Joy knew her mother was worried about her endless busyness. She was forever thrusting sandwiches and flasks of tea into Joy's hands as she rushed out again.

'You must be exhausted, love,' she was always saying.

But Joy was glad to be busy. There was work and the sociable Cadbury's factory life all day – as well as the Cadbury social life, summer afternoons at Rowheath and dances.

She lived in a whirlwind of activity. The last thing she wanted was to have time to stop and think. About Alan. About any other relationship she might have – that was off the cards, so far as she was concerned. About her life in any way, other than looking after Patty, planning with Kay and working towards their dreams.

For weeks now, that was exactly how it had been. She didn't want anything or anyone disturbing her emotions. But that was easier said than done.

That night, as she welcomed her ballroom-dance couples into the hall for the class, there were a few new faces. Four, in fact. Joy was delighted.

A couple in their forties, both sweet and shy, said their kids were almost grown-up and now they finally wanted to try something for themselves – they hardly knew how to dance and thought it looked fun.

'Well, you're in the right place,' Joy said, smiling at them.

As she welcomed the class members she did know, she saw another couple come in. Immediately she liked the look of them as well. And it was obvious that the woman was expecting a child – in not too many weeks. They introduced themselves as Ivor and Phyllis Williams. Ivor was a solid man with thick, cropped brown hair and a gentle manner, and Phyllis had long, darker-brown hair with a wave in it, pinned back attractively from her lovely, smiling face.

'We thought we'd make the most of it – before the little one arrives,' she said, looking down bashfully at her stomach.

'Might not be much chance after that,' Ivor agreed. 'We should have started earlier really, shouldn't we?'

'Well, better late than never,' Joy laughed, thinking how nice they seemed. 'How long is it now?'

'About ten weeks,' Phyllis said. She hardly needed to add, 'We're ever so excited.'

'I bet,' Joy said.

'We're hoping for a girl.' Again she blushed. 'Like Princess Elizabeth.' A few days earlier, the princess had given birth to her second child, a little girl called Anne. 'Do you . . .' Phyllis hesitated, as if wondering whether her question was tactless, 'have any children?'

'A daughter,' Joy said. 'She's five. A bit young for this class.'

They both laughed, and Joy indicated that she needed to go as yet another new class member appeared through the door.

'Have you come on your own?' she asked the tall, lean man with a long face and neat little moustache, who was looking round uncertainly.

''Fraid so, yes.' He smiled. 'Was that the wrong thing to do?'

Well, it doesn't help, Joy was thinking, not having anyone to dance with, in dances that are for couples. But he seemed rather charming. She guessed he would be in his late thirties.

'Don't worry – we'll see what we can do. What's your name?'

'Howard,' he said. 'Howard Fielding.'

Joy asked him to wait aside a moment while she started the class. She gestured to him to sit on one of the chairs arranged round the edge. Howard nodded and perched his tall, lanky figure on the edge of one of the chairs.

'We'll start with a waltz,' she said, as everyone looked expectantly at her. That would be easiest today, she thought, as she was going to have to dance with this Howard chap. 'Most of you probably know it, and I can help anyone who doesn't . . .'

Mrs Parsons only played for the children's classes, and for the adults Joy played records. She went to her little gramophone and a moment later 'The Blue Danube' was streaming out, sounding rather tinny and as loud as the machine could manage.

Even Ivor and Phyllis, who claimed not to be able to dance, had some idea about the waltz, and Joy soon had them stepping carefully around the room with the other couples, beaming into each other's faces. She quickly realized that Ivor really had quite a flair for dancing, though Phyllis seemed to struggle to remember the steps – as well as tiring quickly.

'I think it's the baby,' she said to Joy, blushing as she fumbled on her feet. 'It's addled my brain.'

'Oh, it definitely does that,' Joy laughed. 'I remember – I hardly knew if I was coming or going! Right,' she said, going over to Howard, 'I'll partner with you. Do you know the waltz?'

'Yes.' Again he gave her his charming smile. Suddenly dancing with him felt quite attractive. He added modestly, 'After a fashion, you might say.'

Joy laughed. 'It's all right – it's not a test. We're all here to enjoy ourselves!'

Howard stood up and held out his long arms. Joy hesitated, just for a second. Everyone else came to the class as couples, and it was a long time since she had actually danced with a man, except perhaps to demonstrate a few steps. But she put her right hand in his and accepted his long arm round the back of her waist, feeling suddenly self-conscious.

'You know the timing: one, two, three; one, two, three . . .' she said. 'Right, now!'

Howard kept smiling as they set off into the dance, looking down into her eyes. His were grey, intense in a way she found a little strange, but she put it down to him concentrating hard on what his feet were doing. In fact he was already a rather good dancer, and soon they were circling the room well enough while she called out to the others, trying to keep an eye on them at the same time.

'See if you can find a partner to come with next time?' she suggested as they danced. 'Do you know someone else who might like to learn?' Surely a reasonably good-looking man like Howard could find someone to come with?

'Oh – no,' he said, appearing strangely nervous at this idea. 'Can't say I do, no.'

'Not married then?' She tried to keep things light and chatty.

'No. Married? No.' Then he added, 'I haven't been

lucky enough to find the perfect woman yet. But I live in hope.' Again he smiled intensely down at her.

'Oh, I'm sure you will be one day.' Joy smiled, trying to lighten him up a bit. 'But it would be easier for us in class if you could find someone to come with?'

She got through the rest of the teaching by instructing the others and then catching up by dancing with Howard. They concentrated mainly on the waltz, but Joy did add a run through the quickstep towards the end. She found herself worrying about tiring Phyllis, and she noticed that halfway through she and Ivor bowed out of the dance and went and sat down.

'We really enjoyed that,' Ivor said, with his sweet smile. 'Though I think Phyllis is ready for a rest now.'

'I'm sure she is,' Joy laughed.

'It's surprising how much it takes it out of you, isn't it?' Phyllis said. She did look quite pasty-faced now. As if she felt sick.

'Take it easy,' Joy said. 'But you've done very well. Hope to see you again.'

Everyone seemed reluctant to leave – they were a friendly lot – and stood around chatting. But Fred, the elderly church caretaker, was waiting now, keen to lock up and get home. So they took the hint and left with friendly goodbyes and 'Thanks, Joy – see you next week.'

But, to Joy's surprise, Howard hung back. 'I really enjoyed that,' he said. 'Let me help you to tidy up?'

'Oh, well, there's not a lot to do.' Joy was packing up her record player. 'I suppose you could straighten up those chairs . . .'

'Gladly.' Howard went over and arranged the chairs neatly at the sides of the room. He set each one down with slow care, almost as if they were going to be in a portrait. Fred was starting to look a bit impatient.

'Thanks, Howard,' Joy said. 'That's kind of you.'

'Glad to be of help.' He smiled and raised his long arm to put his hat on. 'See you next week.' With a little bow, he left.

'Quaint bloke,' Fred said, leaning against the upright piano.

'Yes.' Joy pushed her dance shoes into her bag. Howard was certainly an odd mix of charm and slight strangeness. 'Just trying to help, I think. Goodnight, Fred, thanks – see you next week.'

'T'ra, bab.' Fred saw her out and locked the door.

And she made her way home and, for the moment, did not give Howard Fielding another thought.

Thirty-One

'You all right, love?'

'Um?' Joy had been miles away as she gathered her things together to head out to her class, a month later. Her mother stood in the hall, blocking the door, her head on one side.

'You seem a bit – not yourself.'

'Oh, I'm OK.' Joy smiled. 'A bit weary, that's all. I'll perk up when I get there. It's just, there's this bloke coming to the class – tonight's. He's been coming all month and he's always on his own, which is a bit of a nuisance. It makes everything rather hard work.' She pulled the strap of her bag over her shoulder. 'He's pleasant enough, always trying to be helpful. But I was rather hoping he might give up.'

As she spoke to her mother, Joy realized she could not put into words the odd mixture of feelings that Howard Fielding brought out in her. There was her irritation that he came on his own. But once there, he was always charming, anxious to be helpful and – she realized increasingly, week by week – keen on her. Very keen.

The number of long, intense looks he gave her had increased. He was courteous, rather charming, interested in everything she said and forever helpful. It would be hard to fault him. But somehow she couldn't seem to warm to him. While they were dancing and Howard was gazing down at her – he really was quite a good dancer – Joy was relieved to have to keep looking round and calling out to the other couples. It was a way of diluting Howard's intensity.

And at the end he always stayed behind to help, in any way he could – shift the piano, tidy chairs.

'Someone's got an admirer,' Fred kept teasing her, each time they finally got Howard to leave the building, with a gentlemanly tip of his hat. 'He asked you out yet?'

'No.' Joy gave Fred a rueful look. 'I really don't think I want him to.'

'Looks quite a catch,' Fred said cheerfully.

'Yes,' Joy sighed, 'I suppose he might be.' Howard had told her he worked in insurance, in quite a well-paid job. 'But he's a bit' – she searched for a word – 'much.'

She found it all very strange. It was nice to have someone who admired her, was attracted to her even. But why was it that although she couldn't find anything much to say against Howard, she was filled with a chilly sense of dread every time she knew she was going to see him? It was all strange, and she could hardly explain it even to herself.

'Well, you are doing a lot. No wonder you find it tiring,' her mother said now as Joy left the house. As she said almost every day.

'I know.' Joy rallied herself. 'Still, needs must. It's just harder going out of an evening, now the nights are drawing in. Soon as we get dancing I'll be fine.'

And it was true. Dancing was always a tonic for her, something she could lose herself in, no matter how tired she was. And despite Howard Fielding. She wasn't going to adore all her pupils all the time, she told herself as she waited for the bus. That was just how it was.

'Joy?' Phyllis and Ivor came up to her at the end of that night's class. She liked the people in her adult classes to call her by her first name. It was only with the children that she was 'Miss Gilby'.

'I'm afraid this is going to have to be our last class for the moment,' Phyllis said. She looked ruefully down at herself. 'I'm not sure if I got my dates wrong, but I feel like a whale and it's too much for me now, trying to dance. It's a shame, because I know Ivor loves it and he's so good. But they think she might come early – in the next few days.'

'Oh, I'll miss you both,' Joy said truthfully. 'You've both done so well.'

Ivor's vivid blue eyes smiled back at her and, to Joy's consternation, she felt a sudden lurch of emotion that she really did not want to feel. What on earth was the matter with her? She had one man chasing her and could feel nothing; and here was a happily married man, and she was getting all moony and emotional! But Ivor was such a nice man, and a really good dancer. Joy had become really fond of both of them.

'We've enjoyed it such a lot,' he said. 'I expect we'll be back – soon as we can.'

'Oh, I should think that'll be a while,' Joy joked, keeping things light to cover her sadness that she would not be seeing them.

She wanted to tell Ivor that he was very good – he really had a flair for dancing and had come on a lot in the last few weeks. But the same could not be said of Phyllis, so she didn't say it.

'Well, I'm glad you've enjoyed it,' Joy said. 'And the very best of luck to both of you. Let me know who arrives, won't you?'

'We will,' Phyllis laughed. 'We'll drop a note round.'

Smiling, Joy watched them walk away. They were such a nice couple and she could see how much Ivor felt for Phyllis, his arm round her back protectively as they

224

walked off. She was really going to miss them; they always added to the class because they were so friendly and nice to have around.

As she stood watching them, she realized Howard was coming towards her and, in confusion, she turned away, gathering up her things.

'Miss Gilby?'

She turned to see him holding his hat, a brown trilby, which he was moving round and round in his hands.

'It's Mrs, actually,' she said pointedly.

'My apologies.' He gave a little bow. 'What I was going to say was, as it's getting darker these days, I wondered if you'd like me to walk you to your stop?'

This was a polite, gentlemanly offer. It was dark out there now, and the back of the hall could feel quite creepy. It was obvious what Howard's motives were – he liked her and was being kind. So why did she find the hairs standing up on the back of her neck in alarm, as if she was allergic to him?

'My stop?' How did he know how she got home, when he always left first?

'The tram,' he said. 'You go by tram, I believe you told me?'

Had she? It was possible. She was about to say yes – what was the harm? – even though all she wanted now was to walk out on her own, in peace, without having to make conversation with anyone.

'It's all right,' she said, a wave of relief passing through her as she saw Fred come into the hall. 'I don't need to be walked anywhere, thank you. Goodnight, Howard.' She nodded at Fred. Time to go.

'As you like. Goodnight, Mrs Gilby.' Howard gave a little bow, put his hat on and made his way out. Joy gave Fred a relieved look.

'He's not going to give up – not unless you tell him proper,' Fred said. He winked at her. 'Admirers, eh, and no wonder, a pretty wench like you.'

The following week Howard did not say anything and quietly left the class at the end. Joy started off for home, hoping he had finally got the hint. But when she got to the tram stop on the Bristol Road, there were three people waiting – and as she walked up to the stop she saw, with a jolt of surprise and some irritation, that one of them was Howard. She went and stood behind the woman at the back of the short queue, hoping he would not notice her. But he came straight over to her.

'Thought I'd go this way home myself for a change,' he said jovially, before she could ask anything.

For the first time Joy felt really jarred and uneasy. Howard had always been perfectly polite, but he was starting to feel like one of those people who can't take a hint, or take no for an answer. But there was not much she could say. She couldn't accuse him of following her, because up until now he had not followed her anywhere. All the same, she was sure he *was* following her.

'Where do you live then?' she asked, her tone cool and definitely unwelcoming.

'Oh, Selly Oak,' he said. She did not believe him. Why had he not caught the tram before? She didn't want to encourage him by talking. But she sensed something in him, a kind of excitement at being with her.

She made sure she sat behind him on the tram and, sure enough, he did get off in Selly Oak – at the stop before she did. All the same, she found herself looking round as she stepped out, somehow thinking he might be lurking about. She was going to have to say something, but what? So far, he had done nothing very much at all. But the more she saw of Howard Fielding, the more there was something about him that made her feel jumpy. Up until now Joy had not spoken much about Howard, but something about the way he had behaved tonight had really bothered her.

'He's never caught that tram before,' she said, after relating to her mother and Tom what had happened, over a cup of cocoa. 'I don't know what it is about him, but he's starting to give me the creeps a bit.'

'Look, one of us can come and meet you, if you like,' Ann said. 'Couldn't we, Tom?'

'Oh no,' Joy said. 'It's quite a bother for you. I'm being silly. I think it's just that he's a bit keen on me, and I don't feel the same, that's all. Look, if I have any real trouble from him, I'll say, OK?'

But as she settled in bed that night, Joy had to take herself to task about something else. She felt really sad, as if a light had gone out. Had she not started to feel a little bit too fond of Ivor Williams? A lovely man, happily married and not someone she should be having any feelings towards? She knew it was partly that he could dance so well – something she always found strongly attractive in men. But he was also so good-looking in a way she liked, with his kindly, honest blue eyes. And a lovely person.

She drew in a deep breath, trying to calm down.

For goodness' sake, she said to herself, can't you ever get it right with any man? It's a good job Ivor and Phyllis are leaving, if you're going to get silly about it!

Thirty-Two

'So we said we'd go and meet her after the class, if she's worried,' Ann said. She was at Sheila's, the two of them sitting on the sofa, and she was leaning forward to play with Jonny, who had his little train set laid out on the floor. 'I might be worrying about nothing, but Howard does sound an odd sort.'

'Yes.' Sheila put her teacup down. 'Sounds as if he's got a flame lit for her. That's the trouble with being pretty.'

Ann straightened up in surprise. 'Well, she is pretty – but so are you, Sheila.'

'No,' Sheila said. 'Not like that.'

Ann couldn't argue. She knew what Sheila meant. She was a nice-looking girl, but her looks were more homely. Joy had a vivacity and shine, a sparkle about her, especially now she was back dancing and doing the things she loved. Sheila was the one who looked more careworn. That was what having three kids did for you.

'You all right, love?' Ann asked. She seemed to be forever asking that these days, of someone.

'Yeah. I'm all right,' Sheila said gloomily, as she ran Jonny's little loco around the track. 'Well, *he's* up to his old tricks again. But apart from that . . .'

Ann was startled by the bitterness in Sheila's voice, but was unsure if she should say anything.

'Kenneth?' she asked, surprised. She thought everything had long settled down, since they had moved here to The

Grove and their lovely little home and Kenneth had taken that new job.

'Forever wanting to be off – as if none of us are good enough for him.' Sheila's eyes filled suddenly.

'Oh, love . . .' Ann shifted along to put her arm round her. 'I'm sure it's not that – not really.'

'Feels like it, though.' Sheila wiped her eyes. She spoke quietly, trying not to alert little Jonny to the conversation. 'As if having a family is a nuisance to him – and we're holding him back from all his exciting plans.'

'Plans?' Sheila had not opened up about this before.

'Kenneth's been going on about us moving to Australia, for years now. I keep trying to find ways to put him off the idea – keep him busy, you know. The allotment and that. But every so often he starts on about it again. Some feller he knows has gone over there: big house, lots of work, everything marvellous . . .'

Ann felt a terrible plunge of dread. It was like when Joy had been going to go to America with Hank. *Don't go!* she wanted to beg. It meant so much to her to keep her children close. She had already lost Martin – or that was how it felt. She didn't think she could bear it if one of the others took off to the other side of the world.

'It's a very long way to go,' she said carefully.

'That's the thing, Mom.' Sheila was not crying any more. She gave Ann a very direct look. 'I know I should do what he wants, but it's asking too much.'

Ann squeezed her arm. 'Well, he's not going to go without you, is he?'

But Sheila was not consoled. She shook her head. 'Sometimes I really don't know about that.'

Ann had to leave to go and pick Patty up from school. She was mulling all this over as she walked along Linden Road and was so lost in her own thoughts that when a familiar face swam into view – a face she never normally bumped into – she almost squeaked in alarm.

'Jeanette!'

Jeanette could easily have avoided her. She usually seemed to manage to because, despite living only a few streets away, they never seemed to run into each other anywhere. Now, though, she planted herself right in Ann's path.

Ann calculated at high speed how long it had been since she last saw Jeanette. They had come across each other in a shop on the Green – oh, at least eighteen months ago now. Jeanette seemed older; her face had aged suddenly. But then perhaps her own had as well.

'I wanted a word,' Jeanette said.

'Oh,' Ann replied, unable to keep a certain tartness out of her tone. 'Well, it's lucky you ran into me then. You're always welcome to call round, you know.'

This was mostly true, though because of the way Jeanette had acted ever since she set up house with Len, Ann felt differently now about this woman, whom she used to call her friend.

Jeanette ignored this. Ann had a strange feeling that she was talking to a complete stranger, even though the two of them had worked together throughout most of the war; had swum and relaxed and laughed together. Jeanette had been a sweet person, but now and again Ann had been startled to realize that she had a hard side to her. Nowadays it felt as if that side had taken over.

'It's about Marianne.'

Ann could feel tension coming off Jeanette almost like a smell. Marianne, the woman that Ann's husband Len – now Jeanette's husband – had had an affair with. And George, the son she had borne because of it. George was very close in age to Elaine – he would be ten now. He was Len's son, and Len had a responsibility towards him.

'What about her?' Ann said wearily. All this stirred up difficult memories. She sincerely wanted it not to be her problem any more.

'She keeps asking for money. For the boy.'

Ann knew how much Jeanette resented Marianne. Her existence, and the existence of George. Ann and all her family too, for that matter. And she could tell from the way Jeanette was going on at her that *she* was the one Jeanette still blamed for all this. For Len going off the rails. If Ann had been a better wife . . . But then, Ann thought, if I had been a better wife, I suppose you would never have been able to be with Len in the first place, so what have you got to complain about?

'I thought she was working?' Ann said. 'She was doing well for herself.'

'She is working, for Boots the Chemist still. I gather she's been ill. But there's always something – George this, George that . . .'

'Well, he's Len's son, and I suppose George does need things,' Ann said, bewildered. 'I'm not sure why you're telling me all this?'

Jeanette looked her full in the eyes then, and Ann was truly shaken by her expression. She hates me, she thought. She really and truly hates me. Instinctively she wanted to step backwards to get away, but there was a hedge behind her.

'This should be your responsibility as well,' Jeanette snapped. 'All this nonsense I've had to deal with, since I was with Len.'

'Jeanette!' Ann protested. She was about to add, *You knew what you were taking on* . . . But she did not get the chance.

'None of this is my making; it's yours. Everything you put your family through – put your husband through – betraying him like that. It's no wonder Len went off with Marianne. And now we're having to pay for it!'

Ann was speechless for a moment, while the old familiar vibrations of guilt went through her about Len. She had loved Tom all these years – couldn't help herself. Even though she had held off and held off from doing anything about it. Had Len felt unloved, despite her doing her very best? Had she driven him into the arms of another woman? But her spirit rebelled. Len had made the choices he made for himself. And so had Marianne.

'Don't come to me talking like a fool, Jeanette,' she said quietly. 'We're divorced now and you're Len's wife, not me. I never asked you to run off with him, but he's your responsibility now, not mine.'

She stepped round Jeanette and started to walk off down the road, but she heard footsteps hurrying after her. Jeanette grabbed her arm.

'I wish I'd never had anything to do with you or your filthy mess of a family.' She almost spat the words at Ann. 'I had you wrong, right from the beginning. I wish I'd never met you – any of you!' She flung Ann's arm away from her and stormed off again up Linden Road.

Ann turned and watched Jeanette's rigid, furious form striding up the road. She felt as if she had been whipped by Jeanette's voice, the loathing in it. Her eyes stung with tears.

But the next thought that came to mind was, Poor Len – what on earth must his life be like, if Jeanette keeps going on like this? And she even felt a little sympathy for Marianne, or at least for little George.

Thirty-Three

'She really is being completely unreasonable,' Tom said, when Ann told him what had happened.

Ann got home really shaken, and it was the first thing she told him when he came in. He had stopped off for a drink in the upstairs bar at Cadbury's and she had already got Patty down by the time he returned home. 'Jeanette almost sounded as if she thought *we* should be paying for George's upkeep,' Ann said, getting their tea out of the oven.

'That's ridiculous,' Tom said. 'It's not as if he's even your stepson – he's nothing to do with you at all.'

Ann laid his tea in front of him: meat pie, the mince as usual bulked out with veg. Tom smiled as she poured some thin gravy on it as well.

'Looks lovely, thanks.' He glanced up at her. 'She really had a go at you, didn't she?'

Ann sank down at the table with her own plate of food.

'I've been feeling horrible about it ever since, even though I know Jeanette was lashing out at me and doesn't really have a leg to stand on. She was just so . . . hateful.'

Tom nodded, looking serious. They had often talked – with understanding – about how difficult it must be for Jeanette, taking on all the baggage that Len had brought with him. It wouldn't be easy for anyone.

'I don't know what's going on,' Ann continued. 'Jeanette said Marianne was asking for money – I mean, extra money. Len does contribute, of course. But she was . . .'

She shuddered. 'I would never have guessed she could be like that. Not from when I knew her before.'

'Jealousy, I suppose,' Tom said, knifing mustard onto his plate and cutting into the pastry. 'Of Len's past.'

Ann sighed. 'I know. But there's nothing any of us can do about that, is there?'

Tom put his knife and fork down and looked at her. 'I saw him. This evening.'

'Len? Oh, what, in the bar?'

Tom nodded. 'Was bound to happen, sooner or later. Not that I go there often. But I was sitting having a pint with Phil, from the department. And I spotted him across the other side. And then he spotted me.'

Ann felt her heart speed up. 'And?'

'And nothing. He looked at me. I looked at him. That was that.'

Ann stared at him, then started laughing. 'Men – honestly! Still, I suppose I should be glad he didn't come over and lay you out there and then.'

'Yes.' Tom looked thoughtful. 'I must say, though, he did look as if he had a few things on his mind.'

Poor Len, she found herself thinking again. Her former husband was someone she could never think of with bitterness. He was a good man, but he did seem to get himself into some messes.

'Joy all right?' Tom asked. She knew he had a soft spot for Joy – felt protective towards her.

'Think so. It's her Northfield class tonight, bless her.'

'She's certainly got some get-up-and-go, that one,' Tom said. 'I'll say that for her.'

Joy missed having Phyllis and Ivor in the class. Ivor had added a definite flair to the dancing and the two of them were such a sweet, loving couple. But that night as she went into the hall to set up, Fred came in, holding out a note to her.

'For you – arrived today,' he said. There was a smile on his fleshy face, which implied he knew what the note contained.

As Joy read it, a smile spread over her face as well.

Dear Joy,
  Just to let you know we had a little girl – we're calling her Glenys Jane, after both her grandmothers. We're all going along all right; missing your dance class, though.
  Best wishes, Phyllis and Ivor Williams

Joy was reading the note again when Howard arrived, coming into the room so quietly that she didn't notice until he was standing right next to her.

'Good news?' he asked.

Joy nearly jumped out of her skin. 'God, d'you have to creep about like that?' she said crossly. Howard was starting to behave almost as if he expected to have some hold over her, some right to her attention, which he did not have. She would never normally speak to any of her class like that, but there was something about Howard. Despite seeming shy, he also somehow pushed himself on you, invaded you, in a way she really didn't like.

'I'm terribly sorry,' he said. 'The last thing I wanted was to startle you.' And he sounded so genuinely apologetic that Joy felt bad for snapping at him.

'It's from Ivor and Phyllis,' she said, more kindly. 'They've had a little girl.'

'Oh,' Howard said, with his suddenly radiant smile, which forced her to forgive him. 'How nice.'

Joy read the note out to the rest of the group once they

had arrived, and they all cheered and clapped. Everyone had been fond of Ivor and Phyllis.

When the whole class was lined up ready to start, Joy stood in the middle of the floor.

'Oh, I've got another announcement today. I'm afraid there won't be a class next week.' There were some light groans of disappointment. 'I've got to go and take my final dance teaching exam that day. So I hope by the time I've finished, you might feel you are being taught by someone who knows what they are doing!'

Everyone laughed and there were cries of 'Good luck' and 'Break a leg!'

It seemed to put everyone in a good mood and the class went well. Joy even found it hard to keep her mind on what she was teaching, as her mind kept wandering excitedly. Although she had to dance with Howard, who was giving her his usual penetrating stares as he waltzed stiffly round the floor, Joy was miles away. If she passed the exam – and surely she would! – she and Kay could start thinking about how to set up their business properly. At the moment they were mostly working separately, running a class here and there, but maybe soon they could look to hire somewhere and have their own school.

At least that part of her dreams might come true, she thought, as she watched the class glide or stumble their way round the room. With a pang, she thought about Ivor and Phyllis. It was no good musing about meeting the man of her dreams – not now. That was something she was going to have to do without.

'May I walk you to the tram stop tonight?' Howard was saying.

'What? Oh no – no need,' Joy said breezily. God, she thought, this one really doesn't give up.

'It's no trouble really. I'd like to.'

'No, thank you,' she said firmly. 'I'd really prefer not, if you don't mind.'

Howard looked rather wounded by this and clearly did mind, but fortunately the record ended and Joy sped away to introduce the next dance and see to the record player.

When the class ended, to her relief Howard left without a word. Joy watched him go out. She had obviously offended him. But how else did you make someone take the hint? she thought, packing up her things.

'Night, Fred!' she called, stepping out into the gloom at the back of the hall.

Her eyes had not adjusted and she only heard, rather than saw Howard. She had only taken a couple of steps.

'Joy.' His voice was low, almost tender, but there was a command in it – as if she was obliged to stop, to do as he said.

Her heart began to thud, her mind doing rapid calculations. Fred was still here – she could run back inside if she needed help. She tried to get hold of the situation.

'I did tell you not to wait, Howard,' she said briskly, starting to walk on. Of course he was beside her in a second.

'I had to,' he said. His voice was thick with emotion. 'You won't be here next week, and I have to talk to you. I know you're running away from what's happening between us – from the magic of it. I can see it, every time we dance together: it's in your eyes, in your every move . . .'

He was gabbling. He put his hand on her shoulder, forcing her to stop. They had still not quite reached the road.

'You love me just as I love you,' he said. 'You've got to give in to it. I know you've got no one else – I know you live with your family, in Bournville. That you're a widow. We're free to love, Joy. You can give yourself to me.'

Before she could open her mouth to form any words, he had seized hold of her and was pressing his mouth on hers, his tongue forcing at her clenched lips, his body pushing against hers. Joy was overwhelmed by disgust and started to struggle, but he had his arms clenched round her like iron bands.

Feeling desperate, all she could think of was to kick him. She rammed the hard tip of her shoe at his shin, then again. Howard pulled his mouth away with a yelp of pain. Joy kept kicking and kicking.

'Help! Get off me! Go on – get away from me!'

Howard stepped back with a grunt of pain. 'What's wrong with you, you frigid bitch? I love you! How could you?'

'Everything all right out here?' A wedge of dim light spilled out and Fred's dapper figure was outlined in the doorway. Howard immediately took off fast on his long legs, towards the road, and vanished from sight.

'No!' Joy ran towards him. She was not going to pretend everything was all right – not for Howard. 'He just grabbed me.'

'Who?' Fred stepped out sharpish. 'What, that Howard bloke? You all right, bab?'

Joy was panting, almost sobbing now, shaking all over.

'He grabbed me – he was out here and he tried to—' But she was too upset to go on. 'He's run off now.'

'Dear, oh dear,' Fred said. 'We could call the police, I s'pose, but he's gone now. My guess is that we shan't be seeing him again – not now he's shown his true colours. You come on back inside.' He ushered Joy in, fatherly, being careful not to touch her.

Joy felt very cold suddenly, and was shivering as they stepped back into the musty-smelling hall. She was surprised at how shocked she felt. After all, Howard had only tried to kiss her. But it was more than that. It was his waiting there, in the dark. And it was . . . him. Something about him. She hadn't been imagining it. However charming Howard was, there was something about him, and now she could honestly admit that he made her flesh creep.

'I think he's been following me. He seems to know where I live. He might have gone straight there – be waiting near my house . . .' She found her voice going high and hysterical.

'Right.' Fred was decisive. 'We're not having this. I'll lock up and then I'm taking you home.'

'But it'll take you half the night,' she protested, thinking of the tram ride, then the bus, Fred having to come all the way back. 'Please don't worry.'

'No, it won't, bab.' Fred ushered her through the hall. 'That's my car parked out the front.'

'You've got a car?'

'Son works at the Austin. Gets a discount. He lets me borrow it if I'm out nights. Just let me switch everything off and lock up, and off we go.'

As the car smoothed its way along Linden Road and turned into Beaumont Road, all was quiet, as was usual in this Bournville neighbourhood.

'No sign of him that I can see,' Fred said, braking outside the house.

'I feel silly now,' Joy said. She was still shaky, but it felt safe in Fred's car. She was so grateful for not having had to go home on her own. 'D'you want to come in – have a cuppa before you go?'

'No, you're all right,' Fred said. 'My son'll think I'm in a ditch somewhere if I don't get back. Not that it's me he'd be worried about – only the car.' Joy saw the gleam of his teeth as he grinned. 'Go on in. That filthy so-and-so'll keep out of the way now, if he knows what's best for him.'

'Thanks, Fred. Really appreciate it.' She got out and waved him off.

As the sound of the car faded, she saw in the distance a tall figure slip out from the front of a house further along and walk quietly off down the street. Joy jumped, straining her eyes to see, her heart hammering hard.

Was that Howard, coming out of an entry that she would have had to walk past on her way home, if Fred had not brought her? Or was it just someone coming out of their house? She really didn't know, but her nerves were so jangled by what had happened that it felt as if anything was possible.

'I've got to get hold of myself,' she muttered, her hand trembling so much that she struggled to fit her key in the lock.

Thirty-Four

Usually Joy could shake herself out of any blue moods, but she felt very down for the next few days. Ever since Alan died she had tried to keep busy, look after Patty and build a life full of dance and teaching, not leaving her any time to think.

But every now and again the sadness would well up and start to fill her. What had happened with Howard had made her feel horrible – somehow dirty, as if it had been her own fault.

And she knew that her mood was also a result of having heard from Ivor and Phyllis, that note with their happy news. A couple who had done the thing everyone dreamed of: fallen in love, got married, had a child. So ordinary, so straightforward, but from Joy's point of view, something so unattainable. All she seemed to manage now was being followed about by a peculiar creep like Howard.

She didn't want to burden Mom with her low mood, because she knew her mother worried about her all the time. For once, when she was looking after Patty after work and not going out to teach, Joy went down to Sheila's in Selly Oak.

'You all right?' Sheila peered at her as she handed Joy a mug of tea in the little kitchen of the prefab. Her sister had spilled out to her what had happened.

Sheila had been startled at first to find Joy turning up. She had come out with the usual sarky comments, 'Hello stranger – fancy seeing you' and so on, before taking in the look on Joy's face.

'Have you told them, at home?' Sheila asked.

'Yes. I couldn't not,' Joy said, cupping the mug in her hands as if for comfort. 'I was in too much of a state to hide it.'

And she still looked in a state, Sheila thought. Dark rings under her eyes, a pale, shrunken look as if she had received a blow. And Joy had been looking so much better lately.

'Poor Sis,' Sheila said. She put her arm around Joy's thin shoulders for a moment and, to her surprise, Joy leaned into her, looking for comfort. 'That's horrible – he sounds disgusting.'

'He was,' Joy said, 'but,' she looked at Sheila, wide-eyed, 'd'you think there's something the matter with me?'

'What – no! Of course not.'

'It's just . . .' Joy looked down then, embarrassed and still tearful.

Sheila realized how difficult it was for her to speak, but she had been desperate enough to come all the way over her to confide in her.

'With men, I . . .' She shrugged. 'I don't seem to have any luck. Or the wrong ones seem to like me; there's never been one who wasn't wrong, one way or another.'

'Don't be daft,' Sheila said indignantly. 'You've had bad luck, but there was nothing wrong with Alan or Hank as people, was there? It was just how things worked out – the war and everything. The war ruined so many people's lives.'

'I s'pose so,' Joy said. She seemed close to tears. 'But there was a couple who I was teaching. So nice, both of them.' She looked up at Sheila. Why was she talking about this? Her sister would think she was barmy.

Sheila was frowning. She could not make sense of what Joy was saying, either. 'This bloke, Howard,' she said. 'Maybe you should tell the police?'

'I s'pose I could've. But in the end, nothing much happened. And I was too keen just to get home. Fred didn't seem to think . . .'

'If he comes anywhere near you or that class again—'

Joy looked round, startled at the enraged tone in Sheila's voice.

'Yes, if he turns up again,' Joy said uncertainly. Surely to God, Howard wasn't going to, after that?

'Come on,' Sheila said. 'We'd better check on the kids.'

She opened the kitchen door and they could hear the children's voices in the living room.

'Remember,' Sheila said, sounding fierce, 'none of this is your fault.'

Later, after Joy had left – a little bit more cheery than when she arrived, after a cuppa and seeing Patty playing with her cousins – Kenneth was still not back. It was his night for a drink with the other lads at the Austin. Sheila gave the children their tea and later they started on the bedtime routine, for Jonny first of all.

She was in the middle of getting him ready for bed when a great wave of loneliness came over her. It was as if Joy's blue mood had infected her. There was Joy, feeling alone in the world and dreaming about having a man in her life – a nice one . . . Sheila gave a bitter laugh as she thought about this.

She had a man in her life all right, but here she was, on her own again doing all the chores, no Kenneth. The worst of it, these days, was that even when he was here, it felt as if he wasn't. They still had a laugh at times, and he still wanted love-making, once a week anyway. But most of the time he came and went, ate his meals, went to work, went out for a drink – the usual routine – but he seemed miles away.

I might as well be living on my own, Sheila thought as she pulled Jonny's pyjamas up.

'Mom?' The little boy looked intently into her face. Suddenly he put each hand on either side of it, pressing her cheeks, as if forcing her to look at him, to be with him.

'Yes, poppet?'

His blue eyes searched hers as if looking for something. Sheila knew what he was looking for. *Are you here, Mom?* With a pang she realized that she was doing what Kenneth did to her. She smiled, staring back into Jonny's eyes, and he seemed happy again.

'Come on then, monkey, into bed.'

She read him a quick story – *Goldilocks* – then kissed him and slipped out of the room. He needed to be asleep for when the others tiptoed in later. For a moment she stood outside the bedroom door, checking that he was settling. And suddenly she missed Audrey. The old Audrey. Sitting by the fire in the evening, as they had during the war, drinking watery cocoa, talking and talking. All those years when she had ached for Kenneth and longed for him to come home . . . Her eyes filled with tears. And now here she was, missing the years with Audrey. But she had lost Audrey now, she knew. Nothing was the same. All that longing for peace and a quiet life, and now look at her.

Trying to pull herself together, she went into the living room where Elaine and Robbie were waiting, already in their nightclothes. She had a good life, she told herself. Everything she had ever wanted. She needed to pull herself together and not be so ungrateful.

But after she had got Elaine and Robbie down, Kenneth was still not home. Their tea of liver and onions was congealing in the oven and she was hungry. And she started to feel really cross.

I might as well have mine, she thought. There's no telling when he might roll up.

But she was just sitting down, resentfully, to eat on her own when she heard Kenneth come, and she forced herself to smile at him when he came into the kitchen.

'You're late – get held up?'

'A bit, yeah. The tram was an age coming.'

He washed his hands at the sink, then sat down. Sheila put his plate in front of him and went back to the table herself. He seemed in a good mood, she thought with pleasure. Almost excited.

Later, when they were both feeling raw and furious, she thought, if only he had started on this after tea. When they were not both hungry and tired.

'Sheila.' He picked his knife and fork up, but couldn't seem to wait to speak. He appeared lit up; blond, strong-looking. It made her smile, seeing her good-looking husband, his eyes eagerly searching her face.

'You look full of beans all of a sudden.' She wondered if he had been offered a pay rise, or something like that, at work.

'Thing is . . .' He hesitated, as if worried what she might say, but then hurried on. 'I've been looking into it – properly this time. Us going to Australia.'

It was as if he had dropped a bucket of ice over her. Sheila felt herself tense up, rigid, and a fury begin to grow deep inside her. So much so that it was hard to hear what Kenneth was saying as he leaned towards her, talking fast and excitedly about how he could get work at the Austin in Melbourne, and how they could have a whole different life – it would be wonderful for the kids . . .

It was as if there was a wall inside her that her husband

was hitting up against. Sheila's mind was racing. He was not going to stop keeping on about it, she could see. It mattered to him, and she felt terrible that she did not want it. That she could not be the submissive Sheila who, before the war, would have felt obliged to do anything her husband suggested. Who would not have dared to do otherwise, because she depended on him so much.

There was still a lot she would do for Kenneth. She loved him. He was her husband, and a good man. But this, no. And the fury started to bubble faster and hotter because he should not keep asking. Not for this. Not after she had said no so many times. It was as if he thought that because he wanted something, that was the only thing that mattered. As if what she might want counted for nothing.

'No.' She cut Kenneth off.

His face darkened. 'No? What d'you mean, no? You can't just say that.'

Sheila stood up, moved her plate over to the side, suddenly not hungry at all. She turned to him.

'I think I can. Maybe you didn't hear me. No. I'm not going to Australia. I've told you I don't know how many times. I don't want to – and that's that.'

'For God's sake . . .' Kenneth slammed his fist down on the table so that everything rattled. 'I've hardly got a word out, and all you can do is pour cold water on it. You're not even listening. You haven't given it a thought!'

'Oh yes, I have,' she retorted. 'You've mentioned it time and again, and I've thought and thought, tried to persuade myself that I can do it, do what you want. But I can't. This is my home – England and Birmingham – and the home I want for our family. I want to stay here, and that's that.'

Kenneth got to his feet, his face uglier than she had ever seen it.

'You're very uppity these days, Sheila. And I don't like

it. When you're married with kids, you go where the work is – it's not about what you want or don't want. I'm your husband, and you'll come with me if I decide to go.'

Sheila was pressed up against the sink now, with Kenneth standing over her, livid. She could feel a chasm opening up in front of her. In her marriage. All the years she had waited for him during the war; the struggle of living together after the war, all crammed into the family home. Never had they had a sticking point like this. Never had she had a wall inside her like this. And now, just when they had their first proper little home – this . . .

Her anger only increased as these thoughts rushed through her mind.

'That's where the work is? There's jobs going all over Birmingham for the taking, and you know it. You may want to go to Australia, but don't give me all that flannel about going where the work is. You want to go because you want to go – that's the only reason. And you don't even think about what I might want: my family, my friends . . .'

'You can make new friends over there. Don't be such a ridiculous stick-in-the-mud, Sheila! You've always been like this – won't try anything new. Scared of your own shadow. Give it a chance, all right? I'm going to look into making arrangements, whether you like it or not. In fact, you're going to have to like it.'

He started to walk away.

'Kenneth.' There was ice in her voice now. He stopped, but did not turn round. 'You can make all the arrangements you want. Go to Australia. But I'm not coming – and neither are the kids. You want me to make a choice that I don't want to make. Well, that's yours.'

He did turn then, hearing the steel in her voice. His face was solemn and angry.

'You'd leave me? Split up this family – just like that?'

'Oh, for goodness' sake, now who's being ridiculous? We've got a perfectly good life here, without taking off to the other side of the world where we don't know anyone. You're the one who'd be leaving, so don't accuse me. Go on – go, if that's what you want. But I'm staying here.'

Kenneth stood there for the best part of a minute, staring at her, almost as if he had never seen her before. Then, with quiet fury, he said, 'Right, if that's the way you want it.'

He left the kitchen and she heard him go to the front door and leave, slamming it behind him.

Sheila cleared up and sat in the living room, still angry and very tense. What had just happened? Was that the end of her marriage – those moments? But deep down, she did not feel it was. Marriages did not break that easily. And they loved each other, didn't they?

Unable to settle, she sat fidgeting, pulling memories of her life with Kenneth out to examine. Telling herself it was her fault: she was the one who had changed.

When Joy had been about to leave for America at the end of the war – or so they had all thought – Sheila had already known then that she could not do something like that. 'I'm a home bird,' she'd said to Joy. 'I don't *want* to live anywhere else.'

It was a feeling rooted deep inside her. *I belong here.* She had lived with Audrey in the pretty village of Goring-on-Thames, down in Berkshire. It was very nice, but she knew she was not staying there. Never wanted to stay. It was not home. Birmingham, and everything she knew, was home. And it might be braver or more open-minded, or a whole lot of other things, to uproot yourself and go to live in another part of the world. But however exciting or sunny or close to beautiful beaches it might be, however many oranges there were hanging from the trees, she was not going to do it. It was one of the things she knew for sure.

Where had Kenneth gone? What if he never came back? You heard about men who walked out for one reason or another – to buy fags, collect a newspaper – and were never seen again. Maybe he would just go now, straight to Australia, start again, meet another woman . . .

Her mind was running riot. This would be her life. This silence, alone with the children, day and night. The thought made her feel so bad that she burst into tears and sat sobbing her heart out, leaning forward on the sofa.

She waited up until after midnight before dragging herself up to bed, where she lay awake, listening for any tiny sound. But Kenneth didn't come back.

Thirty-Five

The next day Sheila felt completely exhausted. After a night of almost no sleep, her head ached and her nerves were in shreds. It took everything she had not to scream at the children for the slightest thing. However, there was nothing for it but to carry on, get Elaine and Robbie up and off to school, trundle Jonny up to the shops in Selly Oak in the pushchair. It was a long way for him to walk with his little legs, and the pushchair gave her something to hang the bags on as well.

All day she felt as if her innards were weighed down with lead. It was better to keep busy. But wherever Kenneth had gone last night – unless he had truly taken off for Australia – he would now have to be at the Austin, and she couldn't expect to hear anything until the working day was over.

After she'd fed Jonny at dinner time and picked at a sandwich herself, she thought about going down to Bournville: take Jonny down to her mom's and see her grandparents, Margaret and Cyril. But she couldn't face it. It was so tiring getting there and she knew that once there, she would not be able to hide how she was feeling. Nanna and Grandad were frail now, she thought. The last thing they needed was her turning up, blarting all over them.

A wave of desperation hit her as she sat waiting for Jonny to finish his dinner. She put her elbows on the table, resting her face in her hands and trying not to dissolve into tears again.

Where was Kenneth? Had he gone to his mom and dad's? She felt so hurt and angry and worried, all at once.

'Mom, what's the matter?' Jonny tugged at her hands.

'I'm all right, love.' She sat up, uncovering her face and trying to smile at her serious little boy. 'I'm a bit tired, that's all.'

'You're always tired,' Jonny said, rather dismissively, Sheila thought. But it made her laugh a little.

'Yes, I s'pose I am. Not surprising, with you running me ragged all day, is it?'

Jonny gave her a reproachful look.

'Come on – you've finished, haven't you? Let's go and see Auntie Beryl. We could all go to the park or something.'

Somehow she got through the afternoon. Even though she felt close to Beryl, and Beryl confided in her about Sid and his moods, Sheila couldn't bring herself to tell her that Kenneth had not come home last night. She felt too raw and upset.

So they kept things light and on the surface, and when it was time for the school pick-up, they walked down together with the twins in the pram – with Maryann perched at the end for some of the way, and Jonny in the pushchair – to fetch Sally, Elaine and Robbie. And then everything was busy and full of children and tea time, and baths and bedtime.

The time when Kenneth usually came home passed, and Sheila could feel herself getting more and more wound up and desperate. She snapped ferociously at Elaine and Robbie when they wanted more stories at bedtime.

'I can't. Not tonight. Just go to bed and go to sleep!' she almost roared at them.

They both went silent in shock at the fierceness of her reaction. Elaine's face had a definite 'There's no need to talk to us like that – what've we done?' look on it, but for once even she didn't dare say anything.

Sheila was tidying up the kitchen, with dinner warm in the oven, when she heard the door open. Kenneth had waited until he knew the kids would be in bed, she thought. As she heard his footsteps coming closer, the relief that coursed through her was outstripped by her anger and resentment. That he could go off, like that, without a word . . .

'Sheila?' He stood at the kitchen door.

Slowly she turned round. Any thought she might have had of trying to be a sweet, pleading little wife went straight out of the window. 'So where the hell've you been?'

She saw him bite back an angry response. 'I was just over at Mom's.'

'Oh. I thought you'd gone to Australia. So now you've "just" come home for your tea, have you?'

'Sheila.' He stepped closer. She was waiting for 'Sorry', but it didn't come and he didn't sound sorry. Certainly not sorry enough for her to let him put his arms round her, which was what Kenneth seemed to have in mind. She picked up a cloth and went to the oven.

'Right, well, luckily someone stuck around here to look after your children and cook your tea.'

She hoiked the dish of macaroni cheese out of the oven and slammed it on the table.

'And I don't know about you, but I'd like to actually eat it tonight, while it's still hot.' She had scraped the congealed liver into the kitchen rubbish bucket, cursing furiously at the waste.

Kenneth sat down at the table, and Sheila furiously dolloped spoonfuls on to the plates.

'Mustard?' she said savagely. Kenneth nodded.

At last she sat down and they had to face each other across the table.

'I'm not trying to make you angry,' Kenneth said. 'I'm not – honest. I just . . .' He put his elbows on the table, still not having picked up his knife and fork.

Eat your sodding tea, Sheila felt like screaming. *You wasted last night's.* She picked up her own fork and determinedly scooped up a mouthful.

'I don't mind working for us. I don't mind being a father.'

'Well, that's big of you,' she said, through a mouthful of macaroni.

'Can you just listen?' He looked at her directly, and she came up against pain in his eyes, which sobered her a little. 'I know you don't want to go to Australia. And I do want to. And somewhere in between, we've got to find an answer to this.'

'I'm not going,' she said, although more gently. 'I'd do a lot of things for you, Kenneth – for the family. But I'm not doing that. I can't. I don't want to go and live on the other side of the world.'

'You could at least give it a chance . . .' He started saying.

'No,' she went on. 'I'm sorry. Call me weak, or feeble, or whatever you want. But I know I can't do that. And it's better to know than go all the way over there and then find out. If you've got to go – really got to – then you'd best do so, because I can't carry on like this. But I won't be going with you.'

'But you're my wife,' he started to argue. 'And Mom thinks—'

'I don't care what your mom thinks – or anyone else,' Sheila retorted, while at the same time surprised by her own certainty. She didn't feel so sure of a lot of things in life, but of this she really was. 'I may be a bad wife. Have a black mark against me for this. But I'm not going, and that's that. I want to bring our kids up near their grandparents – and my own grandparents, for that matter. They're not getting any younger, and if we leave I'll never see them again.'

'So you'd rather lose me?' To her aggravation, Kenneth still hadn't picked up his fork.

'No. That's not what I said. But I have lived without you here before, and I suppose I'd have to do it again. It's not what I want, but it's not as bad as having to move to Australia. And while we're on the subject, I don't see why what happens in any family always seems to be what the men want. You don't need to go there – there's more than enough work here.'

For a moment she thought he was going to get up and storm off again.

'I can't go on like this,' he blurted suddenly. 'Life being so . . . small.'

'Can we eat our tea?' she said irritably. 'Before it gets cold – again.'

The rest of the evening was quiet. Coldly silent. Kenneth got out his fishing tackle and fiddled with that at the kitchen table. Sheila sat knitting in the other room. Things still felt angry and not right. She clicked the wireless on, fed up with the yawning quiet around her. But she didn't take in any of the programme, as her mind was racing.

He thought I would give in, after he disappeared last night, she thought to herself. Wanted to give me a shock. Blackmail me – that was the word that came angrily to mind.

And she desperately wished she could give in: say yes, make peace and do what he wanted. But there was the wall inside her that this request came up against every time she thought about it. No. Just no. It was too much to ask.

They were going to have to find another solution.

It was gone ten o'clock and Sheila was about to get up and head to bed, when she realized that things were not quite so silent after all. Noises started coming from next door, from Beryl and Sid's house: raised voices.

So they're having a ding-dong as well, she thought. But this was no comfort. She was already scraped raw inside, after arguing with Kenneth, and this only made her feel worse. And he had still not come in. He had stayed in the kitchen all evening, messing about. She put her knitting away and went in there.

'Fancy some cocoa?'

'Ah yes,' Kenneth said sarcastically. 'The answer to everything.'

'All right,' she flared up again. 'I won't flipping bother then.'

'No . . .' He pushed the chair back and stood up. He suddenly seemed very big in the small room. Perhaps that was how he felt all the time. Too big. 'Sorry. I didn't mean it like that.'

'Yes, you did.' She was close to tears now, after all this sitting alone, feeling angry and sad.

They didn't talk as she heated the milk. As they stood in the kitchen, the raised voices next door floated through to them, rising out of control, then dying away, before flaring up again. Beryl shrieking in pain.

Their eyes met, both of them horrified.

'What do we do?' Sheila said.

'Can't interfere, can we?' Kenneth took a mug of cocoa from her. 'Ta. Looks nice.' He was trying to make amends now.

They stood there drinking, united now in listening worriedly to what was going on next door.

'He's a brute when he gets going,' Sheila said.

'Is he?'

'You've seen her – afterwards. D'you think we ought to knock and ask if they're all right? It might put a stop . . .'

Kenneth was shaking his head. 'Can't do that. It's between them, isn't it? I s'pect it'll all blow over in a minute.'

But instead of blowing over, the sounds only got louder. Sheila could hear Beryl. 'Get off me, you pig!' she heard distinctly. This was followed by a shriek of real pain. Sheila made to move, as if to go out.

'No, don't; wait.'

'We can't just leave them. Sid might . . .' She didn't like to finish that sentence. But what would she have wanted, if someone was knocking seven bells out of her?

The voices carried on, more quietly now. There were muffled bangs, of doors being opened and shut. How did their children sleep through this? Sheila wondered. Maybe they didn't. She pictured those little girls lying awake, terrified, hearing the frightening sounds.

Her eyes met Kenneth's.

'We'd best get to bed,' he said. 'They'll be all right in the morning.'

Reluctantly she followed him, already overwrought and exhausted from their own falling-out, from the chasm that had opened. She was longing to lie down in bed, warm and normal – let things settle.

But, as it turned out, she was not going to get to bed for a good while yet.

They had gone into their room and were starting to ready themselves for bed when there came an urgent knocking at the front door. Sheila, in her dressing gown, ran to answer it.

Out in the darkness, she saw several pairs of scared eyes looking up at her.

'I'm sorry, Sheila.' Beryl's voice was hoarse, distraught. She was holding one of the twins, and Sally, her oldest girl, was managing to keep hold of the other, arms clamped around him as if he was a bundle. 'You must've heard us. Can we come in – just for tonight?'

'Course.' She stepped back to let them all in. As they entered, she saw that Beryl, Sally and Maryann had a blanket of some sort draped over each of them.

Kenneth emerged from the bedroom, having dressed again. Sheila was grateful that he had not left all this to her, as 'women's business'.

'Want a hand?' he asked softly.

'You'll all have to bed down in here.' She opened the sitting-room door. 'Beryl, you have the sofa. We'll sort something out on the floor for the kids, as best we can.'

They managed to put together a bed with blankets and cushions, while Sally and Maryann waited, silent, but obviously rigid with emotion after what they had heard. Sheila put the pan on again and made them all a drop of cocoa with the remaining milk. Eventually they got the little girls bedded down on the floor.

One of the twins, Richard, had somehow stayed asleep through all this, but Beryl brought Charlie into the kitchen to feed him, while Sheila dabbed at the cuts on her face with gentian violet. Kenneth made himself scarce then.

'Sorry, you're going to look a bit of a sight,' Sheila said, as Beryl winced and the mauve antiseptic stained her face, to add to the bruises.

'Don't you apologize,' Beryl said tearfully. 'I'm ever so sorry, Sheila, bringing all this to your door.'

Sheila, whose nerve endings were already frayed from her own troubles of the day, as well as Joy's, sat down opposite Beryl, looking at her misery, her injured face, and thought, Men. *Bloody sodding men.*

'Sid doesn't really mean it,' Beryl said, seeing the look in Sheila's eyes. 'Not really. He just—'

'Well, if he doesn't mean it, why does he do it then?' Sheila interrupted, sick to death of Beryl's excuses for her bully of a husband.

'He gets . . .' Beryl looked away, and then her distress started to come out and tears rolled down her cheeks. 'It's like he can't help himself. But he's not like it all the time – he's all right most of the time. He is, honest!'

Her tears were falling on Charlie's face. Sheila got up and put her arms round Beryl from behind, feeling fond, and sorry for her. What choice did Beryl have, with all her kids? Where else was she going to go?

'Look, you go and get some sleep,' she said, feeling defeated. 'Things'll look better in the morning.'

When she slid into bed beside Kenneth, she could sense that he was still awake. As soon as she lay down, he reached out for her.

'C'm'ere.'

Emotionally wrung out, Sheila moved over and they lay holding each other, in silence for a while. She felt Kenneth stroking his hand up and down her back and it soothed her. They both knew the chasm was there. It wasn't only her. But they loved each other and they had to find a way to overcome it.

'Let's never get like them,' Kenneth said eventually. She could feel his breath in her hair.

Beryl's and Sid's latest fight – the worst they had heard yet – had brought both of them up sharply.

'No. We won't get like them.' She lifted herself onto one elbow. But she had to say it, again. To be perfectly clear. 'I'm sorry, love. I really, truly am. But I can't go to Australia. Don't ever ask me again, OK?'

There was another silence in which all Sheila could sense, with a sharp stab of guilt, was Kenneth's dreams shrivelling inside him. But she couldn't do it. Just couldn't. They would have to find some other way to make his life feel more as he wanted it.

After a while, quietly, through the darkness, she heard him say, 'OK.'

Thirty-Six

November 1950

'Cough it up – might be a gold watch!'

Ann dabbed her finger fondly against Patty's nose and she screwed up her eyes, still coughing. She was, as usual, drawing at the kitchen table while Ann got her cooking done. Patty was always happiest with paper and some crayons in her hands.

'She's had that cough a while,' Joy frowned.

'Seems all right in herself, though,' Ann said. 'I'll give her another dose.' She unscrewed the top of the Veno's Cough Mixture and carefully poured some onto a teaspoon. 'There you go – get that down you.'

Patty swallowed, then shuddered at the taste. 'Ugh, s'horrible.'

'Probably good for you then, pet,' Ann said, laughing.

'Mom?' Patty looked up hopefully at Joy. 'Can you teach me a dance?'

Joy took Patty's hand as she slid eagerly off the chair. 'All right, come on then. Just for a few minutes, then I need to come and help Granny.'

Ann carried on cooking the Sunday dinner as music began to float from the record player next door. She had saved up ration coupons for a little beef joint, and the smell was already making her mouth water.

At the sink, peeling potatoes, she looked out at the

garden. Tom was out there, digging, laboriously, but getting it done. Now there was no Alan to help, he had perfected a way of managing the spade with one arm, levering the soil up with his foot pressed down hard on it, then chopping the clod with the sharp edge of the spade.

'Takes longer than it would anyone else, but it gets done,' he would say. And he seemed to like it, out there in the fresh air, with his slow rhythmic movement, as if it helped him to think, calmed him.

She heard Patty's excited voice from the other room. Time with her mom – quite a rare thing in her young life these days. Because Joy was busy, busy. But Ann didn't mind. It was wonderful to watch her daughter blossoming. The only shadow on the horizon was that bloke who was following her about, who seemed to have a bit of a thing for her.

After Joy's next class, she had refused to let Ann and Tom come all the way to Northfield to get her, even after what had happened with Howard springing on her like that.

'There's no need – I'll get Fred to see me out and check there's no one there. And Fred said he'll give me a lift again, if I have any bother.'

But she had come home from that class shaken and indignant. Ann and Tom both leapt up as Joy came into the house. Both of them had been waiting, tense as anything while pretending they weren't.

'Are you all right?

'Have any bother?'

'Guess what?' Joy said furiously, hanging up her coat. 'Howard turned up again for the class, large as life!' She turned to them, hands on hips. 'I couldn't believe my eyes. Comes in, says, "Evening, Mrs Gilby!" all breezy – in fact I've never seen him so full of himself. And he came over to me, all smiles, and said, "I hope I can claim the first dance?" as if we were in some Victorian ballroom. Can I put the kettle on? I'm starved.'

They followed her, agog, into the kitchen.

'He was all lit up as well, as if I'd promised to marry him or something. It was . . . well, sort of frightening, because I started to think, Maybe he's mad, completely bonkers. He must live in some sort of dream world, I think.'

She stood the kettle on the gas.

'Anyway, I said, quite quietly, "Howard, I want you to leave and not come back to this class. After your behaviour last time." And he gave me a really funny look – almost as if he felt sorry for me or something. It was so strange. Anyway Fred was there, standing quite near me. And Howard didn't say anything; but he kept looking at me, all sort of superior, and it was starting to get on my nerves. So I said, "Go, please. Just get out." The others were starting to arrive then and I didn't want to make a big scene. He turned round slowly then, but still with this look as if he was right and I was wrong, and he left.'

'Well, I hope Fred came out with you afterwards?' Ann said.

'Yes, he drove me home again actually, bless him. I told him I thought I'd seen Howard in our road, after the last time. I'm not really sure whether I did, but just in case . . .'

'He sounds a good bloke,' Tom said.

'Yes, he is, but I told him he doesn't need to make a habit of it.'

'Well,' Ann turned, getting cups off the shelf, 'I hope you've seen the last of Howard. He sounds a bit of a case. Don't let your guard down.'

'No,' Joy sank down at the table. 'I won't. I think I was pretty clear with him, though.'

So although there had been no sign of Howard for three

weeks now, the possibility that he might still turn up hung over them like a shadow.

Apart from that, Joy was on the up. And for that Ann gave thanks every day.

Just a few weeks ago, she and her friend Kay Tarrant had sat here at the table, chattering nineteen to the dozen about their plans.

'If we could rent somewhere in town for the school,' Kay was saying excitedly, her ideas getting bigger by the second. 'Imagine it – a big sign, "TARRANT and GILBY DANCE SCHOOL". Are you going to go by Gilby?'

Joy looked at her mother. 'Would that be all right? I feel as if it's really my name.'

Ann shrugged. 'Can't see why not.'

'"GILBY AND TARRANT?"' Kay said.

'What about "JOY AND KAY's"?' Joy said. She frowned. 'No, you're right. Our surnames are better. But we'd better get somewhere out of town – it'll be cheaper. Anyway, we can't afford to give up work yet, so we could carry on renting for evenings and weekends to start with.'

'I s'pose you're right,' Kay said, with a wistful sigh.

'No names up in lights yet,' Joy laughed.

Ann, who was ironing behind them, smiled. She knew Joy didn't mind about the frills. She could see that Joy and Kay would go far. She liked Kay, had really taken to her – she was such a lively, cheerful girl and a great friend for her daughter.

And the two of them were already getting a name for themselves by word of mouth. Invitations had started arriving for them to come and lead tea dances, barn dances, ballroom sessions around the city. Joy was busy – and loving it – and Ann was more than ready to help her to do what she loved best.

*

The music was still going on in the front room and Ann was sliding a pan of potatoes into the oven in the hot dripping-fat, when there was an urgent banging at the front door.

'What on earth?' She slammed the oven shut and went out, to find Joy already opening up. A jaunty dance tune was coming to an end in the front room and it suddenly stopped, leaving the faint sound of the disc turning, the repeating rasp of the gramophone needle. Patty poked her head out to look as well.

'Dad!' Joy said, startled, as the door opened.

'All right, love – is your mother in?'

'Len?' But Ann didn't have to ask. He looked terrible, panicked and upset.

'It's Dad, I think he's had a stroke.'

'Is he . . . ?'

'They've taken him in the ambulance.'

Len couldn't stand still, as if there was something else he should be doing, but he couldn't think what it was.

'Come in.' She ushered him into the kitchen just as Tom came in from the garden. He stood tactfully near the back door, and Len was in too much of a state to notice. He sat, by habit, in his old seat at the table.

'Mom's gone to church and I popped over to see Dad – I often do on a Sunday. Do the garden for him a bit, like. We was both out there. I was digging and he was tidying up a few things, and he suddenly went down like a nine-pin. Couldn't seem to speak. So I ran down to the phone box . . .'

He was almost in tears. Ann looked across at Tom and he tactfully tiptoed out of the room, leaving them alone.

'I'll go up the hospital later. Only I need to get back. Jeanette's expecting me.'

It was Joy with whom Ann exchanged looks now. Patty was staring up at them both with big, solemn eyes.

'It's all right,' Joy squatted down and gave her a hug. 'Grandpa's had a shock because Nandad' – Patty's name for Cyril – 'is a bit poorly.'

'I'll go along to your mother,' Ann said. 'She can come back here for her dinner.'

'Thanks.' Len shook his head. 'I can't believe it. Once minute he was perfectly all right, talking to me about the football, and then . . .' He stood up. 'Look, I'd best get back. I'll be over later to see her.'

They saw him out.

'Shall I go and get Nanna?' Joy offered.

'No,' Ann said. She felt emotional, as what Len had said actually sank in. Margaret and Cyril: people she had hurt, but whom she loved as much as anyone in the world. 'I'll go.'

Taking her apron off, she went down the road without even thinking of a coat, and knocked on the door of the old, familiar house where she had been so many times.

After a pause, Margaret came to the door, still in her church dress. She looked stunned, and for a second it was as if she could not work out who Ann was. Then her face cleared.

'Come in, bab.'

She led Ann to the back room, a stooped figure now, even more so than last week, Ann thought. Though it was not surprising. Cyril's chair still had his crocheted blanket slung over one arm, as if he had just got up from it.

'I'm ever so sorry, Mom,' Ann said. 'Len came round.'

Margaret turned then and crumpled. 'I wasn't even here.' She started to shake. Ann realized she had never once seen her mother-in-law cry. It was a shock now to see tears running down her cheeks. Ann went to her and put her arms round her, holding her close and stroking her back.

Thirty-Seven

Ann walked on to the long Nightingale Ward at Selly Oak Hospital that evening, supporting her mother-in-law as she walked slowly, bravely, as upright as she could manage, towards her husband of nearly sixty years.

Cyril lay on a bed halfway along on the right, flat out with his eyes closed. Even the sight of him laid so low brought tears to Ann's eyes. This man who had greeted her into their family before she and Len ever married, even before the Great War. Cyril, who was always there, looking the same, dapper and cheerful in his frayed woolly jumpers, digging the garden, sitting with the crossword, singing with his Cadbury choir and always keeping out of any of the family ding-dongs, if he possibly could.

It had never seemed that Cyril would ever be any different. He was there in the way a tree is there: strong, permanent and reassuring.

But she wiped her tears away quickly, hoping Margaret had not seen. She was here to be a support to her, not to start blarting all over the place. She stood back a little as Margaret went over to the bed.

'Love?' Margaret sank onto the chair that was squeezed between the beds and took Cyril's hand. He stirred and opened his eyes. There was something not right about his face, Ann could see that straight away. The muscles on one side looked slack. And it became obvious immediately that Cyril could not speak. Not properly. Not any more. He made a sound of recognition, though.

'Hello, Dad.' Ann went up and stroked his arm. 'Sorry you're feeling poorly. I'll pop out and leave you two for a little while . . .'

She smiled at Margaret and left the ward. Looking back from the door, she could see the two of them side by side, quietly holding hands. And she went out into the corridor and burst into tears.

They didn't stay long, as Cyril seemed completely exhausted. As they were walking along the downstairs corridor on their way out, with Ann supporting Margaret by the arm, she saw two familiar figures come in through the far door and head towards them.

'Here's Len,' she said. *And Jeanette*, she didn't add.

'Mom.' Len came up and pecked his mother on the cheek. 'How is he?'

Ann could feel Jeanette's eyes looking her over, but she did not glance back. Not after what Jeanette had said to her – and not now. There were more important things to think about.

'He's going along,' Margaret said bravely. 'Seems very tired. Don't stay long, love – he's asleep mostly.'

'We won't.'

As they parted, Len gave Ann a brief nod and their eyes met. She still did not look at Jeanette.

'Come to ours for tea,' Ann said to Margaret. 'I've the remains of the joint. We'll have a cottage pie.'

Margaret nodded vaguely. She seemed unable to make any decisions, even small ones, and Ann was glad they lived close and could help her with anything she needed.

Joy had gone to tell Sheila, and the two of them and the children were all in the house when they got back. The children were very sweet, hugging Margaret and distracting her. Margaret still seemed stunned, not herself.

'They'll make Grandad better,' Elaine said, very serious. 'They're very good in hospitals.'

All the adults smiled.

'You'd know, would you?' Sheila teased her.

Patty and Jonny showed her drawings they had done, and nine-year-old Robbie, who adored Nanna Margaret, just stood next to her with his hand on her arm, looking solemn and important.

'I'd best get home,' Sheila said after a while. 'Get Kenneth's tea.' She went over and kissed her grandmother. 'Keep us posted, won't you? I'm sure a good rest will sort him out.'

'He did seem tired,' Margaret kept saying. None of them were used to seeing Cyril laid low like that.

They all agreed, trying to be hopeful that after a good rest Cyril would recover. But in the privacy of their bedroom, Ann and Tom sadly came to the conclusion that there might be a bit more to it than that.

The next afternoon and evening they all visited in shifts, keeping it brief. Ann and Margaret in the afternoon, then Joy and Sheila, while Ann looked after the children. Len and Jeanette in the evening. Cyril seemed much the same as the day before.

And Margaret started to come back to herself, to adjust. As she left the ward with Ann, she suddenly said, 'I suppose you're used to these places.'

'Well, not any more,' Ann said. 'It's a long time since I did any nursing – and the home was different. More like a house.'

They walked along slowly.

'I don't think he'll be coming home, you know.'

'What?' Ann was shocked. 'Oh, I don't think you can

be so sure. Cyril's had a stroke – people do recover gradually, you know. It just takes time.'

But her mother-in-law shook her head. As if she knew
something ahead of time.

The two of them were the first to go into the hospital
the next afternoon. The nurse met them as soon as they
appeared, and Ann could tell straight away by her face. She
gripped Margaret's arm, as if to protect her. But Margaret
looked straight into the nurse's face.

'He's gone, hasn't he?'

She gave a gentle smile. 'I'm afraid so. Early this morning. It was very peaceful.'

Margaret nodded for a moment. Then her legs started to
give way, and Ann and the nurse helped her onto a chair.

Margaret said she wanted to be in her own home, to start
to come to terms with things. But Ann insisted that she
come along to them for her tea for those next few nights,
and the family took it in turns to keep her company for
some of the time.

Len helped make arrangements for the funeral at St
Francis's, took care of the details during those strange days
between a death and a funeral, when things felt suspended
between one stage – one reality – and another.

Ann went about her usual daily round, but things felt
peculiar. As if Cyril was gone, but yet not quite. She felt
very aware of him, close to her like a presence, and found
herself talking to him. Thanking him for all this kindness.
'You were like a Dad to me: far more than my own, really,'
she murmured, pegging washing out on the line. And,
walking back from the shops, 'Don't worry, we'll look
after Margaret. But she's going to miss you – my goodness,
she is. We all will.'

And it was as if Cyril was watching over her. And there was nothing bad or unnerving about that; it felt warm and kind.

Early one afternoon, when everyone was at work and Patty was at school, Ann was about to have a sit-down after all the morning chores, when there was a knock at the door.

'Bother,' she muttered. She felt more tired than usual. Had been even hoping to have a little nap.

'Ann.' Jeanette stood stiffly on the step in her neat camel coat. 'Could I have a word?'

Ann looked at her. And did not feel delighted to see her.

'Depends what sort of word,' she said. 'After last time.'

Jeanette looked down at her feet, pulling her handbag in closer to her, as if in defence.

'I've come to apologize.'

'I see,' Ann said. She could feel herself being awkward, not wanting to make it too easy. After all, her few contacts with Jeanette over the last three years had never been pleasant. And what she really wanted was to go to sleep.

'Can I come in?'

Ann held the door back, then led Jeanette into the front room. She sat down and indicated that Jeanette should do the same. She could keep her coat on or not – that was up to her. Jeanette sat perched on the edge of the chair as Ann sat on the sofa.

'I said terrible things to you,' Jeanette said.

Ann waited.

'I am sorry, Ann. We used to be friends, and . . .' Her eyes filled with tears and she turned to look towards the window. 'I don't know what it is. Well, I do. It's just, ever since Len and I've been together, I . . . I've found it very difficult having so much, you know, baggage in the marriage. Even though I knew, of course. Knew what I was taking on. You round the corner. All the children. His parents. And then, on top of everything else, Marianne – and George.'

'It is a lot to contend with,' Ann agreed.

'Len and I've been talking. I haven't made life easy for him, I suppose.'

'Oh well.' Ann found herself being rather relentless, and tried to draw back and find more sympathy.

'Really the best thing would be for us to move away – across town at least, maybe. And we were talking about it. But now his dad's gone, I know he'll want to stay near his mom.'

'Depends how far you go, I suppose,' Ann said. 'You don't have to go to Timbuktu, do you? And we're here. I'll always look out for Margaret.'

'She's very fond of you,' Jeanette said sadly.

'And there's the kids – they help out. I'm not trying to get rid of you, either of you, but if you need to move a bit further away, if it would make things easier. There'll still be Marianne, for a few years yet anyway, 'til George has grown up.'

Jeanette was quiet for a moment, carefully wiping her eyes and looking down at the carpet.

'I do love Len, I do,' she said sadly. 'And I don't think I've made things very easy for him lately. I get, well, jealous, I suppose. Of all of you: the children, grandchildren. Something I'll never have . . .'

Ann's heart buckled for her suddenly. She could see how hard it must be.

'Sorry, Ann.' She looked up then, much more like the old Jeanette, gentle and kindly. 'I miss you as well. We were good friends once.'

Ann gave her a smile, cautiously. But she did feel hopeful now. For the last few years she had felt Jeanette's presence

271

over in Maryvale Road like an unpleasant shadow, glowering at her, and had come to dread meeting her anywhere.

'Maybe if we moved a bit further away – to Kings Heath perhaps, somewhere like that . . . Then we could all see each other, but we wouldn't be on top of one another all the time.'

'Sounds like a good idea, maybe,' Ann said.

'But,' suddenly Jeanette looked truly vulnerable, 'can we try to patch things up? Be friends again? I used to like spending time with you – and Joy as well.'

Ann felt something flower inside her. Relief. Happiness. As if two harshly cut ends of something had been brought back together. She got up.

'Fancy a cuppa?'

Thirty-Eight

'Look at you,' Nanna Margaret said, when they gathered at her house before the funeral. She had taken Martin's hand and stared at it in amazement, stroking it in a way that made his chest tighten with complicated feelings. 'You look like a Lascar.'

Martin laughed to cover his emotion. 'A what?'

'One of those men they used to have working on the ships. So tall – and look at the colour of you!'

In fact the leathery tan that his skin had taken on during months in the heat and dust of Spain had faded over the weeks since they came back, but he did still look dark compared with the rest of them.

And now, seated in St Francis's church, he watched his father – not his father, but Len – lead his grandmother, an arm through hers, to a pew in front of him. Nanna Margaret looked so much smaller than he remembered. Bent and old. Again he felt the swell of emotion at the back of his throat. He was sitting next to Joy, who was already crying, and Patty, who looked round-eyed, sad and bewildered.

Behind all of them, a cluster of older people had come in – old workmates, Martin realized, seeing them in a gaggle outside the church. Cadbury girls and boys. Blokes from his choir. The ones left standing, come to see Cyril off.

At the front of the church, dwarfed by the altar, was Cyril's coffin.

I'll never see him again, Martin thought. He had not

been back in the country all that long, but the time had been filled with his own arrangements. And now it was too late. He had missed his chance and his grandfather was gone, for ever. He quickly pulled the backs of his hands across his eyes, hoping no one would notice.

Mom and Tom were sitting in front of him and once again he found himself examining the back of his father's – *his father's* – neck.

Here I am, he thought, not knowing what he really meant by that. Here. Where I come from. Where I seem to be coming back to. But he had not told them that yet. The organ music swelled louder then, and they all stood for the first hymn.

No one asked him how Jack was. If Jack were a woman, of course everything would be different. There would be constant hints – when were they going to get on and tie the knot?

Instead they asked vague, general questions. *How are things? Getting on all right, are you? How's the job?* Of course no one thought of Jack as his . . . Even Martin's own words ran out at this. His what? Lover, husband, other half . . . None of those felt right. And now they were not right anyway. Not at all. Not any more.

Yet again a lump rose in his throat, but this time grief was mingled with anger.

Their trip had gone along reasonably well until they reached Madrid. Martin had noticed cracks appearing, aspects of Jack that seemed to come out more, now they were away from home. But, he had thought, doing his best to be tolerant, perhaps Jack was feeling the same about him.

In the impoverished, wild countryside they stuck together out of need. Everywhere was a long distance away. It was an adventure and a challenge – finding drinkable water, food, a place to sleep. Although small towns were patrolled by the *Guardia Civil,* you could forget just a little, amid the cowbells and endless fields, the extent of the government's policing of everyone's lives; the fear alive in the streets of the bigger cities.

Once they reached Madrid, Martin at least began to feel very uneasy. Here, where the grey uniforms of armed police could be seen in the tense, repressed streets, it felt as if anything anyone might say could land them in gaol.

'We need to keep our heads down,' he said to Jack. 'I feel as if we're being watched all the time.'

'Oh, we'll be all right,' Jack said. 'We're foreigners.'

Jack always thought he would be all right. As if nothing could ever happen to him. He was keen to see paintings and this they did, seeking out the Prado and smaller museums. But Jack, in his devilish way, wanted to seek out other things.

One afternoon Martin woke after a siesta in the cheap, bug-infested lodging room where they were staying to find that Jack had gone out. This annoyed him – it would be nice to be told things now and again.

But he decided to take advantage of a walk around on his own. He set off wandering in the cooling afternoon: squares and fountains, grand buildings, light and shade cutting the streets in half. The city was just waking after the heat stupor of the middle of the day and he sat in a square, in the shade of a tree, his mind drifting as it tended to do in the heat.

Soon they would go home, back to England. And what was he going to do then? He vaguely imagined going back to the Thornes' house, for the moment at least. He needed a job, to start living an adult life. He could apply to all sorts of companies: ICI perhaps? Somehow he could not focus on the future, though, sitting there with his feet in the pale dust, with the sound of swifts overhead, of distant traffic and of deep male voices, two men talking a few yards away, the smell of fumes and, from somewhere, food frying.

After a time he got up and wandered a complicated way back to their lodgings in a narrow side street. And the moment he pushed open the door of the room, everything changed. He stood as if punched. Horrified.

Jack's naked back arched on the bed over . . . someone. The someone looked young, very slender, blue-black hair, bulging calf muscles in his tanned legs, despite his light build . . . But worst of all was the amount of noise Jack was making. Whenever Martin and Jack made love, they were quiet – Martin made sure of that. Careful, so careful, when they were anywhere where they might be heard.

That was all Martin took in before shutting the door – none too quietly – and hurrying away again, not wanting to be anywhere near this. This betrayal; Jack's self-absorbed, dangerous stupidity – dangerous, above all, for the Spanish boy.

He didn't see Jack until hours later. He hardly remembered what he did after that. Walked and walked. Did not think of eating. Went back to the room, but both the men were gone.

Jack returned later, easy and cheerful from wine-drinking as he came in, this time alone. Martin sat rigid on his sagging bed, beyond being able to speak.

'Oh, hello – you're back! Where've you been?' Jack said easily, throwing himself down on his bed with a clatter of springs. Martin had loved this bare room up until now. It reminded him of their spartan dormitory at the mine. But now it felt like a sad prison. And the place of his betrayal.

Jack lay back, arms behind his head, as if satisfied and

unconcerned about anything. It was this finally, on top of everything else, that finished them, for Martin. He could not stand it any longer.

'You stupid, *stupid* . . .' he burst out, while trying not to raise his voice. He felt genuinely frightened. 'I saw you – and him. Have you any idea what might happen if you were caught?'

Jack looked round, startled. 'What? When were you . . . You saw?'

'You didn't even notice, you were making such a flaming racket.' Martin was so enraged he was almost spluttering. 'It's bad enough at home, but here . . . Catholics, police everywhere. What the hell were you doing?'

He stood up, ready to go over and punch Jack.

'And I thought we were . . . I mean, you and me – that we weren't going to be with anyone else.' And suddenly he was crying and it was terrible. Humiliating, that he felt so deflated and hurt.

'Oh, come on!' Jack swung his legs over the side of the bed. 'It wasn't anything. Just some lad – he was desperate and I . . .' A grin stole over his face. 'You know how it is.'

A chill, hard feeling filled Martin then. Things he had loved and admired at the beginning: Jack's glamour, the way he knew he could draw people in, have power over them and not care about the consequences. The fact that his home and everything about him was different from Martin's own – the art, the family who seemed so relaxed, London. All this had attracted him for so long. Gradually things had started to feel wrong. And now, bitterly at that moment, he loathed Jack with a passion.

'I think,' he said, hating himself for sounding prim, 'we should head home. Before you get us both into terrible trouble.'

*

277

There was no going back. He sat in the church now, thinking, full of pain that seemed to come at him from every direction. He and Jack had stuck together to get home – it was safer, easier. A truce, which helped them get through the journey.

As soon as they reached London again, Martin said goodbye to the Thornes and moved into a tiny bedsit. Jack barely tried to stop him. Things had run their course. Martin distracted himself from his broken heart by applying for jobs, almost at random. There was plenty of work. He could stick a pin in a map and see where it took him . . .

And, as he deep down knew it would, given the subject he had been studying, it was bringing him back to Birmingham.

The rest of the day was a blur of faces and conversations. The Cadbury workers paid little tributes: 'Good lad, your grandad' and 'Oh, I did like Cyril, he was always a gent.' The family gathered at home, a few friends, sandwiches filled with precious tinned salmon, cake and ale and tea.

Everyone paid their respects to Margaret as she sat in the front room. Martin leaned over and put his arms round her. He couldn't think of anything to say.

'Go on with you,' she said, eyes brimming as he stepped back, his own in a similar state. 'Look at you,' she said again, still genuinely astonished that he was now grown-up, a man.

'You all right, little bro?' Joy slipped her arm through his.

He squeezed back. 'Yeah. Course.'

'Look at you. Brown as a berry. Speak Spanish now, do you?'

'Not really.' He smiled. He wanted to tell her, *I'm moving back*. But even that he couldn't face at the moment. 'Poor Nanna.'

'Yes.' Joy looked across the room at their grandmother, and their father handing her a cup of tea. Len stirred the sugar for her, patted her shoulder tenderly, his own eyes red. Jeanette was sitting next to Ann, the pair of them chatting gently.

'Seems those two are getting on again,' Joy whispered.

Martin looked over. There seemed to be no spikes or thorns between Mom and Jeanette now, that he could see.

'That's good,' he said. He felt surprisingly warmed by the sight. What was the point of those two falling out?

Sheila was coming round with a plate of sponge slices.

'Come on, you look as if you need feeding up,' she said. Martin smiled and took a piece of cake.

As Sheila moved away, he said, 'Mom said you and your friend are going great guns with your dancing?'

Joy smiled. 'It was great, meeting Kay. We're going to set up our own school – that's the plan.'

Martin nudged her, fondly. 'My sis, the business-woman!'

Joy nudged him back. 'I could run a business!'

He grinned. 'Course you could.'

It was nice – always had been with Joy – and it felt like old times, starting to rag each other.

Out of the corner of his eye, Martin felt Tom Somers's eyes on him, but when he turned, Tom looked away.

'Can't be too easy for him, this,' he said to Joy.

'Listen to you, all understanding all of a sudden,' she teased. But he could hear a note of real reproach in her voice. 'He's a good man,' she went on, even more quietly. 'You should get to know him.'

Martin felt a blush rising in his cheeks. He glanced at Tom again, but he had moved away and was – a jolt of surprise – talking to Len. Suddenly he felt left behind, out of it. If Len and Tom could manage to have a civil conversation, as well as Mom and Jeanette . . . It was as if he had been stuck, for years, while everyone else flowed on past him. It was about time he had a word with Tom Somers.

That night Martin slept in his old room for the first time in many years. It was not as bad as he had expected. Now that he was no longer with Jack, it was as if something in him had softened. Was more sympathetic towards himself – who he really was and where he came from. He didn't have to keep seeing things through Jack's eyes, criticizing (he had always assumed this, though he could not be sure what Jack really thought). It made it easier to look calmly at everyone else.

The next day was Saturday. Over breakfast Mom said she was going to see Margaret for a little while.

'I'll come,' Joy said. 'And Patty. Take her mind off it.'

'I think I'll finish the digging,' Tom said. 'Before the frosts set in.'

Martin was at the table. He swallowed a mouthful and managed to say, 'Want a hand?' Then he felt mortified. Tom really *was* in want of a hand. 'Sorry, I mean . . .'

His father actually seemed amused. 'It's OK. That would be a help. If you can spare the time.'

Martin could see that Tom was still nervous of him – and he felt the same. They didn't know each other well enough. But there was something about the man that seemed to say, 'I am who I am, take it or leave it', which Martin found himself respecting, despite himself. Tom never tried too hard to impress him. Didn't suck up to him. And after draining his teacup he followed Tom Somers outside.

It was a sunny morning, the shadows sharp-edged. Tom started digging and Martin watched the way he had perfected a technique of pivoting the spade and lifting the soil clod with one hand, then chopping down on it with the sharp blade. But it looked hard work.

'D'you want me to do that for a bit?' Martin offered shyly.

'All right. If you like.'

Tom came over with the spade. As he handed it over, he smiled. Not in a way that meant anything much. Just the sort of look of thanks he might have given anyone. And again Martin was impressed by him. Briefly he smiled back.

'I can get on and cut back those brambles down at the end.' Tom headed towards the old air-raid shelter, which was gradually being engulfed by long thorny switches. Martin watched him in his ancient tweed jacket, worn at the elbows, and his patched grey flannel trousers.

Words had burned in him, so many times; things he wanted to say to Tom: accusations once, but now that had faded. Recently it had been going to be justifications for his own behaviour; and things he was going to demand to be told.

But now, seeing this lightly built but strong, mild, admirable man walk down the garden and start snipping at the tangle of brambles, without demanding anything of this son of his, but seeming glad all the same that Martin was there, he could not think of a single one of them. Suddenly none of it seemed necessary. Here they were, working away in silence, side by side – almost. Father and son. The words pulsed inside Martin. *That is my father.* There would be questions, later. But for the moment there seemed nothing else to say.

III

1952–3

Thirty-Nine

Summer 1952

'Sorry!' Joy mouthed to Kay across the dance hall, which echoed with piano music and the clickety-clack of tap shoes as she came flurrying in, horribly late, with her bags.

Thank heavens Kay had taken charge of the first class, a slowly growing group of children learning to tap-dance after school.

'That's it, Linda – one and two and . . .' Kay turned and winked at Joy as she hurriedly put her things down, pulled on her own tap shoes and came to help, beaming at their little charges.

The children, all between eight and ten, turned eagerly towards her. They looked up to her and Kay, Joy could tell: both of them attractive, active women who were beginning to make a name for themselves. A lot of the girls almost worshipped them – you could see it in their eyes.

'I want to be like Miss Gilby when I grow up,' she had heard one girl say to her friend after a ballet class. 'I'm gonna be a ballet teacher.'

'Well, you'll need to put lots of work in, Susan,' Joy said to her, and the girl blushed and giggled, mortified and pleased at the same time that she had been overheard. Susan was already a good dancer, so Joy wasn't just stringing her along. 'When I was a little girl, I used to dance and dance. So if you keep it up, maybe your dream will come true.'

They worked through the class, with Mrs Parsons, who had happily become a permanent fixture in the school, plinking away on the piano. When the tap session ended, some of the children would stay on for the ballet class and other girls started coming in.

A flustered-looking mother, plump and pink in the face, seemingly having hurried like mad to get there, came in with a little girl who was similarly big of build. They had not seen her before. The child, who was eight or so, had round, pink cheeks, long brown hair and a sweet expression. But she looked unsure of herself and embarrassed.

'Could I have a word?' the mother panted, hefting shopping bags that were cutting into the flesh on each of her forearms. Joy could see rings of sweat under her arms and beads of perspiration on her forehead – it was a warm summer day.

'Why don't you put those down?' Joy suggested.

Gratefully the woman lowered them to the floor.

'I'll round everyone up,' Kay said quietly. She turned to the little girl. 'Are you joining the class today?'

The little girl looked uncertainly at her mother.

'She hasn't got any shoes,' she said.

'Never mind.' Kay shepherded her gently along with the others. 'She can start in bare feet today – that's all right. And then, if she likes it, we can see about her getting some, all right?'

Joy took the woman to one side. She seemed worried, upset almost.

'Is it all right if our Gillian comes – dancing, like?'

'Of course it is,' Joy replied, bewildered, although she was puzzled by how the child managed to be such a little pudding when there was so little food to be had. Most of the children (and adults) were as thin as lamp posts.

'See, 'er's my only one and I want the best for her. And

I thought . . . Thing is, she gets called names – it's because of her being on the big side, like. I was the same. Dunno why, it's just the way we are. And some say she shouldn't do things like dancing and it ain't right for her, but she wants to do it and . . . I'm worried she's going to shut herself away, feel she can't do anything, like I did.'

The woman was suddenly close to tears, and Joy felt a surge of anger. People could be so nasty.

'We'd love to have her. Dancing's very good for anyone; it's good for coordination and balance, and for learning about music and keeping your body fit. And it's fun! Of course she can come.'

The woman seemed almost more tearful at this. 'Well, if you're sure.'

'Course I'm sure.' Joy touched her arm kindly. 'We'd love to have her.'

'I just don't want the others . . . You know what kids can be like.'

'I do,' Joy said. And adults too, she thought, when they should know better. 'I won't have any of that in here, you can be sure. We want Gillian to come and learn and to have a nice time, like all the others.'

'Oh. Thank you.' The woman seemed almost overcome.

'You come back in an hour, all right?' Joy said.

The woman went, giving Gillian a little wave before she carried her bulging bags and heavy body to the door. Gillian waved back uncertainly. Then she turned to Joy and gave a shy, delighted little smile.

Joy and Kay had finally rented their premises in town only in the past few months, though Joy still continued to teach a few sessions in halls in Northfield and Stirchley.

'But if we could get somewhere in town, it'll mean people can come from all over if they want – once we're famous,' Kay said, laughing. As ever, she was the optimist, full of laughter and enthusiasm.

When they started looking at places to rent, Joy realized how little she ever went into Birmingham these days. Doing so shocked her every time. She had seen the bomb damage, of course. But even so, the bare, bleak bomb pecks she saw on the way into town, cleared of rubble, were now rough wastelands used as kids' playgrounds. The bulldozers that were starting to clear further gaps for rebuilding the city also left swathes of open land, and all this made the city seem broken open and strange.

Eventually, after looking at decayed warehouses and one private house renting out rooms in Edgbaston – dank and depressing, and too far from town, they both agreed – they had found a wide upstairs space in a building in a street behind New Street station. It had previously been offices over a machine-tools firm, which had moved. The upstairs had a wide window facing over the street.

Joy stood in the middle of the big, drab room. Flakes of paint showed the original colour as cream, but it was a jaundiced nicotine-stained shade, grubby with furniture marks. The wooden floor was filthy and pitted where desks and chairs had stood for years. It stank of stale cigarette smoke and a shut-in mustiness – but as well as a couple of small back offices, there was a good, long, light space.

Joy grimaced at Kay. 'I suppose it's got promise.'

Kay nodded. 'Lick of paint – some lino. We could partition it in two, if needs be.'

'And the light's not bad.'

They went over to the window, which overlooked the narrow street and the dust- and soot-clogged windows and marauding pigeons on the sills of the buildings opposite. Kay managed to shove the stiff window open until fresh air streamed in.

'Glamorous, eh?' They both laughed, a bit hysterically. 'We can get ourselves a nice sign. They should be able to get the piano up here – just about.'

The girls had debated long and hard, sitting around Kay's family's kitchen table and around Joy's as well, as Kay often came there, about various aspects of the business. They had finally settled on 'Gilby and Tarrant' as their business name.

'Gilby and Tarrant sounds more professional,' Kay's mom said, folding a teacloth and putting her head thoughtfully on one side. 'More professional. Glamorous almost. Like a stage duo.'

'Can you afford the rent?' Mr Tarrant asked. 'I s'pose we could loan you a very small amount . . .'

Joy's mother and Tom had said the same, but the two girls were determined to be independent.

'Thank you, Mr Tarrant, but my stepfather helped us get a small loan from the bank to set up,' Joy said. 'And with any luck, we can soon pay that off. So long as we get enough customers!'

And so the Gilby and Tarrant Dance Academy was born. Walls were painted white, stiff grey linoleum laid on the floor, the windows cleaned, the piano lugged up the stairs and a folding partition installed to divide the room in two, if necessary.

The city was booming, and more parents had money in their pockets for dance lessons. And the girls were making a name for themselves at demonstrations and shows. There were pictures in the newspaper.

Pupils had started rolling in. The women taught children after school in the afternoon – almost all girls, but a couple of boys were keen to tap-dance after seeing films with Fred Astaire and Ginger Rogers. So far, none of the lads would own up to wanting to learn ballet. And Joy still taught adult ballroom classes in the evening.

Week by week they were starting to pay off their loan. Both of them were still working the morning shift at Cadbury's, waiting to take the plunge of giving up that work altogether. It was a big juggling act, but Joy was loving it – it was everything she had dreamed of.

'Sorry to come crashing in so late,' she said to Kay, during their break after the children's afternoon classes, before the adult class started.

They sat in one corner, eating their sandwiches, and they had each brought flasks of sweet tea to keep them going. Mrs Parsons usually only played for the children – after that, Joy relied on her record player for the ballroom music.

'Only Mom had to go and fetch Patty from school this morning. She's a bit poorly, so I've left her in bed – I lost track of the time.'

Patty was usually round for most of the classes these days and, now that she was seven, she was shaping up into a nice little dancer herself.

'It's all right,' Kay said with a wink. 'We can survive without you, you know.' She looked closely at Joy, who seemed more flustered than the situation would account for. 'What's up?'

'Is it that obvious?' Joy asked. She sagged in the seat. 'I saw . . . *him*. Again. I'm almost certain. No, I *am* certain. I'd just got off the tram and he was crossing Navigation Street.'

Kay looked solemn. 'Did he see you?'

'I don't know. Don't think so. I mean, I don't think he was there deliberately this time. But still . . .'

After the nasty incident with Howard Fielding, when Joy had told him not to come back to her classes, she had spent months feeling uneasy. It was not as if a great deal had happened – Howard had tried to kiss her and she didn't want him to. On the face of it, it didn't sound like much.

But there was something about him: the way he sneaked around and always seemed to know where she was going to be. And that night in Beaumont Road – had that been him, slinking away along the street, or had she been mistaken?

He had not come back to the class in Northfield after that and gradually she had begun to relax, and not to need Fred the caretaker to take her home or check out at the back of the building every time she left. Howard had gone – and all that was two years ago now.

But a number of times she had seen him. Today, at the lights, she was fairly certain he had not seen her. But a few weeks ago she had been crossing the Bristol Road in Selly Oak. Waiting for a gap in the traffic, she had suddenly become aware of a tall figure on the other side of the road in the fawn raincoat that Howard always wore – come rain or shine. And he was staring straight at her.

Joy felt her body chill all over as, for a second, their eyes met. She started to shake and looked away, pretending she had not seen him and that her eyes had just passed over him as if he were a stranger. But she *had* seen him. And she knew that Howard knew she had.

She had turned into a chemist's shop, watching out of the window, worried in case he followed her inside. But Howard had crossed over and walked off down the road towards Bournbrook. Only after waiting for a time, and even feeling obliged to buy a pot of Vicks VapoRub, did she feel safe to go out again.

Every so often he turned up. And every time she got a shock. But as ever, with Howard, it was impossible to say whether he was actually doing anything wrong. There he was, going about his business – what else could she say?

'It's so odd,' she said. 'There's just something about him . . .'

'He's a creep,' Kay said briskly. 'Don't let him get inside your head.'

Joy sighed. 'You're right, I know. It's silly. Hey, how're things with Eddie?'

Kay attracted men like a honey jar – even more than Joy. But Eddie, a new lad on the scene, seemed to be special. He was cheerful, dark-haired and good-looking and a fine dancer. Joy liked him as well, and she could see that this might be someone who would stick around.

'They're all right,' Kay said coyly. She blushed slightly and gave Joy one of her sidelong smiles. 'I'd say they were very all right.'

Joy smiled, pleased for her. Her own track record with men had been a rocky path, and for the time being she was concentrating hard on getting the business going and bringing up her little girl. After all, who was going to want her, when she had already had another man's child? It was wisest to put matters of the heart well to one side.

But seeing Kay so happy with Eddie made her ache inside. She spent all her days now keeping frantically busy. She had Patty to bring up, a dance school to run and try to grow, as well as the invitations to other dances as a demonstrator. She revelled in it – it was her dream. But it was also a way of trying not to think about anything, ever.

Because in those few quiet times, late at night when Patty was asleep, or on Sunday mornings when she woke and for once did not have to rush to work, the thoughts seeped in. Memories. How it felt to be loved. Alan. Lawrence. Their eyes looking into hers, their arms around her. It would be so good to be loved again, and to love in return. It felt as if she had had that chance and it had passed her by.

Forty

'So – is today the day?' Margaret said.

Sheila was washing up the breakfast things in her grandmother's house. She turned and winked at Margaret.

'Yes. D'you want to come? Stop me doing anything stupid?'

Margaret sat down at the kitchen table, finishing off a last drop of tea. Her hand, the knuckles swollen with arthritis, trembled a little as she lifted the cup. 'You don't need me dragging along, silly old woman, slowing you down.'

Sheila tipped the water away and turned, drying her hands on a cloth.

'Nan, don't say that. It's not true. Go on, come with me. He only lives in Northfield – we can get the bus.'

Margaret smiled, wiping her lips on her hanky.

'Go on then. It'll make a change.'

There had been a number of changes over the past few years. After Cyril's death, Margaret mourned him in her quiet, stoic way. There were not many tears – not that the others saw anyway – and certainly no histrionics. But she aged, became frailer and more uncertain. They had been married for so long that living without him now, she seemed stripped bare.

A year later, almost to the day, once she had started to come to terms with things, Margaret asked Sheila and Kenneth to come round. She sat them down and said to them, 'Look, it seems ridiculous, me rattling round in this house while you're all squeezed in that prefab, like peas in a pod. And there's others all desperate for a place to live. Why don't you think about coming to live back with me? It'll save us all on rent, and I'll keep out of your way . . .'

Sheila glanced nervously at Kenneth, thinking he would want to refuse straight away and hoping he would do so in a way that would not hurt Nanna's feelings. But she was surprised.

'That's nice of you – to offer,' he said. 'Very nice. We'll have a chat about it at home, if that'd be all right?'

'Of course, love, take your time,' Margaret said. 'There's no rush; only it seems daft, this situation, when you think about it.'

Once they were back home and the kids were in bed, they sat huddled by the fire in their sitting room. Things had been uneasy between them off and on for a long time now, what with Kenneth's itchy feet. But that night, things felt relaxed again and she felt as if they were close.

Kenneth leaned forward to poke the fire, then turned to her.

'So what d'you reckon? About what your nan said? Why don't we do a swap? If the council'll let us. She could come and stop here?'

Sheila had expected him to say no straight away, so this was a good start. She leaned forward in her chair. 'Thing is, love, that's not what she asked us, was it? She won't want to leave her house, not after living there all that time, with all the memories of Grandad there. And her neighbours – she's known some of them for years. It'd break her heart.'

Kenneth was nodding. It would be the same with his mom and dad in Greet. Their neighbours were a big part of their lives.

'It's getting cramped in here,' he said. 'And to be honest,

it'd be nice to get away from all their carry-on . . .' He jerked his thumb towards Beryl and Sid's house next door.

Beryl and Sid had six children now, and Sid was as handy with his fists as ever. Beryl had involved Sheila in all sorts of crises over the years, and this had brought about conflict between Sheila and Kenneth as they kept getting dragged into it. Nothing ever seemed to change. It was like a horrible pattern that the two of them were locked into, and neither could think of a way of stopping it. Even Sheila was losing patience with their neighbours now.

'Nanna's house is so much bigger,' she said. 'We can help with the garden. And it won't be the same as last time, with you just home and . . .' She kept the rest of that thought to herself: You being in a foul temper so much of the time.

'Anyway, living with one person's different from living with a couple. I think she's lonely – but she's said she doesn't want to go and live over with Dad and Jeanette, away from everyone, in that prim little house.'

So in the spring of 1952, more than a year since Cyril's death, they had given up their little prefab. Sheila was sad to leave it – they had had mainly happy times there and they had made it into a lovely little home, after its raw beginnings. But now the three children were growing and were all squeezed into one room, it was time to go.

'Come and see me, won't you?' Beryl said tearfully when Sheila told her she was going.

'Course I will – we'll be over all the time,' Sheila said. 'And we're keeping the girls at that school, so they'll still see each other there.'

And they had moved back to Beaumont Road.

Margaret was very kind about the rent – they went half-and-half. And with the money they saved on rent and by being very careful, they saved up and managed to buy a car.

Kenneth got a discount at the Austin and he was now the proud owner of a grey Austin A30. The car was his pride and joy and it helped solved the problem of his wanderlust. With the kids squeezed in the back, they would go off on jaunts at weekends, and Sheila saw Kenneth's eyes light up whenever they were off and away on the road. And he spent hours cleaning and polishing it.

'I reckon you love that car more than me,' she teased him.

But Elaine, Robbie and Jonny loved being outside, sloshing water over this exciting new toy and climbing inside as well, using it as a den to play games in. Kenneth was quite relaxed about that, so everyone was happy. And he seemed more contented – more loving and relaxed. Sometimes, as they went bowling out of Birmingham and along the country lanes, he would glance at Sheila with a smile and a wink, as if to say, 'This is the life.'

And now that their travels did not mean her dragging heavy bags and grumbling children on and off buses or trains, and they could glide along singing songs, Sheila was beginning to appreciate getting out and seeing new places herself. She was starting to get used to the idea of widening her horizons.

And now, to her own surprise, she was hatching other plans – which might mean they could take their adventures a bit further.

She had not told Kenneth yet, but she was thinking of going back to do a morning shift at the Cadbury works, now Jonny was at school. She had made enquiries and found they were quite happy to take her back.

Joy was still working mornings at Cadbury's and it was

she who had told Sheila about the lady on the line with her whose husband worked at the Eccles factory in Stirchley. It piqued Sheila's interest.

'She said he was there through the war,' Joy had told her recently, when they were helping make Sunday dinner over at Mom's. Joy was rooting around in the cutlery drawer, getting ready to lay the table. 'It was talking about the war that brought it up. They were making mobile workshops – a bit like caravans with no wheels, I s'pose; ambulances too, I think she said. But it's back to caravans now, and they're all the rage apparently.'

'So how many people can you fit in one of them?' Sheila asked.

'Well, it's going to depend on how big a one you have, isn't it?' Joy teased.

Sheila turned and put out her tongue and Joy did the same – as if they were both suddenly little girls again. Joy laughed, walking off with fistfuls of knives and forks.

But the idea had stuck in Sheila's mind. Once they had bought the Austin, they had carried on putting a little bit of money aside each week – thanks to Nanna Margaret. For a rainy day. For something. And then she had seen a small ad in the *Evening Mail* . . .

'You all right, Nanna?' Sheila said as they limped along, arm-in-arm, in the warm sun. She was starting to regret asking Margaret to come with her – it all seemed to be a bit much for her. Two buses, and now a walk.

She quite often went out with Margaret, now they shared a house, and it was nice. Sometimes Mom came as well. They had taken all the children out a few Saturdays ago to see the last tram run along the Bristol Road from Northfield to the depot at Selly Oak.

'I'm going to miss the trams,' Ann said, as they watched it go swaying past.

And they went for picnics: to see the little railway in Cannon Hill Park or by the boating lake in Bournville. Margaret managed very well, but it was especially hot today.

'Sorry I'm slowing you down, Sheila. But I'm all right – and it's nice to be out.'

Sheila smiled round at her. 'There's no hurry, Nan. Let's just enjoy the sun. And we're nearly there.'

The house was in a back road, and they could see the caravan parked on the strip of drive before they even got there.

'Ooh,' Margaret said. 'Imagine having to pull that behind your car.'

The door was answered by a small, tense-looking man with slicked-back black hair, who looked out suspiciously at them. But he softened and became much more pleasant when Sheila reminded him why they were there.

'Oh! Yes, sorry, I thought you was one of them door-to-door people . . . I'm fed up with them. Right, you'll want to have a look.'

He unlocked the boxy-shaped caravan with its oval window in the door.

'See, you can have it half open – very nice touch, that.' The door was in two halves, so that you could close the bottom half and swing the top half open.

Sheila immediately loved the cosy little caravan with its miniature gas stove and sink, its pretty grey-and-white fabric covering the seats and its neat little curtains tied back on each side of the windows in cream fabric with red spots. The area where the table was could be made into a double bed, and the back seat had a top bunk that you could pull out to make bunk beds. There was even a wardrobe and a cubicle for a chemical toilet.

'Oh, Nan – it's lovely, isn't it?' she cried.

Nanna Margaret was sitting at the front by the table, looking round her in amazement.

'I've never been in one of these before,' she said. 'Amazing what they can pack in.'

'Fancy a cup of tea while you're here?' he asked. 'You look a bit weary. Have a proper look round and I'll bring it out to you.'

They all sat at the little fold-down table with the tea. Sheila soon realized that the man was glad to have some company.

'The wife and I had all sorts of plans,' he told them sadly. 'She made all the curtains and everything.' He looked round fondly. 'We took it down to Devon, just the once. Oh, that was a lovely holiday! They let us park on a farm right near the sea. It was heaven. Eating pasties on the beach; and of a morning there'd be this delicious smell of bacon frying, drifting right across the campsite!' He laughed, but then his thin face fell into sad folds.

'We didn't know it then, but she was already ill . . . I lost her in January. After that, well, I haven't got the heart.'

He gestured around him at the caravan.

'We loved it in here. But I don't want it now – not without Jean.'

'I can understand that,' Margaret said. 'I lost my husband not long ago.'

They smiled at each other with understanding.

'I think it's lovely,' Sheila said warmly. 'It would be perfect for us – but I'd have to ask my husband.'

'Got kiddies, have you?'

'Yes, three. We could all squeeze in here. They'd love it.'

'Jean and I never managed to have children.' His voice

299

was so sad that Margaret touched his hand for a moment. He looked round at her gratefully. 'Look, I'm not in a rush. It's not even about the money. I want it to go to a good home. So let me know, all right?'

'You did *what*?'

Kenneth was annoyed the second Sheila started telling him about it, all excited. She knew it was because she had taken the lead, and he didn't like that. But she wasn't going to be put off. Her mistake, she realized, had been to start on him the moment he got home. She was so keen to talk about it she had forgotten that starting on a man about anything at all before he had eaten his tea was never a good idea. She should have waited until Kenneth had some shepherd's pie inside him.

'Just come and see,' she argued. 'You'll like it – and the man selling it is ever so nice. His wife died and—'

Kenneth waved a hand at her as if to say, *I don't want to hear it* and disappeared to the bathroom.

After tea, he was in more of a fit state to listen. And it all came pouring out. They agreed that they had saved almost all the money, but might have to borrow a tiny bit off their families, but then if Sheila went back to work, only part-time of course . . .

Kenneth wasn't keen on that at first.

'Thing is though, love,' she said, 'if we want to travel a bit, have adventures, we could do with the extra money. I'd always be back in time for the kids after school, and for you after work.'

She soon talked him round. It had been a long time since Sheila had been out to work, and now that the house was empty for so much of the day she was rather looking forward to it.

*

Sheila saw Kenneth's eyes fasten on the caravan as he parked the car just short of the drive. Sheila looked at it with excitement: this little travelling home, which might soon be theirs!

'We could go anywhere,' she said. She was surprised at herself – she, the woman who never wanted to leave home.

Kenneth leaned forward, hunched over the wheel to look.

'It's ever so clever, the way it all fits in – there's enough room for all of us.'

'And you can cook in there and everything?'

'Come on – come and see.'

As she prepared to jump out of the car, she saw a spark of excitement light in his eyes.

Forty-One

It was late, gone midnight, the next Saturday night. The weather was hot and stifling. Sheila and Kenneth lay together. They had just made love and things were sweeter, calmer, between them than they had been in a long time.

They had talked in low voices for a while about plans to get away. There was the caravan – where might they go with it, once Kenneth had got used to towing it behind the car? It was exciting, a whole new adventure. Of course Kenneth hadn't been all that sure at first, probably because it had not been his idea, Sheila thought with a wry smile. But once he had had a look inside, and a chat with the man about towing the thing, he was dead keen.

And she was starting to feel that as long as he was not going to drag her to the other side of the world, it would be fun to have adventures.

'A travel fund,' she said, smiling into Kenneth's eyes. And he smiled back. He liked to talk about 'travel' and not 'holidays' – it sounded more manly and daring.

Now, though, they were lying apart, trying not to touch each other because it was so hot. The room was dark, except for a rim of light at the top of the curtains from the street light outside. She could tell he was still awake beside her.

'I can't get off to sleep, can you?' Sheila whispered.

'No.' Kenneth flung even the sheet off him. 'It's stifling in here. Is the window open as wide as it'll go?'

Before she could answer, he jumped up to look. She saw

his strong frame silhouetted for a moment as he pulled the curtains back and yanked at the sash.

'Flaming thing . . .' He managed to inch it a little further up and was coming back to bed when they both heard a thunderous hammering on a door outside. Kenneth stood, halfway back to bed.

'D'you hear that?'

'Well, of course I did,' Sheila sat up. 'I'm not deaf, am I? Is that ours?'

They waited. Again someone was hammering on the door with what sounded like the flat of their hand.

'God almighty, who can that be?' He went and stuck his head out of the window.

'Who's that?'

'Let me in – please, just let me come in.'

Sheila heard the sobbing voice from below. 'Is that Beryl?' She jumped out of bed. 'How did she get all the way over here?' She was running downstairs before Kenneth could even answer her.

Beryl almost fell in through the door. Sheila took her into the front room, clicking the light on, and gasped in horror at the sight of her. Beryl's face was swollen, a mess of cuts and bruises, and her left eye would hardly open.

'Oh my God, Beryl.' Sheila went to put her arm round Beryl's bony shoulders to guide her to a chair, but her friend flinched as if she could not bear to be touched. 'Look, sit here . . .'

Kenneth was standing, stunned, in the doorway.

'Can you make some tea?' Sheila mouthed at him. Without Beryl saying anything, she could sense that she would rather not have a man in the room.

Sheila sank down at her side. Beryl sat with her arms clamped round herself as if trying to hold herself together, and she was shivering violently. Sheila gently put one of Margaret's crocheted blankets round her.

'Look, love, Kenneth's making tea. How on earth did you get all the way over here?'

'How d'you think? I walked,' Beryl said, between chattering teeth. 'I couldn't stand any more – can't. Had to get out.'

'What about the kids?' Sheila said. 'He won't . . .?'

'He won't touch them. They're asleep anyhow. It's just me, he . . .' For a moment her breathing became so shallow and panicky that she could not speak. It took her a while to get it under control. 'He's . . . It's as if he's got to punish me,' Beryl managed. 'I'm the one in the wrong. All the time. And I don't even know what for.'

Her distorted face turned to Sheila and looked directly at her.

'I can't have any more kids. I don't want to – I can't stand any more. But he . . . I can't stop him. He . . .'

Sheila felt the clench of cold dread inside her tighten further. 'He forces you?'

Beryl nodded, eyes down, washed in shame. 'But tonight I couldn't. I tried to fight him off, and he just . . .'

Weak sobs began to come out of her, but Sheila could see how much it hurt her to cry. Sid must have given her a real pasting, all over.

'I've tried so hard. But all he ever does is what he wants.' Her voice rose high, out of control. Sheila silently prayed that Beryl wouldn't wake her children. 'He's no idea about me, what I feel or what I want. What it's like – he's a pig,' she burst out. 'A vile pig and I hate him.'

Sheila had no idea what to say. She squeezed Beryl's hand gently, and Beryl winced, as if every inch of her was hurting.

'Let me get some water, bathe that eye,' Sheila said. 'And your face – I've got some witch hazel somewhere.'

She went into the kitchen where Kenneth was keeping out of the way, waiting for the kettle to boil.

'I'll just take a bit.' Sheila tipped the kettle. 'Bathe her eye.' She turned to him. 'I don't know what to do. Should we tell the police?'

'They won't take no notice. It's between him and her.'

'But where can Beryl go? She can't stay with him – he's an animal.'

Kenneth shrugged. This was not his sort of thing; he had no idea. Nor did Sheila, for that matter: something like this, normally kept behind closed doors, suddenly spilling out.

She ran upstairs for some cotton wool and went back in to see to Beryl. As she came down, Kenneth was filling the teapot.

Sheila sat with Beryl as she sipped a cup of sweet tea, still shaking. Looking at her there, in the light of the overhead light bulb, Sheila was shocked at how much Beryl had aged. She had only known her three years and she had been a strong, lively-looking woman in the beginning.

Now she had six children and she was as thin as a rake, her hair neglected and scraggy down her back, and she was missing several teeth – on top of having been used as a punchbag, Sheila thought, with a surge of rage against Sid.

Looking at poor Beryl, she wanted to march over and give Sid a piece of her mind. Tell him exactly what she thought. Threaten him with . . . But with what?

This was the sort of thing people didn't talk about. Women hid their bruises and soldiered on. Who were they supposed to tell? Wouldn't people say that Beryl had somehow brought it on herself; that it was Sid's right as a husband? She felt a wave of gratitude towards Kenneth wash through her. They had had their difficulties since the war, but he had never raised a hand to her.

As if reading her thoughts, Beryl, with the cup cradled in her hands, shoulders hunched, said, 'Sid wasn't like this before the war. Least I don't think so. We got married so quick, and then he went.' Tears ran down her cheeks suddenly, but she ignored them. 'He was all right. But now it's . . . He's so . . . I only have to open my mouth and I'm in the wrong.'

She raised her tear-filled eyes to Sheila. 'I always wanted to get married, have kiddies. That's all I ever wanted. And I try and love him – I do. But,' she looked down, shaking her head, 'nothing much I can do, is there? Except stick it out until the kids are old enough.'

Sheila wanted to offer something else, to say, *No, you can take the children and go* . . . But she could not think of anything. She knew Beryl would never move back in with her mom in her cramped back-to-back. The council said they were knocking it down soon anyway. And Beryl loved her little home. And she couldn't ask Sid to leave – he'd never agree to that. What on earth was she supposed to do?

'Look, let's get some sleep,' she said, feeling useless. Her own mind was becoming blurred with exhaustion. 'You can settle down on here.' She patted the sofa. 'I'll go and get you some covers.'

The next morning, Beryl's face looked even worse as the bruising came out. She wouldn't eat anything for breakfast.

'I need to get home – to the kids.' Her voice was full of panic. She seemed almost annoyed with them, as if they had brought her here against her will. 'I'm sorry, for coming over like that. I don't know what I was thinking. I've got to go . . .'

She was about to go tearing out of the front door, but Kenneth stopped her.

'Just give me one tick – I'll run you over there.'

Beryl looked fearfully at him. 'Don't let Sid see you.'

'I won't.' Kenneth picked up his car key. 'Come on.'

'I'll come and see you – soon, bring the kids,' Sheila said. She already felt guilty for not going over more often.

She didn't try to embrace Beryl, as she could see it was not welcome. Beryl seemed angry, as if she was regretting everything about the way she had broken open her private struggle and suffering and shown it all to them and now she was full of shame.

From the window Sheila watched as Beryl went outside, keeping her head right down. She slipped quickly into the Austin's passenger seat. The engine started and Kenneth pulled away. Sheila moved away from the window, feeling completely helpless. There was nothing Beryl could do but go back, keep on trying to dodge Sid's fists and his sexual relations by force. And hope to God she didn't get pregnant again – not this time.

'Who was that?' Elaine was standing behind her.

'Oh . . .' Sheila had no idea what to say. 'Just your dad, going off.'

Forty-Two

Autumn 1952

Ann stood stirring gravy in the roasting pan and humming along to the sound of the *Billy Cotton Band Show* streaming loudly from the wireless. The Sunday dinner time programme was her favourite and she liked to turn up the sound and have a good singalong while she was cooking.

She still found the music that moved her most was a lot of the songs that had kept them going through the war: Vera Lynn, Glenn Miller, Anne Shelton. It tapped into all those intense emotions of the time – and now all the uncertainty and fear were over, it somehow felt good listening to them still.

Joy and Patty were getting the table ready, there was a beautiful smell of roasting potatoes and Ann joined in the chorus of 'Down by the Old Zuyder Zee!' as loudly as she felt like.

She was caught round the waist suddenly from behind and jumped, laughing, as Tom kissed her cheek.

'For goodness' sake – you nearly got gravy all down you!'

'Someone's in good voice.'

'Yes, I am.' She was surprised that her voice still seemed to come out clear and in tune. A sing-song always lifted the spirits.

Tom put his lips close to her ear. 'It's lovely to see you so happy.'

Ann put the spoon down and turned to face him. They held each other close. She was happy. She was buzzing with delight, in fact.

'Yes – and you know why.'

All the family was to be together again. All of them. It was lovely having Sheila back living close, so that Elaine, Robbie and Jonny could pop in whenever they felt like it, after school or for a play in the garden. It was company for Patty on the days when she was not at her dance classes with Joy. Tom had been thinking about taking the air-raid shelter down, but the kids loved using it as a den, so instead he had cleaned it up a bit. So there it stood, a reminder of the war, with flowers and weeds sprouting from the top of it in the spring.

But there was one other thing that had completed her happiness. Most weekends now the family gathered for Sunday dinner. It was becoming a tradition: pooling rations for a big enough cut of meat, all squeezing into the front room, specially laid with a smaller table for the children. Sheila was glad of it, now that she was back working mornings and she was spared having to cook a Sunday dinner. And the family was complete now, because Martin was here as well.

'Have you put that extra chair in?' Ann called through to Joy. She looked up at Tom. 'Martin said could he bring a friend?'

'Oh yes?' Tom smiled teasingly.

'I wonder who she could be?' Ann said, beaming. 'About time, isn't it?'

The first job Martin was offered was in Witton – at the old Kynoch Works, now called ICI Metals Division. So he had taken this as a sign indicating his destiny and had moved back to Birmingham.

He had found lodgings in Erdington: a room at the top of a house, which worked happily for him. The landlady, a Miss Eagle, left him alone once she could see that he was a 'nice boy', quiet and inoffensive, who paid his rent on time. And the room, though shabby and a little musty, was pleasant, a good size, south-facing and looked down onto a little garden.

After his years in London, living with the Thorne family, with all their academic and arty friends in their lavishly sized house, followed by Spain, it had been a shock coming back to Birmingham. The place was – like parts of London – a building site. And the workaday drabness of this side of the city especially at first made him wonder if he had made a mistake. In some ways he missed London, and all that was available in terms of art and entertainment.

The job was a challenge at first as well. Not that Martin was not up to it. But it was his first time going into a big works like this, his first proper job, finding his way around, knowing how to behave, to tease and be teased. But he liked it. The more he saw of it, the more proud he felt: here he was in this city that had given the world so many new and practical things. Which had made a difference to people's lives, even when they often had no idea of it – what it took to develop metals for various uses that everyone took for granted.

After a short time, he started to settle in and enjoy himself.

And there was the family. He was safely removed from everyday contact by living across on the north side of town. But he could soon hop on buses or the train and visit them. See his mother, sisters, nieces and nephews – and his father. In fact, it was more of an effort to see Len and

Jeanette in Kings Heath and Martin found that he rarely did that.

Tom took a close interest in his work, and Martin found now that when he went over at the weekend, he would often be helping Tom with something practical in the garden, and then Mom would bring out mugs of tea and they might sit perched on the back step, or in warm weather on the grass, and talk.

'So how's the job going? What exactly are you up to at the moment?' Tom might ask, his gentle face turned to Martin, the one eye covered under his spectacles, the other directed at him with keen interest. And Martin realized that although he had never once heard Tom Somers complain about losing his own chosen career path, which meant that he was now having to work in purchasing – which was hardly the same thing – he was deeply interested in how Martin's career was developing.

And he was the only person Martin could talk to in detail. Len and his mother would say, 'Job all right?' To which he would reply, 'Yes, all going well, thanks.' Beyond that, they had no idea, and neither had his sisters. But with Tom he could really get into the detail and felt that he wanted to know.

And after a time Martin felt he could begin on questions as well. Last summer, when they were sprawled on the grass, he had plucked up the courage to ask something he had always wanted to know.

'Mom's never really told me exactly what happened, when you were wounded?' He felt himself blush as he asked. It was a very personal question.

Tom looked ahead of him, his mug of tea clasped in his remaining hand.

'Actually I don't have much memory of it. Just as well, probably. She told you it was in the Gallipoli area? It was a shell – I can remember feeling something, that rushing sensation. And when I woke up . . .' He shrugged. 'I was being carted off on a stretcher. I didn't know what had happened at that point. To my arm, or my eye. I was in shock, I suppose. It wasn't really until I got back here – to England – that it all started to sink in.'

Martin wasn't sure what to say. But to his surprise, Tom turned to him, smiling.

'That was where I met a certain Nurse Williams . . . Volunteer nurse, anyway.'

At the time when they had this conversation, Martin had been in the first throes of love again himself. Not that he was letting on to anyone about that.

But for the first time he felt a deep awe for all the adults in his life. Mom had kept her promise to the man she was engaged to, Len Gilby, who in his turn had brought Martin up, a cuckoo boy he discovered was not even his son. And Tom, this man who had stayed away, left them all alone, but carried on faithfully loving his mother all these years . . .

He wanted to say this, but he had no idea how to begin and stared back towards the house, at the climbing rose that Tom had planted, now beginning to snake up one side of the window, blossoming into deep-red flowers.

'Funny how things work out,' he said, feeling silly as he said it.

Tom nodded. 'Certainly is.'

But, Martin realized, with a stab of pain that was closer to anger, the way things seemed to be working out for him could only ever remain unspoken.

He met Simon in the works canteen quite early on. The place was huge, specializing in non-ferrous metals, and he and Simon worked in different departments. But they met queuing for food at dinner time, side by side. Simon, though tall, looked young, had brown hair and freckles and a sunny smile. There was something cheerful and carefree about him that Martin immediately took to.

'Make sure you don't go swimming after you've eaten that,' Simon commented, as a slab of rice pudding landed on his plate.

Martin turned and smiled.

'Probably tastes better than it looks,' Simon went on. 'You won't need to eat for a fortnight afterwards. Want to sit here?' He jerked his head at the end of a table where there were free spaces.

They talked – and, above all, laughed – all through that first meal. Martin learned that Simon was from Sutton Coldfield, had done his degree in physics here in Birmingham and was interested in all sorts of things: he must take Martin to the Barber Institute, the art gallery opened at the university just before the war. And did he fancy coming to the theatre one night?

Martin warmed to him more and more as the days went by. In some ways it was like being with Jack. Like Jack, Simon was quick and clever under his jokey exterior. He was interested in the world, in life and in politics. But unlike Jack, he did not give off the feeling that in the end he was superior, with his big family house and confident parents. Simon still lived at home with his mother, a dinner lady in a school, and he had worked for everything for himself.

And when Martin met his mother, Mrs Hollis, he could see that this warm-hearted, welcoming woman had bent over backwards not to make her son feel tied down by her, or bad about anything.

Their friendship had blossomed over the months. They had been out drinking, watching plays or chatting endlessly in a coffee bar in town. Both of them liked going into Birmingham, being part of the night life of bars and pubs.

What Martin had not been sure about, had taken a long time to ascertain, was whether Simon was . . . like him.

He supposed he should have guessed by the way they were instantly attracted to each other. It was there right from the start. There was never any mention of a girl – or of girls in general. Martin had felt almost straight away that he and Simon . . . But it frightened him to death, the thought that he might get everything wrong, misread the signs and mess everything up – or worse. Everything about his kind of love was against the law.

One night last winter, when it was far too cold to hang about on the streets, he had said to Simon, 'Why don't you come back to mine for a drink? Miss Eagle won't mind. In fact she's so deaf she most likely won't even notice.'

Even so, they had crept along the silent hall and up the stairs, giggling like schoolboys as they closed the door of Martin's room behind them.

'I'll put some water on.' He had one electric ring in his room and soon a pan was hissing its way to boiling.

'Nice place.' Simon looked round, with real appreciation. 'Cosy, isn't it?'

He made straight for Martin's little book collection on the shelves and leafed through them as they waited for the pan to boil.

That evening, in the dim light from Miss Eagle's side-light with its little faded pink-tasselled shade, they sat and talked quietly so as not to disturb Miss Eagle. And in this private, intimate space, things opened out and became clear between them.

Martin had given Simon the one chair and he was sitting on the bed. They were talking about *High Noon*, the picture they had seen the week before, and how it stood for the Cold War, even though it was a western.

After a while they ran out of words. There was a silence. A tense, electric feeling grew between them. Martin stared down at the brown linoleum on the floor between his legs, his whole being inwardly trembling with emotion. With desire – equally balanced with terror.

God! he thought, his cheeks burning. The ache of longing rose inside him and he allowed it to. Simon – he was in love with Simon. But suppose he was imagining that Simon felt something in return. What if he had got it wrong, had got the wrong person, and it was only him full of these feelings? *I want to kiss you. I just want you . . .*

He heard a creak of the floorboards and looked up abruptly as Simon stood up. Holding Martin's gaze, he sat himself on the bed, close beside him. Both their faces were solemn. A kiss was more than a kiss. It was a terrible risk. If you got it wrong, said anything to the wrong person, even with your eyes . . .

But Martin could see it in Simon's eyes, in his face – so often joking, but now solemn, vulnerable. *I want you too.* This was not the wrong person.

Neither of them spoke. The *yes* was granted with their eyes. And Martin was the first to risk, to reach out and gently lay his palm on Simon's cheek, as their lips moved closer to each other's.

They were careful at work. They were so very careful everywhere. But since that night, Martin knew – deeply, fully, joyfully – that in every respect he had come home.

'They're here!' Joy called from the upstairs landing, as there was a light knock at the front.

Ann hurried along the hall, still in her apron, and flung the door open. The young woman she had been expecting to see on the doorstep beside Martin, perhaps looking bashful, was in fact a fresh-faced young man.

'Hello, Mom.' Martin grinned happily at her. She was slightly startled by how happily. 'I did tell you I was bringing a friend, didn't I?'

'I don't eat much, don't worry,' Simon said winningly.

'Yes, of course – Joy told us. Come on in!' Ann stood back, smiling, to let them in.

Martin leaned in to kiss her and, as the two lads came into the house, all the children came rushing out of the front room, led by Elaine – 'It's Uncle Martin!' – and started to mob him.

Ann quelled a slight feeling of disappointment that she was not meeting a possible future daughter-in-law. But Martin's friend looked a nice enough lad and it was good to have new company.

'Right,' she said, shutting the door. 'Come on then, everyone, dinner's ready!'

It was lovely being there. Martin felt his heart expand as they sat round the table – he and Simon, Mom and Tom, Sheila and Kenneth and Joy; the kids were squeezed at a little table in the corner. He smiled across at Simon, who had hit it off with Joy and was chatting away.

'We thought you were bringing a girlfriend home, Mart,' Sheila said. Then over her shoulder, 'Robbie, leave Jonny alone!'

Martin looked up at his elder sister as she turned back, cut herself another forkful of roast potato and shoved it into her mouth. He felt a moment of rage and resentment. Sheila was so stolid, so sure of how things should be. *Just so*, as they had always been. Could she not see anything outside the way she thought? See *him* for who he was? But he told himself not to be unreasonable – and unkind. Sheila had had her own struggles.

'You don't find many girls at the works,' he said, keeping it light. 'Only up in the offices, I s'pose.'

'You could've come and worked in the labs at Cadbury's,' his mother remarked. 'You're a scientist. Sheila's back there now – did you know?'

'On Easter eggs,' Sheila said.

Martin laughed and saw Simon smile at him. He loved these moments – the two of them could say so much with their eyes. It made him feel warmed: both of them in a secret place against the world, which was solely theirs. 'I'm a metallurgist, Mom. Testing foodstuffs isn't really my thing.'

'Oh.' She smiled, making fun of herself. Science was all science to her. 'Oh well. It'd be nice to have you living this side of town, that's all.'

Martin's eyes met Simon's again, a flicker of recognition. Living over in Erdington suited him down to the ground. A lot of things about his life felt very good: beginning to get to know his father, for one, and the way he felt better about everything, able to accept the situation. But all the same – living further away was definitely for the best.

Forty-Three

Joy stood on the line at Cadbury's, the bright-red wrappers of the slim little fudge bars streaming in front of her eyes while all sorts of chatter was going on around her.

'Ooh, did 'e say that? You're onto a good thing there, bab . . .'

'And then he said, "I've got the biggest one in the family . . ."'

Ooohs and cackles of laughter followed this.

'Well, I told him he was a dirty so-and-so – and he looked at me, all big-eyed, and said he was on about his motorbike. "It's a Bantam, I'll have you know" – as if I care!'

Joy smiled vaguely, while the others booed and laughed on each side of the line. Her own head was buzzing with things she needed to remember. *Make sure Lizzie gets some proper shoes . . . This afternoon's ballet class – they could move on a bit now, they seem to have some of the basics. I'll ask Mrs Parsons to bring different music . . . And tonight's ballroom – let's concentrate on the quickstep, everyone has a job with that.*

'Oi – Joy? Wakey-wakey. Break time!' One of the other girls tapped her on the shoulder. 'Bet you're thinking about your dancing, aren't you?'

'There's a lot to do,' Joy admitted, thinking, Crikey, I hope Kay remembered to get the rent in on time. A sudden panic seized her, so that her heart was thumping as she took her first sip of tea. The landlord was a stickler, and Kay was marvellous at most things, but she was not the most organized – especially since Eddie had been around. Joy didn't see Kay during the day any more. And right now Kay was probably sitting in front of the belt filled with Milk Tray chocolates, nattering away, not fretting the way she was. Kay lived in the present, all the time. Maybe the rent was another thing she should take on herself . . .

'You going to be at the tea dance on Saturday, at Rowheath?'

'What? Oh!' That was another thing Joy had forgotten about. She tried to drag her attention back to the present. 'Yes – yes, Kay and me.'

In the bathroom to which she hurried, before going back on the line, Joy looked in the mirror, adjusting her white cap. With her hair taken back, she looked pale-faced and austere. Patty had had a bad cold and had been up and down last night, feverish. Joy leaned closer to the glass, examining the dark rings under her eyes.

But it was not only lack of sleep that had made her look pale and drawn. Something else had happened that morning that she was trying not to think about.

On her way into the works she had suddenly found a woman hurrying to catch up and walk alongside her. Joy, lost in her own thoughts as ever, had jumped, startled when the woman spoke to her suddenly.

'Are you Mrs Bishop – Alan Bishop's wife . . . Well, you were, I mean?'

The woman was in her forties, solidly built, with brown eyes and an almost country face, sympathetic-looking. Joy did not know who she was. And her words were like a punch, the sudden reminder.

'Yes?' She only just managed to speak, through her suddenly dry throat.

'Sorry to startle you.' She reached out, for a second, to touch Joy's shoulder, a sympathetic gesture. 'I used to look after your husband. I work in the medical room. I didn't know you were working back here until recently – I mean, we've never met. I just wanted to say . . .'

The woman stopped. There were tears in her eyes.

'He'd been through such a lot – terrible. I mean, you'll know.' She looked down, as if in sudden embarrassment.

'Yes,' Joy managed to say again. Although she thought, No, I don't. Not really.

She didn't know what to feel. The nurse meant to be kind, she knew, but all Joy dearly wanted at that moment was for her to go away. She was in a storm of confused feelings. Had Alan confided in this person in a way he never managed to do at home? The woman looked very upset, considering that Alan had been one of the many employees she would have seen in the medical room.

'I wanted to say, I'm so sorry. That's all.' She now looked as if she was regretting stopping and saying anything. Joy stood numbly, staring at her. 'I know it was a while ago now, but . . . Terrible. For you. And your family.'

'Thank you,' Joy said huskily. She could not find anything else to say and turned away. The woman took the hint and hurried off towards her entrance to the factory.

Joy had felt in those moments as if she had been cracked open again. She stopped, fighting to get her emotions under control. She remembered Dr Saloman saying to her, 'The war will never end for some, you know, my dear.' And she had spent the morning forcing herself to think about other things.

But here in the bathroom mirror she could see the strain in her face, which looked pinched and tight. All she ever seemed to do was run. Run to work her dance school into flourishing existence. Run to forget, so as not to feel.

'I can't go on like this much longer,' she whispered. 'Not doing everything.' There were not enough hours in the day, and she was exhausted.

'Gillian seems to be enjoying her dancing?' Joy said carefully to Mrs Cooper, the little girl's mother, who always arrived looking flushed and harassed and seemed to worry endlessly about Gillian. About having passed on her own shape and size to this child, with her round pink cheeks and well-padded limbs.

'Is she?' Mrs Cooper said. 'She don't say much when she comes back and . . . They're not, you know, being nasty or anything?'

She looked round at the other girls in the ballet class, mostly slender as little colts on matchstick legs. There had been a few remarks, but Joy had made sure she scotched those straight away.

'Now, girls, in this class we have a rule. No one is to comment or make remarks about anyone else's body, do you hear? Your body is your business, and so is everyone else's. So I don't want to hear it.'

'But you can't be a ballerina if you're fat, can you, Miss Gilby?'

It was Amanda, a girl who seemed to think that the fact she was pretty, with a head of the most beautiful thick blonde hair, made her lord of all the world. If anyone was going to be a troublemaker, it was her.

'Ballerinas come in all shapes and sizes – they're not all built like fence posts,' Joy said, feeling herself getting really annoyed. Although she knew as she said it that this was untrue (ballerinas did all tend to be thin as fence posts), but she wasn't having this young madam putting someone else down. 'Enough comments, thank you – let's get to work.'

She saw Amanda smirking with one of the other girls. Goodness, this was hard, teaching girls you actively disliked! Joy tried hard to treat everyone the same.

And Gillian was a tryer. She was slow to learn, not especially graceful and was carrying too much weight to make her own movements easy. But Joy was determined that young Gillian was going to enjoy dancing. Enjoy her life, for that matter, without little madams like Amanda judging what she should and should not be allowed to do.

'Gillian's doing very well. Aren't you, dear?' She smiled encouragingly as Gillian came over to her mother, her new, pink ballet pumps in hand. Joy saw her glad smile fading as she got closer – perhaps afraid of what her mother was going to say about her. 'You're a good little dancer, aren't you?'

Gillian glowed at this praise. Joy spotted Amanda watching them across the room with a contemptuous expression. How did anyone get to be so nasty so young? she had wondered – until she met Amanda's mother, Mrs Rowse. She was also blonde (though not naturally), came staggering in on heels so high she could hardly get up the stairs and with a smell under her nose.

As they all left, Joy sank down on a chair, tired out.

Kay came in then, full of beans as usual. 'What's up with you? You look all in.'

'I am. I never knew what we were getting into here – teaching dancing's one thing. It's dealing with the parents that wears you out! They can't all be Margot flaming Fonteyn.' She got to her feet, feeling anxious again. 'You did pay the rent? Please tell me you didn't forget?'

Kay pretended to think, stroking her chin. Then put Joy out of her misery.

'Yeah, I went to see old face-ache this morning. God, he is a miserable sod. But we're all right for another month. Come on, break time – you've earned it. I brought you a treat.'

They sat with a cup of tea and a couple of cream horns that Kay had splashed out on.

'Oh, my word, this is heaven,' Joy said through a mouthful of sweetness, cream all over her lips.

Kay laughed. She had already wolfed hers down. She opened the window, lit a cigarette and leaned on the sill, looking down over the street.

'Looks like you need feeding up.' She watched the street below idly. She was a great people-watcher. They chatted about practical things, the classes yet to come, while Kay smoked. She was nearly at the end of her cigarette when she stood up straighter.

'Hey, look at this. What's he up to? D'you think he's from the papers?'

Joy got up and squeezed in next to her to look. Following where Kay was looking, she took in the camera pointing up at their building, at the sign announcing their dance school. And then her blood froze. She immediately drew back from the window, pulling Kay with her.

'Oh my God.'

The man's face was mostly covered by the camera, but there he was. Tall, the long face, the fawn raincoat.

'What's up with you?' Kay demanded.

'It's *him* again.'

'What, that . . . that weird sod?'

'Yeah. Howard something-or-other. Fielding, that was it.' Her heart was pounding horribly. 'What the hell is he playing at?'

Kay stood back as far as she could to look out again,

trying not to be seen. 'He's going now. Gone – round the corner.'

'Was he taking a picture of here? It looked like it.'

'Maybe.' Kay looked at her, puzzled. 'Come on – can't do any harm, can it? He's gone now. Forget it.'

'He's just . . .' Joy cleared away her tea things. 'I don't know what it is with him.' She found it hard to put her discomfort into words. But it seemed a peculiar coincidence that Howard should be out there, taking a picture of a building, with her name on it. When she was inside it.

Only the adults' ballroom-dance class to get through, Joy thought later, wearily. She taught this class on her own and Kay had gone home. She changed her shoes and got the record player set up, and the classmates started coming in. To greet everyone and get them in the mood, she put on a cha-cha-cha rhythm at low volume.

'Evening, all!' She managed to find the energy to be her usual chirpy self as they arrived, and in fact the sight of the class lifted her, with all her pupils coming in looking enthusiastic, keen to do something different after a day in offices and factories. There was a new couple, and Joy chatted to them and found out they already knew a lot of dances, which was a relief. They could join in with everyone else, instead of her having to teach them separately.

And amid these arrivals suddenly appeared a familiar face, though – strangely, it seemed to her later – she could not immediately place who it was.

'Hello?' she said. 'You've been before, haven't you? I know I recognize you.'

'Yes.' He gave a sad smile. 'Used to come a few years back with my wife, Phyllis. I'm Ivor. Williams.'

'Oh yes, I remember!' Joy exclaimed happily. Of course it was Ivor – how could she have forgotten? But there was something about him that looked very different. His face was thinner, his hair shorter than she remembered. He looked older, not like the fleshy, almost boyish man she had known before. And Joy realized that she hadn't been able to place him at first because she had always known him as part of a couple.

'You used to come to the class in Northfield – and you and your wife were expecting a baby. How are they both?'

'Well,' he spoke very quietly, 'our Glenys is doing very well. She's two now. But . . .' He was finding it hard to speak and, when he looked up at Joy, his face was full of sorrow. 'We lost Phyllis. It was very sudden. She was expecting again. It was her heart – we had no idea there was anything wrong. It was eighteen months ago now.'

Joy gasped in shock. Beautiful, vivacious Phyllis, and they were such a lovely couple.

'My goodness, I had no idea,' she said, feeling immediately ridiculous. How could she have had? But it seemed so unlikely, so awful. 'I'm so sorry.'

Ivor nodded his thanks.

'It's taken me a while, what with looking after Glenys and everything. To get out – do anything apart from work. But I saw your advertisement in the paper and we – I – always used to enjoy your class. Now you're in town, I thought it would be nice to come along, otherwise I never go anywhere except work. Phyllis's mom said she'd have Glenys. Only I don't know if it's a problem, my coming on my own? I remembered there was that bloke who used to come . . .'

'Yes,' Joy said. Howard. That bloke. 'Of course it'll be all right. I can dance with you – unless anyone else arrives without a partner. From what I remember, you were a really good dancer.'

'Very rusty now,' he said bashfully. 'But it would be nice to get into practice again.'

'Well,' she said. 'It's time we all got going. Right, evening, everyone. I thought this week we'd start with a quickstep!' With a smile, she said to Ivor, 'Just let me put the music on and I'll be over.'

Forty-Four

Joy had thought Ivor's keenness to dance might soon wear off, as he had to come all the way into town from North-field. She was only doing the children's classes out of town now. But over the following weeks Ivor came faithfully. And every week they danced together.

As he had said, he was rusty, at first. But Ivor was nat-urally good at dancing. In fact he had the makings of a very good dancer indeed. He was light on his feet, somehow held himself correctly, and his body leaned into the music and flowed with it in a way that not many of her pupils ever managed.

Of course anyone could learn to dance and go out and have a good time – that was mainly what her classes were about. But Ivor improved quickly and naturally. Joy realized that he had something more to him than almost anyone she had ever met – even Alan.

She didn't say anything, not at first.

'You're really coming on,' she said at the end of one class, when he had been attending again for a few weeks. 'You're very good at learning the steps – it seems to come back to you very quickly.'

'Oh,' he replied, seemingly unaware this was anything unusual. His rather woebegone face broke into a smile. 'I like doing it. Cheers me up. You can forget everything when you're dancing, can't you? It's the best thing in the week.'

Ivor did seem lit up by coming to the classes. But Joy

watched him leave that night, her heart aching. However much he enjoyed dancing, and even if this was his happiest couple of hours in the week, a veil of sadness hung over him all the time. Joy could sense it every time they were together. It was almost as if Phyllis was still in the room, her happy, smiling face, and their love for each other so plain to see. A love they thought would go on for years and years.

She knew what it was like to lose someone. But she knew that to some extent, she had lost Alan before he died. There had been those precious times of closeness, of joking together and him being sweet and loving. But Alan had been difficult at times, even before the war. He had had a lot to contend with, with his bully of a father and his mother driven to the edge of sanity. But after he came back at the end of the war, he really had been almost a complete mystery to her. So much of the time he had been strange or locked up in himself, trapped by experiences he would never share. Only in small glimpses did she ever see the Alan she had known before the war.

But Phyllis, that was a completely different situation. Joy remembered the lively woman with her dark, flashing eyes who had come dancing with Ivor, excited about their baby, glowing with health. Tears rose in her eyes. Phyllis had died so suddenly, just when she was expecting another child. And Ivor and poor little Glenys were left without her. How cruel life could be.

She had told Ivor about Alan, and it made it easier for him to talk because they had both experienced loss. But, Joy thought, as she cleared up after the class, it was going to take that poor man a very long time to get over his loss – if he ever did.

*

By the time they were in the run-up to Christmas, the two of them were dancing very well together.

Kay was still at the school that particular evening. She had stayed on to do some work in the office and said she would wait until the end of the class, travel back with Joy, as she did occasionally.

'Right,' Joy said to the class. 'Now, the quickstep . . .'

There were groans all round.

'It's so difficult!'

'Slowstep more like. That's all we'll ever do!'

Joy laughed. 'Come on, all you need is a bit of practice. So we're going to show you how it looks when you manage to speed it up a bit.'

'What, me?' Ivor mouthed at her, looking worried to death. 'I'm not sure about—'

'Yes, you,' she said. 'You can do it.' She moved her lips closer to his ear. 'Follow me – I'll talk you through, where you need it.'

The others stood round good-naturedly. Ivor was no show-off and he looked terribly nervous at being asked to demonstrate the steps.

As she was talking, Kay came out of the back office and sank onto a chair. Joy could tell she was impatient for the class to be over, so that she could go home, and she felt a tinge of annoyance. What was wrong with Kay these days? They had just got their business on the right track, but some days now she was like a black cloud covering the sun.

Joy took no notice and went to put the record on, saying as she did, 'Now I've mentioned before – with the quickstep, the idea is to move smoothly across the floor. Like a swan.' She looked up with a grin. 'Your feet'll be working away like mad, but on the surface you will be gliding serenely.'

Self-mocking laughter came from the gaggle of dancing couples. 'Swan in hobnailed boots!'

'Good luck with that, Ivor!' one of the other men called, and Ivor gave him a terrified wave.

'Come on . . .' Joy held out her arms.

It was not all plain sailing, but considering the tempo at which she was making him dance, Ivor did very well. She could almost hear the sound of ticking in his head: *slow, slow, quick, quick . . .*

'Lockstep,' she murmured as they reached one end of the room. And then the ticking stopped. She could see in his face that he had reached a point where his feet took over. They swirled and glided along the room again and it was working, the way sometimes everything came together when their feet just knew what to do, knew the music. Joy experienced a moment of pure happiness. As Ivor whirled her round, she felt her full skirt swirl about with her. She had not danced so well with anyone for a long time – and it felt very good. 'Well done!' she said as they took a bow, both breathing heavily at the end, and the others applauded, all saying they hadn't a hope of ever dancing like that, and other such comments.

'Why don't you ask him to come to one of the demos with you?' Kay said, when the others had all gone. 'He's really come on . . . It'd be better than them seeing us dancing with each other. Anyway I get sick of dancing the man's part!'

'Kay?' Joy shut the faded red lid of the record player and rested her hand on top of it. She'd been holding back from saying anything, but Kay really didn't seem herself. 'Are you saying you don't want to come? What's up? You've been in a funny mood lately. It's not like you.'

Kay, who was moving the few chairs they had into a tidy line, paused for a moment, but didn't look round.

'Nothing,' she said, turning away irritably. 'I'm perfectly all right.'

But a moment later she turned back and sank down onto one of the seats. Her shoulders began to shake.

'Kay!' Joy was beside her in a second. 'Hey, what's happened?' She had never seen cheerful, optimistic Kay like this before.

Her friend put her hands over her face for a moment, then sat up, wiping her eyes, as if she had decided something.

'It's no good me keeping on,' she said, a little bit more like her normal self. 'Blarting won't cure anything. Only . . .' Her face crumpled as she turned to look at Joy again. 'I know I can tell you, because you understand what it's like. I've not been feeling too good – and now I know. I'm expecting a baby. And we're not even married!'

'Oh, Kay.' Joy put her arm round her friend. 'Does Eddie know?'

Kay nodded tearfully. 'I'm no good at hiding things. And anyway, it takes two – why should I have all the worry of it while he sails on with his life?'

Joy found herself smiling faintly. This was more like Kay. 'Are you going to – you know . . .'

'Get married? Oh, yeah. Eddie's going to do the right thing.'

But she didn't exactly sound overjoyed. She stared gloomily ahead of her.

'Well,' Joy said hesitantly. 'That's good, isn't it? Aren't you happy?'

Kay gave her a watery smile. 'I am really, yeah. Eddie's over the moon – said he was about to ask me to marry him anyway. We're going out to buy a ring tomorrow. He couldn't be nicer, and I'm just being stupid. Only, it's a lot to adjust to. And I can't help thinking, you know how it goes, men and women . . . He's got his job at Kalamazoo and his life'll go on much the same, because that's how it is for men. And here am I, trying to run this school with you, and now I don't know how I'm going to manage. It's not fair, is it?'

For a second all Joy could feel was envy. A husband with a nice steady job at Kalamazoo the office equipment place, not having to worry about everything on your own – what did Kay have to moan about? But she could understand what Kay was feeling and tried to be comforting, even though it certainly set her own mind whirring over how they were going to cope.

'We will, somehow,' Joy said. 'Don't you worry.'

'Also,' Kay added with a wry grin, 'I don't want to go round being called Kay Bottoms all my life.'

'Well, you should have thought of that,' Joy laughed.

'And everyone'll expect me to stop and stay at home and do the washing and cooking all the time.' Kay reverted to sounding gloomy, and Joy could quite understand why. Once you had a baby, everyone thought they had something to say about it and how everything should be.

'Look, we'll find a way – OK?' Joy gave her friend's shoulders another squeeze. She had no idea how they were going to manage, but they were going to have to, somehow.

Christmas was a happy time. Now that Sheila was living back in the street and Patty had her cousins near, it made Joy's life much easier. Sheila and Mom could share out looking after the children, and Patty always had company.

'All the same,' Sheila said to her one day, a bit snippily, Joy thought, 'Mom and Tom deserve to have some freedom now as well – with you living with them, they've ended up looking after Patty all the time.'

And Joy took this to heart. But she was so busy it was hard to do anything but rely on her mother.

Having Martin back in town was nice as well. When they were all together, with the kids playing in the middle of the room, Joy had joked to Martin about herself and him being the 'old maids' of the family.

Martin laughed at this, even more than she had expected. 'I rather like the idea of being an old maid.'

He waggled his eyebrows at her in his jaunty way, and Joy couldn't help feeling there was more to the joke than she could make any sense of. But then Martin's face became serious.

'What about you?' he said. 'Anyone special, Sis?'

'No.' She grinned bravely. 'I don't have any luck with men – I'm steering well clear. I just want to make my school the best dance academy there is, and bring Patty up. That'll do me. Time's passing me by anyway.'

Martin looked sadly at her. 'Come on, Sis, you're not that old. I know you've had some rotten luck – but give yourself a chance, eh?'

She reached over and ruffled his hair.

'You're a fine one to talk. I know Mom's waiting for you to come home with a nice girl on your arm.'

Martin gave her a strange look, almost as if he was about to say something. He looked down, then back up at her with a twisted smile.

'Ah well, she might have a bit of a wait for that.'

Forty-Five

Coronation Day 1953

'ALL THIS – AND EVEREST TOO!'

Sheila held up a copy of the *Daily Express* as she hurried into her mother's kitchen, with Elaine coming in behind her.

'Look at this: they've done it!'

Ann and Tom both pored over the paper.

'"Briton first on roof of the world",' Ann read. Everyone had been waiting to see if Edmund Hillary and Tenzing Norgay would succeed in a climb that many others had failed at. 'Rather them than me – it gives me the shivers every time I see a picture of that mountain. Ooh . . . "Three girls made the Queen's dream dress."'

She and Sheila pored over the picture.

'Looks beautiful,' Sheila said. 'We'll see the real thing later.'

'Are we going to see what colour it is?' Patty asked, pushing between them to look at the picture.

''Fraid not,' Ann laughed. 'Only black-and-white. But they'll tell us. Anyway it must be white. The Queen's not going to get crowned in red, is she?'

Joy came in then. 'Hi, Sis. Everyone ready? Shall we start cutting sarnies? Ooh, can I read "The Gambols"?'

As Joy chuckled at the cartoon, Ann beckoned to

Elaine and went back to cutting slices of bread as thinly as humanly possible.

'Put a scraping of marg on for me, will you, love? Patty, you can help as well.'

Elaine smiled happily and set to with the spreading. Patty piled all the slices neatly for her mother to put fillings in: egg-and-cress and fish paste.

Tom melted out of the room. 'I'll check the television,' he murmured. 'Wouldn't do if it pegged out today, would it?'

'Too many females!' Sheila laughed, lifting the teapot lid off to see if there was anything doing. 'Nanna said she'll be along a bit later – she didn't want to get in the way. Right, we'd best crack on. I've left Kenneth with the lads.'

She rolled her eyes jokingly, but, Ann thought, she looked content. Those two seemed to be settling down again at last. And Kenneth was really good with his two boys. Robbie was eleven now and Jonny five, and he taught them all sorts of things and played football and cricket with them.

'Stick the kettle on again, will you, Joy?' Ann said. She looked round the kitchen happily – there was a heap of rock-cakes and a plate of jam tarts ready for the coronation party outside, and now they just had to do the sandwiches. Everyone had been saving rations for today, so that the street could have a good party and let its hair down.

Joy stood by the front door looking out, having a break from all the goings-on in the kitchen, not to mention Sheila bossing her around. She lit a cigarette and stood in the doorway, blowing smoke into the damp air. She'd never smoked much, but lately she found it a comfort.

'Shame about the weather, isn't it?' the lady across the

road called, as her husband and son wrestled with a trestle table on the pavement. 'Let's hope it clears up later.'

Joy waved and agreed with her, before she went back in. It was a shame, though. A light rain was falling, and all the miles of bunting and Union Jacks, their colours brightening every street, were hanging limp, water dripping from them. The city had been preparing for weeks, and the centre of Birmingham was full of decorations and flowers and flags.

Poor old Kay had had the same sort of day for her wedding back in March – wet and much colder than today. But she and Eddie made the best of it, and Kay seemed happy. By the time their little wedding took place she had adapted better to all the changes facing her.

Joy thought back fondly to the day. Eddie was a good bloke, she thought. And that counted for a lot. She and Kay were going to have to work out how to manage, once the baby arrived in August. But for now, Kay was still teaching and was feeling better than she had at the beginning.

Thinking about work, Joy could not help her mind drifting, as it did so often now, to Ivor Williams. Her star pupil was still coming regularly to classes. And with Kay feeling tired and heavy, Ivor had helped Joy out at various dance demonstrations and had come to a couple of tea dances with her around town as well.

At first he had been very shy and hesitant at these events, but he was gaining in confidence. Now, when they danced, she looked forward to linking arms with Ivor as an equal. Someone she could count on for his footwork, who would not let her down. He was solid, gentle, his blue eyes looking down at her as they danced with a tender concentration. His face moved her. He was a loving man, she could see. A man missing and longing for the woman he had loved so deeply. Sometimes she felt almost guilty for not being Phyllis. And she was moved by him, and found herself looking forward to being held in his arms.

She sighed, flicked ash out to the side of the wet doorstep and took another deep drag on it.

No good thinking like that, she decided. Ivor was grieving for Phyllis. Perhaps he always would be. Joy's heart buckled. Sometimes she felt almost jealous of Phyllis. How awful that was – being jealous of a dead woman! What a loving husband he must have been. And, in her own loneliness, she ached to have someone look at her in that way.

The afternoon did not get any warmer, but the rain did let up some of the time.

'Well, we've been through worse than a drop of rain,' Ann joked as she and the girls carried out the plates of food they had prepared as their contribution to the party.

They had all sat round the television, with everyone squeezed in, the children in a gaggle on the floor. Sheila sat on Kenneth's lap.

'And I don't want any comments about my weight,' she said, plonking herself down. Kenneth gave an exaggerated groan. 'Oi – stop it!'

Miss Prince from along the street and a couple of other neighbours came to watch as well. Everyone sat spellbound at the astonishing carriages drawn by beautiful horses, the cheering crowds and all the rest of the pomp and ceremony transmitted to them from London – a miracle in itself, because they had not long had a television and it still felt like magic, seeing those pictures moving in their own living room.

'She looks so young,' Ann said.

'Bless her,' Margaret agreed. 'What a job! I don't think I'd want it.'

When the moment of the vow came, everyone fell silent. It seemed to Ann they were all holding their breath, frightened for this young woman with the eyes of the world on her, willing it to go well and for nothing to go wrong.

'Ooh, thank goodness,' Sheila said on an outrush of breath, once it was over.

And now the party could begin: the hats and bunting and cakes and laughter.

Ann carried another plate of sandwiches out from the house. It was drizzling, but no one was taking any notice. The party was in full swing and she heard bursts of cheering from further along the street. Someone had a penny tin whistle and was playing a fast, jigging tune. The rest of the street was full of chat and laughter and everyone was enjoying themselves, tucking into this unusual feast.

As she came to the table, Ann's eyes met Tom's. He, like everyone else, had the day off. And the two of them had even more to look forward to. The children were being good about letting them have a break now and then, and they had managed a weekend away in Malvern not long ago. And they had been to the Hippodrome to see Alma Cogan – Ann had decided she liked 'Hold Me, Thrill Me, Kiss Me' even better than she liked Billy Cotton's band.

But this week Tom was to have his sixtieth birthday.

'You should get away,' Sheila had said to them. 'You can go to the caravan if you like, but I expect you want something a bit more luxurious!'

Ann and Tom had looked at each other. Sheila and Kenneth had their Eccles parked on a site in the countryside between Birmingham and Redditch. And it was nice to go out there – they had spent many happy afternoons down at the caravan.

'I think we can do a bit better than that,' Tom said. 'But thanks, Sheila.'

They had decided to go to the seaside and had booked into a guesthouse in Aberystwyth. Ann had hardly ever been to the sea, and the thought of a few days of just her and Tom together, with no cooking or pressure to do anything and a whole new place to explore, sounded pure bliss.

As she came up to the table now, Tom looked up and their eyes met. His face creased into a smile – one of those special smiles of his, solely for her.

I am so lucky, she thought, smiling back, laying a loving hand on his shoulder for a moment. My dearest love. And once again the very fact that the two of them had a life together now seemed like a miracle.

Joy chatted to the neighbours on each side of them and smiled as she watched Patty and Elaine wobbling their plates of red jelly about and giggling their heads off. Patty was eight now and always looked up to thirteen-year-old Elaine, who was definitely leader of all the children. Patty was lucky having cousins so close. Because, Joy thought with a pang, she was not likely to get any brothers and sisters now.

Her mind drifted, despite itself, to Ivor and little Glenys, who was nearly three. Ivor's mother, and sometimes Phyllis's, looked after her while he was at work. Glenys didn't have any cousins, so far as Joy knew. Poor little girl, she really was going to be on her own. Ivor was going to have to be everything to her: both mother and father.

'Three cheers for Her Majesty!'

Joy, startled from her daydreams – she really must stop thinking about Ivor – raised the mug of beer she was drinking, jolted back into her surroundings. She watched all the couples along the street, including Mom and Tom, linking arms, kissing, cheering.

'Hip hip hooray!'

As soon as the cheering was over, her mind drifted straight back to Ivor again and a swell of longing rose in her. She didn't want to be alone for ever, however much she tried to bury herself in her dance business. She wanted love and a family – and increasingly she knew who she wanted it with.

But it could not be. Not with a man who still loved someone else.

She could no longer hide from herself that she was developing very tender feelings towards Ivor Williams. And she was going to have to work hard to keep them to herself.

Forty-Six

'Aaah, look – she's waking up.'

Joy leaned over the carrycot where Kay's baby, the young Sandra Bottoms, three months old, was snuggled, curled up plump and pink under the fluffy primrose-yellow blanket that Joy had given her when she was born.

'Little monster,' Kay said fondly.

They were in the dance studio, and Kay was already desperate to try and get back to work. Sandra had been born bang on time in August, but Kay had been struggling. Joy was surprised. She had expected Kay to take to motherhood like a duck to water, the way she seemed to do everything else. But she had had problems with feeding Sandra, a breast abscess that made her very sick for a time, not enough sleep and had been generally feeling lonely and down in herself.

And it showed. Kay was definitely looking thinner, with dark half-moons under her eyes.

'You'll be all right,' Joy had kept trying to encourage her. 'It's really hard those first few weeks, but you'll get through it.'

She thought back to when she had had Patty. Hank had been away at war and she didn't know if he would come back. There had been all the preparations and the ups and downs about her going to America. And then Alan coming home . . .

There had been so many problems, one way or another. But in fact she had not suffered too much, when it came to actually having Patty. She was the one who had taken to being a mother easily and naturally. Mom had been there to help, of course. And now Joy realized how lucky she had been, when she saw Kay all exhausted and weepy in those first weeks – not helped by Eddie feeling left out and getting impatient with her, saying she needed to pull herself together. Things had been fraught.

'Go easy on her, Ed,' Joy had said, trying to sound friendly instead of annoyed and indignant, which was what she felt. He hadn't had to do much towards having the baby, had he – typical bloke! 'She'll be all right; it just takes time to adjust. You need to be nice to her.'

To give Eddie his due, he had tried harder. And he could see that Kay needed to get out of the house. So between them, he and Joy had encouraged Kay to go against the grain – and against what her own mother thought was the right thing – and come back to work as soon as she felt ready.

'I know you're tired, but it might perk you up,' Joy said.

Kay was not one to be stuck in on her own. And being back here, she was already starting to show a spark of her old self.

In the meantime, Joy had had to work incredibly hard running the school by herself. She had to cancel some classes, had doubled up on others so that she was teaching large numbers, and had generally worn herself out. And it was no fun on her own – the school was hers and Kay's, and she wanted her partner back.

'Little 'un will be all right once we put the music on!' she laughed, going towards the office. Sandra already loved music. Her eyes would go wide and she would lie still with her mouth open, listening, or would sometimes wave her arms about. 'You OK to do your tap class?'

'Yes, I think so,' Kay said gamely. 'I'll just top her up first – she's such a guzzler. I don't want milk all down my front while I'm teaching.'

She sat down to feed Sandra. Joy went into the office and picked up the post. Bills, all boring-looking stuff, except for one rather classy-looking white envelope. She frowned. A moment later she was dashing back into the hall, letter in hand.

'Hey, guess what!'

Kay looked up at her. 'Not a clue.'

'This is from the Alex – they've heard about my demos and everything and they want a couple to dance in their Christmas show!'

The Alexandra was one of Birmingham's main theatres. Joy was bouncing about on her toes with excitement.

'My God, that's wonderful!' Kay burst out laughing, making Sandra pull back, startled for a moment. 'Sorry, petal. Hey, you're getting really famous, you are.'

She did not seem at all jealous or put out at Joy getting all the attention; or, if she was, she tried never to show it. Kay knew what bad times Joy had been through and she was glad for her.

Joy's mind was racing. The letter said they needed a couple who could dance – 'excellently', as they put it – with a jive, a waltz and quickstep to be included in their show *The Days of Lydia,* which was to open just after Christmas. A couple . . . She racked her brains. She could have asked them to find a partner for her. But her mind immediately turned to the person she most loved to dance with.

'I could ask Ivor Williams,' she suggested hesitantly.

'Don't they want a professional?' Kay said. 'They could get someone for you . . .'

'I s'pose they could,' Joy replied.

343

'He is good, though. I mean, I haven't seen him dance for a while, but if you think he's up to it?'

'I'll ask him,' Joy said casually. As if Ivor was nothing to her. As if he was anybody – someone who happened to be a good dancer. Because that was what he had to be.

'I don't know.' Ivor sounded really worried, though he blushed in amazement and pleasure at being asked. 'I'm not good enough for that, surely? I'd mess it up – embarrass you.'

'I don't think you would,' Joy said. She had noticed that when Ivor set to on a dance and practised, he hardly ever made any mistakes after that, as if he could programme himself and never go wrong. 'I'd say you were made for it.'

'But it'd mean a lot of rehearsing – timewise, it might be difficult.' He immediately found reasons to refuse. 'I see little enough of Glenys as it is.'

'We'd have to rehearse mainly at weekends, obviously,' Joy went, 'because of work. But we could practise after your Tuesday class, if you don't mind staying late. And Sunday afternoons – bring Glenys along? Patty likes coming over here and she'd love to play with Glenys. And Elaine, my niece, she's always angling to come over here – she could help.'

'That sounds nice,' Ivor conceded. 'It would give my mom a break too.' He stared ahead of him as if dazed for a moment. 'The Alex! You sure about this?' He looked at her, awed, then they both started laughing. Ivor's face lit up with laughter, his blue eyes and his strong-featured face looking even more handsome.

'Sure as eggs is eggs, as my grandad used to say,' Joy laughed. Suddenly she was flooded with happiness. 'We must get to work.'

*

344

They did work hard, on those available evenings and Sunday afternoons, dancing together until their steps knew each other's and fitted the music perfectly. By the end of the year, their dances really did feel like two swans gliding perfectly together.

They smiled into each other's eyes. You were expected to look happy when you were dancing, but Joy certainly did not have to put it on. Sometimes, as they jived or waltzed around the room, she thought she saw something in Ivor's eyes that was not simply a professional smiling-dancer's mask. They fixed on hers deeply, almost questioningly. Sometimes, in a dance, there were moments out of time when the two of them, absorbed in the music, in the rhythm of the dance, seemed to work perfectly together, as if they were in another world where no one else existed.

Once or twice, as the music stopped, they stood panting in each other's arms, their eyes fixed on one another. But Ivor would come back to himself abruptly. He would release Joy, look down and away – anywhere except at her. And each time, even though she knew not to expect anything else, it felt to Joy like a cold shower.

On Sundays the children were there, Patty and Elaine, entertaining themselves and little Glenys with dolls and games. And they would bring their parents back to earth like no one else.

'Mom, Glenys needs a wee!'

Christmas was already busy. Joy, with as much help from Kay as she could manage, put on a Christmas dance show with the children. She scoured the Rag Market for bits she could use for costumes and sat up late sewing and adjusting, and her mother helped with some of them.

The children were doing a little dance version of the

nativity. Joy made sure that plump, under-confident little Gillian was given the part of Mary. This was of course the part that Amanda Rowse, of the abundant blonde hair and figure like a young model, thought she was entitled to, no questions asked. Joy cast her as a shepherd.

'That's not going to go down well,' Kay said, laughing when she saw the cast list. 'You'll have that mother to contend with.'

Mrs Rowse and Amanda were very put out.

'Who's going to be Mary then?' Amanda asked, furiously sulky when she was allotted her part.

'And Mary . . . will be played by Gillian Cooper,' Joy announced.

'What?' Amanda gasped. She gave a mocking snort of laughter and, to Joy's extreme annoyance, some of the others joined in.

'You'll have to be careful not to giggle at the wrong time in the play, Amanda,' she warned. 'Because you'll end up not having a part at all.' Amanda's face straightened and she stared with loathing at Joy. And Joy really didn't want to be at odds with any of the children, but Amanda did seem to expect everything to be automatically handed to her on a plate.

Sure enough, Mrs Rowse teetered in on her perilous heels and demanded 'a word'.

'I want to know why my Amanda's been put as a shepherd,' she said. 'She's ever so disappointed. With her looks, she ought to be playing Mary – not that one . . .' She gestured dismissively towards Gillian.

Joy gave her a sympathetic smile.

'The thing is, Mrs Rowse, I know Mary's the main part. But if you think about it, she's just had a baby and she's not going to be doing a lot of dancing. The shepherds will be doing more, so Amanda will enjoy that.'

In fact Mary did have a little dance of her own to do – a gentle little solo to show her joy in holding her new baby.

'I didn't point out to her that Mary wasn't exactly likely to be blonde,' she said to Kay afterwards. 'I think Amanda's more bothered about the costume than the dance. Anyway, that sorted her out. For the moment.'

Kay laughed, holding Sandra up in the air and making faces at her as she gurgled. 'You're a one. When this one's older, I fully expect her to be given all the best parts, of course,' she joked.

Joy rolled her eyes. 'Honestly, I'll be glad when Christmas is over, with all this going on.'

The Days of Lydia, a new, light musical about a poor girl who finds life and love through learning to dance, opened at the Alexandra Theatre on 28 December, by which time Joy was almost a nervous wreck.

She and Ivor spent a short time rehearsing with the cast once they arrived in Birmingham, for everyone to get the measure of the stage, and everything went reasonably well and the cast were kind and encouraging, said they looked good and fitted in well, which was reassuring.

Then suddenly the show was upon them. They walked in at the back of the theatre on opening night, both as nervous as anything.

'I feel like a jellyfish,' Joy said. 'My arms and legs have gone all weak.'

'You're even worse than me,' Ivor commented as they headed for their separate changing rooms backstage. He seemed to have passed through his terror and doubt into a sort of state of calm unreality. Joy was still stuck at terror and doubt. 'You'll be really good – you always are.'

In the changing room, glowing from this compliment, she put on her favourite dance dress, a new white one that she had had made with a floaty skirt, tiny white beads sewn into the seams at her shoulders and waist, and gold sequins scattered over the whole dress. She put her make-up on and fastened her shoes, feeling excited and nervous in equal measure. It felt fantastic being here in the proper performers' changing room.

She sat for a moment, amid the bustle of the actors, waiting for the woman to come and do her hair. She did not know any of the other performers well, though some of them smiled and said hello. The hairdresser came and fixed her hair back into an elegant chignon.

Looking at her terrified face as she powdered her face one more time, her lips a bright cherry colour, hair beautifully arranged, Joy had a moment of complete unreality. This is me, here . . .

And then it was time to get on with it.

When the two of them walked onto the stage, they both experienced a moment of frozen terror. Joy could just make out the people in the front couple of rows, but the sea of faces behind them were all invisible, ahead of them in the shadows. All those people staring at them! But the moment the music started, it was as if they both stepped into the dream they already knew.

Joy swung about the stage in Ivor's arms. He, with his amazing gift of precision and rhythm, made her feel completely confident, and soon they relaxed into the dance. They could have been anywhere, the two of them together. It went well – she could feel it. It was a good start.

The last dance, and the climax to the show, was the happy, playful, triumphant jive. Joy and Ivor led it, but other cast members were dancing behind them. This was the moment when she really started enjoying herself. She and Ivor knew the dance backwards and they beamed at each other.

She even became aware that they were dancing in front of an audience, who cheered them enthusiastically as it ended, and she and Ivor flew off into the wings to enthusiastic applause, laughing, panting and hugging each other in amazement.

The rest of the cast followed them, dancing off the stage, laughing as well.

'We did it!' Ivor said, amazed, as they all waited for the curtain call. Clasped for a moment against his chest, Joy could feel his entire body pumping, just as hers was, from the effort.

'It went like a dream!' she said. She did not think she had ever felt so alive.

And then they were swept back on to the stage to take a bow.

The musical was playing for two weeks and the days passed quickly and successfully. On one of the nights Ann and Tom came to watch, bringing Patty, with Sheila and Kenneth and their children and Nanna Margaret. Len and Jeanette got tickets for a different night. Joy loved the whole thing – dancing her very best and knowing they were all out there, watching.

'I could get used to this,' Ivor joked.

As the last night approached, there was a rising feeling of triumph and enjoyment. They had done it. They had done it well – and they had loved it!

But that night, amid the songs and chorus lines, and after Lydia's poignant solo despairing that she would ever find love or a place in the world, when Joy and Ivor were to dance a waltz enacting Lydia's fantasy of how she longed for her life to be, Joy had a shock that almost knocked her right off her stride.

As she and Ivor stepped, hand-in-hand, on to the stage, a face seemed to jump out at her from the second row of the audience. She almost gasped. The lights were, of course, focused on her and Ivor as they positioned themselves to begin the dance, but in the split second as she looked round, she had seen *him*. Howard Fielding. She knew it was him. The long, thin shape of his head. The set of his shoulders. Him, again. Joy's heart started pounding.

Don't let him spoil everything, a voice seemed to say in her head. *Just shut him out. He's allowed to come to the theatre if he wants to. Forget him.*

She pulled herself together and, as usual in this first dance of the story, they were watched by the ring of cast members, the dance expressing the longing and togetherness of love for which Lydia longed, but which always seemed to elude her. Joy danced, concentrating on nothing but the steps, on herself and Ivor, feeling the crispness of his white shirt under her fingers, the swell of the music playing through her body, forcing her to be nowhere else but here.

As they left the stage she clutched at Ivor's arm.

'Ouch!' he protested, startled.

'Sorry.' She hadn't realized how hard she was digging her fingers in. She was trembling. They were in the back corridor, with other members of the cast pushing past, hurrying in both directions.

'Did you see him?' She still couldn't seem to let go of Ivor. 'He was right there, in the second row.' She looked into Ivor's baffled face. '*Howard.*'

'No,' Ivor said, bewildered. 'I'm not sure I'd even recognize him.'

She tried not to let it spoil the rest of the performance.

There were several encores, as it was the final night. And a wonderful feeling of celebration – the run had gone well and everyone was pleased.

The two of them stepped forward for their applause, holding hands, arms outstretched to give a graceful curtsey and bow. They beamed at each other. There were cheers and whistles. Ivor's face was alight with happiness and relief, and Joy was sure hers must look the same.

Once they were changed and the rest of the cast were hurrying away to celebrate, Ivor was waiting for her near the backstage door, as she had asked him to. Of course she wanted him to wait – this was the last night. Might they go somewhere and celebrate?

But there was also another reason. She was not stepping out into the dark street on her own – not with that screwball Howard hanging about. Thinking about him as she got changed, she felt the hairs on the back of her neck rising.

Why was Howard here? She had been trying to reason with herself: Howard liked dance; he had come to classes and was actually not a bad dancer. It was probably nothing at all to do with her. Except that she knew her name had been advertised on the bill outside, along with the main members of the cast.

Joy gathered up her things and went out to meet Ivor. As she did so, a gaggle of cast members came past on their way out, laughing and calling goodnight to them.

'You were fantastic, both of you!' one of the women said. 'You coming for a drink?'

But she was gone, without waiting for an answer. None of them knew each other well enough.

'It's all right,' Ivor said, before Joy had even said

anything else about Howard. 'Come on, let's go and check if the coast is clear.'

They stepped outside. Immediately Joy saw a movement to her right and a tall figure straightened up from leaning against the wall and came towards them. A feeling of horror spread through her. The tall, lanky figure, the long jaw, the top half of his face in shadow from the street light nearby, under a trilby . . . She tried to reason with herself. What was it about this man that gave her the shivers so much? But then, what had he been up to, outside their dance premises with a camera that day? As he came closer, her skin came up in goosepimples.

'Ah, my old dancing pals,' Howard said.

Joy clung to Ivor's arm.

'All right, mate?' Ivor said cautiously.

'Just came to say congratulations – you've come on a lot, I must say.' He laughed, a bit too much. 'Miss Gilby was excellent, as ever.'

He gave a little bow. Joy's mouth seemed to have seized up. She barely managed to whisper, 'Thank you.' Ivor said something similar. Then there was a long, awkward pause.

'Right,' Howard said. 'I assume you don't want escorting home, Miss Gilby?'

'We're all right, thanks,' Ivor said.

They waited for him to leave. Howard took his hat off, gave another of his courtly bows and walked away, soon disappearing round the corner.

'Oh my God,' Joy said. 'He doesn't half give me the willies, that one. If you hadn't been here . . .'

'Yeah, he's certainly an odd bloke,' Ivor agreed. 'For all he's been through the charm-school.'

'I'm glad you're catching the same bus,' Joy said. 'I don't trust him an inch.'

They walked on a little, with Joy still jumpy. Howard

did truly seem to have disappeared, but an awkward silence grew between herself and Ivor.

For Joy, it was full of feeling. As if the next thing she wanted was for Ivor to take her in his arms. As if that was simply what had to happen next, even though she knew it would not. She could never make out what Ivor felt. Sometimes, the way he looked at her . . . *But it is not very long since Phyllis died*, she kept telling herself. She had to stop thinking of Ivor in that way. But she did not know what he was feeling and could only ever guess.

'D'you fancy a quick drink?' she said, trying to lighten things up. Make it seem they were just friends – because that is what they were. 'To celebrate?'

Ivor hesitated, looked at her quickly, then away again. 'I'd better get back.'

'OK.' She tried not to let her disappointment show in her voice. She wanted Ivor to wish to spend time with her. 'Look, I just wanted to say – you've done a wonderful job. Congratulations. You're a really talented dancer. You never even hesitated.'

'Well . . .' The light was dim, but she could sense him blushing. 'I had the best teacher.' He looked round at her and she heard the warmth in his voice. 'It was good, wasn't it?'

They walked on a moment, then he stopped again and Ivor turned to face her. He seemed in a state.

'It's not that I don't . . .'

They were at the back of the station, with people coming and going, but Ivor seemed not to care, as if he could hold back no longer. He stepped towards Joy, pulled her close and they were kissing, both strongly and passionately as if they had been waiting for a long time and now there was no hesitation. Joy held him close, feeling the weave of his coat, his warm lips on hers. I love him, was all she could think, full of happiness. She already knew that, but now, raising her hand to stroke his neck tenderly, it was all so obvious and she began to relax into it. She had loved him for a long time now, and it was good, *he* was good . . .

Then he pulled away and suddenly it was terrible again and full of pain.

'Oh God . . .' He started to move away. 'I can't. I'm so sorry, Joy, I just can't. I like you, so much – more than like you. But . . .' He was stumbling over his words. 'I still feel as if I'm married to Phyllis.' He stood at a distance and, even in the gloom, she could sense the upset, haunted state of him. 'It feels as if she's watching everything I'm doing. I'm sorry. So sorry . . .'

They had to sit on the bus, side by side, in silence, all the way to her stop in Selly Oak. Joy would walk home along Linden Road; it would give her time to recover. Her chest was hurting, as if she had been hit, physically. Her heart felt bruised and battered. As she got off, she patted his shoulder. He could not even look up.

'Thanks, Ivor. See you.'

IV

1955–6

Forty-Seven

Summer 1955

'Ooh – very classy!'

Kay, with Sandra on her hip, joined Joy outside the studio where their new sign was being fixed across the building: 'GILBY AND TARRANT DANCE ACADEMY' in swirling black-edged gold letters on a grape-red background. Kay had said she was damn well not renaming her dance school 'GILBY AND BOTTOMS' and, anyway, Joy was using her maiden name.

'Looks better, doesn't it?' Joy squinted up at it, shielding her eyes from the morning sun. 'And it does look classier than the last one.'

They had had a sign painted when they first opened – green and white – and Joy had never liked it. This one did look classy, an image they were promoting as much as possible. Their dance lessons for children were crowded now, and they had laid on extra ones for ballet and tap. And the adult classes were a big success as well.

With all this going on, Joy had finally taken the leap of giving up her part-time job at Cadbury's. The business – hers and Kay's – was her work and her income now, and she was going to throw everything into it. Invitations were also coming thick and fast, for both of them. Kay did not feel in a position to take on much extra yet, with

Sandra still so young, but she had done some modelling for Faulk's, the fur shop: fur coats and jewellery.

'You look like a film star!' Joy had laughed, seeing pictures of Kay, her head turned slightly, laughingly, back over her shoulder and the collar of a luxurious fur coat. 'Like Leslie Caron, only with red hair!'

'Not red – auburn,' Kay corrected her and Joy laughed. Kay, tall, striking and vivacious, was perfect for modelling.

'You could do it as well,' Kay said.

'Oh no,' Joy said. 'That's not me, really.'

They were talking about the latest invitations as they went up to the studio that morning. Joy was already up to her eyes with work and worried about taking advantage of her mother and Tom too much. She had already felt she must turn down some of the demonstrations and performances and the judging of dance competitions.

'I'll stick to the dance invites,' she said on the stairs. 'I'd never be at home or see Patty otherwise! Just as well I'll probably never have any more kids.'

'Oh, you never know,' Kay said from behind her, holding Sandra.

'It does tend to take two,' Joy joked, though there was a melancholy edge to her voice.

'Well, I'm not having any more.'

Kay had decided this, almost from the minute Sandra was born. Not that she didn't adore the little girl, now nearly two, with the same carrot top, vivid blue eyes and vibrant personality as Kay. 'I want my life back, thanks very much.'

They had brought a playpen into the studio so that if Sandra was there, instead of with Kay's mom, they could teach more or less in peace. And Sandra seemed to love being there during the children's classes, watching and cooing and squeaking at them, and they all played with her and talked to her whenever they got the chance.

'You, though,' Kay added, rather breathless as they reached the top of the stairs, 'are just being dense. Anyone can see Ivor's head over heels in love with you.'

'Oh,' Joy said, trying to make light of it. 'I've had more than enough man-trouble without him messing me about.'

But she went into the office with Kay's words piercing her. All these months she had forced her feelings towards Ivor down inside herself. He had made himself clear – or as clear as he could manage. She was not going to risk feeling love again and all the pain that went with being rejected. She had fought hard to tell herself to forget him, at least in that way. Ivor was a friend, a dancing partner, that was all.

Well, she thought, if he is in love with me, he'll have to be the one who flipping well does something about it.

After that last night of the performance at the Alex, nearly a year and a half ago now, Ivor had stayed away from the adult dance classes for several weeks. Joy had thought that was it – that she would never see him again. There was nothing she could do; she could hardly go and beg him to come back. But it was very upsetting. Ivor was so talented.

More than anything, she missed his company. As a friend. All right, she was in love with him, and that was something she was going to have to deal with. But Ivor was a friend, that was what really came home to her during those weeks.

And he did come back. One summer day he suddenly appeared again. When Joy saw him walk in, her heart started hammering so hard she had to fight to behave normally with him in front of the other dancers.

'Hello, Ivor,' she said, managing to sound as if he was just another class member. 'Nice to see you back.' It was at this point, though, that she realized Ivor had come on his own. She was not going to be able to avoid dancing with him again.

So instead of keeping her distance, as she had hoped to, she was thrown straight back into being with him in a way that could only be described as intimate – with their arms round each other.

He didn't say anything during the class. He concentrated hard, as he was a little out of practice, but being Ivor, he was soon back in the swing of all the steps. Joy confined anything that she said to the matter in hand. But he came up to her at the end, looking hesitant and worried.

'Is it all right – me being back here?'

'Yes.' She knew her voice sounded cool and she did not like herself for it. It was not how she felt, but she had to protect herself. She had pulled up the shutters, was trying to speak to him as she might have to anybody. 'Course. Why not?'

'Right. OK then. Good. See you next week, Joy.'

He looked a bit . . . what? she thought as he walked away. Hurt? Taken aback? What was he expecting?

It wasn't that she didn't understand that he was still in love with his dead wife. Having met Phyllis, she could see what a loveable woman she had been. But there was nothing she could do about that, was there? She needed to keep her distance.

Gradually, as more invitations arrived, Joy softened her stance. She just could not help it.

She and Ivor went and demonstrated ballroom steps at the Tower Ballroom, the Casino. They were invited to the Austin, to lead the dancing at a big social at the works, and they held tea dances at Rowheath for Cadbury workers. Now that rationing had finally ended last year, the city was booming and everyone wanted a good time – whether it was sitting in coffee bars in town, listening to rock-and-roll or going out dancing.

Even though Joy had given up her job at the works, Sheila was back there now, and Joy and Kay's Academy was becoming well known. Quite a few of the kids in the classes were the children of Cadbury workers, and Joy and Kay often found themselves presented with chocolates from the misshapes shop or bags of broken biscuits.

'We thought you might be missing your rations!' they'd joke.

And the invitations kept coming. Everyone commented on how good Joy and Ivor were as dance partners. At first Joy would go along to wherever they were invited, do whatever was asked of them and then make sure that she and Ivor had no chance to spend time together afterwards – for her own protection.

'I need to get home. Mom's got Patty, and she needs to go out.' Or, 'I'm very tired – need an early night.'

Ivor never argued. Maybe he was relieved, Joy thought. And so it had gone on for the whole of last year. Then an unusual invitation arrived.

'It's from a miners' club – in Yorkshire.' Joy frowned at the letter. 'They want us to come up and teach them to dance.' She looked round at Kay. 'You'd think they could find someone closer to home, wouldn't you?'

Kay smiled. 'It shows you're getting to be a well-known demonstrator. I mean, you can do the lot – like Arthur Murray.'

She did a jokey curtsey, as if Joy were royalty. American Arthur Murray was well known for his television dance programme, *The Arthur Murray Party*.

'That's a nice invitation,' Kay encouraged her. 'You should go.'

Joy hesitated.

'With Ivor,' Kay said meaningfully.

The first miners' tea dance was something Joy would never forget – not least because they had had so many invitations to come back. And because she and Ivor had to travel up to Barnsley together by train.

They found themselves in a hall where eager couples welcomed them with overwhelming warmth. Amid the steam from the tea urn and the inviting smell of sand-wiches and cakes, she and Ivor demonstrated steps to begin with. Everyone was so nice and so enthusiastic that Joy quickly began to relax, and she and Ivor started to enjoy themselves.

They taught the couples new dance steps, encouraged everyone to join in and generally have a jolly afternoon.

'That were right nice,' the ladies said to them as they left. 'I've enjoyed myself – are you coming back? You'd better be, lass; we've only just got started!'

To Joy's amazement, they were gifted with a silver cig-arette case, and agreed that yes, they were coming back. Of course they were. And in the end they would be coming back to quite a number of miners' tea dances as the word spread.

That evening as they left Barnsley, the two of them had to tear along the platform and just managed almost to fall into their seats before the train set off. Getting their breath back, they looked at each other, laughing.

'Well, that wasn't what I was expecting!' Ivor said.

'What lovely people,' Joy replied. Everyone had been so welcoming that she had felt almost tearful. And it had made her feel useful as well. Their travelling all the way up there had meant so much to these warm, hard-working people – and if there was one thing she loved, it was teaching people to dance.

It was the beginning of things starting to relax between herself and Ivor. They sat back, going over the events of the afternoon they had shared, discussing things coming up in the next few weeks. There they sat, side by side, with Ivor's muscular legs in his black trousers, the dark grey sleeve of his jacket, that strong hand resting on his thigh, his kindly face turned to her, laughing every now and then. Everything about him was so familiar now.

And Joy realized after a time that she had managed to sit chatting without feeling tense and rejected by him. They were both there after sharing the afternoon, talking and laughing like old friends.

And, she thought afterwards, on her way back to Bournville, she really was probably better off without a man in her life – like that. And what a precious thing it was to have a friend with whom she could share so many things.

Forty-Eight

'Joy's in tonight, for once – shall we go out for a bit?'

Ann stood in the doorway talking to Tom, who was weeding in the garden in the summer evening. He straightened up.

'Why not? Where d'you fancy going?'

'Oh, nowhere in particular. It's a lovely evening. Shall we walk down to Rowheath, after tea?'

It had been a beautiful, golden July day and they strolled arm-in-arm down the road in the low-angled sunlight and into the green space, where other couples were scattered across the lawn and around the little lake. The whole place had finally been returned to playing fields now, though parts of it had gone on being farmed for some time since the war.

They settled on a sunny patch of grass near the trees by the lake. Children were playing, running about happily in the evening sun, and cigarette smoke and laughter drifted over to them. Ann smiled.

'Reminds me of when our lot were that sort of age.'

Tom returned her smile. 'Nice to have this.' A sadness crossed his features for a second. He had missed all of Martin's childhood. After a pause he added, 'They seem to be sorting themselves out all right now, don't they?'

He knew how much of the last few years Ann had spent worrying about her children. Joy's heartbreaking experience with Alan; Sheila and Kenneth trying to get used to each other again; and Martin being away so long. She sighed. That was what mothers did, she thought: worry. But she tried to make light of it all.

'I s'pose everyone does in the end – or not!'

They both laughed.

Tom narrowed his eyes suddenly, looking over Ann's shoulder. 'Is that . . .' He nodded in the direction in which he was looking, and Ann turned. At a distance, sitting on the grass, she saw Len and Jeanette. It felt strangely shocking seeing them there.

'I wonder why they're over here? It's a bit of a way to come from Kings Heath of an evening. Old times' sake, I suppose.'

'We ought to go and say hello,' Tom replied.

Ann was surprised. They could have stayed where they were, but of course it would be better to be friendly. 'Well, if you like.'

Tom jumped up and helped Ann to her feet. As they walked over, Ann saw Len catch sight of her. He looked away for a moment as if unsure how to react, then looked back. Jeanette glanced round and smiled.

'Hello, you two.' Her eyes met Ann's. She seemed to have completely got over whatever was biting her in the backside before, Ann thought. 'Come and sit with us for a bit?'

Ann and Tom hesitated for a second, before settling on the grass beside them. Ann and Jeanette had made up from their bad feeling some time ago, but things still felt a bit awkward. If Len and Jeanette had not moved away, it would have been easier to see Jeanette more, break the ice properly. But at least now, after all this time, it had become possible for the four of them to have a polite, if stiff conversation for a while. All of them were content with where they were. Len and Tom could get along; past hurts and resentments were finally fading.

'Kids all right?' Len asked. 'No news is good news, I s'pose?'

'Yes, they're all doing OK,' Ann said. She knew that none of them went to see Len and Jeanette often, but it was more because of the busyness of life than any hard feelings. 'I didn't expect to see you two over here.'

'Oh, I'm back doing some shifts at the works now,' Jeanette said. She looked happy, Ann realized. 'I can get round easily on the Outer Circle, and I missed the company. Len and I are saving up for a nice holiday. He deserves a good break.'

Ann was not certain if this was said with an edge of some jealous emotion – *I* look after my husband – but she did not want to dwell on it or choose to read anything bad into it.

'Oh, good for you,' she said.

'Well, now I'm back over here quite a bit, I could pop in for a cuppa – after work maybe?' Jeanette suggested. Ann could hear her hesitation. Would she be welcome?

'Course you can,' Ann replied, the warmth that she felt as a sudden inward rush also coming out in her voice. 'That'd be lovely – like old times.'

Jeanette looked her directly in the eyes and smiled. 'I'd like that. Thanks, Annie.'

There was a silence between them for a moment in which they took in that Len and Tom were discussing something about a piece of machinery at the works. The women rolled their eyes at each other and smiled. Things were all right; they could relax. It felt nice, Ann thought. They went back a good way now, she and Jeanette.

'I suppose you know Sheila and Kenneth bought a caravan?' Ann commented. 'They go off all over the place – Scotland this summer, they said. Sheila's back at the works now, so you might see her around. She seems to save up her wages for them to have holidays as well; she's getting quite adventurous!'

They exchanged a bit of chat about the works, and Cadbury girls whom Jeanette had caught up with and they knew in common. Len and Tom were talking about sport now, Ann realized; although Tom could not participate in all sports, he was a keen spectator. She moved closer to Jeanette.

'Any news of Marianne?'

As the cross that each of them had had to bear in their marriage to Len, this was something they could now sympathize with each other about.

'She leaves us alone mostly, now she's remarried. They're in Nottingham still.'

'And George? I s'pose he must be leaving school?' Like Elaine, George was fifteen now. 'Elaine's just finished at Dame-o's,' – the nickname the children gave to Dame Elizabeth Cadbury School in Bournville. 'She wants to go on to learn shorthand and typing.'

'George doesn't seem very sure.' Jeanette sighed, seemingly impatient. 'He's a sleepy sod, that one. I think he's going to look for some sort of apprenticeship. Maybe at Raleigh, the bike place.'

'Oh well, good for him,' Ann said.

They chatted for a while as the sun sank lower and Ann started to realize she was getting cold.

'Best be off,' she said to Tom. All four of them got to their feet. 'Drop in when you like, Jeanette? I'm mostly in.'

'Let's have a walk round before we go, shall we?' Ann suggested, when they had said their goodbyes. She watched as Len and Jeanette walked off, arm-in-arm. Len now felt like someone from so long ago that it was strange. And all she could feel was glad – that he seemed to be happy.

They strolled round the lake. A few ducks and geese glided lazily across the surface and one or two men sat fishing silently.

'I was asking Jeanette about George,' Ann said. 'Funny that he's so sort of placid, when you think what Marianne's like. Born survivor, that one.'

'Sounds as if she needed to be,' Tom commented. Ann glanced at him fondly. That was Tom: always slow to condemn.

'Jeanette was a proper madam.' She thought for a moment. 'In some ways, though, I can't help admiring her.'

They walked on, close together, in comfortable silence. But something kept nagging at Ann's mind. As ever, her thoughts strayed back to her children.

'It'd be nice if all our lot could get settled,' she said. 'Poor Joy – after all she's had happen. She works herself into the ground, and there never seems to be anyone for her. And when's Martin going to bring someone home?' She nudged Tom, half joking. 'Give you a grandchild, eh? It'd be nice to see him settled.'

There was a pause as they walked, then Tom said quietly, 'Don't you think he is? Settled?'

'What, living in a bedsit? And he never has girlfriends. He seems to spend all his time knocking about with that Simon lad – just like—'

She had been about to say, *Just like he spent all his time with Jack, that artist person he was in the mines with, who we never even met . . .*

Tom kept quiet and Ann frowned up at him. Only gradually, as Tom looked directly into her eyes, did she even begin to get an inkling of what he was trying to say.

'What? But . . .' It was as if a whirlwind was blowing in her mind. What did Tom mean? Surely not that Martin

368

was one of those . . . No. Not that – that was ridiculous. 'What d'you mean?'

'Just that . . .' Tom was struggling for words. In the end he settled for saying, 'Martin seems – happy. And settled. As he is. That's all.'

She laughed it off. 'Well, I'm sure he'll sort himself out sometime or other. They did lose a lot of time because of the war – I mean, he hardly ever met any women. But he is knocking on thirty. He'd better not hang about too long.'

Tom looked tenderly at her. He put his arm round her shoulders and they strolled on in the warm dusk.

A few weeks later Martin and Simon sat sprawled on a warm, flat rock, looking out from the top of Helvellyn in the Lake District. They had eaten the sandwiches and apples they had brought, and were full of well-being from the climb and contentment in each other's company. Their strong legs were stretched out in front, both having caught the sun, both in shorts and stout hiking boots.

'This is the life,' Martin said, unscrewing the top of his Thermos and swigging coffee from it. 'I love being able to get up high like this. Maybe we should just keep walking – see where we get to.'

'The edge of the world.' Simon lay back, eyes closed in the sun. 'Or maybe Glasgow, at any rate.'

Martin laughed. 'I'm not sure which would be worse.'

Simon sat up again and they both stared out at the view, high now, as if they were looking out at a relief map of the land rising and falling, dotted with shining eyes of water in the lakeland landscape.

They sat shoulder-to-shoulder, looking out, breathing in the fresh breeze. Below them, hovering and dipping, a buzzard hung in the air, beautiful, solitary.

Heaven, Martin thought again. All this – and him. A whole week of just the two of them, walking, staying in youth hostels. Finding isolated spots deep in the countryside where for short periods they could be themselves, kiss out in the open, throw their arms round each other. Freedom!

The two of them had settled into this relationship that, for the moment, it seemed was the most they could have. Simon still lived with his mother, Martin in his bedsit. Everything about their being together had to be careful and discreet. But it was lasting. Solid and strong. They visited each other's families, acted like good pals, hoped no one suspected. Or, in Martin's case at least, sometimes hoped they did. Hoped a little.

But their love – as it was vital, for their own safety, to keep reminding themselves – was wrong in everyone's eyes. It was illegal. Deemed filthy, perverse, although they knew otherwise, and sometimes Martin ached to tell people so – to be able to live without hiding. Thinking about it now, with Mom going on about girls and weddings and grandchildren, he felt like crying. Or punching something. Why did it have to be like this? Why did he? At other times it felt adventurous – their bold, secret love; he and Simon against the world and its sad, narrow ways of thinking.

He looked round at Simon and felt the same surge of affection, or rightness, of passion that had grown in him since they first met.

Because it was a weekday, there were not many people around. Martin looked carefully behind them and to each side: there was no one. He leaned round and kissed Simon on the lips. They did not linger. A quick kiss, just in case. Then both of them looked nervously round again.

'I suppose it's always going to be like this,' Martin said, holding Simon's gaze.

Simon stroked his hand up Martin's back for a second. 'Yeah, I suppose it is.' A moment later he added, 'I hope so.'

Forty-Nine

The Tower Ballroom was packed with couples, all in their best dance outfits, standing expectantly round the edge.

'Now,' the compère announced, 'we are going to have a demonstration of the steps for the jive.'

'Let's have the jitterbug,' someone called out. 'Go on!'

'Well, perhaps that will be next. But for the moment, the jive – danced by our local dance experts, instructor Miss Joy Gilby and her partner, Mr Ivor Williams.'

Joy took the microphone, smiling as the crowd clapped. She had made a new dress out of a golden-yellow rayon, with a lovely full skirt, and she knew it looked good with her dark hair and eyes. She beamed round the room.

'Right, I'm sure a lot of you know these steps already, but for those who don't . . . The girl leads with her left foot, the man with his right – there are four beats to the bar.'

She explained the basics of the dance as Ivor stood smiling beside her. He had bought a new suit for dancing in and looked very handsome, with his upright figure and vivid blue eyes.

'So we will now demonstrate . . .'

She handed the microphone back, and she and Ivor took up their dance position as the music started.

'You see,' she called out loudly, 'one, two, three and four.'

Once again she was in Ivor's arms and they danced together in the smooth, almost clockwork manner they had developed over the months – in perfect time with each other. When they finished their brief demonstration, the waiting dancers clapped. Joy stood back, so that the couples could all take their places on the dance floor. She guided them, taking the microphone once again to call out the time and the steps.

They progressed through the jive, with some couples almost expert, others stumbling to remember the steps. As they all danced, Joy remembered, slightly uneasily, the request for the jitterbug.

It wasn't that they could not do it. She and Ivor had learned pretty much any dance that came along. It was simply that there was something about the jitterbug. They did not perform it often – a lot of dance groups wanted to master more sedate waltzes and foxtrots. The jitterbug was fast and raw, and for some reason she felt nervous. She looked at Ivor.

'OK to do it?'

He curved up the right side of his lips in a way that said, *Well, it's a challenge.*

'All right,' she said, with her professional smile. 'Is the band ready for this?'

And off they went – the fast-stepping, stomping, whirling jitterbug, Joy, held by Ivor, was slipping along the floor between his legs one moment, jumping high, her legs around his waist the next. It was invigorating, exhausting, with the lights seeming to whirl round her head as she danced; and, once again, it felt as if she and Ivor were in a world of their own. They were fast and sure. They were good. They knew it, could feel it. At times their eyes met. It was magical, like flying.

As they finished, the room exploded into applause and wolf whistles.

'Come on – ask her to marry you!' a cheeky lad's voice hollered from the crowd, and everyone cheered.

As Joy and Ivor, red-cheeked, both breathing heavily, took a bow, she knew she could not look him in the eyes, not straight after that.

They were rescued by the general chaos of trying to teach the dance to everyone else, a young, energetic group, all eager to learn.

After it was over, they stepped out into the night, feeling the air cool on their cheeks, seeing the moon almost full between the branches of trees circling the reservoir close by. The other couples went off, and they could hear a lot of chat and shrieks of laughter in the darkness. Joy stood looking out at the moon's face reflected like a spotlight in the water.

Everything about that night already felt electric. The dance, the bright silvery atmosphere outside. They really needed to get going. To find their way to their bus stops, to get home, be fresh for work in the morning, for looking after their little girls. The last of the other dancers had left and they were locking up the building.

'Best get going then,' Joy said briskly, pulling her bag onto her shoulder.

Ivor didn't say anything. He just stood for a moment, looking out over the reservoir. She was about to speak again when he said, 'Shall we have a walk round – before we go? It's a lovely night.' He turned to her. 'Your bag'll be all right there, if you put it down.'

Joy hesitated. Her emotions were already near the surface and she did not want to be played with. She almost said something to that effect, but bit back the words because they felt unkind. Ivor was not someone who ever deliberately set out to hurt her. That was not what had happened. But she did feel she had to protect herself.

She hesitated, then nodded and placed her bag down by the wall.

Slowly they walked side by side round the reservoir, now restored to its normal size. It had been drained during the war, as its reflective surface acted like a beacon for German bombers flying over the city. The water was high and still, cradling the moon's silver image on its surface.

For a few moments the only sound was the gentle fall of their footsteps on the earthen path.

'That went well, I thought?' Joy said, trying to break through the atmosphere, which felt intense, as if something, which she both wanted and did not want, was about to happen. Ivor didn't say anything and the tension grew even greater.

He must have realized that not answering her might seem rude and strange. Eventually the words seemed to burst out of him.

'Joy – stop a minute, will you?'

She did as he asked. They were on the far side of the reservoir, away from the ballroom's entrance. She heard a little sound, perhaps a moorhen in the water.

'I . . .' Ivor ground to a halt, then forced himself forward again. 'I'm just going to say it, all right? I don't know what you feel about me, now. There was a time, but I know I wasn't ready. And it must have felt as if . . . felt as if I was messing you about. It was bad of me. But it was too soon. The way Phyllis died, it was such a shock, and I couldn't . . .'

He stopped and shook his head, half turning away. He sounded very emotional.

Joy waited. She realized she had to remind herself to breathe. Because however much, and for however long, she had told herself not to have feelings for Ivor, to refuse them to herself, at this moment she wanted him to say the words that she had longed to hear coming from his lips for so long. Words that she already knew she wanted to respond to with all her heart.

'I didn't behave very well to you back then,' he went on. 'I was so . . . confused. And I missed Phyllis. Terribly. I just wanted her back. I couldn't get past her, and part of me wanted you to replace her, to stop that feeling . . . I'm sorry. It was selfish and wrong. But I couldn't seem to help it.'

He reached out for her hand. After hesitating, Joy took it, feeling the strong warmth of it closing around her own almost like a shock. Ivor gently tugged and they both started walking again, which seemed to make it easier to talk.

'But you . . .' He stopped again, trying to choose his words carefully. 'You are so beautiful, so special. I've been in love with you for ages, Joy. You must know that. Sometimes when you look at me, when we're dancing, it's all I can do to hold back. But I wanted to be so careful, not get it wrong and then regret it. And hurt you again. Because now, I'm not sure if what I'm saying means anything to you. Whether you could possibly . . . Whether you feel—'

This time it was her turn to take Ivor's hand and stop him, gently pull him round to face her.

'I do,' she said, moving closer to him in the darkness. And once again they were in each other's arms, as they had been so often in the dance. She felt his familiar shape, his smell. She knew the feel of him so well by now that he felt like home.

'I do,' she said, reaching up to kiss him. 'My dear love.'

Fifty

June 1956

'Well, the mother of the bride is supposed to have a little weep,' Ann defended herself, half-jokingly, as Martin put his arm round her shoulders and gave her a fond squeeze.

They had all just come pouring out of St Francis's church, the organ still blasting out inside.

She looked across at Joy and Ivor, both now sprinkled with confetti, talking and laughing happily. Joy wore a long, beautiful ivory-coloured dress and Ivor was in his smart suit. They looked such a handsome pair.

'Wasn't that lovely?' And tears ran down her cheeks all over again.

'Oh, Mom,' Martin said fondly.

Ann had almost wished she was not seated at the front of the church. Sheila and Kenneth and Martin were all behind her, and she would have liked to be able to see them all at once, take in her whole family, gathered here together.

But of course she and Tom and Jeanette were all in the front row. Len was waiting nervously at the church door.

To her surprise, she saw a young man she did not at once recognize arrive with Jeanette. It took her a few moments to work out that he was George, Len's son with Marianne. George, all grown-up! He would be sixteen now, like Elaine. For a second she felt angry that he was here. But, she reasoned with herself, George must have said that he wanted to be – and in the end, he was related to all her children. How else was the poor lad going to have any family? Marianne had turned her back on all of hers.

Ann had kept turning round as they all came in. Sheila walked slowly down the aisle supporting Margaret on her arm, who was hunched over and beaming from underneath the wide brim of her hat. Ann's mother-in-law – that was still how she thought of Margaret – was eighty-eight now. She was altogether smaller and stooped, but still impressively spry and very definitely all there.

'It's living with all these young 'uns – keeps me on my toes,' she would say. 'And Sheila looks after me. She's a good 'un.'

Margaret searched Ann out as they advanced slowly amid the sound of the organ, and the two of them exchanged a knowing smile. *Finally*, the happy smile said, *after all she's been through, things have come good for Joy.*

Ann turned to face the front, already close to tears. She knew Margaret had, naturally, had strong reservations about Tom when that truth had erupted into her life. Len was her son, after all, and she had seen him suffer. Not to mention her own views on how things should be. All of those had taken a severe battering over the years, what with her sister Ida turning up like that and the sheer sadness and betrayal contained in her story. And then all the troubles that had gone on in Margaret's own family.

But Margaret was a straightforward, fair-minded woman. She had never been slow to let them know her views, but she had been won over by the sheer goodness of Tom, as well as by being able to see what this long-enduring situation had cost him. He had held back for years, waited loyally without ever interfering in the family. Margaret respected him. In the end, she had been able to rise above judgement and not take sides. She did her best just to love everyone, and they loved her.

Ann had welled up, thinking about this as she saw Margaret come in. Tom noticed that she was getting emotional and took hold of her hand and gave it a squeeze. Ann gave him a grateful and slightly watery smile in return.

She had to pull herself together, as she noticed Ivor's parents coming down to sit on the opposite side of the aisle. She had only met Sylvia and Dai Williams a couple of times, but she had liked them. Dai, a Welshman, was short and solid in build, with a bow-window tummy and a wide, friendly smile. Sylvia, Birmingham-born, was as tiny as a little bird, with dark hair and a quick smile.

Nice people, Ann thought. Joy would be all right there. And they had accepted Joy and the fact that she already had a child. Both of them were widowed, after all. And Ivor had a daughter too, a dear little thing.

Just then Ivor, all smart in his suit, his thick hair – like his father's, Ann realized – freshly cut for the day, hurried down the aisle. He gave his mother a peck on the cheek, shook his father's hand and gave Ann a smile, before going to the altar steps, where he stood looking nervously back towards the door.

As the wedding march started up, she turned to see Joy, on Len's arm, appear in the doorway. Joy had decided not to wear a long white dress and veil. 'After all, I'm hardly a virgin bride, am I?' she had said.

She had made the dress, with its swinging skirt, lined lacy bodice and stylishly capped sleeves, herself. Cream was in any case a shade that flattered Joy's dark hair and eyes, and it was obviously going to come in very handy as a dance dress afterwards.

Ann started to well up again. There was Len, uncomfortable being in the limelight, but proud as punch, and

Joy, her eyes dancing with happiness and a glow to her cheeks. She was so beautiful, Ann thought.

And then, as everyone saw who was walking behind her, there was a long, collective 'Aaah.'

Elaine, sixteen, and Patty, eleven, both in pretty yellow dresses, were both holding hands with little Glenys, who was now five and in a matching frock that covered her feet and made it look as if she was gliding along on wheels. Elaine was becoming quite a young lady now – blonde, like Kenneth, steady, sensible and mature for her age. Patty beamed round at everyone, her brown hair up in a little ponytail, and Glenys had little bunches sticking out on each side of her head.

Behind them, looking very serious in dark trousers and white shirts, walked Robbie and Jonny, Sheila's boys.

Joy and Len reached the altar and Len retreated to his seat beside Jeanette. Joy and Ivor gave one another adoring smiles as they took each other's hands. The lump in Ann's throat swelled. This was so lovely, so much what she had hoped for her little girl.

And then the organ struck up with 'Praise, My Soul, the King of Heaven' and, as she stood up, Ann was off. Tears poured down her cheeks. She just couldn't help it.

The next day Joy and Ivor sat on the train as it moved out of New Street station. Ivor had his arms wrapped around her, and Joy leaned into him, as happy as she had ever been. She was wearing a new full-skirted pale-blue dress and white cardigan. Their suitcases were stashed on the luggage rack.

Nearly a whole week they were going to spend together, off work, in a little guesthouse on the South Devon coast. It felt like utter bliss. Kay had said she would take over the running of the school for a week, and Joy had to hope that she would manage. Mom was having Patty; and Sylvia, Joy's new mother-in-law, was looking after Glenys. It felt like an incredible amount of freedom.

'That was so lovely,' Joy said dreamily. 'Just having everyone together like that.'

'It was perfect.' Ivor kissed the top of her head.

Joy laid a hand on his thigh. This lovely, loving man that she had come to know. More right – somehow more inevitably the right person, she knew now – than any of the other men she had known in her life.

The previous afternoon had passed in a dream: the church service, and then they had all gone to Rowheath for the wedding party. The adults sat eating and drinking on the terrace, and there was a sun-drenched lawn for the children when they got fed up with the grown-up talk.

They had all watched, amused, as George – at first very shy and stiff – unbent in the company of Elaine. In terms of the family, George was her uncle, despite them being only days apart in age. But in terms of who was in command of the situation, it was definitely Elaine. She was used to being the oldest and telling the others what to do, and George was soon being marshalled about – 'Right, you go and stand over there' – and seemed to love every moment of it. They played ball games and tag, and soon George was laughing and throwing himself around with the rest of them.

Being with her family, Sylvia and the kids, and having Martin back, looking happy with himself, and her new family, Ivor's parents and aunts and uncles, and them all being there with time to sit and talk and laugh – all that had been bliss. And now, on top of that, she had a week to spend, solely with Ivor, her love, at the seaside.

After they had been travelling for a while Joy dozed, worn out from all the excitement. But she was quickly woken by an exclamation from Ivor.

'Oh, my word!'

Joy raised her head muzzily. 'What's the matter?'

Ivor had opened the newspaper he had bought at the station and was now staring at it in horror.

'Sorry I woke you up, love. But look . . .'

Joy sat up and peered at a grainy photo in the paper. A long, thin face. Before her mind had even made sense of what this was about, her heart had begun to bang in instinctive alarm.

'Dear God, to think he was following you about . . .' Ivor was well ahead of her.

She pieced together the words: ARRESTED FOR MURDER. *Howard Fielding, resident of Northfield. Murder of a Maureen Roper, 28, who had worked in Grey's depart-ment store. Had been cautioned for persistently harassing her* . . . Joy's eyes raced through the text: *Obsessive nature. Fixated on women. Dangerous. Home searched. Cache of photographs of other local women* . . .

A sick, terrible feeling filled her. The sinister, black horror of it. She could feel herself go all shaky, a sick dread twisting in her stomach. Howard! Those keenly staring eyes. That face. That day Kay had seen him outside – with a camera. Taking pictures of their studio. Did he have pic-tures of her hidden away in his vile rooms?

'So I was right,' she breathed. 'I always knew there was something . . . He was just horrible. Worse than horrible.'

She looked up at Ivor. She didn't have to say any more. It could have been her. So easily.

'It's all right, my love. They've got him. He won't be doing anyone any harm from now on.'

But the way he suddenly held her so tightly, she knew

382

he was thinking the same: how close she had come. How poor Maureen Roper had not managed to escape the distorted darkness that Joy had sensed in Howard.

'Thank God,' she said, her arms tightly around this miracle of a husband at her side.

'When we get off this train,' Ivor said, 'I'm going to take a match to that newspaper – and to him. He's gone: he can't hurt you. And we are going to enjoy our honeymoon, my love.'

She looked up, smiling into his eyes. 'Yes. Of course we are.'

Fifty-One

August 1956

'Mind how you go!'

'Don't eat too many snails!'

Ann stood with Margaret outside her house in Beaumont Road, waving as Sheila and Kenneth finally took to the road. The caravan, on its site near Redditch, was waiting for them to go and hitch it up and be on their way to their new adventures.

Sheila had spent the last couple of weeks, when she was not at work, getting all prepared. She'd packed up the family's clothes, gathered supplies: tea, sugar, flour, tins of this and that, games for the children, bedding . . . They had a set of picnic cutlery and melamine plates and cups that would not get broken, and various airtight tins and boxes for keeping supplies in. Most evenings they had driven out to the site to deliver more items for the journey awaiting them.

Sheila wound down the window and waved happily from the passenger seat, holding up her own and Kenneth's dark-blue passports – Sheila was proud to be the first person in the family ever to have one. The three children were all squeezed in the back.

'We're catching the ferry tomorrow and heading to Boulogne, and then we're going to stay at campsites in France,' she had told them all excitedly. 'We're going to try

384

it out. Kenneth wants to get all the way to Italy one day, but we thought we'd try France first and see how it goes.'

Kenneth started the engine.

'Bye, Mom. Bye, Nanna!'

'Have a lovely time,' Ann said. 'Be careful, won't you?'

Sheila grinned. 'Aren't I always?'

'Bye!' Kenneth leaned over to say. He looked all lit up as well. He loved getting away on a journey. The kids all called out their farewells and the Austin drew away and off towards Linden Road.

'Well,' Margaret said, amused, 'that's not something I'd have predicted a few years ago, would you?'

'No,' Ann laughed. 'Sheila seems to be getting quite a taste for it.'

'At least they've got that extra awning to put up at the side,' Margaret said. 'They'd be like wasps in a bottle, else.'

'Yes,' Ann replied as she and Margaret walked slowly along to her own house. Margaret was going to stay with them, to be looked after for the fortnight that Sheila and Kenneth were away. 'Rather them than me. But good luck to them.'

That afternoon Ann left Margaret resting at home. Tom was at work and the street outside was quiet. It was a sultry, close day, mostly sunny.

So much had happened lately that Ann felt the need to catch up with herself. With a cardigan thrown round her shoulders, she wandered slowly to the end of the road and up Bournville Lane to the Valley Pool. It was high summer and the grass was dotted with mothers and children picnicking. Clusters of kids stood round the shallow pool, feeding the ducks or floating little boats on the surface.

Ann found a spot to sit down on the slight rise further up from the pool, looking across at the new Dame

Elizabeth Cadbury school that Elaine had gone to, and where Patty would be starting too, after the holidays. She watched the shifting movement of children.

This place held so many memories. So many times she had brought Sheila and Joy and Martin here, when they were little ones. She smiled, images flashing through her mind of all of them, their little backsides padded out with napkins; running about playing when they were older, ice-cream on their faces; sitting with a picnic of sandwiches and crisps and beakers of squash. Her kids.

Her mind flowed over her life. Len. Tom. Things to be ashamed of and things to be proud of and, either way, she could not undo them now. But at least for the moment life was going well for her children, whatever she had or had not done in the past. Seeing Joy and Sheila both so content filled her with a deep happiness.

She hovered around the one uneasy thought that she had long been avoiding. Her lovely Martin. That conversation she had had with Tom about him had been the start of it. For a long time she had been unable to face bringing up the subject again. Her hopes for him – a nice wife, more grandchildren and, above all, grandchildren for Tom – seemed unlikely to come about. There was still plenty time of course, in the normal run of things, if Martin had been . . .

But she was having to start facing up to things. Deep down, she knew that to love her son properly – and she did love him, of course she did, deeply and proudly – she had to face reality. Come to terms with all the signs that had been there his entire young life, if she looked back honestly.

She had just not wanted to see it. There had been Ian. And later Jack. Now Simon. Not one girlfriend that she could recall, ever, even though Martin had been quite friendly with some girls. For years she had told herself that he was shy . . .

A dog barking on the other side of the green distracted her. A golden retriever, demanding that a boy of about six throw the ball he was holding. The boy lobbed it, the red ball arced in the air and the dog chased, happy as anything. A little lad who looked very like Martin had at that age. Her heart twisted with pain for a moment.

She dragged her mind back to her difficult thoughts. She had always regarded herself as the one who understood her children before anyone else. Had been the one really to see them, know them. But now, at least with Martin, she had realized that she was the one who needed to catch up. Something that had happened at the wedding had forced her to start doing exactly that.

It had been such a happy day, perfect in its way. They had all lingered at Rowheath as the shadows lengthened into evening, everyone happy and relaxed, talking and laughing together. But of course there came a time when it all had to end.

She had been leaning over to pick up some glasses from one of the tables when Martin came to say goodbye. Tom was behind her, so Martin reached him first. They both spoke quietly, but she heard almost every word.

'Lovely day,' Martin said. His tone was polite, shy, but not unfriendly. Tom must have nodded in agreement, because Martin added, 'Nicest wedding I've ever been to.' He gave a laugh. 'Not that I have been to very many.'

Ann turned then, to join in the conversation, but as she did so she saw Tom and Martin looking at each other in silence, in that instant. There was meaning in their eyes – she could tell, not because she could see clearly, but because of the way they held each other's gaze, as if both were really seeing each other in a frank way. Then Tom reached out his hand and laid it on Martin's shoulder for a moment.

'You're all right, son. OK?'

Martin looked down quickly, as if Tom's remark had hit a nerve. It took him a moment to reply. Finally he managed to look up again and when he spoke, his voice was thick with emotion.

'Thanks. Dad. And so are you.'

And their eyes met again. They smiled at each other. The heartfelt smile of two people who could see each other deeply and accept what they saw.

Ann froze, almost stunned. This was no time for her to interrupt. Tears slid into her eyes. She saw her two beloved ones give each other a little nod then, and Martin came over to hug her. She could see that deep emotions were working in him and she held him tight, hardly able to speak, her heart was so full.

'Love . . .' She held him close, so that she could speak without looking into his face. 'You do know . . .'

Martin was standing very still.

'Whatever happens, you're my boy.' And then she could not stop her tears, try as she might. 'I love you. And everything's all right. Everything. We're always here – if you need us. Whatever. OK?'

There was a silence as he held her, before he managed to make any words pass his lips.

'Thanks, Mom.' His voice was rough and he was so close to breaking down that he drew back rather roughly, but for a second he held her arms still and managed to look into her eyes. Then he gave her a little squeeze and let go.

Ann and Tom stood side by side, watching as he walked off. And Tom reached for her hand. They didn't need to say anything.

She could not help asking herself over and over again if

Martin – the way he was, which was considered so bad – was her fault. Or hers and Len's. Was there something they should have done? He was her only son; she had no others to compare him with. But, above all, she was so afraid for him; afraid of what his nature, as it seemed to be, might mean.

She was not going to stand watching as he married his bride. He would not bring home grandchildren. Those were also her losses, her own selfish thoughts. But she was so frightened for him as well. His love for Simon – nothing about it was seen as right or within the law. How terrible that was: that what made Martin so happy was somehow beyond the pale. And my God, they were going to have to be careful.

Even so, looking at Martin these days, seeing him at the wedding – he had not brought Simon, which, now she thought about it, was rather a shame – she could see that her boy really was happy. He was back home, he liked his job. And whatever else was going on in his life, he was all of a piece. It was obvious. And she had to enlarge her heart to take this in – her Martin, her boy as he really was. And Simon too.

After a while she got up and wandered slowly back across the grass, past the children and the wandering geese in the warm afternoon.

Everyone would be who they would be, she thought, walking back along Bournville Lane. It was not up to her. All she needed to do was love them, all of her beloved family. And she knew that she was greatly blessed.

Acknowledgements

My grateful thanks go to all the former Cadbury work-ers who came to our reminiscence session at Northfield Library in the summer of 2022 and shared memories of working at the Cadbury works: Kate and Robin Shaw, Marilyn, Yvonne Riley, Barbara Bagby, Bridie Johnson, Ann Belcham, Chris Ullmer, Mary Cutler, Paddy Gin, Maureen Thornhill, Janet Ryan, Gill Judge and Pat Francis.

To Laurence Inman, for also letting me come round and pick his brains about his time working at Cadbury's.

Also to Mollie Champ, a former chocolate girl who spoke to me in her home in the Quadrangle, the beautiful Bournville Almshouses.

Thank you also to Emma Louise Tighe, for sharing details about her glamorous grandmother Maureen Lewis, both a dancer and a model in Birmingham. And to Kathlyn Lovell for other dance-related details.

To Pat Hayward, who recalled one of the Polish ser-vicemen's parties held by Dame Elizabeth Cadbury.

My thanks to the Cadbury Archive at Birmingham University for access to copies of the *Bournville Works Magazine* for the late 1940s and early 1950s.

As ever, there are historians who have made my life a lot easier by doing studies of aspects of life in the city. For this particular story, these were Carl Chinn's *The Cadbury Story*, *Chocolate Wars* by Deborah Cadbury, *A History of Cadbury* by Diana Wordsworth and *My Place in Chocolate Heaven* by Ray Barrett.

Important also were *Stranger in the House* by Julie Summers, about families with a father and husband returned from Japanese internment camps, and *Austerity Britain: 1945–51* by David Kynaston – as well as many other general histories and books more specifically about Birmingham.

My huge thanks to the wonderful team who work on my books: my agent, Darley Anderson, and all the agency staff. And at Pan Macmillan, my lovely editor Gillian Green, brilliant publicist Chloe Davis and all the talents in the marketing and art departments who do their very best to deliver stories to their readers. Thank you to you all.

Do keep in touch . . .

If you would like to receive my free e-newsletter with book news and any other interesting bits that catch my eye, you can find the sign-up on my website, here: annie-murray.co.uk – then all you have to do is wait for it to drop into your in-box three or four times a year.

There's a friendly conversation on Facebook, too, if you would like to follow, at facebook.com/Annie.Murray.Author.

And on Twitter you can find me at twitter.com/AnnieMurray085.

Hope to see you there!